YOU ARE ABOUT TO WITNESS AN EXECUTION.
AND YOU'LL NEVER BE THE SAME.

The son of a senior corrections official,
James McLendon literally grew up in prison.
Now he has created the moment-by-moment
drama of an execution morning as it soon may
be enacted across America. From the electrician's first test of the dreaded chair to the
final, agonizing seconds of the condemned—
it's an unforgettable experience that sears
every page with terrifying reality . . .

"A POWERFUL BOOK. THE FINAL CHAPTERS
ARE STUNNING."

—Robert Daley
Author of **Target Blue**

DEATHWORK

JAMES McLENDON

*This low-priced Bantam Book
has been completely reset in a type face
designed for easy reading, and was printed
from new plates. It contains the complete
text of the original hard-cover edition.*
NOT ONE WORD HAS BEEN OMITTED.

▶

DEATHWORK
*A Bantam Book / published by arrangement with
J. B. Lippincott Company*

PRINTING HISTORY
*Lippincott edition published September 1977
Literary Guild of America edition published Fall, 1977
Serialization appeared in* Argosy, *December 1977
Bantam edition / September 1978
2nd printing*

*Bantam Books are published by Bantam Books, Inc. Its trade-
mark, consisting of the words "Bantam Books" and the por-
trayal of a bantam, is registered in the United States Patent
Office and in other countires. Marca Registrada. Bantam
Books, Inc., 666 Fifth Avenue, New York, New York 10019.*

This book is for my wife
ANN RASH MCLENDON

We went off
To find the dragons
Didn't we Lady.
How innocent
It all seemed
At the time.

And for my father
R. P. MCLENDON

Forty years a distinguished
Prison official and a man
Who, in his time, knew deathwork
As well as any prison man in America.

CONTENTS

DEATH WARRANT

EXECUTIVE DEPARTMENT
STATE OF FLORIDA

To HONORABLE HUBERT L. GREENWOOD, _Warden of our State Prison,_
and HONORABLE D.C. McCOMB, _Sheriff of our County of_ DUVAL

Greeting: Whereas, at the _____ NG _____ term of our Circuit Court
for the FOURTH _____ Judicial Circuit _____ in and for our said County of DUVAL
begun on the 31st _____ day of MAY _____ A.D. One Thousand Nine Hundred and
SEVENTY-THREE _____ , one _____ ALICE FULLER
was convicted of the crime of _____ MURDER IN THE FIRST DEGREE,
and thereupon by our said court the said

was sentenced for said crime to suffer the pains of death by being electrocuted by the passing through her
body of a current of electricity of sufficient intensity to cause her immediate death and until she be dead, all
of which by an exemplification of the record of said conviction and sentence, which I have caused to be
hereunto annexed, doth fully appear

Therefore, I, MORGAN J. KING, _____ Governor of said State of Florida,
command you, the said Sheriff of said County of DUVAL _____ , that not less than
five days prior to the 24th _____ day of JULY _____ , in the year of our Lord One
Thousand Nine Hundred and _____ you deliver the said
ALICE FULLER _____ to _____ the HONORABLE HUBERT L. GREENWOOD,
_Warden of the Maximum Security Prison in our County of Bradford, by him to be kept securely until the
sentence of death shall be executed, and that on such day, so to be decided by the said Warden_

of the State Prison, in the week beginning with Mon_____ the 21st day of FEBRUARY in the Year of Our Lord One Thousand Nine Hundr__ d SEVENTY–SEVEN within the permanent death chamber of said Max_____ Security Prison in our said County of Bradford, agreeably to the Six Thousand One Hundred and T_____ y-fifth Section of the Revised General Statutes of our said State, as amended by Chapter Nine Thou_____ One Hundred and Sixty-nine, of the Laws of our State, Acts of 1923, you cause the execution of th___ d sentence of our said Court, in all respects to be done and performed upon him, the said ALICE F____ER, for which this shall be your sufficient warrant.

You, the said Warden of our State Pris___ r some deputy by you to be designated, shall be present at such execution. Such execution shall be c___ d out by the First Assistant Engineer at the Florida State Prison, deputy executioners, and such deputy _____lectricians and assistants as he may require to be present to assist, and shall be in the presence of a j___ f twelve respectable citizens who shall be requested to be present, and witness the same; and you shall _____ve the presence of a competent practicing physician or of the physician of the prison, and all persons c_____tion such jury and physician, the counsel for the criminal, such Ministers of the Gospel as the cri_____l shall desire, officers of the prison, deputies and guards, shall be excluded during such execution.

Hereof Fail Not, at your peril, and _____ e return of this warrant, with your doings thereon, as soon as may be after execution.

In Witness Whereof, I have hereunto placed my hand _____ caused to be affixed the Great Seal of the State of _____ rida, at Tallahassee, the Capital, this 14th _____ of FEBRUARY _____ the year of Our Lord One Thousand Nine Hundred _____ SEVENTY–SEVEN

Reubin O'D. Askew

GOVERNOR OF FLORIDA.

"And the Lord spake unto Moses, saying,
And he that killeth any man shall surely be put to
  death.
And if any man cause a blemish in his neighbour;
  as he hath done, so shall it be done to him;
Breach for breach, eye for eye, tooth for tooth."

LEVITICUS, *Chapter 24,*
Verses 1, 17, and 19

Lake Cuitzeo, Mexico

Far out above the horizon the great flock of birds arched up into the sky. They moved as one, a giant whip through the clear blue void. A surging fishhook motion sent them higher and higher, until they appeared as white specks over the barren mountains that stretched west as far as the eye could see.

The burnt-brown mountains ringed half the ancient volcanic crater whose sides had been blown off in an explosion untold thousands of years before. Now an enormous shallow lake called Cuitzeo filled the crater. Two dugout canoes, poled by Tarascan Indians, moved on the lake, pointed in the direction of the mountains and the birds that climbed ever higher.

In the strong morning light, with the sun just above the ridges to the northeast, two men sat in the bows of the canoes—one a white man, the other a Mexican. The white man, Lincoln Daniels, sat on a squat, cane-bottomed chair, an excellent vantage point as the canoe made its way easily across the lake. He gripped the shotgun he was holding between his legs with both hands and continued to watch the freshwater pelicans. At noon, when the heat of the sun would drive the birds down to the lake's surface, he and the hunter in the other dugout, whose name was Palo Reyas, would be obliged to kill four of them.

1

It would not be sport. The pelicans would have no chance. On instinct, for survival against the blazing dry-season sun, the birds would seek relief on the cool mountain lake. As they swooped in, dropping down in their long line, the two hunters would take four of the largest with four quick shotgun blasts. By custom, they were expected to take the birds as food for the village of St. Agustín de Pulque, the village of their Tarascan polers. St. Agustín was very old and very poor, and the birds, each of whose wingspans was almost seven feet, would be skinned and dried and eaten by the villagers for protein.

For all the years Lincoln Daniels had lived in Morelia and hunted Lake Cuitzeo with Palo Reyas, the number of pellicans expected by the Indians had always been four. Now the number played on his mind with the kind of irony he detested. In five days he and Palo Reyas would be in a small room inside the Death Facility at the Florida State Prison's Maximum Security East Unit watching three men and a woman die in the electric chair. Executions had returned to America after a thirteen-year absence, and Florida, the first state to put the death penalty back on its lawbooks, was beginning again with four in the same morning. "A show of force," the governor had said. Lincoln Daniels, one of the last of America's expatriate Whiskey Generation writers, would be there to describe the act in a 30,000-word article commissioned by *Esquire*. The magazine had also signed Palo Reyas, Mexico's leading sculptor and muralist, for his drawings of the deaths.

Palo Reyas, who sat in the bow of his canoe twenty feet from Lincoln Daniels, also watched the birds, but he did not concern himself with their killing. To him, it was like the bullfight. It was not sport; it was ceremony. He knew this absolutely without thinking about it, because he was a Mexican who had been a peasant boy under the rule of the dictator, Porfirio Diaz, and had fought Diaz as a young lieutenant in the cavalry of Pancho Villa's Division del Norte. The thought of the executions five days hence did not for a second invade his mind.

At noon, the pelicans came. The polers anxiously pushed the dugouts into a narrow clearing of brown water in the reeds so the hunters could get excellent wing shots. Lincoln Daniels stood and waited for the birds to come in. Along with Reyas, he stood slowly and deliberately, and as he took his first shot his mind froze on the faces of the four condemned prisoners he would see electrocuted on Monday at 8 A.M.

PART ONE
MONDAY

THE DEATH WORKERS

The electrician got up early. He had been awake since three, turning the thought over in his mind: *How would it be to do four again? To kill four in the same morning?* He had forgotten. It had been so long since the last time that the reality had grown dim. Now, on this Monday morning, after so many years, they were beginning again with four. *How would it be to again see four people walk into a room alive and be carried out dead?* His mind would not fashion an answer. His bedclothes were soaked with sweat, and he felt acid in the hollow of his stomach. With only a handful of other men still in the prison business, he knew how the thing was done; he was one of those who had made it work.

Cabel Lasseter was a tall, thin man with big bones but tight features. He had been born one sixteenth Cherokee Indian to a large family of dirt farmers in 1918, born in a four-room, two-story log cabin in the little nondescript village of Pigeon Forge, Tennessee, in the western Great Smoky Mountains.

Like generations of the Lasseter family before him, he would have remained on the family's three hundred hilly, half-productive acres and been a farmer if it had not been for the Great Depression and World War II. But, as they did for almost everyone else in America, the depression and the war altered Cabel Lasseter's life completely. With no money to operate the farm, the Lasseter family—mother and father, eight

7

boys and four girls—moved to Florida in the summer of 1941 to plug themselves into the war effort.

They moved to Gainesville, and the girls took jobs in two ammunition factories that had sprung up outside the sleepy little university city. All eight boys were inducted into the Army at Camp Blanding, thirty miles away, outside the town of Starke, but only three of the brothers fought overseas; four others remained stateside for the duration, and one brother, Cabel Lasseter, was discharged without completing basic training, excused from military service at age twenty-three because of varicose veins in his right leg.

Lasseter, neither happy nor disappointed at his rejection by the military, joined his sisters in defense work, and in the fall of 1941 he was hired at one of the Gainesville ammunition factories as an apprentice electrician. From the first day, he found the work fascinating. In 1943 he married Sarah Elizabeth Douglas, a comely if not beautiful brunette, whose family lived in nearby Brooker. A year later they had the first of their three children.

When the war ended in September 1945, Lasseter had finished his apprenticeship. In the postwar building boom that descended on north-central Florida, and bolstered by the considerable sum of money he had saved as a defense worker, he opened his own small electrical contracting firm on 13th Street in Gainesville.

Cabel Lasseter was a fine electrician but a poor businessman; two years after he began his business, he was bankrupt. At age twenty-nine he found himself dead broke, with a wife and child to support. In the want ads of the *Jacksonville Journal,* he found the job of "prison electrician" advertised by the Florida State Prison at Raiford. He was hired the day of his interview, on December 12, 1947, and went to work three days later at a salary of $225 a month plus the standard prison-system amenities: free house, free utilities, six pounds of meat a week, free milk, free vegetables in season from the prison farms, and a black inmate house servant.

Although he was not an overtly religious man, Lasseter viewed the job and the various benefits as a godsend, and he threw himself into his work with the vengeance only a drowning man possesses. In a short time Cabel Lasseter and the position of prison electrician were one and the same.

Lasseter stretched rigidly in bed and massaged the sockets of his eyes with the knuckles of his first two fingers. Beside him his wife, Sarah, lay in warm sleep, face down, with her arm under her pillow. Lasseter's careful movements did not wake her, but she gave a short, sleep-worn groan as he pushed himself from under the covers and stood on the cold bare floor. He replaced the covers around his wife's neck. In the darkness he found his flannel robe at the foot of the bed, slipped it on, found his bedroom shoes, and then laboriously made his way out into the narrow hall and down to the bathroom, his teeth chattering as he walked.

Lasseter flipped the light switch in the high, narrow room, a switch that activated the wall heaters on either side of the sink. He splashed cold water on his face and delicately cleaned the sleep from his eyes with the tips of his long fingers. He dried his face and lit a cigarette and ran hot water for his shave as the warmth of the heaters began to fill the room. He shaved mechanically, undressed, and then walked into the shower stall without wiping his face clean. He stood under the hot shower jets and let the scalding water on his long neck take the place of sleep. It felt good and put the thoughts of the executions out of his mind. After five minutes, he dried himself, put his robe on, and walked in the dark back up the cold hall to the bedroom.

For the twenty-nine years he had worked at the prison, Lasseter had affected the same dress: gray work clothes and a zip-up leather jacket in winter; white short-sleeved shirt and gray work trousers in summer. But automatically on this morning, as he dressed in darkness, the electrician put on a blue suit, a white dress shirt, and a black tie. It was not until he finished dressing that he realized what he had done. He had dressed for a funeral. He had dressed as he always did for executions. The old pattern had come back automatically.

He took no pleasure in that knowledge, but he did not dwell on it. He moved across the floor as quietly as he could, intent on getting out of the house without waking his wife, but in the bed in front of him she stirred and fumbled for the lamp on the bedside table.

"Cabel . . . Cabel . . . what?" she muttered groggily. Her eyes were closed against the lamp's sudden light; as she adjusted them to the light she saw her husband. "Oh, Cabel," she said, her soft, maternal voice pained.

She needed no more words; instantly, the routine started to come back to her. Lasseter saw the look on her face—knew her thoughts—and tried to smile, but failed.

"I'll make breakfast," she said, pushing back her thick gray-brown hair.

"No," he told her, his voice subdued. "You go back to sleep. I'll get coffee inside."

Sarah Lasseter looked at the clock on the bedside table and saw the hour. "It's so early," she said, getting up and reaching for her housecoat at the foot of the bed.

"I have to go now," Lasseter replied.

"You can't leave without your breakfast," she said, catching her words, remembering that he never ate on the execution mornings.

"Go back to bed," he said gently.

Sarah put on the housecoat, stepped into her slippers, walked over to her husband and touched his hands. "I hate this for you so," she said thickly.

"I know," he answered. "I hate it too. But it's here and that's the fact."

She walked with him to the back door and helped him on with his black prison-issue raincoat and handed him his battered felt hat. She stood on the cold, damp back porch as he walked down the steps.

"Cabel—" she said, as he stepped out onto the wet lawn into a drizzle of freezing rain.

He turned back and looked at her.

"The house seems so empty now that the children

are all gone." She tried a small half smile. "I haven't thought about that in years."

"I know," he replied, avoiding her eyes. "It's time to think about leaving," he added. "Everything is beginning to seem empty. Everything."

Lasseter drove out of the wet, rutted driveway in his blue state pickup truck marked on the sides of the cab with the stenciled block letters: EAST UNIT ELEC. SHOP. It was 33 degrees, and the wet cold inside the cab was oppressive. His hands felt frozen to the steering wheel. He lit a cigarette for warmth, remembering that the truck's heater had been broken for a week. It was unlike him not to have fixed it. He was a stickler for detail; order was the cornerstone of his life.

He turned out of the rows of reservation houses onto State Road 16, the two-lane blacktop that divided the prison compound into half residential area, half prison. He turned east and went on line past the Main Prison, a vast series of long, high concrete buildings with rows of narrow barred windows. The buildings stretched for a mile-and-a-half front, enclosed by three thirty-foot-high cyclone fences topped with barbed wire and three strands of hot electrical wires and punctuated at quarter-mile intervals by tall concrete guard towers that always seemed to Lasseter like huge concrete spears.

Almost immediately Lasseter encountered the first of the roving National Guard patrols, a jeep that passed him slowly in the opposite direction, the soldier on the passenger side fanning his truck with a searchlight. The National Guard, the Florida Highway Patrol, and Bradford and Union County sheriff's deputies were everywhere. Since the riot and sit-down strike on Saturday, the whole prison complex had been like a battlefield. Six inmates had died in Big Max, the Maximum Security East Unit, east of the New River in Bradford County; and in the strike at the Main Prison, across the river in Union County, forty-seven had been wounded and nineteen badly beaten. One prison guard was dead and five were injured, one with a broken back.

It had been a sympathy riot and strike for the

condemned, something that could have stopped the
executions cold, but Major John McPeters, Big Max's
chief correctional officer, and the prison system's head
prison inspector, R. G. Hayes, an iron fist like Mc-
Peters, had prodded the respective wardens into action. While Hayes spearheaded the action at the Main
Prison, McPeters had moved into Big Max with a riot
squad of fifty guards, armed with riot shotguns loaded
with .00 buckshot and aided by snipers in the towers.
In less than twenty-five minutes they took Big Max
back from the four hundred rioters who had roamed
C, D, and E wings and the ball field for two hours. By
the time Big Max warden Hugh Greenwood had per-
suaded the governor to call out the National Guard
and the Highway Patrol and the two sheriffs' depart-
ments, the last rioters in both prisons had been returned to their cells, or to the prison hospital or the
morgue, all while national network and local TV cameras and the national and local press recorded the
events as if they had been staged for a movie.

Lasseter drove through the cold dark past the
Main Prison, down a slight incline into the start of a
broad dogleg curve, and over the time-scarred concrete bridge spanning the New River. The searchlights
from the guard towers fell behind, and to Lasseter's
right front, just beyond the quarter-mile-long bridge,
he picked up the lights of Little Max, the Isolation Unit,
a squat, windowless concrete pentagon encased in a
miniature fencing like the Main Prison. As he cleared
the far side of Little Max, he saw the lights of Big Max
to his left.

Closer in, as he traversed the half mile between
the two maximum security prisons, Lasseter began to
make out shapes and forms despite the blaze of the
strong stationary floodlights and oscillating searchlights.
The first distinguishable cellblock wall he saw was that
of the Death Facility. Ahead, too, were more National
Guard jeeps and a Highway Patrol car. Lasseter
snubbed his cigarette in the truck's ashtray and set
both hands on the steering wheel as he came up to the
roadblock at the two-lane entranceway to Big Max.

There were four jeeps, two on either side of the

entranceway, with the Highway Patrol car positioned to the left so that only one vehicle at a time could negotiate the entrance. Two guardsmen sat inside each jeep. Two highway patrolmen were in the patrol car. All ten men were helmeted and bundled in overcoats.

The guardsmen in the first jeep eyed Lasseter and his truck for a few moments, training their spotlights on him, and then reluctantly lumbered out into the cold rain, carrying M-16 rifles in gloved hands. Before they reached him, he saw one of the highway patrolmen get out of the patrol car. The patrolman carried a riot shotgun in one gloved hand and a clipboard in the other.

The highway patrolman, a big-bellied six-footer, was the first to confront Lasseter. Like the two guardsmen, he was sleepy, cold, and irritated. "Get out of the truck—please," he ordered hoarsely, grudgingly adding the "please."

Lasseter complied silently and stepped out of the truck, his movements deliberate and authoritative.

"State your business and show me some I.D. And get the I.D. slowly," the patrolman said, reluctantly adding another "please."

Lasseter unbuttoned his raincoat slowly, as he had been told, reached into his back trouser pocket for his wallet, opened it to his driver's license and prison employee's I.D. card, and handed the wallet to the patrolman.

The heavy-set man tucked the shotgun under his arm, hunter fashion, and studied the documents carefully, matching Lasseter's face with the small photo on his I.D. card, and then returned the wallet to him.

"What's your business?" the patrolman asked, obviously following a set routine.

"I'm the electrician," Lasseter replied.

"I got that, dammit. Says so on your card. What *detail* you with? I got details, not alphabetical names or jobs."

"The Death Committee," Lasseter said evenly.

"What?"

"The Death Committee," he repeated in the same voice, looking the man squarely in the eye.

The patrolman made a quick search of the clipboard's papers and found Lasseter's name on the execution detail. His eyes darted back to the electrician's face, his indifference instantly replaced with admiration and curiosity.

"God-a-mighty-damn! The Death Committee! Mr. Lasseter, why didn't you just come right out with it? Damn!" The patrolman grinned, slapping the clipboard on his thigh. "Man-oh-man, what I'd give to be in there. Go on in, sir! Doggone, I sure as hell envy you. Whew!"

Lasseter's only response was to nod his head. He turned and got back into his truck.

Like the patrolman, the two young guardsmen were on fire with curiosity. As Lasseter rolled up the window, he saw one of them race to a nearby jeep.

"Goddamn! That's one of 'em!" he heard him say. "One of the Death Committee. Goddamn, boy! Look at him."

A few yards beyond the roadblock, Lasseter stopped his truck again. He rolled the window down and announced his name into a call box in the center of the roadway. The main tower's searchlight focused on the truck.

"Go on in, Mista Lasseter," the tired voice in the tower drawled over the two-way phone. "Cold mornin', ain't it?"

Lasseter did not answer. He rolled the window up again against the biting cold and drove around the entrance circle to the left toward the large parking lot in front of the prison Administration Building. The lot, which would have been all but deserted on any other Monday morning at that hour, was half full. TV mobile-unit trucks were everywhere, and the National Guard and Highway Patrol had set up small headquarters tents. A huge revival tent had been commandeered to house the guardsmen and troopers. Most of the men were in the tent, and all TV and other media people had been banned from the prison grounds until seven fifteen. At equidistant points around the lot, armed national guardsmen walked sentry duty in the thin, freezing rain.

Lasseter found a vacant space beyond the headquarters tent on a line with the entranceway walkway.
When he cut the truck's motor he checked his watch:
five thirty exactly. *Two and a half hours until the
thing begins,* he said to himself. He locked his truck,
turned the collar of his raincoat up against the drizzle,
and walked briskly toward Big Max's main gate. He
gave up all thoughts and simply addressed himself to
getting inside the prison and down its halls to the
Death Facility. His steps were heavy and he heard
only the crack of his tapped heels on the wet sidewalk.

There had never been an escape from Big Max.
You knew why the moment you stepped up before it.
The prison hit you in the face like a baseball bat. Its
thudding concrete bulk stretched for a mile: seven rows
of three-story, barred-window cellblocks to the right,
the one-story Administration Building to the direct
front, and, to the left, a solid, windowless, three-story-
high concrete mass that was the beginning of the prison
shops area. One hundred acres, and all, like the Main
Prison, engulfed by three thirty-foot-high cyclone
fences, each topped with thick rolls of gnarled con-
certina barbed wire, plus the usual three top strands
of hot electrical wire. And around Big Max, inside the
two runs made by the three rows of cyclone fencing,
there were dogs—German shepherds, Rhodesian
Ridgebacks, and pit bulls—all gone mad from isolation, boredom, beatings, and doses of hot pepper in
their faces.

Finally, in Big Max's guard towers there were no
shotguns as there were in the Main Prison's towers.
Big Max towers were arsenals: one Springfield .03
sniper rifle for long shots, a .30-caliber carbine for
close-in shooting, an M-16 machine gun, a tear-gas
launcher, and a .357 magnum pistol as each guard's
personal handgun. Each tower held a combined total of
one thousand rounds of ammunition. There were nine
towers spread out along the two and a half miles of
fencing. It had been estimated that it would take a
fully armed company of marines to crack the de-
fenses, and then, it was said, the attack force would
suffer three-fourths casualties.

Lasseter stopped in the cold, slow rain and said his name into the call box just out from Big Max's first electrically controlled, sliding cyclone-wire gate. The gate hummed open, and he stepped inside and said his name into another call box at the head of the small cage formed by another electrical sliding gate as the first gate slammed shut behind him. When he said his name this time, Lasseter took off his hat and stared up into the blinding lights of the far guard tower so that the man inside could see his face. He put the hat back on when he heard the voice in the call box say, "C'mon, boss."

The second sliding gate opened then, leaving his path clear to the doors of the Administration Building thirty yards ahead.

As he entered the head of the prison yard, Lasseter could see the debris of the fierce riot on Saturday. All down the line of the cellblocks were broken glass, toilet paper, chunks of mattresses and pillows, sheets, discarded prison garb—ten thousand bits of waste spread out on the dead brown grass of the yard. Lasseter negotiated the distance quickly and entered the warmth of the Administration Building's offices beyond its unlocked double glass doors. He was in Safe Ground now, a mid-area between the rigid security of the first of the cellblocks and the equally tight security of the Main Gate.

The hallway was brightly lit, as it always was for security, but the rows of offices off to the right were in darkness; to the left Charlie Amos, the old black trusty who cleaned the Administration Building on the midnight-to-eight shift, leaned back against the pea-green concrete wall in a folding chair, positioned under a line of scalding 500-watt light bulbs encased in dark-green wire mesh cages on the fourteen-foot ceiling. Amos was sixty-eight and had been sent up from Tampa for the first time for armed robbery in 1940, when he was a mean young buck of thirty-two. He had done eight years, been paroled, and had come back in 1949 with a life sentence for murder. After seventeen harsh years at the "Nigger Gun Camp," the State Road Prison outside the town of Deep Lake near the Everglades, he again made parole in 1966. Two years later he returned to prison—this time with his busted life sentence and thirty years on manslaughter charges for cutting a black woman in a bar in Ocala, where he had been working as a groom on a thoroughbred ranch. He was an old man now, a broken, shriveled little monkey with no teeth and a slick bald head and a little tuft of wispy gray hair under his short lower lip, hair that gave him his nickname of the Chinaman.

The Chinaman was an institution rat, a "white man's nigger," curled up safe and sound in sleep, possessed of one of Big Max's gravy jobs, a job that gave him his own time in a place where there was no *own* time. He could sleep through anything, but on this morning, deep in sleep, he had his con's radar working. The instant his mind registered footsteps, his head popped up from his spidery neck and his tiny broganed feet slapped the waxed finish of the tiled floor. Before he opened his eyes, he knew it would be the electrician standing before him.

The old man's eyes widened as they focused on Lasseter. The tall, thin electrician looked like what the old con pictured as death itself. Lasseter stared straight into the black man's face and shook the water from his raincoat with fierce tugging motions at both lapels. He beat the icy rain from his hat with a slap against the wall. The Chinaman stood up before the electrician and bowed his head so that their eyes could not meet.

It was the look, the response Lasseter had seen all week—as if looking on him, looking into his eyes, would somehow drag the beholder into the thing with him, would somehow bring the other into the realm of death that hung over the prison like a bad smell.

"Mista Lass-ter. Yessir. Good mornin', sir," the Chinaman mumbled, quailing against the wall, his eyes never leaving the floor.

"Morning," Lasseter replied, setting his hat back on his head, starting off down the lighted hall without another word. He cleared two more sets of electric gates and a final three-inch-thick steel door and then was in the main cellblock corridor, an equally brightly lit, sixteen-foot-high passageway as wide as a four-lane highway that stretched the length of the seven rows of three-story cellblocks.

He stopped momentarily at the long, barred, safety-glass-enclosed Control Room at the left of the entrance corridor, and the shift lieutenant, a burly, crew-cut ex-strawberry farmer from the nearby town of Starke, passed him on down the line with a short, respectful wave of his hand. As Lasseter turned and made his way through the maze of steel and wire doors to the Death Facility at the far end of the last cellblock, the lieutenant picked up a phone and dialed a three-digit number. At the other end of the line, Major John McPeters answered on the first ring.

"Mr. Lasseter's inside," the lieutenant said.

"All right," McPeters answered.

He carefully lowered the receiver back into its black cradle. Then he stood up and walked over to the line of coat pegs next to the doorway of the office, where he stood and took his heavy blue wool uniform coat from one of the pegs. He slipped the huge garment on with studied ease, buttoned it, then took his triangular Sam Browne belt from the next peg, fitted the wide belt around his considerable waist, flipped the thin shoulder strap across his right breast, and clipped it into its hook to the left of the belt's large, shiny brass buckle.

He stepped in front of the narrow, full-length wall mirror to the left of the row of coat pegs and checked his dress, adjusting his black tie slightly. The check and the movements were automatic; John McPeters did not respond to his hard, block-like face in the mirror, only his appearance. When he was satisfied with what he saw, he turned and walked back to the only desk in the small, windowless room. He sat down in his high-backed wooden swivel chair, set his booted feet on the desk top, pushed himself back into the chair, crossed his heavy arms across his belted chest, and fixed his hawk's eyes on the open doorway as he waited for the electrician.

Major John McPeters was untouchable. He was fifty-nine, the last of Florida's hard-bitten chain-gang guards. The state would retire him in a few years, and when he was gone there would be no one to take his place. He was of the old school, the school of prison thinking that looked on rehabilitation as a joke and on every convict who passed through the gates as something less than human, a dog, an animal to be beaten and cowed into submission as if he were being trained for a sideshow.

He would be replaced by a member of the new school, one of the younger, college-trained, retired military men who had taken over the Florida prisons in recent years. Everything was changing within the prison system. It was not even called a prison system any more. It had been labeled the Division of Health and Rehabilitative Services, implying that the people there were sick and could be cured, an idea that had come to prevail in Florida.

John McPeters was not a man given to big words or big ideas, but a quote he had heard once, at one of the annual Florida sheriffs' conventions, had stuck with him for more than ten years. He knew it verbatim and would recite it with the finality of an end-all philosophy, because to him it was the last word on prisons and gave him open season on every convict in his charge, linked what he did to them with reason and made his actions official.

"The word rehabilitation," he would drawl in a hard-boiled monotone he reserved for the quote, "presupposes habilitation. But the people who come to prison are not habilitated in the first place. Therefore there is no such thing as rehabilitation, because you can't rehabilitate a nonhabilitated man.

"This crowd," he would say of the convicts, "ain't sick. They're just fuckups. But by God I'm gonna make 'em sick when they get here. You can cash a goddamn check on that." And there wasn't a listener who doubted his sentiments. They had been passionately sandblasted on McPeters's face by his own personal battle for respectability.

He had been born on a fifteen-acre farm out from the Florida Panhandle town of Jay, almost within sight of the Alabama state line. The year was 1917, and two months after he was born his father did his second one-year stretch in the federal penitentiary in Atlanta for moonshining. Young John lasted fourteen years in the confines of the family's slatboard and tar-paper shack and the grinding poverty that came in regular sessions as his father went off to prison three more times for moonshining.

The misery of his early life taught John McPeters four things: the way to make good corn whiskey from a submarine still on the banks of the Escambia River not far from their played-out farm; the silent, secret ways of the hunter; the closed-mouth stoicism that bone-crushing poverty imposes; and the brutal meanness that is the only defense of the permanently down-and-out. He abandoned the first of the teachings when he was fourteen, after he ran for two days to evade federal revenue agents who jumped him while he was tending the mash barrels at his father's still. But the others stayed with him the rest of his life. He had gone to the sixth grade, but for the life he would lead he would not need books. The lessons of his father were all the education he would ever require.

On the second night of his run from the revenue agents, the fourteen-year-old McPeters, already a man's size at an even six feet and one hundred and fifty pounds, doubled back through the scrub-oak woods behind his parents' shack. While his mother and father lay drunk in the bedroom, he collected his few belongings from under the sagging living room couch where he slept, stored them in the family's one cardboard suitcase, took all the money, $67.43, from his father's wallet and his mother's kitchen fruit jar,

and walked ten miles across the state line to Pollard,
Alabama. At noon he caught the Greyhound bus to
Mobile, and after a repairman in a jewelry store had
altered his birth certificate for five dollars he enlisted
in the Army.

The Army was the perfect home for John McPeters. He took his basic training at Fort Benning, Georgia, and was assigned to an infantry company two
months before his fifteenth birthday. On December
7, 1941, when the Japanese bombed Pearl Harbor, Mc-
Peters was a ten-year Army veteran, a three-stripe
sergeant in an infantry battalion at Fort Bragg, North
Carolina. When the Germans surrendered uncondition-
ally on May 8, 1945, he was a decorated master sergeant in the 503 "Rock" Battalion of the crack 82nd
Airborne Division, but homeless again at almost twenty-eight, as he bewilderingly found himself mustered
out of the Army after fourteen years, a sterile number
in the massive peacetime cutbacks that followed VE
Day.

McPeters was discharged at Fort Dix, New Jer-
sey, on Friday, September 21, 1945, and after a wild,
drunken weekend with a whore at the Gove Hotel on
42nd Street between Sixth and Seventh Avenues in
Manhattan, he bought a black 1938 Ford coupe with
half the $900 he had to his name and drove south to-
ward his birthplace near Jay, Florida. All during the
four-day trip he kept trying to decide what he was
going to do with his life and why he was pointing himself toward home. He had not seen or written his parents since he left them. But for reasons he did not
understand, he suddenly felt the need to link up with
some sort of roots, some sort of order—the order that
discharge from the Army had wrested from him.

Nothing had changed in Jay during the fourteen
years of his absence. McPeters found the dirt road to
his parents' shack with no trouble and pulled up in
front of it late on the afternoon of September 28.
He stopped his car a hundred yards from the shack and
sat looking at it across a bare field of plowed-under
brown summer cornstalks. The narrow, sagging front
porch was empty except for a rusted-out refrigerator

that had no door. The wooden windows of the shack were closed against the late-afternoon cold that came in with a burnt-red sunset against a dull gray sky. McPeters watched the shack for a long time; it was almost full dark before he saw an old woman come out onto the porch. She looked at his car for a few moments and then stepped down off the porch and walked around the side of the shack to the outhouse. McPeters knew the old woman was his mother, but he found that he felt nothing for her, no emotion whatsoever. Looking at her and the shack and the desolate farm, McPeters tried to figure out why he had come back. He couldn't. He only saw why he had left in the first place.

He started the car's motor, put it in reverse, and backed out the dirt road. At the junction with the highway, he put the Ford in neutral and got out and walked over to his parents' mailbox. He counted out seven $10 bills from the roll he had in his right uniform pocket, folded them together, and put them inside the mailbox. Then he got back inside his car and headed east through the Panhandle into the heart of the state. He did not give a thought to what would become of the money; it was simply an old debt he had paid. He drove all night, and in the morning when he stopped for breakfast he found himself in the north-Florida town of Lake Butler.

He had breakfast at the Coffee Pot, a small café on the main street of the little Confederate one-street town. He was the picture of the American war hero returned home: a big man, scrutinized by people at the tables with curiosity and envy as he sat at the counter like a great tree trunk in his Army winter browns, his immense chest embossed with four rows of battle ribbons and topped with a silver combat infantry-man's rifle badge and silver paratrooper's wings with two battle stars, the arms of his uniform dominated by his master sergeant's three-up, four-down stripes and, beyond them, at his cuffs, lines of hashmarks and combat bars.

Before he finished his breakfast, the editor of the

weekly *Lake Butler Journal* had been summoned by
the café's owner for an interview complete with Mc-
Peters full-length photo, for the front page of the paper's next edition. The editor of the small paper, a
would-be blood-and-guts war correspondent, wrote
John McPeters up as if he singlehandedly won World
War II. McPeters, for his part, was so awed by the
possibility of having a story written about him and,
more importantly, of seeing his picture on the front
page of a newspaper, that he took a $2-a-night room in
the Hotel Butler and waited the five days until the
Journal appeared on Thursday.

The five days from September 29 to October 4,
1945, were the finest, the fullest, the happiest in John
McPeters's life. He walked along Main Street and
talked with the admiring shopkeepers. In the after-
noons he sat on the long, shaded porch of the Hotel
Butler and drank beer from the bottle as the crisp
fall days turned to cool evenings. At night he ate at
the hotel or at the Coffee Pot, and then before he went
to bed he would walk down to the town's namesake
lake, a little oval in the center of the residential section
north of Main Street. He would stand and look at the
lake and the light of the full yellow moon on it, and
at the lights of the fine, respectable houses that rimmed
the lake, and feel good, a feeling he had not experienced since his first days in the Army fourteen years
before. Looking at the lake and the houses, John Mc-
Peters began to forget about his childhood and the last
four years of war in Europe. He began to think of
respectability, of amounting to something, of being like
the safe, secure people in the houses on the lake. Lake
Butler might have been dreary by almost anyone else's
standards, but to John McPeters it was the finest place
he had ever seen. When his article appeared in the
Journal on Thursday, October 4, under the glowing
banner headline: WANDERING PARATROOP
HERO RECALLS WAR'S HELL, he felt as though
the small town and all it contained were his.

The owner of the Coffee Pot closed his café at
noon on Thursday and, in the innocence of the time,

opened its counter to free beer in McPeters's honor for the afternoon. The town's dignitaries—the mayor, the city clerk, the chief of police, the county sheriff, the newspaper editor, the local dentist, and the town banker—were there, and at the end of the affair, McPeters was asked by the newspaper editor what he wanted to do now that he was out of the service.

In a voice filled with half-drunken good cheer and emotion, the giant soldier told his attentive listeners, with proper dignity, that what he wanted most was to be like them, "to be respectable" and "to stay in Lake Butler" among the "finest people" he had ever known.

McPeters's audience was stunned by his answer. To them he embodied the carefree romance of the battlefield, the essence of swashbuckling wanderlust itself. The fact that such a man wanted to share what they considered their drab, unfulfilled lives burst their illusion of him completely, and to McPeters's bewilderment his party broke up with cool indifference.

Only the county sheriff, Joe Fergus, seemed to know what McPeters had meant by his outburst. After the party, the meaty-jowled, handlebar-moustached Fergus took McPeters back to his office in the county jail just off Main Street, and they had a long talk built around a bottle of I. W. Harper.

"Don't pay no mind to that bunch of peckerwoods," Fergus told McPeters, sizing the soldier up past the brim of a weathered Stetson pulled down over his wide, wrinkled forehead. "They just want a hero. No offense, but one out of the goddamn funnies would do 'em just as well—better, probably, because then he couldn't talk to 'em and bust their bubble like you did."

He gave McPeters a tight-lipped smile.

"No sir," the sheriff went on, "fellow like you— big fellow, tough, not afraid of no damn body—man like that won't have no trouble at all getting a job out to Raiford Prison, 'bout eight, nine miles from here, right on through town and due east on Highway Sixteen. Hell, I'd put you on myself, be damn glad to, 'cept deputy jobs is for local boys, generally boys that can't make a go of nothin' else, if you know what I mean."

Prison! The word, the thought, threw a fright into McPeters that sent the color out of his face and brought the misery of his childhood, the lack of respectability of his life, in on him like a thundercloud which the sheriff saw descend on him.

"What in hell's the matter with you, boy?" Fergus asked. "You ain't afraid of nothin', are you? You ain't got some skeleton in your closet? You ain't been in the jug yourself?"

"No. No sir," McPeters protested loudly. He tried to smile his way back to composure. "I mean, I just . . . maybe had something else in mind. I mean, I didn't know nothing about a prison around here, nothing about a prison at all."

"Had somethin' in mind like the banker's daughter, eh?" Fergus's laugh bellowed out. "Gonna make your fortune and your bed all at once? Hell, it's not a bad idea." Fergus toasted the notion with a long drink of bourbon served up in a jelly jar. "But forget it, son," he went on. "The banker's got two boys, and judgin' by the way they look, if he had a daughter, money or no money, he'd have to marry her off to a blind man.

"No sir, soldier, Raiford Prison's the place for you. That is"—he laughed—"*outside* Raiford. I know Warden Blackshear myself," he went on. "As fine a Christian gentleman, as fine a *man*, as ever lived. I'll call him tomorrow mornin' and you go out and see him."

So the next afternoon, Friday, October 5, John McPeters drove through the dense slash-pine woods from Lake Butler through the little pulpwood railhead town of Raiford and onto the fifteen thousand carefully worked-over acres that made up the Florida State Prison, FSP, or the State Farm, as it was known when it was under the jurisdiction of the Department of Agriculture in Tallahassee.

In those days the prison had the true look of a great Southern plantation: a place of long fields, immense stretches of turpentine pines, pastures, hog farms, a great dairy, and neatly laid-out rows of big, white, wood-frame employees' houses in the center of fine, well-kept lawns.

At first, as he drove onto the prison reservation, McPeters took it for a farm, and the warm October afternoon and the peace and order of the place erased his dread. But as he parked his Ford near the Main Gate, walked into its enclosure, and went up to the uniformed guard inside, standing back as the guard methodically went about frisking two tired blacks dressed in dirty stripes and shackled together with a heavy four-foot-chain, the realization of where he was came in on him like a bad dream, and although he towered over all three men he felt as small and insecure and out of place as a child.

The gate guard went on clearing the two blacks, looking at McPeters but not speaking to him. When he was done with the two men he opened the heavy barred gate with a thick brass key and roughly sent them on their way into the maze of barred gates that led into the prison's great yard. Then he turned to McPeters, grudgingly regarded the rows of battle ribbons on his chest, and, in the same rough tones he had used with the two convicts, inquired his business. McPeters responded lamely that he had been sent by Sheriff Fergus to see Warden Blackshear. The guard, a thick man with close-cropped gray hair and a jar full of chewing tobacco, made no reply but picked up the telephone on a wooden stand next to the gate and called the warden's office. After a brief conversation he hung the phone up and told McPeters to wait where he was.

"They'll come out and get you," the guard said in a hard, nasal drawl, spitting tobacco juice into a coffee can stuffed with toilet paper which was standing on the floor by his feet. And in ten minutes, another uniformed guard, one who looked much like the gate guard, emerged from the maze of gates and took McPeters inside.

The prison yard was a contradiction. Like the prison grounds it had the look of a plantation: rows of great live oaks, plotlike flowerbeds, and manicured shrubs. But now, for the first time, John McPeters saw the actual prison. At first it sent genuine fright through him. As far as the eye could see in either direction there were huge concrete buildings with barred windows; to the left, as he entered the yard, loomed the Rock, the great three-story-high main cellblock building that had been built thirty years before in a time when a prison was supposed to look like a prison.

McPeters saw the lines of convicts, straight lines of gaunt, bent men who looked not like men but like pegs on a giant gameboard. At closer range, they resembled scared rabbits, and as McPeters and the guard passed them they slapped the sides of their legs with their blue caps and mumbled the word "boss," staring down at the ground. Here was the feel of army basic training for McPeters, and of the authority he wielded as a master sergeant, but at once he knew it was different. This was a completely different world with a completely different set of values and rules. There was venality everywhere.

As he walked along with the silent guard, John McPeters knew—without understanding why—that he had found his world, the world his life had molded him for, as surely as if he had studied for it in college. His uneasiness passed as quickly as it had descended upon him, and by the time he was ushered into Warden Blackshear's grandly appointed office he was composed and more solidly assured of himself than ever before. The courtly, graying warden, who had once been pastor of the Old Stone Church in Key West, hired him on the spot, and John McPeters reported for his first day of work as a $90-a-month tower guard the following Monday, October 8, 1945.

John McPeters was days away from his twenty-eighth birthday when he went to work at Raiford Prison, but the birth certificate he had had forged to get into the Army as a fourteen-year-old showed him to be just short of thirty. His age, his commanding size, and his war record immediately set McPeters apart from the other guards, most of whom had been deferred from the war because of their prison work. And the fact that he had had virtually no formal education bothered no one, as there was not a high school graduate among Raiford's hundred and fifty guards.

From the start, the older guards and the guard officers broke tradition and sought out the tough, silent, authoritative McPeters. Within six months he was taken off the midnight-to-eight shift on his tower and used by Major R. D. Crews as a day utility man, roving Raiford's fields, checking the various squads, in particular the notorious 8-Spot, the big work gang all new prisoners—Newcocks—were put on for their first ninety days of hard labor, and the equally tough Grist Mill squad. If there was trouble there was John McPeters; then, minutes later, there was Bulldog Crews.

In the fall of 1947, Crews made McPeters a shift sergeant in charge of the Rock from midnight to eight. No other guard had ever risen so fast at Raiford, but no one, guard or convict alike, dared question the promotion; by then, with the sole exception of Major Crews himself, John McPeters was the most feared man at the prison. When an all-black cane-cutting squad sat down in a cane-field ditch in the spring of 1946, saying they wouldn't get up until they had personally seen the governor, John McPeters arrived in his truck, got out with a 12-gauge pump shotgun, and blew a leg off one black convict with a single blast of .00 buckshot and took the right arm off another as the group burst back toward the field.

"You've seen the governor," he bellowed after the terror-stricken blacks as they raced back to work. "Don't call me again till you want to see Harry Truman himself!"

It was in the Rock, while he was sergeant for two years, that the cons labeled John McPeters "Peeping John." He earned the name because he knew everything that went on in the massive cellblock complex. There was not one single thing that did not pass before him, either through his intense network of stooges or from his own relentless pounding of all the floors, all the cells, all night long, and around the prison yard during much of the morning and early afternoon.

John McPeters never left the prison. As a bachelor

he took his meals in the officers' dining room just off the main prison dining hall, and he slept in the bachelor officers' quarters, the BOQ, a three-story antebellum type of structure fifty yards to the right of the Main Gate. The prison was his whole life, and he knew everything any guard could know about it: all but its darkest, most private consecrets, the evil root fungus not even the grapevine could penetrate.

During the morning it was his custom to sit in one of the cane rocking chairs under the great oaks that fronted the Rock and read the *Jacksonville Times-Union* and drink black coffee brought to him by a trusty from the prison canteen, a fine little wood-frame structure that sat at the edge of the visiting yard behind him. He would sit and read the paper, the sole source of any printed information he might receive, and at the same time observe all movement around the Rock and on the yard as the various squads checked in and out: a front-row seat to the prison's daily business. He would read until the prison band played its daily concert in the band shell in the center of the visiting yard, and then he would eat his lunch and stroll through the main dining hall among the convicts seated at the long rows of benched tables, and afterward he would make a round out in the athletic yard on the far side of the dining hall for more observations. He slept six hours during the cool afternoon and was back inside the walls of the prison by nine in the evening for his dinner and more personal rounds, until he took over the inner workings of the Rock at midnight.

The guards and convicts alike had a saying about John McPeters when anyone asked where he was: "Peeping John," they would say, "is everywhere."

Bulldog Crews made McPeters the Rock's night lieutenant in early 1950; in 1952, he elevated him to day lieutenant. In 1955, he made him captain of the guards, his number-two man, directly in charge of meting out day-to-day inmate discipline. And in late 1959, when Major Crews retired, Peeping John McPeters, at age forty-two, became the prison's major without one word of dissension.

By 1957, Florida's prisons had been taken out of the jurisdiction of the Department of Agriculture and were under the separate Division of Corrections, headquartered in Tallahassee, with a director of cabinet rank. More than half of the original thirty-five roadcamp chain-gang prisons had been closed, but work was under way to add five additional state prisons to the Main Prison at Raiford and the prison at Belle Glade near the Everglades. Everything about the closed prison society, both for inmates and guards, began to change in the late 1950s. The crackers, the hard-nosed, ill-educated descendants of the rough Scotch-Irish immigrants who had settled north Florida in the 1850s, pushing their teams of mules and oxen through the dense palmetto underbrush with thick leather whips which had sisal crackers on the ends for added noise, were being edged out of jobs at Raiford and the other prisons by the new school of young, retired military men and college graduates: two types of people who had never before ventured into the closeted domain of Florida's prisons.

Peeping John McPeters, although he had been a much-decorated World War II veteran, immediately found himself at odds with the new group. He was solidly of the old school, a semiliterate cracker linked to the old ways of brutality and repression. And there was the added thorn that McPeters had never married. He had absolutely no outside interests beyond the prison. The members of the new school were clumsily playing out the first stages of what came to be called "the middle-class-leisure myth." They were golfers, fishermen, and would-be country clubbers. To them, John McPeters was a too-painful reminder of their very recent past.

But for all his enemies, and his cross purposes with the new school, John McPeters was on solid ground. He was not simply tolerated, he was a totally necessary part of the prison structure: a bulldog, as Crews had been, someone to keep order when the going got tough, someone whose very presence stood for order.

McPeters, for his part, accepted his situation with characteristic indifference. He had no desire, no thought, no frame of reference to change the ways he had learned. His only defense, if it could be called that, was to isolate himself further from everything but his work.

During his first fourteen years at the prison, McPeters had lived in the BOQ, first near the Main Gate and then in the newer quarters near the eastern entrance to the prison reservation on the highway to Starke. His small rooms in both buildings had been more than enough, as he was rarely in them, but with his appointment as major and his estrangement from the growing number of newer prison employees, he seized the opportunity in late 1959 to move into a cavernous, nine-room colonial-style house on the grounds of the old dairy. He tended his prison duties with the zeal he always possessed, but by early 1977, as a fifty-nine-year-old man, although he was still the prison's bulldog in spirit and in body, he was able to spend more time tending his own house and its surrounding isolated acres. By then his stooge grapevine system was unimpeachable, and he, as man and officer, was someone apart, someone the warden and the cabinet-post Director of Health and Rehabilitative Services dared not tamper with, dared not cross, dared not offend, for fear that, without McPeters's old-style discipline, all their forward-thinking reforms and carefully laid-out college plans might fall apart.

By 1977, he was Peeping John the relic, but no one dared tell him so or stand up to him, not even Florida's boy-wonder Republican reform governor, Morgan Kingsly, who would have liked his head in a truly biblical manner.

In the style of reformers, the thirty-nine-year-old Kingsly tried to change everything about state government with a new set of laws, but when it became apparent that Florida's conservative, rural-oriented Democratic legislature would not go along with his ideas, Kingsly resorted to the tactic taken by most would-be reformers: he reworked the intent of the state agencies and controlled them by executive action. If an agency was doing *white,* he set them to doing *black,* and the tactic caused so much excitement that the media immediately jumped on his bandwagon, largely because they had something new to report. Florida's prisons had long been among the hardest in the nation, with little or no emphasis on rehabilitation, so Kingsly naturally made political hay with his adamant reversal of prison policy. "From retribution to rehabilitation," he would intone in his throaty west-Florida revival preacher's delivery.

By 1976 the media had abandoned Kingsly and what they had come to call his "milk toast" reforms. It was a presidential election year without a war, and Law and Order, that great peacetime catch-all, was the hot state and national issue. The death penalty had been upheld by the U.S. Supreme Court in its landmark five-to-four *Santos* v. *Florida* decision in September 1976, leaving Kingsly saddled with his reformed Division of Health and Rehabilitative Services and encased by his lofty and hastily put-together maxims on rehabilitation. But Kingsly's political instinct landed on a solution for all his problems. The true campaigner, he found the perfect way to have his public cake and eat it too.

In November, two months after the *Santos* v. *Florida* decision, when it became apparent that almost every public voice in the state—the legislature, citizens' groups, the courts, and most of the powers of the media—favored starting executions all over again, Governor Kingsly rose like a fallen warrior out of a dime novel, more throaty, more evangelical than ever, proclaiming a newly reworked slogan: "Retribution *and* rehabilitation." Overnight, Morgan Kingsly was the state's favorite son again. Before the presidential election in November, Kingsly, a lawyer by profession, was being touted by the Republican candidate as a likely U.S. Attorney General, the "new voice of the enlightened South, a voice that is not afraid to tell it like it is."

The U.S. Supreme Court had struck down capital punishment with its precedent-breaking *Furman* v. *Georgia* decision on June 29, 1972, but six months later, on December 8, 1972, Florida became the first state to put the statute back on its lawbooks. In the five years since, 240 people had been sentenced to death in Florida.

"One hundred and ten convicted felons had their sentences commuted from death to life under *Furman versus Georgia*," Kingsly said in his thunderous campaign speeches. "If this be justice, then I shall see the same justice for the unfortunates who inhabit Florida's Death Row today. . . . There," he said, as if he had invented the phrase himself, "but for the grace of God go we all."

Then came serious mention of the attorney generalship and a renewed courtship with the press, and everything changed in Kingsly's life. There were those in Florida and Washington who saw him as a cabinet officer for the incumbent president. To ensure himself a place in that inner sanctum, Kingsly knew he not only had to stand firm on the big issue of law and order, he had to prove beyond the shadow of a doubt that he had the fortitude to do something positive for the cause.

Capital punishment arrived as an issue giftwrapped for him, as the A-bomb had come for Harry Truman. The spectacular idea of killing four people in the same morning came with equal ease. Three times, during Florida's forty-year history of electrocutions, they had done four in a morning, and four times they had done three. Although it made him physically ill to consider the possibility of signing even one person's death warrant, the chance to sign four at once was an opportunity no born politician could turn down. It was Morgan Kingsly's future, and he seized it. And in the person of Major John McPeters, the most feared man in the prison system—a man Kingsly despised above all others—he had the perfect instrument.

"Let that bloodthirsty sonofabitch bear the brunt of the thing," Kingsly would tell whatever sympathetic ear he could find. "He'll be gone in a year or so, and maybe the old school will go with him; maybe the whole issue of capital punishment will go with him. I'm not a man to sign death warrants willfully, but John McPeters can go after the killings with all the enthusiasm the public can demand."

John McPeters *had* kept the old ways. His home resembled an Old South plantation, complete with black retainers who served him with both fear and respect. Against all opposition, he had retained the same blue wool winter guard uniforms with their Sam Browne belts and the khaki summer uniforms with the same belts. In an age when police forces wore fashion-designed jumpsuits, John McPeters said no; he said no in an age when the word "no" had all but been erased.

He was untouched by the ebb and flow of the last part of the twentieth century, and now, on the morning of the first executions he would preside over since he had personally supervised the death of Eugene Burns, a black murderer from Gadsden County who, at 9:08 A.M. on May 12, 1964, had been the last to die in the electric chair in Florida, he sat in his office and waited for the day to unfold with the self-assurance of a man who has no questions, only the answers.

5:45 A.M.

The Death Facility occupied all three floors of the last cell-block building. Its entrance was two hundred yards from the Control Room as one entered Big Max's main hallway. It was a prison within a prison and its cells were cells within cells.

Big Max was the final confinement for Florida's hard cases—touch hogs, in the language of the cons—but the Death Facility was beyond that: beyond written words, beyond spoken words. The Death Facility was a place like no other, a place not to go and live but a place to go and die.

Cabel Lasseter approached the final maze of doors before the Death Facility, a maze not of bars, as before, but of solid steel punctuated only by five-inch slits of bulletproof glass.

All along, the steamy main hallway was permeated with the stench of male sweat, industrial disinfectant, stale cigarette smoke, and the distant aroma of breakfast bacon and strong coffee. Because of the riot on Saturday, all privileges had been suspended and the hallway was bare of its usual clumps of trusties, a fact for which Lasseter was thankful.

At the end of the hall, Lasseter pushed the buzzer on the right wall by the first steel door.

Two small eyes, below a meaty forehead, appeared in the glass slit and looked him over.

A second later there was the hard metallic clank of a key being rammed into the door's lock, then the sound of the lock's tumblers being depressed. The door began to open, sliding sideways into a wall recess; it opened only wide enough to let the electrician pass.

The guard, one of McPeters's hand-picked Death House crew, a hulking six-footer, gave no greeting but concentrated on ramming the heavy steel door shut a brief second after the electrician was inside.

From this point on, Lasseter knew everything would be different, sterile, completely barren: concrete walls covered with glossy pale gray paint and gray steel doors, all illuminated, held somehow out of focus, it always seemed to the electrician, by the hard white light of 500-watt bulbs in green wire mesh cages on the ceiling.

Everything was totally measured, absolutely deliberate. Each of the two cubicles formed by the three-door maze was five feet wide, seven feet long, and eleven feet high. Big Max had the look of confinement, but the Death Facility went past that, past reference, past definition.

From the first maze to the second, the same procedure was repeated: the eyes of another silent, sullen guard, a second clanging of steel on steel, as Lasseter entered the second box of the maze. Not stopping to indulge a feeling of complete alienation, he finally cleared the last steel door and stood inside the gray-walled Death Facility itself.

From the final door to the Death Facility office it was only two paces. Bob Griffis, a Death Facility shift sergeant, met Lasseter at the last door and escorted him the nine feet down the hall to McPeters's office. Griffis, now that Lasseter was inside Deep Lock, greeted the electrician in the easy combat-zone manner familiar to all prison guards on safe ground.

"It's the right kind of a mornin' for a hangin', or at least it was when I came on at midnight." Griffis grinned, flexing his shoulders.

"It still is," Lasseter responded, knowing his part but saying it with difficulty.

"Mr. Lasseter," Griffis said with a countryman's unprefaced solemnity, as they came to McPeter's door, "I just want you to know that we all feel better about this thing, knowin' you're with us."

Lasseter studied the tough young guard's already old face and, despite his own inner thoughts, responded with the words the younger man wanted to hear.

"It's all right," he said simply, nodding.

Bob Griffis had come to work at the prison three months after the last execution in 1964; he was a good prison man and he had seen much in his dozen years at Raiford—riots, killings, stabbings, homosexual rape, a vast and sordid spectrum of prison life—but at age thirty-three he had not seen legal death, the one thing only a prison could deliver.

McPeters explained Griffis's dilemma best: "He's like a half-back who's never scored a touchdown." Of course there was much more to it than that, but, as with all other things concerning the prison, McPeters had touched the heart of the matter.

When Cabel Lasseter entered McPeters's office, he found him seated behind his desk with his feet stretched out on the desk top. It was a pose that was clearly for effect—McPeters's simple and direct way of conveying that all was under control—and Lasseter, with much the same difficulty he had had in replying to Griffis's remarks, responded to the pose.

"Things not so quiet you can go to sleep, are they?" he said, straining to keep his face pleasant.

It was the kind of remark McPeters wanted, and when it came he quickly got back to the business at hand.

"Not that quiet," he said, swinging his feet to the floor and standing, "but we're ready to go. Bob," he went on, without pausing, adjusting his coat and Sam Browne belt as he spoke, "get us some coffee in here."

The guard appeared in the office doorway, mouthed a respectful "yessir" and departed, as Mc-Peters walked over to where Lasseter was standing before his desk.

"Give me your raincoat and hat," McPeters said, holding out his hand. "Rain still coming down?"

"Yes," Lasseter answered, shedding his coat and hat.

"Hell of a night," McPeters replied, hanging Lasseter's coat and hat on two wall pegs. "I've made rounds three times, each time worse—colder and more rain."

"Rain's slacked off some." Lasseter came back, sitting down in the single chair in front of McPeters's desk, a gunmetal gray, bolted-to-the-floor folding chair.

"You been up long?" McPeters questioned, going back to his swivel chair.

"All night," Lasseter answered simply, in the style of a man who has nothing to hide.

McPeters looked hard at the electrician's face and started to speak, but he held back his first words, obviously searching for alternates. "Everything's okay here," he finally said. "It doesn't look like trouble."

Lasseter took out a cigarette and lit it; he inhaled deeply before responding. "What do *you* think?" he asked, seemingly ignoring McPeters's words.

Cabel Lasseter was one of the few men at the prison who spoke to McPeters in such a fashion, one of his few equals in the ancient and disappearing society of prison men.

McPeters regarded both the speaker and the question for a few moments. "Who can say?"

"Yeah," Lasseter agreed, drawing hard on his cigarette in lieu of more words.

McPeters let out a small laugh, a sound foreign to the surroundings. "Well," he said, "we both know who *can* say, but they ain't talkin'."

Before Lasseter was obliged to reply, the coffee came.

They had their coffee—thick, gritty, pungent, industrial-price coffee, laced with syrupy-sweet condensed milk and a pinch of salt—in silence. They had known each other for almost thirty years; whatever they had to say, professionally or privately, either had already been said or did not need to be put into words. And, as well as any two men alive, they understood what had to be done in the four hours to come.

Lasseter knew McPeters's philosophy on capital punishment. "You get the bastard's attention," McPeters would say. "That's important. Because generally you're dealing with a sonofabitch who hasn't given his attention to God, man, or beast. It's the last thing—probably the only thing—the bastards ever learn. But by God they finally learn something, and that something is just plain and simple that we have all got to answer to somebody here on earth before we answer to the Lord on high. I've seen the sorry sonsofbitches go out so wide-eyed you knew it wasn't from fear. By God, you knew it was because they finally got the message of this life, the message that says, *Don't fuck up!*"

Lasseter drank his coffee as quickly as was decorous. He did not like Deep Lock; in the prison business you either fancied it or not. He stood up to leave, but McPeters did not stand up with him.

"They don't know their ass from a hole in the ground," McPeters said, on cue, leaning his thick arms on the desk top. "Technicians!" he boomed. "Horseshit! There's one job here, and before this morning's over a hell of a lot of free riders around here are gonna find out what it is. They think they're better'n me. Smarter. More in touch with the times. Shit." He snorted. "The times are right here and right now, and the business of our business is getting rid of four of God's sorriest mishaps."

Lasseter did not want to respond to McPeter's words, but he did, reluctantly. "Everything is changing, John," he said. "Nothing is like it was—here or anywhere. I don't understand it. It's just not the same."

There was a silence. Then McPeters stood. "Cabel," he said, "that may be true; I feel it *is* true. But does change make it right?"

Lasseter looked at the big man; it was one of the few times he had ever heard McPeters ask a question. "Probably not," he said finally. "Probably not," he repeated, and he turned and walked out of the office into the hall toward the Death Chamber to start his work, with Bob Griffis in step behind him.

6:02 A.M.

The first floor of the Death Facility was called the Death House. It was a long rectangle with six rooms that had no windows.

Past the third steel door there was a solid wall at the left down the six-foot-wide hall, broken only by the steel door at the end that led to Death Row. At the end of the hall was the steel door that led into the Death Chamber. To the right was McPeters's small office, then the even smaller Preparation Room, and finally the Ready Cell, a steel cage in the center of a small room where those about to die were kept under constant guard during the final sixty-five hours before their execution. Past the Ready Cell, the hallway made an L to the right, with the Death Chamber sitting at the left and the Witness Chamber farther along. The small Circuit Room, where the electrical guages and mechanisms of the Death Machine were housed, was at the end of the second hall to the right. The death switches were in the narrow Executioner's Booth between the Death Chamber and the Witness Chamber.

With the sole exception of the Ready Cell, the three stories of Death Facility cells—Death Rows, they were called—were like Big Max's other cells: nine by six by eight feet with barred doors that looked out onto five-foot-wide catwalks onto walls lined with narrow barred windows.

In an irony no one seemed to notice or care about, the walled-in exercise yard where the Death Facility inmates exercised for two hours a day was located directly behind the Death Chamber itself. If you went up for a lay-up shot in the yard, you and the ball came down in a spot directly across from the center of the chair, five feet away.

The door to the Preparation Room was closed as Lasseter walked past it. He walked on by the door of the Ready Cell where the woman, Alice Fuller, had been kept since she had been transported from the Women's Prison at Lowell on Friday. In another three paces Lasseter and Griffis had traversed the open hallway between the Ready Cell's door and the closed steel door of the Death Chamber. Lasseter stood back while Griffis opened the chamber's door with one of the heavy brass keys on his wide key ring.

The Death Chamber was in complete darkness, but the room was warm; the heat had been on all weekend. Lasseter entered the dark room first and fumbled along the wall to the right for the light switch. When he tripped the switch the boxy room was invaded by the harsh glare of two rows of flourescent lights on the ceiling.

The Death Chamber contained four things: the Executioner's Booth immediately to the right of the door; the Lead Line Cabinet that held the two electrical leads attached to the condemned person, in the center of the near wall; the Black Box, a large black wooden box that held the death implements—the Death Cap, with its Contact Plate and chin strap, and the Ground Pad—and the electric chair.

The electric chair was like no other chair ever made. Everything about it exuded evil. It was sterile and inflexible, yet totally physical. All wood. Solid oak, with a grain that arced out in ribs that formed garbled zigzag patterns that made no sense. A chair with only three legs, giving the false impression that it was rearing back like a bucking horse.

Convicts built the chair in the spring of 1924, after the state legislature changed Florida's form of legal death, in 1923, from hanging at county courthouses to electrocution at Raiford Prison. They cut down a giant live oak on the banks of New River where it bellied out in a wide U past the prison. The lumber was milled at the prison sawmill, and the chair took shape in the rear of the carpentry shop near the Rock.

It was bolted to the floor, all twenty-one broad slats that made it a chair. There was a high back with four ribs down to the broad seat that was covered with thick, finely ribbed black rubber. At the center of the high back, two vertical spikes waited as a headrest. The armrests were irregular Ts, and there was a final T at the bottom of the third leg, a pillory for the ankles. Leather straps padded the insides of the ankle cups. There were wrist straps, a waist strap, a chest strap. The tile floor under the chair was covered with thick, black, ribbed rubber like that of the chair's seat. It was an implement with no frame of reference. A singular thing.

Ol' Sparky, or the Thunderbolt, Raiford's inmates called it.

"Run ol' Sparky . . . ride the Thunderbolt," they would joke—gallows humor with a history as old as execution itself.

Around the base of the chair, screwed into a detachable wooden housing, there were twenty-three clear glass 100-watt light bulbs used for testing the chair's current. The instant the executioner threw the Death Switch, 2,250 volts of raw household current would tear into the condemned inmate's skull, grounded by a second power line attached to the right ankle. The moment the current made contact with the copper wiring of the Death Cap's Contact Plate, the condemned's thoughts would be erased and there would be no pain as the automatic eight-cycle Westinghouse Death Machine took over for each of its 5–25–5–25–5–25–5–25–second killing cycles that stopped the heart and lungs and brought death within two minutes.

Lasseter circled the chair and made sure each bulb was carefully secured in place. He walked behind the chair to the right side of the Lead Line Cabinet and checked to see that the L-shaped fail-safe bar was turned to the right, in the open-circuit OFF position; the bar disengaged the executioner's controls. Next, Lasseter unrolled the two rubber-coated leads from the cabinet and attached them to two copper connection points on the electrical line that encircled the light bulbs' wooden housing. He made sure the connections were secure, and then he walked back to the fail-safe bar on the side of the Lead Line Cabinet and moved it to the left, to the closed-circuit ON position, so that it could receive the 2,250 volts of electricity from the Death Machine and transmit the volts along the two leads to the chair.

"Go down to the Circuit Room and see that there are eight clicks when I throw the switch," he told Griffis, who was standing nearby.

The guard went out with a respectful "Yessir."

When Griffis had gone, Lasseter turned off the Death Chamber's lights; in the darkness he made his way the short distance along the wall from the light switch by the door to the narrow opening of the Executioner's Booth.

There were two rectangular panel boxes in the Executioner's Booth, both just below the long, thin, eye-level slit that ran across the width of the booth, looking out onto the electric chair. Lasseter felt the left box, passed it, and found the right box. With his thumb and first two fingers he located the circuit-breaker switch, itself a thumb-shaped device, and felt above it for the transfer button, the device that passed control of the Death Machine's lethal electricity to the Death Switch on the left-hand panel.

He set his fingers on the circuit-breaker switch and gave it a sharp turn to the left to the ON position; from the Circuit Room where Bob Griffis stood, Lasseter heard a *thump* as the circuit closed. Without pausing, Lasseter moved his finger above the switch and pressed the transfer button; there was another *thump* from beyond the Witness Chamber as the transfer of controls was made, and concurrent with the thump the red Ready Light came on above the Death Switch on the left-hand panel. In the eerie crimson glow the electrician could just make out the outline of the Death Switch.

Lasseter reached out and grasped the switch between his thumb and forefinger. He lowered his eyes in the dark to the point where he knew the eye-level slit was and got ready to throw the switch.

He had made tests of the electric chair for the past six months, and although he was disturbed to be associated with it again, he had not given the matter any detailed thought until the past weekend. Then, when he saw they were all finally bound to the thing, old memories of the seventy-one executions he had helped perform came back to him. As the weekend progressed, as the time of the executions grew nearer, the memories had become more vivid, a condition that had reached its peak at midnight Sunday as Death Monday, as they had called it in the old days, materialized.

Now, alone in the darkness of the Executioner's Booth, with his hand on the Death Switch, a switch he had helped throw—there were times when he had actually held the hand of reluctant or new executioners —the old sights and sounds and smells of electrocution flooded in on Cabel Lasseter's mind like a rip tide. Quickly, as if to rid himself of the plaguing thoughts, he jerked the Death Switch to the left, instantly sending 2,250 volts of electricity through the two lead lines to the test bulbs at the base of the chair.

A blinding light came into the room from the chair's twenty-three bulbs, leaving the chair itself suspended ghostlike over a raw white halo of electric light. Lasseter kept his eyes on the sight, checking the front bulbs to see that each was perfectly lit; then he walked to the chair and circled it, checking each of the remaining bulbs. They were receiving the proper current.

He returned to the Executioner's Booth and waited for the eight killing cycles to run their course. On the two round dials of the left-hand—Death Switch—panel, in the strong light provided by the twenty-three 100-watt bulbs at the base of the electric chair, he could see the 5- and 25-second cycles change, with the

5-second, 2,250-volt high-range cycle registering on the left, and the 25-second, 1,000-volt low-range cycle registering on the right. On the square dials of the right-hand—circuit-breaker—panel, he could see the voltage readings as they went from 2,250 to 1,000, and the amps as they went from 0 to 20. He watched the dials intently; when the Death Machine cut off automatically at the end of two minutes, he was satisfied that the entire killing mechanism was in order.

In the dark once more, the electrician retraced his path along the wall until he came to the light switch by the door. He turned the lights on and walked quickly to the Lead Line Cabinet and threw the fail-safe bar to the OFF position; behind him he heard Bob Griffis's heavy boots pounding the tile floor of the hall.

When Griffis walked back into the Death Chamber there was a smile on his square face. "Works just like it came out of a Sears 'n' Roebuck catalog," he said.

Lasseter didn't answer. "That's it," he said, instead. "If you'll take the platform loose and store it in the Circuit Room, we're through."

"Yes, sir," Griffis responded, but his face showed that his mind held a curiosity he could not contain. "Mr. Lasseter," he went on, facing the electrician, "what's it like? I mean," he continued self-consciously, "what will it be like this mornin'? I've thought about it all weekend. I can't figure out what it will really be like."

Lasseter studied the guard's hard face. His mind flashed back to his first execution almost thirty years before. "Like nothing else in the world, Bob." He paused. "I can't describe it to you. You have to see it, to *feel* it, yourself."

The big, unschooled guard thought for a second. "I suppose I knew it was like that." He frowned. "The major says everything goes so fast you don't really have time to think about it; just act."

"He's right," Lasseter agreed. "But you think about it later. You think about it a great deal."

"I figured that too," Griffis said slowly. Then he set about disassembling the test base around the electric chair and carrying it down the hall to the Circuit Room.

As Griffis began his chore, Lasseter walked behind the chair to the Black Box on top of the Lead Line Cabinet; inside the box was the Death Cap, with its chin strap, and the Ground Pad.

The Death Cap resembled the top piece of an ancient Turkish warrior's battle helmet. Like the other death implements, it was homemade, and, like the other pieces, it had that slightly imperfect homemade look. The cap was four pieces of thick brown leather sewn together in a concave shape that became an inch deep at the center. The four pieces were fastened together by four half-inch-wide strips of thinner, darker leather so that all four sections met at the top where a quarter-inch-diameter hole had been punched. The stitching on the strips had been done on an industrial sewing machine at the prison. The sewing machine operator was unskilled, and the thick cotton stitches weaved in shaky lines along the binder strips. A nine-by-four-inch piece of black leather was sewn across the front hemisphere of the cap as a mask, and at the sides of the mask, fastened to the thick leather of the Death Cap, there was the neck strap, stationary to the left, with a buckle at the right.

The chin strap was constructed from the same material as the Death Cap. Its chin cup was made of heavy tan leather with straps of black leather, and in places it too was sewn together with no skill.

But of the three implements in the Black Box, the Ground Pad was the most poorly constructed. It was eight inches long and three inches wide, made of thick, dark-brown leather on the outside, with a soft, almost silky, inside of pure lead hammered paper thin. The leather outside and the lead inside were fastened together by wide, erratic stitches of white nylon fishing line, handsewn over and around the edges. On each end of the pad there were five metal hooks and in the center of the pad, built into it between the leather covering and the lead lining, was a thin square piece of copper attached to a copper screw post that extended two inches to the outside.

All the leather implements had cracked slightly and been covered with a thick layer of mold after almost thirteen years of storage since the last execution, but Major McPeters had personally seen to their repair and restoration.

Lasseter examined each of the three items carefully—a check he had made more than twenty times during the past months—and returned them to the box, closing it. Beside the box there was a large clear-plastic bag that held two new pairs of thick, reinforced telephone lineman's black rubber gloves. He took the bag down and removed the gloves. He examined the outsides carefully, then blew into each one. They could have no holes, in the event he had to make any adjustments to the chair, or to the condemned themselves, after the Death Switch had been thrown. When he was satisfied that the gloves were flawless, he placed them in the plastic bag again and returned it to the top of the cabinet.

Now there was only one other object to be checked, the Contact Plate. It was round and concave, four inches in diameter, formed of copper mesh that was welded in the center to a three-inch copper screw post. The under side was covered with thin sponge rubber so constructed that the plate sat solidly inside the one-inch-deep concave recess of the Death Cap.

The Contact Plate was hooked to the left electrical lead line by a large round copper wing nut and was the device that transmitted the lethal electricity to the condemned person's shaved skull.

The Ground Pad was hooked to the right electrical lead line by a smaller copper wing nut, at a point four inches above the condemned's right ankle. It was the passage of electricity from the Contact Plate across the heart and lungs to the Ground Pad that brought about death.

The Contact Plate was in a five-gallon galvanized bucket at Lasseter's feet just behind the left side of the electric chair. Lasseter bent down before the bucket to examine its contents. The afternoon before he had half filled the bucket with water and put in two pounds of common ice cream salt, because the saline solution would ensure good electrical conduction. Now the water was a milky, translucent paste. You could smell the salt. He stared at the bucket's contents and then reached his hand down into the water.

The sponge circle of the object felt soft. Lasseter picked it out. In the hard light of the room he could see its delicate creamy-yellow color. Turning it over he grasped it by the metal rod that was anchored to its center. He dipped the object in the bucket and swirled it around in the thick salt water for three circles and then brought it out again.

At first glance it appeared to be simply a concave yellow sponge with a short metal handle. It looked perfectly harmless, absolutely pedestrian; you might use it to clean dinner dishes or the bathroom bowl. But this piece of hardware was more important than any other single instrument in the execution.

The sponge, a fine-grained, natural elephant-ear sponge imported from Greece, had been sewn by hand over the concave webbing of copper wire with wide nylon-thread stitches like the Ground Pad. A Jacksonville doctor had designed all the death implements in the late 1930s. In the early days they had attached the bare metal electrode to the condemned's head, but it burned the skin, and the stench of burning flesh sickened the witnesses, who sat in the same room at that time. With the sponge there was no burn and no odor.

The delicate plate Lasseter held in his hand had killed more than half the 196 inmates who had been executed in Raiford's chair. Lasseter always thought of it as a sleeping cobra, something that might strike out at any moment, and he was also aware of the black irony that, of all the complex machinery that went into the act of execution, it was a household sponge and ice cream salt, as much as anything, that killed the condemned.

Lasseter checked the sponge for breaks or tears. There were none. He kneaded the sides with his fingers to make sure there was proper contact with the copper wiring. The device was in order. He took a steel emery board from his coat pocket, one he had used on the object the day before, and went over the grooves of its metal post. *There would be proper contact,* he told himself. But a persistent fear invaded his mind: *Would the fragile sponge hold up through four executions in a row?* He intended to re-dip the sponge each time. *Would it continue to hold the conducting salt? Would it crack?* He didn't know. There was only one sponge. No like substitute could be found. *So much could go wrong with four,* he said to himself. He whirled the plate in the saline solution a last time and then let it fall back to the bottom of the bucket. Two final checks remained.

On the floor of the Executioner's Booth, in the right front corner, there were two boxes. One was Lasseter's own personal electrician's toolbox. He shook the salt water from his hands, walked to the booth, bent down by the box, and carefully examined its contents. The other box, cardboard and slightly larger than a shoebox, contained the executioner's robe, a black robe like a judge's, and the executioner's thin, black rubber gloves. Lasseter opened this box and saw that the robe and gloves were inside. He replaced the box top and stood up. He was through. He had made his checks. He had started the thing. The death apparatus was ready.

He turned and walked out of the Executioner's Booth and found Bob Griffis standing outside the Death Chamber's doorway.

"You ready, Mr. Lasseter?" Griffis asked.

Lasseter nodded that he was through and walked out of the room, leaving the guard to cut off the lights and close the door. As he walked out, his mind was behind him in the chamber.

If the water content of the four condemned is sufficient there should be no problem, Lasseter said to himself as he walked toward McPeters's office. The killing amperes, in large measure, were a function of the condemned's body water content. But the electrician wondered how the amps would take with two of the four they were about to execute. The woman, Alice Fuller, was small and frail, but he thought the amps would take with her. But one of the white men, George

Kruger, was like a madman. He would go for days without eating or drinking; the amps might not take with him.

It could all go wrong, Lasseter told himself.

When he came in line with the Ready Cell, he turned and looked in as he walked past. The look was only for a brief second, and he saw nothing but the glaring light in the door's glass slit. *Anything could happen,* he said silently, as he moved on toward the open doorway of McPeters's office.

6:18 A.M.

McPeters was on the phone when Lasseter came up to his door. The electrician stood back to allow him time to finish the call, but McPeters motioned him inside, pointing to the bolted-down folding chair, and continued his call, hunched over his desk, leaning on his elbows in his habitual manner. He was talking with the warden, and he said Greenwood's name several times for Lasseter's benefit, never looking at him but appearing to be talking directly to him.

As Lasseter watched McPeters on the phone, he was stuck, as he had always been, by the big blunt man's capacity for subtlety and measured deception; watching McPeters operate always seemed like watching a spider weave his web.

"Right. That's exactly right, Mr. Greenwood. We're on schedule here. Cabel Lasseter just came into my office." McPeters looked at Lasseter for the first time, his big face pleasant but unsmiling, his eyes quiet. "We're all set on this end," he went on. "No problems at all. . . . Yessir, that's correct. . . . Yessir. I'll see you in twenty minutes. . . . Yessir," he ended respectfully, pausing to let Greenwood hang up before he replaced his receiver.

When he had put the phone down, McPeters sat

back in his chair and rubbed his eyes and his forehead with the palms of his open hands. He had removed his blue uniform coat; his bulk was enormous inside his finely starched and pressed khaki shirt with a major's gold oak-leaf insignia on each collar. His chest and upper arms looked like a single piece of granite.

"Yeah." He exhaled, reaching down to grip the side of the desk top between his thumbs, his meaty fingers spread out on the top. "I got to get some sleep when this thing is over. I'm an old man. The young bucks are gonna get me yet," he told Lasseter, his face still pleasant but unsmiling.

"They'd best bring their lunch, when they start," Lasseter replied, reaching inside his coat for a cigarette.

McPeters shook his head in reply to this, then said, "So you got your work done?"

Lasseter lit his cigarette and nodded, exhaling a long deep line of smoke. "The apparatus is ready," he said, crossing his legs and sitting stiffly back into the chair, "but are we?"

"You and me," McPeters answered instantly, "we're ready. And that's all that really counts. The rest is just window dressing."

Among the twenty or so people present at each execution, only three actually made the thing happen: the Chief Correctional Officer (McPeters) and his three-man Death Strap Squad, who prepared the condemned inmates for death and delivered them into the Death Chamber; the electrician (Lasseter), who made the actual electrical attachments; and the executioner, who worked the controls of the Death Machine. Of the three, the executioner remained anonymous behind a mask and robe and did his deathwork shielded from view inside his Executioner's Booth, while Lasseter and McPeters did much of their deathwork in plain view of the assembled officials, witnesses, and the condemned. Lasseter and McPeters were acting as officers of the prison; the executioner was an officer of the courts. How Lasseter and McPeters performed reflected directly on the prison system itself; what the executioner did reflected on the law in general. Like most prison workers, John McPeters and Cabel Lasseter had no real knowledge or understanding of or *identity* with the law. Their minds focused instead on the code of discipline of the prison.

"It's been a long time," Lasseter finally replied. "People change." He went on with some uncertainty, keeping his eyes on McPeters. "Me," he said slowly, "I thought the thing was over for good. I haven't thought about it for years. I'd put it out of my mind.

"I don't know," he went on, drawing hard on his cigarette, his voice becoming grim, "I guess I've gotten a little soft and lazy with all the rest—*most* of the rest," he amended, regarding McPeters's now icy eyes.

"They've made executives out of us, John," he continued, his tone clearly indicating he regretted his words. "A far cry from the old days when we got meat 'n' potatoes and a few dollars spending money—"

"The work, our job, is still the same," McPeters broke in firmly. "You and I know that as well as anybody. Right's still right and wrong's still wrong. There's no in-between, no matter how hard people try to make it so; there's still just two sides of the coin.

"A man's job is his honor," McPeters went on. "Without a job, a purpose, a man's nothing. That's what's wrong with these people here: the ones we'll execute this morning, and the new ones who've come to work at this prison. They've got no job, no purpose, no honor. But we do, Cabel, and we go all the way." He paused, then continued, locking his fingers together before him on the desk top. "That's the trouble with people today. They don't want to go all the way. That's the biggest problem. I've got when I hire a new guard. I've got to find somebody who'll go all the way. An' that's almost impossible to do, because about all I get is gravy-trainers and screw-ups. Drunks, who've sandbagged twenty years in the Army and are out looking for another meal ticket to go with their government retirement.

"So I had to adopt a new system. Yessir. I got myself a *modern system* just like all the bushy-headed geniuses running around here. And Cabel, this is my system: Most of the time I just settle for a man who'll do what he's told when I know he won't go all the way. That's right"—McPeters allowed himself a little smile—"I just find me a strong back who'll do what I tell him.

"Not these boys here," he added quickly, gesturing with his open hands toward his office door. "Not my Death House crew. These boys will go right down the line to the last man. They're good boys. The best in the system.

"We're walled off here from the screw-ups." McPeters locked his fingers again, fixing his cold brown eyes on the electrician. "We've got a good strong chain. No weak links." His eyes searched Lasseter's for agreement, demanded it.

The electrician knew McPeters's system very well. He both understood it and understood why it was needed. The old-timers of the old school had been taken into the prison system at the end of World War II, which was to say the end of the Great Depression. The prison had been both a haven and the end of the line for men like Lasseter and McPeters; theirs had not been a generation of choices. The retired military personnel of the prison's new school were the "straights" of the Beat Generation; theirs was the age of options and greener pastures. The loyalty McPeters and Lasseter felt for the prison had its roots in the breadlines of the thirties, a time the new school studied in history books or watched on TV documentaries.

"You're a wizard, John," Lasseter said, attempting a thin smile. "You never cease to amaze me. You've got one half the world in one pocket, and the other half in the other. You're a lucky man."

McPeters stood from behind his desk and returned Lasseter's slight smile. Lasseter stood, too. "Not lucky," McPeters said, coming around the desk adjusting his starched shirt in his trousers as he moved, "just persistent."

He was standing even with Lasseter when he finished his sentence; he took Lasseter by the shoulder, an odd thing for him to do, and led him out of the office to the beginning of the Death Facility's deep-lock maze.

"But don't tell anybody I know a big word like 'persist,' " he added as they came up before the maze.

Lasseter smiled fully and turned to face McPeters head on. "The wizard," he said. "The lucky, *persistent* wizard."

McPeters didn't respond directly. "Right," he said, releasing Lasseter's shoulder. "We go all the way. All of us—you, me, the warden, even the governor himself. We do what we're told because of our jobs, because of our honor.

"So," he went on, shifting his weight from foot to foot, motioning for Bob Griffis to open the first steel door that led into the maze and back to Big Max's main hallway, "the Death Committee will assemble here right at seven forty-five. I'll see you then. And don't you worry, Cabel," he added. "Let me do the worrying. That's part of *my* job," he ended, sending the silent Lasseter on his way into the maze.

Alone in Big Max's vast and empty main hallway, Lasseter made his way toward his office in the heart of the industrial shops area on the other side of the prison. As he walked, he became aware that the muscles in his neck and shoulders were beginning to relax, to soften like rocks breaking up. It amazed him that he had not been aware of the tension. Then he remembered that it had always been so when they executed.

THE DEATH WATCHERS

Starke, Florida, was a Civil War town that had always been on the way to somewhere else—never much more than a wide spot on the road, but the first real city you saw among the line of hardscrabble filling-station towns past the Georgia state line thirty miles to the north.

It was founded by Hard-Shell Baptists and then transformed into a hell-raising boom town during World War II when Camp Blanding sprang up in the pine flatlands ten miles to the east, on the highway to Jacksonville. For thirty years after the war it had floundered between boom and bust. Now, according to a University of Florida study, it was "a place that was losing its folkways."

Those folkways were the bitter foundations of the tough-nut cracker ethic, an unwritten doctrine that had ruled supreme for more than a hundred years. But the customs and the old-time crackers themselves were being devoured by outsiders, Yankees who once would have been called Carpetbaggers and were now called Suitcasers, people who used Starke as a cheap, clean, safe bedroom for their lucrative jobs in Gainesville and Jacksonville or as an equally cheap place for light industry, fast food restaurants, chain motels, and "last chance" souvenir stands.

Like most towns of the Old South, Starke began with two streets of commerce, a courthouse square, and ten back streets lined with slatboard and brick houses and oaks. By the 1970s it had four streets of commerce, about fifty back streets, and one shopping center, and it was encircled by subdivisions whose names generally favored the word "estates" and featured ranch-style yellow brick houses where boats and campers replaced trees and shrubs. It was one of those unimposing, uniquely American places about which it could be said that it was a good, quiet place to live and raise children. A place where nothing ever really happened.

But now something was happening. There was a frenzy in the air. Starke was filled to overflowing with the media: TV, radio, newspapers, wire services, magazines. All their representatives and paraphernalia were there. The executions at the prison ten miles distant were suddenly the biggest show in the world; headlines were calling Starke "Death City," and nameless, faceless farmers and merchants and housewives were being stopped on the freezing sidewalks by radio and TV crews and asked probing questions about the executions—something they and the questioners knew nothing about but endlessly elaborated over.

Starke was suddenly big news, suddenly a firm place on the map, and the city and its citizens basked in newfound glory like a pug after his first winning fight. Seemingly overnight the shops and stores filled up with new merchandise. Service stations started selling glassware and towels hastily imprinted with *The Starke Four*, and hundreds of T-shirts went on sale with the same words set underneath a fearsome drawing of the electric chair. Motels advertised "Special Event Rates," and one bar, the Lone Pine, just north of the city limits, was featuring the Thunderbolt Cocktail, a combination of four kinds of rum and fruit juices, for its working-class patrons. Everywhere you looked the locals were coming out of their habitually leaden shells and getting into the act. For twenty years TV had conditioned them for the "media event," and now there was one in their own back yard and they were taking it for the longest ride possible.

Lincoln Daniels and Palo Reyas entered Starke on Saturday at 5 P.M. exactly. In the way Lincoln's

mind worked, his thoughts split in half when he first
confronted the city again after a month's absence, one
half focusing on the frenzy before him, the other half
going back to the pleasure and ease of Mexico, which
he had left only five hours before. Looking out the car
windows, Lincoln Daniels had the sick feeling that he
had made a great mistake in coming to witness the
executions. He knew that it would only last for a few
minutes as they progressed through the cold, damp
streets, but he held on to the pleasing image of Mexico
as long as he could.

It had been a bright 50-degree morning in Mexico
City as the olive-drab train that carried Lincoln Daniels and Palo Reyas wound its way through the outlying adobes past Tlalnepantla. Since the first morning light hit the smoky industrial city of Toluca, the
train, which had traveled ten hours through mile-and-
a-half-high mountains on a treacherous boot-toe route
from Morelia, northeast to Acámbaro in the state of
Guanajuato, and down the high passes of the Sierra
Madre Occidental to the capital, had inched along,
stopping every mile or so to pick up day laborers for
the Federal District.

Lincoln had come to think of Mexico as his
home, which was odd, as he was one of America's most
decorated war heroes and one of the country's most
successful money authors—odder still because he set
great store by each recognition and had actively
worked for each in the spontaneous but planned manner of such enterprises. Now fifty-two, he had lived in
Mexico for four years, since the end of his last marriage, his second, trying to adjust to a life without, as he
said, "a full-time, sleep-in woman."

Daniels had moved to Mexico for three specific
reasons: because of the end of his second marriage,
because of his long-standing friendship with Palo Reyas, and because he wanted, as he said, "to go back
in time," to appropriate "an older, simpler momentum."

Mexico was a thousand sights, sounds, and tastes,
a thousand feels: the singular Latin look of four-hun-
dred-year-old buildings, arches, cracked walls lined

with flowering vines, granite columns, narrow stone
streets, cathedrals rising up from nowhere; cactus,
palms, wildflowers, high-mountain evergreens, bone-
hard deserts; the rainy season coming in and eating up
the winter dust; small boys, armies of them, waving
red handkerchiefs at railroad crossings and hoping for
pennies, standing with shoeshine kits marked with the
names of saints, washing cars, selling colorful balloons
and rubber balls painted with gay faces; ragpickers,
paper pickers, men and women plodding along dusty
roads with burdens fit for horses or burros; sidewalk
cafés and gentle music, or the fire of the mariachis.

Daniels had baptized his new life in the country
and, in the way a place can, Mexico had healed the
wounds that had sent him there. He had retreated into
the unseen past. But his writing was constantly calling
him out. In a sense, his whole life was like the train
ride from Morelia to Mexico City: long, secure, his
needs seen to, fine quiet moments to sit and read or
make notes, or time for conversation and drinks. But
always, running through the scene like a rattlesnake
slithering through the night, was a hint of insecurity
and foreboding, the idea of disaster. And, at the end of
the journey, the price.

As the train had wound its slow way through the
high red-clay banks down into the open plain that was
Mexico City and into the outlying cardboard slums, the
price was a sea of poverty and despair: people huddled
inside the packing crates of refrigerators and stoves,
inside rag-wall huts or cardboard and stick lean-tos;
sad faces that lined the railway and watched the train
as if it were from another planet. *Always a price,*
Daniels had thought to himself as he looked out from
his warm Pullman compartment at the scene. *There is
always a price to be paid. Nothing we do, no matter
how good or bad, is without its price,* he had said silently, as the train moved on toward the regal heart of
the ancient city.

Before him, now, there was nothing regal, nothing serene; there was Starke, Florida. From the coastal
lowness and lushness and the muggy heat of the Tampa
airport, where they had landed two and a half hours

earlier, Lincoln and Palo had driven through Florida's interior rolling hills and the state's neuter midsection of pines and palms and slight middle-air winter chill. Now the land had flattened out again and closed in with long stands of slash pines and scrub oaks. The ground was an unfertile gray, and the air was biting cold. They had entered the venal remnants of the mythical Kingdom of Dixie.

Mexico City was in one world, Starke, Florida, in another. And as Starke bore down on them, Lincoln was forced to give up the images, the peace of Mexico, and come back to the frenzied reality of the city and the thing he and Palo had come to watch and describe.

"It's no accident that prisons are where they are," he said to Palo as they drove on through the city on Route 301. "We are a very orderly race, after all," he said. "We always keep things in their proper place."

Palo nodded his head in agreement and stared straight ahead at the dank landscape.

Starke had a population of just over 5,000, but it seemed to Lincoln Daniels, as he drove into the center of the city, that the figure had doubled or tripled. On his first visit to the prison, a month before, he had passed a pleasant week in the little city. He had even fished once in nearby Cross Creek where Marjorie Kinnan Rawlings had lived in a fine little sectioned-off wood-frame cracker house and written books like *The Yearling*. It had been warmer then, with some days in the high 70s, but now it was 38 degrees, a bank clock-thermometer reported, as Lincoln came to the second of Route 301's three stoplights in the city.

"All we need now is some lions to throw these Christians to," Palo said, seeing the streets jammed with people and cars.

Lincoln chuckled. "I imagine there are lions enough, amigo; it's my hope that we avoid them ourselves."

"The TV and newspaper boys." Palo laughed too. "They will be our own personal lions, no doubt."

"No doubt," Lincoln said heavily, as he pulled into the wide oval driveway of the Holiday Inn past the traffic light at the northern edge of the city.

The hundred-room Holiday Inn looked as though it were under siege. Like Starke itself, the motel had been overrun by four times as many people as it could accommodate. All three major TV networks had their headquarters and mobile units there, the major U.S. and foreign papers and wire services had staked their representatives, and along with these, never far from the action, was the crushing crowd of the curious, milling around in the biting, damp cold.

Lincoln and Palo quickly ducked inside the inn and made their way through the glut of bodies and equipment in the smoke-filled lobby to the reception desk. Lincoln was spotted several times by journalists he knew, and he shook hands and spoke briefly with them and introduced Palo, but he got the desk clerk's attention as soon as possible. The month before he had made arrangements for a first-floor suite for himself, and now he would share it with Palo because of the overflow. He registered for the two of them and then quickly led the way back outside to their car. But as he and Palo returned to the motel's double doors he gave up all hope of the immediate sanctuary of their rooms. NBC had spotted him, and their legal correspondent, Fred Billings, was waiting with a three-man mobile crew by the door of his car.

"As my old friend Orson Welles said so eloquently," Lincoln told Palo under his breath as they approached Billings and the TV crew, "the Martians have landed."

Billings and Lincoln knew each other, and the small, well-dressed man approached Daniels with a wide smile and a one-liner that was nearly bursting from his lips.

"You've committed the unpardonable sin," Billings announced. "You've missed my deadline for the six o'clock news."

"Forgive us, for we know not what we do," Lincoln came back quickly, forcing banter of his own and a tight-lipped smile. "How do I get straight?"

"You come through with the goods for tomorrow's special or my hide goes up on the wall on Forty-ninth Street."

"We can't have the weathered pelts of two-hundred-and-fifty-thousand-dollar-a-year newsmen dangling over the rooftops of Manhattan," Lincoln rejoined, his narrowed eyes showing the strain of the effort.

Finally, a handshake and Palo's introduction brought an end to the ice-breaking.

"Can you bail me out?" Billings asked, seeing that Daniels was intent only on getting to his suite and out of the crowd.

"I'll do my best," Lincoln replied, trying to sound pleasant but not completely pulling it off. "Just give me a couple of hours to get my bearings and make a few phone calls. Say about nine; that too late?"

"Fine. Nine it is," Billings agreed, extending his hand to Lincoln again and then to Palo. "It's good to see you, damn good," he added, almost as an afterthought.

Lincoln picked up the words deliberately. "Likewise," he said. "But this whole mess is starting to smell. And when a thing smells bad before it's had time to turn sour, that's about as bad as it can get."

Billings didn't answer immediately. He just stood and looked at Lincoln; for a second he didn't get Lincoln's meaning. He was too conditioned to the media circus going on around him, too conditioned, without knowing, to starting circuses. Finally Lincoln's meaning hit him and he cracked a short, sharp laugh. "Hell," he said, "this is nothing. The fun's just beginning. We haven't even warmed up yet."

Lincoln shook his head and tried to laugh but couldn't. "Well," he replied with much effort, "we'll fan the flames a little tonight."

"Now you're talking," Billings said.

Lincoln didn't reply as Billings and his crew broke and moved away swiftly back to the lobby.

"The Martians?" Palo said when Billings was out of earshot.

"The green-eyed, five-footed, six-peckered variety," Lincoln answered, as he turned for their suite.

2

In their suite, Lincoln and Palo mixed drinks and unpacked; they were sitting in the small living room watching TV and drinking when the six o'clock news came on. Lee Bozeman and Michael Reddish led off with the Florida executions and stayed on the subject for much of the program. They began with a remote broadcast outside Big Max and then went to stock shots of the interior of the Death Chamber and the electric chair and some hands-through-the-bars shots on Death Row. Then they cut back to New York for a taped interview with Paul O'Dell, a senior *New York Times* editor and author of *Death in D-Yard,* the Pulitzer Prize-winning account of the Attica rebellion of September 1971.

"Damn good man," Lincoln said as O'Dell came on. "But from the clippings *Esquire* sent me, he's made up his mind on the thing way before the fact."

Palo said nothing; he knew Lincoln did not want to talk about his own right or wrong views.

On the TV screen, Bozeman was trying to pin O'Dell down without success; Reddish came on, laconic and unhappy and not obliged to give his own personal views on capital punishment, although one would have guessed by his delivery that he thought the electric chair was too easy. After O'Dell's many public pronouncements that he was "totally against capital punishment for any reason," Reddish took the opportunity to list the crimes of the four, crimes probably everybody in the United States knew by heart after the month-long media bath they and capital punishment had been given.

"George Kruger raped five women; Charlie Parker killed his wife and his mother-in-law with an ax and then shot and killed one of the policeman who tried to arrest him; Mrs. Alice Fuller poisoned her husband and her three children, ages six, four, and one; and José Santos, around whom the test case on capital punishment, *Santos* versus *Florida,* was lost, bombed a pro-Castro social club in Miami and killed eight people, half of whom were women and small children, at a Saturday-night bingo game.

"So"—he crossed his hands and looked off past the camera—"you don't believe in capital punishment, and you don't believe these four should die this coming Monday morning?"

"I can give you the hypothetical situation"—O'Dell scowled, adjusting his considerable frame in his chair—"of a fiend who disembowels an entire orphanage filled with virgins. But for the state to kill the guilty party does not set the thing right, and, as I've said before, I don't think the state has the right to take lives." He paused.

"Don't get me wrong, I'm not excusing the criminals," O'Dell went on. "I'm for their being punished, but punished within the bounds of human rights, regardless of the fact that they go beyond those rights themselves. The state, after all, has the higher responsibility. Should the state *lower* itself to the level of criminals?"

Reddish responded only with his icy eyes; Bozeman, the picture of dozing urbanity, stepped in and switched both the tone and the approach to O'Dell and began probing him about the book he had contracted to write on the event. Rawson and Company was reportedly giving him a six-figure advance to write a biography of the condemned.

O'Dell half-heartedly denied the figure, but for the first time publicly announced that he was indeed under contract to do a book on the executions, as well as to cover the event for the *Times.* Since the book would obviously be on the side of the abolitionists, Bozeman moved on to another strong rumor that was making the rounds of New York's literary rumor mill.

"You and Lincoln Daniels are the principal writers

who will be covering the event," he said. "What do you think about Daniels's refusal to say whether he is for or against the executions?"

Before O'Dell could answer, Bozeman looked at his note cards and read a quote.

"His only statement thus far has been, 'I'm going to Florida as a reporter, not a book author. Reporters shouldn't express opinions,' end quote."

O'Dell thought a moment; in his seat in front of the TV, Lincoln Daniels stiffened at hearing himself quoted and not being able to take his own part.

"Well, of course Lincoln is a stubborn, secretive cuss, and I respect his opinions," O'Dell said, obviously distressed that his own position of vehemence against the executions put him in a seemingly less respectable position. "But we're not talking politics, or business, or even crime. We're talking about life and death. There are times when the reporter must have an opinion, and this in my judgment is one of them. Dammit!" he roared. "I don't uphold these people. They're the dregs of the earth. But we've got to stop before it's too late or we as a society—we, the state—will be no better than they."

Lincoln had heard enough. He got up and started to turn the TV set off just as Bozeman switched to a live on-the-scene broadcast outside the prison. The reporter was standing out from the cyclone fence in front of the long row of cellblocks. There was great noise and confusion; debris was pouring out of the barred windows of the cellblocks.

"My God," the reporter was sputtering. "Lee . . . Michael . . . they're tearing the prison apart! It's a full-scale riot! My God. . . ."

Lincoln forgot about defending the quotes and the stance attributed to him on TV. He and Palo were both dashing out the door of the suite, part of the mad rush to the prison to cover the bloody sympathy riots.

Sour from the first, Lincoln said to himself as he raced for his car. *Sour from the first. . . .*

3

Lincoln Morgan Daniels was born in a two-story log house outside Kalispell, Montana, on March 7, 1924, the son of Michael Dean Daniels and Kay Winston Daniels, both of whom had been born and raised and lived all their lives in the Flathead, as that part of northwest Montana was called.

The Flathead and the small town of Kalispell sat in the shadow of Glacier National Park to the northeast and the dense Kootenai Forest to the west. The country was still wild and untamed at Lincoln's birth—Montana had been a state then for only thirty-five years—and Mike Daniels was building the largest timber company in the Flathead. A boy could not have wished for a better place or time for an American childhood.

Leaving home at the age of seventeen, like a legion of others at the time, to join the Marines and fight the Japs, Daniels took with him two great gifts: from his father he got knowledge, skill, understanding, and love of the wilderness; from his mother, he learned great kindness and a love of books. All his life, he judged other men and women by Mike and Kay Daniels, and he found few who measured up to their standards. Both lived to see their son honored in the military and a successful writer. In later years Daniels would tell an interviewer, "A man ought not to expect more luck than that."

In war and in writing Lincoln Daniels had good luck, but not with his marriages. When his second marriage ended in tragedy in the winter of 1972 and he moved to Mexico, he tried to analyze the failure of his first marriage and the senseless end to his second. He found no pat answers. He was able to reason only that he was the victim of his own folly and the victim of fate. Nothing more could be said, he had decided in the end. But to guard against recurrence, he had resolved never to marry again, a resolution he hoped he would keep.

Lincoln had married his first wife, Andrea de Clovis, almost two years to the day after he resigned his commission as the "boy colonel" of the Marine Corps on January 1, 1954. He was living in Paris at the time on Île Saint-Louis at the corner of the Quai d'Orléans and the rue le Regrattier. He was almost thirty-two when they married, and Andrea, delicate, and champagne-blond, was twenty. He was the dashing war-hero-become-world-famous-novelist; she was feminine illusion itself, the youngest daughter and pride of Baron Guy de Clovis, whose vast fortune centered around the tenth generation Chateau de Clovis cognacs. The match seemed perfect, but it was "a union ordained to failure," as a Paris newspaper reported when Andrea sued for divorce on the grounds of mental cruelty four years later in Monaco.

They had met in a box at the races at Auteuil in the fall of 1955 and were inseparable for the fifteen months before they married. She was everything in a woman he had ever imagined; in his wildest fantasies he had never allowed himself to believe that he would possess such a creature. The words were trite and he knew better ones, but he always thought of her as "a vision": her delicate, high-cheekboned face, pale with a mouth always pouting; nose upturned; brown eyes, the majestic, staid, haunting eyes of the always rich, at ease as eyes can be only if the bearer has never known a single hint of insecurity.

The marriage was in Nôtre Dame, the reception at the Ritz, and the honeymoon in Rio. Six months later when they returned to Paris, Daniels found that movers had transplanted his belongings, writings included, to a villa at Cap d'Antibes on the Mediterranean north of Cannes—all compliments of his father-in-law.

True to his nature and his heritage, and truer to his own pride, Lincoln balked, but silently, accepting the gifts gracefully, hoping that after the six-month

interlude he would be able to return to work, hoping
that the gifts would end, hoping to settle in with his
wife, raise chldren, write books, and grow old and fat
and happy. But of course it was not to be. He had
been let into the de Clovis family as a symbol, and it
was that symbol—the writer, the war hero—the Baron
was financing, not the husband or the man. The de
Clovises' life-style set the pace of what came to be
called the Jet Set, and Lincoln Daniels was exhibited
like a painting between Saint-Tropez and Nice for a
third of the year, in the Swiss and Italian Alps for
another third, and on a shuttle between Paris, Ven-
ice, London, Rio, Buenos Aires, and New York for the
final third.

From 1947 to 1949, as a Marine first lieutenant,
Daniels had produced his first two books, *The Island*
and *The Village,* the second a best seller. But it was
his sad comment that, freed from any hint of money
worries and set up in a secluded villa that could have
afforded absolute peace and quiet, from 1956 to 1960
he produced not a single book.

"It was impossible," he later joked to a friend.
"My fingers hurt so bad from opening and closing
my suitcase I couldn't type."

The four unproductive years were a grim joke to
Daniels. They shamed him and made a mockery of his
labored decision to give up his Marine Corps commission after a brilliant twelve-year career that had
seen a seventeen-year-old farm boy develop into a so-
phisticated, self-educated twenty-nine-year-old Marine
captain with the unprecedented temporary war-time
rank of full colonel.

If there was anyone who seemed destined for a
career in the military, it was Lincoln Daniels. The ideas
of service, obedience, discipline, and dedication came
as easily to him as the act of putting on his uniform.
The lessons of his youth and his own inner sense of
duty made him a natural soldier, a fact that was immediately apparent to his superiors from his first action
as an eighteen-year-old PFC with Lieutenant Colonel
Chesty Puller's Seventh Marines in the Point Cruz

Landing on Guadalcanal in August 1942, until he was wounded some weeks later in the disastrous battle of Matanikau River.

A year after Guadalcanal, after he had recuperated from gunshot wounds in his left arm and shoulder at the U.S. Naval Hospital on Fiji, Buck Sergeant Lincoln Daniels, decorated with a Navy Cross, a Purple Heart, and a row of campaign ribbons, got himself assigned to the First Marine Division in time for the New Britain campaign that began with the Cape Gloucester invasion the day after Christmas 1943. In the relatively light fighting on New Britain Island Lincoln again distinguished himself, this time as the leader of a hastily put-together five-man raider team. By the summer of 1943, not yet twenty, Lincoln Daniels was a seasoned Marine staff sergeant with two Navy Crosses on his three rows of combat ribbons, a trooper who had caught the eye of no less a person than stone-faced Major General Alexander Vandergrift, the commanding general of the First Marines. From the summer of 1943 to the summer of 1944, Daniels served as head of the security squad that accompanied Vandergrift on his inspection and combat rounds of First Marine installations.

In early September 1944, privy to top-level Marine strategy in the Pacific by virtue of his proximity to Major General Vandergrift, Daniels again got himself attached to Colonel Puller, who had just been given command of a brigade of the First Marines. On September 15, at age twenty, Daniels went ashore on the first wave at Peleliu. During the first week Puller's men suffered 1,749 killed and more than 2,000 wounded. In the devastation, Sergeant Daniels was given a battlefield promotion to second lieutenant and was in command of a company when he was shot in the right leg on October 2 in the bloody Battle of the Umurbrogol.

World War II ended for Lincoln Daniels in the grim island wastes of Peleliu on that October day in 1944, but his wound cemented his bond with the Marine Corps and with Colonel Puller and General Vandergrift, two of the corps' most influential officers.

He was flown directly to the San Diego Naval Hospital and on to Bethesda Naval Hospital outside Washington, D.C., in an effort to save his badly shattered right leg, which had been ripped open two inches above the knee by a Japanese machine gun.

General Vandergrift next caught up with Daniels by chance as he lay in Bethesda undergoing extensive rounds of prolonged surgery to save his leg. Vandergrift had been brought home from the Pacific to be Commandant of the Marine Corps. He took a personal interest in the twenty-year-old battlefield lieutenant, giving him the rank of a regular Marine second lieutenant in a ceremony in his hospital room.

The regular commission was clearly a token gesture, intended to help Daniels receive the greater officers' benefits rather than the enlisted man's disability compensation when he was mustered out of the corps because of his leg injury. But after a year and a half of surgery, and through his own grit, Lincoln made his leg heal, and a week after his twenty-second birthday he presented himself at the Commandant's Office in full winter dress greens with an invitation for General Vandergrift to accompany him for his first postoperative drink of whiskey.

The bar of the Hotel Jefferson was selected for the auspicious occasion, and after a half-drunken afternoon, the brash young lieutenant convinced his commanding officer that no other career except that of a Marine officer was good enough for him.

General Vandergrift had Daniels transferred to the 8th and I Guard Command in Washington and personally saw to it that he was enrolled in appropriate junior officer courses at the nearby Quantico Marine Officers Training Station.

In the fall of 1947, at the fatherly insistence of General Vandergrift, Daniels, a newly promoted first lieutenant, enrolled in night school at Georgetown University. Intent on exposing himself to college-level courses only, he enrolled in only two classes: American history and Freshman English.

He attacked both courses with his usual vigor, but when he enrolled for the second semester in January 1948 he had narrowed his field of interest to English. Like most wounded, he had read widely during his two wartime convalescences, and suddenly something clicked inside him. Lincoln Daniels discovered that words had a genuine fascination for him.

The first great books and novelists from World War II were beginning to emerge, and for someone with the inclination to describe what he had seen in that war it was a rare time of communal encouragement. That winter and spring of 1948, Lincoln read everyone he could find—novelists, poets, biographers —and in the summer he timorously enrolled in a creative writing class at Georgetown. While his eighteen-and nineteen-year-old classmates wrote about skiing vacations or crushes on finishing-school girls, the twenty-four-year-old Marine first lieutenant wrote about the Battle of the Umurbrogol on Peleliu. Encouraged by his professor, Norman Sutter, who had developed name writers for thirty years, Lincoln finished a short, rough, book-length manuscript on the island battle in six months.

In October 1948, the author and his pile of badly typed manuscript was delivered via Sutter to R. L. Cranston's William Rockbridge, a wiry little forty-year-old New Englander who had just taken over the unpublished James Jones from Maxwell Perkins, who had died the previous summer. *The Island,* as Lincoln was calling his would-be novel, was not of the size or scope of Jones's work-in-progress, *From Here to Eternity,* but all the spark and originality of the Jones manuscript was there. After a modest advance and a herculean rewrite effort by both author and editor, *Island,* to Lincoln Daniels's astonishment, appeared on Cranston's fall line of titles in 1949.

The book was hailed by *Life* as a "brilliant first novel," but the review in *The Atlantic* got to the heart of the matter with its praise. "The Marine Corps' gain," it said, "is literature's loss." And from the fall of 1949, until he resigned his commission four years later, that was the dilemma Lincoln Daniels faced: the choice between continuing his career as a Marine or pursuing the tenuous craft of writing.

Of course Rockbridge and Sutter urged him to resign his commission immediately, but such a move was impossible so long as General Vandergrift, Lincoln's virtual sponsor as an officer, remained Commandant of the Marine Corps. To leave the corps in the face of his World War II combat record, simply because he had written a slim novel that had barely sold 5,000 hardback copies, seemed so preposterous to Lincoln that he could not even form the words of an imaginary resignation speech to Vandergrift.

He contented himself with the knowledge that he had been able to exercise his newfound skill and interest with speed and good luck, and, under the admiring praises of both his fellow officers and some of the literary world, he almost immediately began a second novel, *The Village,* a love story set on Fiji, where he had recuperated from wounds suffered on Guadalcanal in 1942.

The second slim novel—both were slightly more than two hundred pages—was completed between November 1949 and April 1950 and was hastily included among Cranston's 1950 fall titles.

Whereas *The Island* had been a critical success only, *The Village* was an immediate critical and financial blockbuster. The Book-of-the-Month Club picked it up before publication as its major selection for December 1950, it was sold to the movies in May, and the paperback rights were acquired in the same month for a hefty sum—all before the first hardcover book was sold.

Lincoln was astounded at the success of the novel and the sums of money it brought—astounded and a little embarrassed. The Commandant of the Marine Corps made less than $20,000 a year; Lincoln himself barely made $6,000. In his frame of reference, the six-figure money he was earning would keep a battalion of Marines in the field for a year. It seemed impossible that such overnight recognition and such wealth had come to him.

"It's just a matter of time," Rockbridge would announce in his New England twang. "Better now than later. Best all round. The best, the very best," he would say past tight blue lips that were always wrapped around words, a drink of Jack Daniels Black Label, or a Lucky Strike cigarette.

While *Island* developed into a phenomenal success, the question of Lincoln Daniels's leaving the Marines was resolved by the North Koreans when they invaded South Korea on June 25, 1950. When the novel was officially published on September 25, Captain Lincoln Daniels, a newly promoted company commander, had been ashore in Korea for ten days after the Inchon landing. That winter, surrounded in the Chosin Reservoir near the low-skyline North Korean factory town of Hagaru, his battlefield mentor, the mercurial Colonel Puller, kidded him grimly that the North Koreans were not after the reservoir but his money.

"If things get too tough," Puller would tell him, "I'll ransom your ass and get the rest of us out of this."

When the Armistice was finally signed near the 38th parallel at Panmunjom on July 27, 1953, and Lincoln was an acting full colonel at twenty-nine, Puller, by then a brigadier general, took great delight in telling the man he considered his prize pupil in the "stand and fight" school of warfare that he had been made a "boy colonel," as the press dubbed him, because he was "too goddamned rich to be anything else, and not old enough to be a general."

But the kidding only made the paradox of Lincoln's situation more apparent. Of course the exaggerated sum of money, and the popular acclaim that came with the two novels, was an important factor, but clearly—even in the face of his military accomplishments in two wars and his certain career as a Marine officer—he had to leave the service and pursue the full-time vocation of an author.

As soon after the armistice as he could, Lincoln got himself shipped home, and he resigned from the corps with the permanent rank of major on January 1, 1954. Three months later, he left for Paris.

His next book, *A Marine's Journal*, a novel based on the Chosin Reservoir fighting of 1950, appeared in 1956 and was well receveived, but more than anything it was an attempt by Daniels to repay the Marines for the sense of guilt he felt at resigning his commission.

In light of such deep feelings, the jaded years with Andrea de Clovis were all the more hurtful to him. After four years and two children, Guy II and Christiana, and sixteen laps around the earth, Daniels pulled out of the de Clovis whirlwind and took a small cottage on the four-thousand-acre Neville Chamberlin estate on North Andros Island in the Bahamas. Alone on the island and sobered by the realization that he had made a monumental ass of himself for four years, he settled in by himself for two years and wrote what was generally considered his best novel, *The World Did Not Come to an End,* a Pulitzer Price-winning story, appropriately enough, of a failed writer who broke free of a gilded cage and a consuming love affair and regained his strength as a man and as a novelist.

The novel proved to Lincoln and to the world at large that he might "go all the way" as a writer. But from the spring of 1962 to the fall of 1967 he floundered, wandering aimlessly between the Bahamas and Europe to visit his children, and to Montana to try and link up again with the strength of his youth. Finally, in October 1967, he moved to London. He took a small studio apartment in Mayfair and sat down before his typewriter for six months and pulled himself together.

He returned to his first theme of war and wrote a superb 138-page novel entitled *The Battle,* a more or less factual account of the grim Battle of Matanikau River where he had been wounded on Guadalcanal. The novel was excellent. It was not well reviewed in America because of the tide of resentment over the Vietnam War, but the book served its purpose: at forty-four Lincoln Daniels was back in business as a writer, having come to grips with the reality of his bad marriage and of the regimen of writing and living alone. Then came Lady Alice Douglas, the one great love of his life.

They met at a cocktail party on Drury Lane, a cautious, casual meeting and conversation that ended short of an exchange of telephone numbers but teasingly close to curiosity. They were neighbors, it turned out. He lived on Piccadilly across from St. James Palace; she lived three blocks away on Park Lane in the center of Hyde Park. He thought he remembered seeing her; she thought she remembered seeing him. She was forty and had been married once. Both approached members of the opposite sex with a wariness only a bad divorce can bring. A week after they met, Lincoln got her number from a friend and called her for dinner. She was receptive to the call, but reserved.

That was how their courtship developed: with reserve. She had two children, he had two children; neither wanted to make another mistake with marriage. She was a woman of wealth and position by virtue of her father's title and steel mills, a large, shapely, hearty-looking woman with deep-set eyes and thick, curly black hair that she wore parted at the side and at a medium length. She was educated, worldly, witty, and a deeply religious Roman Catholic. She was the first woman, apart from his mother, that Lincoln Daniels admired as well as loved.

They were married on February 14, 1968, in a small graceful stone church in Mexico City and honeymooned at the Villa de Montaña 190 kilometers distant in Morelia.

They honeymooned for six weeks, and during that time Lincoln met Palo Reyas, after he bought one of his sculptures at a private showing at one of the great mansions on Santa Maria Hill overlooking Morelia. Lincoln and Palo became firm friends because of their similar backgrounds in war and in the arts. Lady Alice and Palo's wife, Frances Howes, a wealthy Chicago heiress who had married Palo while both were students at the Chicago Art Institute in 1924, became equally good friends.

It was a fine, settled marriage, with Lady Alice's two young sons away at boarding school in Scotland and Lincoln at work on his sixth novel. They moved into an elegant three-story townhouse on Berkeley Square, a central point in Mayfair halfway between their old residences, and by 1970 Lincoln had completed his 780-page novel *Mr. Pearson's Wall*, about a middle-aged man coping with the pressures of modern life, another sound book and a movie success. By then he had also fathered a boy and a girl by Lady Alice, and his life was full and expansive: a good wife, lovely children, successful writing, and a true lifetime friendship with Palo and Frances Reyas that was built around several reciprocal visits a year.

Then, a week before Christmas in 1972, Lady Alice and his two children were senselessly killed in an airplane crash while returning to London from two weeks of skiing at Gstaad. By the spring of 1973, Lincoln had put their affairs in order and moved to Morelia, feeling it was the only home left for him.

Lincoln passed a quiet forty-ninth birthday on March 7, 1973, at a small dinner party given by the Reyases. The next day, after two months of mourning, he sat down before his typewriter once more and went back to writing, to the only thing he clearly understood and the only thing that had never gone sour for him. On June 1 he finished *The Dogs*, a short, savage novel about a pack of wild dogs that raided a Mexican village. The book was one of America's all-time best sellers, a thriller filled with gore and violence and hatred, a book that, on the surface, seemed to fulfill William Faulkner's flippant quote—"A cheap idea to make a lot of money"—about his own novel *Sanctuary*. But it was not so. The dogs in Daniels' novel were the same as the sharks in Hemingway's *The Old Man and the Sea,* the blind, mindless brutalities of life that chip away until there is nothing left, or until what is left is either no longer wanted or too difficult to recognize. In every respect, the book was Daniels's own sanctuary. Once more he had retreated into his writer's shell when life became too unbearable. *The Dogs* cleansed him, rid him, as much as could be expected, of his grief and hatred, and set him again on an even keel.

In the summer of 1974, when he was in New York plugging the new novel, the chance beginning of another book embroiled him in yet another torturous struggle that tested the balance of his sanity.

He was having lunch with William Rockbridge at

the Café Pierre when he was sheepishly approached by a New York State policeman, a paunchy man with long sideburns, who had trouble getting past the captain because of the cut of his wrinkled seersucker suit. The man showed Daniels his identification and then produced a telegram that had Daniels's name lumped with sixteen others. Although Daniels had never heard of either the town or the prison, he was one of the sixteen observers originally requested by the rebel leaders at Auburn Prison that muggy August afternoon when the convicts seized their hostages and began a bloody three-day drama that proved to be a shorter, bloodier reenactment of the Attica uprising three years before. Lincoln was staying at the Algonquin Hotel seventeen blocks away, and although it was a sweltering 90-degree day outside, because his lunch was at the Pierre he was decked out in full suit and tie. A State Police helicopter was standing by atop the Pan Am Building to ferry him and several others on the list to Auburn, and so Lincoln had to arrive at the prison dressed in a black pinstripe suit with a heavily starched white shirt and a maroon tie.

"I looked," he said later, "like I'd come to arrange a loan, not a truce."

The truce, like Attica's, failed. Forty-two hours after he arrived, State Police and National Guard troops stormed L-Yard, and in nine minutes twenty-two inmates and eighteen guards lay dead or dying. But despite the failure, the reason why he had been sent for by the inmates, and the fact that he had gone, had a profound impact on Lincoln Daniels's life.

Cletus Dempsey, one of the rebel leaders, had served under Daniels as his driver during the last days of the Korean conflict. Dempsey, a small, articulate black man from the East Bronx, had read his colonel's first two novels and made it known to his commanding officer that he was an admirer and an aspiring writer himself. The colonel and his driver spent many hours of travel time in near-sophomoric discussions of life and writing, and they developed a small friendship, but the end of the war and Lincoln's resignation five months later had ended all contact between them. Exactly twenty years to the month since they had last been in each other's company in Seoul, Korea, the two met again in Auburn's riot-strewn L-Yard.

Daniels did not immediately recognize the black man, but he remembered his name. They were a striking contrast that first meeting on August 10: Dempsey, frail and wary, dressed in prison trousers, a New York Jets sweatshirt, mirrored sunglasses, and a turban made from a prison towel; Daniels, robust and imposing in his business suit, fresh from his lunch in one of the world's most expensive restaurants.

They shook hands with reserve in the crush of the Brothers that formed a gauntlet of inmate security from K-Wing out into L-Yard. Lincoln tried to make small talk, but he was totally confused as to why he had been included on the list of observers, and uneasy in the chaos around him.

"Two reasons," Dempsey told him with a staccato ghetto delivery that seemed too fierce to come from such a slight speaker. "I'm one of the leaders, and you are the only straight white man I ever met. Ain't that some shit?" He had laughed. "I been on this stinkin', fuckin' earth for thirty-eight years, totin' this little black ass of mine like a five-hundred-pound sack of shit, an' I only met one straight white cat."

"If it's any comfort to you," Lincoln told him, staring him straight in the eye, "I haven't met all that many either, black or white, and I'm fifty."

They shared a small laugh over that and shook hands again, warmly. From that moment on there was a bond between them that had nothing to do with the Marines, or writing, or Auburn, or anything else except two people reaching out to each other.

The courts added two consecutive twenty-year sentences to Dempsey's ten-year armed robbery sentence for his part in the Auburn riot. In the twenty years since Korea he had done fourteen years behind bars for robbery, breaking and entering, and dealing cocaine. He was a self-professed habitual criminal, a prison rat who subconsciously preferred life behind bars. Although he was con-wise, his articulateness and political fervor constantly plunged him, solidly and irreversibly, into conflict with prison authorities. He would probably be in prison for the rest of his life, but that fact did not deter his militancy; if anything, it acted as a cushion that enabled him to channel all his energies inside the prison rather than wishing and scheming for the outside.

During the Auburn uprising, and in the three years since, the name Cletus Dempsey had become synonymous with inmate participation in American prison militancy. And Lincoln Daniel's nonfiction book on the riot, *The Short Summer of Auburn,* and his friendship and involvement with Dempsey, had placed him in the forefront of public figures associated with proposed prison reform and firsthand knowledge of prison life.

The fact was that Auburn had brought Daniels completely out of the shell that followed the death of Lady Alice and their two children. He despised causes generally, and the people they attracted specifically, but in his own stolid way he joined the cause of prison reform, and although *The Short Summer of Auburn* was not a great financial success for Daniels, it earned him his second Pulitzer Prize and set him up as the most knowledgeable contemporary writer on the subject of prisons.

When the Supreme Court ruled in favor of reinstating capital punishment in the five-to-four *Santos* v. *Florida* decision in September 1976, Lincoln Daniels had been the logical major writer to get the plum from *Esquire* to cover the execution, but once again the situation had placed Daniels between the paradox of his life-style and his surface interests and his deepseated and much more restrained inner feelings.

In Mexico, during the past four years, Lincoln believed he had finally come to grips with life, as well as such an abstract thing could be accomplished. The life—the perfect, measured life—that might have been his with his wife and their two children still lingered in his mind—he imagined that it would always remain there—but he had learned to live with it. He was not happy, not complete, but he had adjusted to life, not death. And with the assignment to cover the executions on Florida's Death Row, his mind had been piqued by a nagging that had to do with the idea of death over life itself.

4

It was almost midnight before Billings came for the interview. Big Max had been sealed off to cameras and reporters by prison guards before Lincoln and Palo and the others from Starke arrived, and as a consequence they spent the rest of the night chasing down the details of the riot, finally recording Warden Hugh Greenwood's press conference on the steps of the prison at 10 P.M. Billings and Daniels had changed into fresh suits for the filming, but strain and deep fatigue showed plainly through their well-tailored façades.

"Let's just go for the meat," Billings said, as he and Daniels took their places on the sofa in Daniels's suite, "and hope we don't go to sleep on camera."

Lincoln grinned limply and agreed, as Billings cleared his throat, straightened in his seat, and nodded for the cameras to roll.

"You've lived outside the United States for most of your adult life," Billings began in his nasal southern accent, "but your themes could be described as genuinely American. As an expatriate observer of the U.S. scene, how do you think the rest of the world sees these executions?"

Daniels shifted slightly on the sofa and set a blood-and-feathers look on his face.

"I don't know that they *see* anything," he answered. "This is a lawful execution of convicted criminals: murderers and rapists. *If* they see anything," he went on, "I suppose it is that we are simply carrying out the lawful sentence of our law."

"Well," Billings said, "are you aware that many European and South and Central American countries, notably Holland, Germany—and Israel in the Mid-East—Argentina, Brazil, Columbia, Ecuador, Venezuela, Uruguay, Costa Rica, the Dominican Republic, Panama, and even your adopted homeland of Mexico, all have abolished capital punishment? And that England and France, who *have* capital punishment, rarely if ever use it?"

Lincoln said he was aware of Billing's information.

"Do you think that these countries, many of whom we tend to think of as turbulent and unsettled, will not regard the U.S. as barbaric? Especially when we begin our executions again after thirteen years with four deaths in the same morning?"

"As a writer," Daniels answered, "I have lived with public opinion and criticism for twenty-five years. I do not play to public opinion. I play to my conscience. That is probably good advice for nations as well."

"Are you saying that the conscience of America demands these executions?"

"No, sir," Daniels said forcefully. "I am saying that nations need not play to public opinion. You give me instances of nations giving up capital punishment. In Bangladesh you can be hung for burning jute. Bangladesh is very poor and jute is very important to the national economy. So jute takes on the capital status of rape and murder.

"It's a matter of degree," he went on. "I don't think anyone in Kansas has ever been hung for burning wheat because there's so much wheat that burning some wouldn't really matter. In Taiwan there is much overcrowding and much robbery and so robbers are shot publicly and often; in this country no such overcrowding exists."

Under Daniels's hard stare and obvious knowledge of the subject, Billings changed his tack. "You've said publicly that you would not express an opinion for or against capital punishment," he said. "Is that still your position?"

"Yes," Lincoln answered. "I'm here as a reporter, and, as I've said, reporters ought not to express an opinion, only report the facts of the event. The facts are their own opinion," he added, looking directly into Billings's eyes.

"Well," Billings went on, "do you find capital punishment itself offensive?"

"The U.S. Supreme Court has said that it is not," Lincoln answered quickly. "As a reporter who's done his homework, I can tell that to you verbatim."

Lincoln paused but took the floor again before Billings could comment.

"Florida is an extremely bloody state. It is eighth in the nation in lynchings, with one hundred and seventy-eight, and fifth in legal electrocutions, with one hundred and ninety-six.

"It is a conservative estimate that about ten thousand people have been put to death in the United States, either by illegal lynching or by legal execution, either by hanging, shooting, asphyxiation, or electrocution. There are no exact figures, because of the nature of lynchings. Even with executions, before say, 1925 most legal executions were carried out at county courthouses and not logged on a national level.

"From 1899 to 1919, three thousand two hundred and twenty-four people, mostly blacks, were lynched in the United States. The top ten lynching states were, predictably, all Deep South states, and Georgia, just as predictably, was the leader with almost four hundred killings.

"Interestingly enough, lynching does not confine itself to hanging, as I had imagined; it includes burning at the stake. About half the three thousand two hundred people lynched in the United States were burned at the stake and afterward cut up in pieces and their various body parts parceled out as souvenirs."

Lincoln stopped speaking abruptly. "Wait a minute," he said into the camera and the glaring ring of lights around it. "Am I getting too rough or going into your own legal territory?"

"Hell, no," Billings answered quickly, with the

camera still rolling. "We'll just cut the raw parts. Listen," he insisted, "if you've got facts and figures, they'll sound a hell of a lot better coming from you than me."

"All right," Lincoln replied. "You want facts and figures; I'm loaded with them. Maybe they'll be just what we all need to put us to sleep."

"Go," Billings said, both men straightening up before the camera.

"The U.S. Department of Justice gives the figure of three thousand eight hundred and fifty-four people, thirty-one of whom were women, as being legally executed in America, but, as I said, the figure is good only from about 1930 on.

"Florida's electrocutions began at the State Prison at Raiford on the afternoon of October 7, 1924. Frank Wells, a black man from Jacksonville, was executed for murder. They didn't even list Wells's age at the time of his death," Lincoln said.

"Three years and thirteen deaths later, they finally listed the age of the executed, and then the irony strikes me as so gray I can't even laugh at it. The man's name was Fortune Howard. He was a sixteen-year-old black from Gainesville who went to his death at two thirty on the afternoon of April 27, 1927, for the crime of rape. It was 1932 before the state got around to keeping full records on the condemned, and after that all their ages were listed.

"The oldest person Florida ever executed was a seventy-two-year-old white man named Charlie Penn, and they executed eleven teenagers, all black. The last time Florida used its electric chair was May 12, 1964, and they killed two that morning. Sam Fallon, a white man convicted of murder, died first at eight forty-nine in the morning, and Eugene Burns, a black man convicted of murder, was the last when the switch was pulled on him at nine-oh-eight."

Lincoln stopped, rubbed his forehead, and then picked up again. "Interestingly enough, my own introduction into prisons at the Auburn riot in '74 was also my introduction to capital punishment. Between the fruitless bargaining and negotiating sessions, one of the guards who was assigned as my escort gave me a running history of capital punishment in general and of its introduction at Auburn Prison in specific.

"The inception of electrocution as a form of legal death goes back to 1890, a truly fascinating period in American history, or at least a fascinating period to me, partly because it is so obscure. Benjamin Harrison, 'Little Ben,' as he was called, five foot six and the grandson of another president, William Henry Harrison, was president at the time. It was said that Harrison was liked neither by his own Republican Party nor by the U.S. citizens. People were advised to wear overcoats in Harrison's icy presence so they wouldn't catch cold."

Lincoln laughed. "The point is, it was twenty-five years after the end of the Civil War, and the 'Age of Progress and Prosperity,' as it became known, was about to descend on the United States. The country was shifting from agriculture to industry. The horse, and everything it stood for, was on the threshold of losing to the automobile and automation."

Lincoln forced a smile. "All that progress and change had to start somewhere. I apologize for regarding it so, but I find it typically American and highly amusing that one of the first advances of the Age of Mechanical Marvels was the invention of the electric chair."

He continued without any hesitation, swept up in his own thoughts. "The first death by electrocution occurred on the hot, muggy, rainy Wednesday morning of August 6, 1890, at Auburn Prison, south of Syracuse, near the village of Auburn in western New York State, and the first person to die by the induction of electrical current into his body was William Francis Kemmler, a convicted ax murderer.

"During his trial in 1889, the state prosecutor kept saying Kemmler was 'born to hang,' a cliché that had had a very pragmatic meaning in New York State and the world at large at the time. But Kemmler cheated the gallows. The usual waiting time for a condemned person in those days was about six weeks to three months, but Kemmler waited a full year on Auburn's Death Row before he was executed."

Lincoln went on, staring straight ahead.

"Kemmler thus became the first modern criminal, or, rather, the first criminal to be dispatched in a *modern* fashion. You have to ask yourself the *why* of the thing. Why and how did men come to choose electrocution as the new form of legal death? History itself is the answer.

"Edison had perfected the light bulb only nine years before, and, discounting Ben Franklin's kite trick in 1772, electricity itself, as a form of power, was only eight years old. Edison began the first central generating system in America in New York City in 1882. In 1890 electricity was like moon landings or the space shuttle today. To be associated with it was to be associated with the future, with progress, with modernization itself.

"And here is the grim kicker," he added, without pausing. "There was a raging debate at the time between rival AC and DC electric companies as to which type of current was better. The DC company, possessed apparently with a better public relations staff, had begun touring the country with a sort of medicine show in which dogs, cats, monkeys, and even horses were electrocuted before various audiences of business and civic leaders to show that direct current was best for future home use. The logic of the show has always escaped me, but nonetheless it had a positive effect on a group of New York State legislators who happened to catch the act in Albany in the spring of 1889.

"That same year there happened to have been a particularly gruesome hanging at the Auburn Prison where a convicted murderess dangled in full consciousness for twenty minutes—without the usual broken neck and the ensuing unconsciousness—before she choked to death on her own spittle. The press raised hell about the woman's execution, and soon the floor of the State Legislature in Albany was on fire with rhetoric for a 'more humane' method of execution.

"Enter the modern marvel of electricity," Lincoln said with a wave of his hand. "And just to put everybody's thinking straight on the salient worth of their product, the DC company sent off to Thailand for a load of man-sized orangutans and executed them for the pleasure and edification of the legislators.

"Kemmler, for his part," Lincoln went on, "took the debate over the form of his death in relative good stride, but on the morning of his execution he balked in the doorway of the Death Chamber at the sight of the chair and the ten rows of bleachers set up before it, filled with wonder-struck onlookers. And Kemmler was not the only one who balked. His executioner, E. F. Davis, and the prison's warden—even the officials of the DC electrical company themselves—did not really know that the household current would kill a man.

"They strapped Kemmler in the chair, dressed only in his undershorts, and then they went to work hooking him up to the crude device. They used one conducting electrode, an implement shaped like an inverted metal soup bowl. This they fitted to his head with a chin strap. Next they fitted a second flat grounding electrode to his back with a chest strap. And at ten nineteen that morning, Kemmler got himself into the history books when Davis threw the death switch, sending two thousand volts of raw current directly into his body.

"Kemmler's body lunged up out of the seat and into the chair's leather straps. A buzzing noise filled the room. The chair, which had not been properly bolted to the floor, began rocking up and down in a sickeningly grotesque death dance. While the horrified Davis and the spectators looked on, the bare electrode on Kemmler's back dried his skin out and his flesh started to burn, sending a pungent blue smoke out over the witness gallery.

"For five minutes this kept up, with most of the witnesses becoming sick or turning away in terror. Finally the current was turned off, but, to the total horror of those present, Kemmler's chest seemed to be moving and a purple liquid bubbled from his gray lips.

"His whole body had turned a bright red," Lincoln continued, the description obviously causing him pain. "Quickly the warden signaled Davis to turn the current back on. Over and over again for four minutes Davis gave Kemmler's body a series of short charges of voltage, a procedure that caused a blue flame to run up and down the dying man's spine.

"Finally the thing was over," Lincoln said, his fist tight from the strain of his words. "When they got Kemmler into the autopsy room that had been set up next to the Death Chamber, his brain was like a loaf of burned bread. The blood in his head had turned to charcoal, and his back had been burned black.

"Understandably," Lincoln ended, turning to look directly at Billings, "the press had a field day with the execution, but the doctors swore that Kemmler had felt no pain. By 1906, more than a hundred criminals had been electrocuted in the United States, and the act had been perfected to a point where the condemned person usually could be pronounced legally dead within two or three minutes."

Billings shook his head at the dizzying array of facts Lincoln had rattled off and for a few seconds genuinely tried to let them sink in. But he was too tired for anything but the physical act, the motions, of the interview. Realizing he had all the information he needed, he pressed Lincoln as to what, as a student of constitutional law, he personally considered to be the heart of the matter. "Is capital punishment cruel and unusual?" he asked, both he and Daniels aware that the question was the end of the interview.

Lincoln answered with almost no hesitation. "For me, no," he said. "Legal death for me is not cruel and inhuman. I am convinced, as well as such a thing can be told to another, that the deaths are instant·and as free of pain as they can be.

"But"—he used his hand for emphasis—"it is the changing of the courts and the changing of people's minds on the question of legal death that angers and distresses me with regard to the Eighth Amendment of the Constitution.

"Specifically, in the case of William Kemmler, the Supreme Court said that electrocution, the new form of capital punishment, was *not* cruel and unusual. And historically the High Court has said that the Eighth Amendment does not even apply to the death penalty as meted out by the states.

"Look. In 1972, when the *Furman* versus *Georgia* decision struck down capital punishment, the sentences of about a thousand of America's most repugnant scum were commuted to life imprisonment, and some are eligible for parole right now or will be in the next few years. Vermin like Charlie Manson and Sirhan Sirhan, the scum of the earth, walked off Death Row laughing. And when the *Santos* versus *Florida* decision reversed the Furman case last year, a time span of just over four years, Death Rows were holding condemned prisoners in thirty-five states.

"In the *Furman* versus *Georgia* case in 1972," he went on, "the Supreme Court struck down capital punishment not because it violated the Eighth Amendment but because they said that laws giving so much power to juries in deciding whether a convicted criminal lived or died were unconstitutional. So the states came back six months later with tighter laws that let the trial judge fix the life or death sentence, and essentially, in *Santos* versus *Florida,* the court bought that plan.

"To me, it's six of one, half a dozen of the other, whether the judge or the jury decides the matter," Lincoln said. "The important question is to determine whether to have legal death or not, and then, by God, once the matter is decided, to stay with the decision."

"If the U.S. Supreme Court believes it is capricious for a jury to decide death and not so when the sentence is imposed by a judge, how the hell do they reconcile their own capricious decision to put death in and take it out over and over again? Think of all the poor bums now sitting on Death Row knowing that that they were a day late and a dollar short."

"But," Billings broke in, "the Supreme Court does not rule by itself; it acts on cases presented to it, cases that arise from the will of the people. If there are changes, no matter how frequent, are they not changes of the will of the people, changes of the times?"

"You missed your calling," Lincoln answered swiftly, half smiling. "You should have stayed a lawyer. But yes, you're right." he went on. "The court acts on the will of the people. I suppose what I'm really saying is that I like my truths a little better packaged than most. To me, right is right, and fair is fair. I've never been able to see that gray mid-ground philosophers babble about. Two and two is four, and all the philosophy in all the libraries won't ever make it five."

"That is the novelist in you, my friend," Billings broke in, also smiling. "You want your truths to remain true. You know, of course, that it is not often so."

"I give up, counselor," Lincoln said, nodding his head in submission to Billings, forcing a tight grin. "Maybe I'm just a damn fool who wants to make himself feel better about the rotten thing he is about to participate in. In any event, I've said my piece; maybe that will be counted in my favor if things like this are ever taken into account."

"I give up too," Billings shouted, waving his hands for the camera and lights to be turned off. "I thought TV journalists were talkative bastards, but you win the prize hands down, Lincoln. By God, you've just put the lid on a day's work I won't have to do tomorrow."

Lincoln gave a tired laugh and stretched as the lights and camera went off. "Comes from being shut up in my studio all the time. Minute I get out in public I'm a walking encyclopedia."

"Just one thing you said," Billings cut in, dry and serious.

"What's that?"

"The thing about being a day late and a dollar short. About one man sitting on Death Row and another walking off to serve a life sentence and hit the streets again. It bothers the hell out of me too."

Lincoln shook his head. "Yeah," he said, "and

you can bet it bothers the hell out of the four out there on Death Row tonight."

Billings did not answer; he turned away and stared at the floor. Like so many others on the outside, his thoughts never really seemed to leave the four condemned prisoners inside Big Max's Death House.

PART THREE
MONDAY

DEATH'S RHYTHM

The Chinaman scurried to his feet as Warden Hugh Greenwood entered the double glass doors of the Administration Building.

"Good mornin', boss," he said, rushing to hold back one of the doors.

Greenwood grunted a reply and paused long enough to hand the trusty his rain-soaked hat and overcoat. Then he resumed his bull-like charge toward the deep lock of Big Max.

Hugh Greenwood was a thickset, humorless man of thirty-seven, a man whose life read like a guideline to the ambiguous but real American situation called the middle-middle class.

He was born in Baltimore, Maryland, and grew up in the tough southeastern section of Brooklyn in a brick rowhouse whose mortgage was paid on but never paid off by his father, a city policeman who died of a heart attack while walking a beat during his thirty-second year on the force. On an Army ROTC scholarship, Greenwood went to Baltimore University from 1957 to 1961, graduating with a degree in criminology and a letter as a second-string linebacker. He served in Germany with the military police for his two-year ROTC obligation and was discharged as a first lieutenant in August 1963, the month he married Joan Embry, a Brooklyn girl he had dated since high school.

With connections he had made in the Army, Greenwood applied for a job as a classification officer —the prison's executive trainee position—at Florida's Main Prison at Raiford and was hired in September 1963. Thereafter he rose in the system at two-year intervals from classification officer to prison inspector in one of the southern districts to deputy warden at the harsh Belle Glade Farm Prison. In 1971, he was appointed warden at the medium-security Sumter County Correctional Unit. After his ruthless put-down of Sumter Prison's bloody 1973 riot, he was made head of the Maximum Security East Unit, becoming Big Max's youngest warden at age thirty-five and the finest example the prison's new school had to offer.

Greenwood had put on thirty pounds since college; his wife had added five pounds after the birth of each of their four children. He was sober and distant, his wife plump and prematurely gray. Both dressed cheaply and had no real interests beyond job and family, except TV and halfheartedly attending the First Baptist Church in Starke twice a week. Both were absolutely content with their lives and shared the belief that they had bettered themselves.

Greenwood was always all business; this morning he was also formal. He moved down Big Max's halls at a pace meant to give assurance to all who saw him, but he had no taste for the business at hand. Only months after he had gone to work at the prison he had seen Sam Fallon and Eugene Burns electrocuted in 1964, and he had had nightmares about the thing for two years.

Thirteen years later he could still hear the crisp humming sound that came from the electrodes on their bare flesh; he could still see the bodies of the two men heaving up into the chair's leather straps. There were still times when he walked into an empty room that he thought he saw the two men sitting there, looking at him.

Greenwood also had no taste for confronting Major John McPeters on this morning, but the meeting was as unavoidable as the deaths themselves. Governor Morgan Kingsly had become paranoid about

the executions going off right: "without incident," he
kept repeating by phone to Greenwood.

"You have got to make this thing work like clock-
work," the governor would say to him, his voice
strained and high-pitched. "Your executive record in
the prison system is flawless. I am putting myself in
your hands, to see that there is no incident. To see that
somehow—God help us all—those four poor unfortunates are made to walk into that room and sit in
the chair and be killed with no commotion, no mess,
no incident."

Kingsly would say the word "incident" as if you
could touch it. Greenwood could see that the word
was the thread, the hope, that was thinly holding
things together for him, but the word was a sinister one
for Greenwood. It set him squarely between Kingsly,
on the one hand, and John McPeters on the other.

Kingsly's idea was to have the four walk into the
death chamber and be killed with all the quiet and
dignity of actors in some movie or play. McPeters's
method was to prepare them to do just that. Kingsly
vaguely imagined that the four would do it on their
own. McPeters knew how to make them do it.

"Peeping John" was only one of McPeters's nick-
names. The convicts also knew him as "Curing Salt
John" and "Castor Oil John." The first name he got on
his own; the last two names he inherited from his pre-
decessor, Major Bulldog Crews. One of Crews's favorite punishments was to take a man and strip him naked
and handcuff his hands over his head through the bars
of his cell, and then sit him in an inch-thick pile of
curing salt spread on the concrete floor of the cellblock corridor; sit him there so he could walk by each
day and watch the sores form on the prisoner's buttocks, watch him sitting there in his own excrement
and urine. Or strap a man into a straightjacket and not
feed him for two days and then give him a dose of castor oil.

They were ways to "get a con's mind right," as
the saying went, and they always worked. Always.
You could break a convict before you killed him, and
once he was broken, he was broken for good.

McPeters had also inherited ways from Bulldog Crews to make men or women get up out of their cells and walk down the hall and be strapped into the electric chair and killed. Like the other methods McPeters knew, those for Death Row worked. Only three times during the 196 executions at Raiford had there been any real trouble. Twice, two big blacks had put up a fight as they were being taken from the Ready Cell, but only one man, Jake Dane, a stocky, forty-three-year-old white man sent up from Levy County for murder, actually delayed his execution by fighting in the Death Chamber itself.

Bulldog Crews had been in charge of the execution, and Dane, a violent, muscular man, had taunted Crews all along, telling him he would never get him strapped into the chair. At 9:00 A.M. on the morning of November 23, 1943, Crews and two guards entered the Ready Cell and fought Dane to the door before they could get iron-claw clamps on his arms. They fought him across the hallway to the Death Chamber and wrestled him into the chair, and they strapped him in while he bit and kicked and cursed. Then they stood back and Warden Blackshear asked Dane if he had any last words.

Dane's face got red and his arms bulged; with the cry of a wounded animal, he broke both wrist straps.

For fifteen minutes Dane wriggled in the chair, swinging his arms and trying to free himself from the other straps while a guard was dispatched to General Supply for a coil of thick hemp rope that Bulldog Crews personally used to lash him to the chair.

At 9:27 A.M. Dane went to his death, roped to the chair like a side of beef tied to a butcher's block, begging to kiss the Catholic priest who had given him the last rites.

Bulldog Crews had prepared Dane as he prepared all the other condemned, but it had not taken. Dane was the only real exception. The Preparation worked on all except fanatics, and it was the opinion of the Death Committee that none of the four—Mrs. Fuller, Parker, Kruger, or Santos—was a fanatic.

McPeters had used the Preparation from the time
he was made captain of the guards, in 1955, until the
last two executions in 1964. This morning he meant
to use it again.

That was Hugh Greenwood's dilemma. Everything had changed since the last executions. You
couldn't use things like the Preparation any more. Now
there were civil rights and the media, and both were
conducting a circus outside the prison, a circus that
would begin again at seven fifteen, when the press
and TV people were allowed back on the prison
grounds.

Since the murderous sympathy riot on Saturday,
everything the prison officials did had been under microscopic scrutiny. The ACLU was already calling for
a federal investigation of the riot and McPeters's immediate suspension for his bloodthirsty quashing of
the rebels.

The Preparation would largely erase the possibility that an incident would occur, but Greenwood knew
he could not allow McPeters to use it. Nonetheless, as
he approached the maze of locked doors to the Death
Facility, Greenwood didn't know if he could keep Mc-
Peters from using his methods, and he didn't know if
he really wanted to stop McPeters.

Greenwood entered the Death Facility under the
watchful and respectful gaze of the three maze guards,
but, as always, he knew he was no longer really in
command; this was not his turf, it belonged to Mc-
Peters.

McPeters had a well-appointed office in Big Max's
Administration Building, but he was seldom there. He
used the small, bare office in the Deep Lock of the
Death Facility, and from it he dispensed his justice to
the convicts of Death Row and Solitary Confinement
and Big Max itself. From the seclusion of the Death
Facility he could run both the convicts and his guard
force in private, in his own time and manner, in his
old-school style.

The gap between old school and new school was
immediate and graphic the second Greenwood and Mc-
Peters came into contact. Greenwood, for all his stodgy

appearance, affected long sideburns and slightly longish hair that had the defiant unruliness of hair that is usually worn short. His dress was trendy, with cheap doubleknit suits, wide-striped shirts, $5 imitation-silk ties, and patent leather shoes. McPeters's brown hair was clipped off bare to the ears in military fashion and worn just long enough on top to afford a slight part. His block face was meticulously shaved, and his uniform was always fresh and creased, with his boots finely spit-shined.

As Lasseter had been minutes before, Greenwood was ushered into McPeters's office by Bob Griffis; McPeters stood when the younger, smaller man entered the room.

"Good morning, sir," McPeters said formally, articulating his words, his face and his huge upper body tight, almost menacing. "Get the warden some coffee," he said to Griffis before Greenwood could respond.

"Good morning, major," Greenwood answered with equal formality, but not with equal tightness. Before McPeters—and he despised himself for it—Greenwood always felt loose and ill at ease.

The two men faced each other across McPeters's desk, a ritual it seemed to Greenwood that McPeters played out each time he was obliged to come to the Death Facility, a ritual that only heightened the fact that he was not warden here. After a silent, uneasy interval, McPeters asked Greenwood to sit down. Greenwood smiled halfheartedly at the offer, feeling, as always, defeated and angry at being treated as an inferior but, at the same time, as always, smiling limply.

Griffis came back with coffee for Greenwood and then departed quickly. Greenwood sipped the hot, bitter liquid that was always given to him without sugar and cream—the way, as McPeters knew, he preferred it. And in McPeters's presence you always drank alone. McPeters never held anything in his hands when he spoke. It was as if he always had a defensive plan in his mind, as if he always wanted to put his opposition at a disadvantage.

"Are we ready?" Greenwood asked, squaring off in his seat, trying to seem forceful.

The big man was sitting back in his chair, gripping its arms with his hands so that his whole mountainous bulk faced the warden; he studied the younger man for a few moments, long enough to make Greenwood shift his weight in the armless folding chair.

"We're ready," McPeters answered, his face stony. "They've been quiet on the Row since midnight, and the cellblocks have been quiet too."

"Do you still have guards on the blocks with tear gas grenades?" Greenwood asked.

"You're damned right," McPeters came back bluntly. "That's why the bastards have been quiet. I've personally been on every floor, and my message has been the same: Start raising hell again and you'll get gas till the doctor says I've got to quit."

Greenwood squirmed in his seat and looked in vain for a place to set his coffee cup, knowing he should not have asked McPeters about the tear gas, he should have *told* him; knowing, as always, that McPeters was in control. "Yeah," he said. "Well, we've got to keep the upper hand until after the executions. I mean, dammit"—he explained his choice of words—"we've *always* got to keep the upper hand, but especially until we get through this morning and get the goddamned newspapers and TV out of here.

"Morgan Kingsly started calling me at five thirty this morning," Greenwood went on, his face pained. "He called twice before I could get out of the house. My ass—your ass," he ventured cautiously, looking directly into McPeters's face, "is on the line here."

McPeters did not move a muscle of his stony face. "Well," he said evenly, "you know what I have to do to carry this thing off without trouble."

Greenwood frowned and set his coffee cup roughly on the bare concrete floor. "John," he said, "we've been over that till I'm blue in the face. I don't interfere with you. I don't tell you how to handle discipline. I look the other way when you get rough, but dammit, John, what you want can't be, and you know it can't be."

"Well, then," McPeters replied, still stone-faced and immobile, his cold eyes drilling Greenwood, "you and that Boy Scout governor ain't gonna get what you want."

His articulation was gone, and Greenwood knew his rage was building. "Just a minute," he said, pushing himself forward in his chair. "For once you've got to listen to me. For once you've got to curb your Wild West routine. You run roughshod around here like you owned the damn place"—he stormed on, gaining courage as he went—"like the prison was yours, yours to do with just as you damn please. Well, dammit, John, the place isn't yours. It isn't mine either," he added, his voice easing somewhat, his eyes looking for some sort of understanding from McPeters, an understanding that was not there.

"I know what you want to do. Goddammit, I've heard it enough times." He crossed his legs nervously and went on immediately, feeling the weight of McPeters's granite face. "But John," he said, "just how the hell do you think you're going to get away with kicking the shit out of those four people, roughing them up so bad that they'll walk into the Death Chamber like zombies and let us kill them without a whimper?"

"Get away with it?" McPeters slapped his hands down onto the desk top in front of him. "Goddammit, we're talkin' about dead people anyway. Who the hell are they gonna tell? The best shyster civil rights lawyer in the world can't milk a corpse."

"Dammit, you know what I mean. They'll come in looking like hell, and before we can get the death mask on them they'll sing to the press like canaries."

"Let 'em have their fuckin' say," McPeters came back. "All you do is say you don't know what they're talkin' about. The press sure as hell can't wake the bastards up for a rebuttal. By God, it's just like I told you Saturday when you and everybody else was standing around with your fingers up your asses while the place was gettin' ripped to hell. Either we got the institution or we ain't. And that goes double for the motherfuckin' newspaper and TV queers."

"Jesus Christ!" Greenwood moaned, uncrossing

his legs, facing McPeters head on. "You think like somebody in a cowboy movie. You are *not* Judge Roy Bean and this is *not* the 1850s—"

"Oh, horseshit," McPeters raged, his fists clenched. "I don't even know what the hell you're talkin' about and I don't give a damn. Save that college bullshit for the fuzzy heads in the Administration Buildin'. Goddammit! I'm talkin' about runnin' this institution like I know how to run it. I've told you a hundred goddamned times, you give these fuckers an inch they'll take the box the tape measure came in. There's only one way!" he boomed, his finger thrust out toward Greenwood like a spear. "One goddamned way to do this thing, to do anything in a prison, and that's it. Take it or leave it."

"No! No, John," Greenwood bellowed, standing as he gathered steam. 'I don't have to sit here and listen to you cuss me. You work for me! Can't you get that through your thick skull? You work for me! Not the other way around."

McPeters eyed him coldly, keeping his seat, his meathook hands on the desk top. "You tellin' me you're gonna do it by yourself?" he said evenly, after a pause that had Greenwood shifting his weight unevenly. "You gonna go in there and fight these cocksuckers into the chair with your fuzzy heads? You want it that way, I'll take my boys and clear out of here right now."

"John!" Greenwood pleaded, shaking his head in exasperation. "I can't reach you. I've never been able to reach you. You say just one way, and that's the only way you know. You just look at one part of the problem. I've got to look at the whole problem—outside *and* inside."

To his surprise, McPeters nodded his head in agreement. Greenwood sat back down.

When McPeters spoke, his voice had eased somewhat. "For the inside I tell you there's only one way," he said. "I told you that the first day we met; I'll tell it to you the last day I see you. One way for the inside. For the outside," he added with scorn, "all the ways, all the choices, are what fuck it up. You do what you want with the outside. Just let me run the inside."

Greenwood sat lost in thought before him; Mc-Peters went on quickly.

"What the hell do you think is keepin' the cock-suckers on all the tiers quiet? The press? TV? A lot of college bullshit? No goddamned way. They're quiet because my boys got 'em by the balls, because *I* got 'em by the balls. And because we got the tear gas and the guns. Tear gas and guns, and me and my boys. They understand that.

"Books!" he bellowed, banging his fist on the desk top. "Goddamn books! Nobody ever stopped a riot with a fuckin' book or a college degree."

Greenwood sat dejectedly in the bolted-down folding chair and stared at the floor, his forearms poised on his knees. "How in the hell can I turn you loose, John?" he said to the concrete floor. "For once, use your head. How can I let you drag those people into the Death Chamber all screwed up for the whole world to see? The world, dammit!" he exclaimed, looking up into McPeters's unyielding face. "We've got reporters from England and France and West Germany. Jesus Christ, for a week the Administration Building's looked like the fucking UN."

McPeters sat back in his chair and crossed his legs, his big boot jutting out from the side of the desk like an anvil. "There'll be no mess," he said quietly, his articulation returned. "Nothing that will show," he added, with a total lack of emotion.

Greenwood straightened himself up in his chair and looked at McPeters with dark anticipation.

"I just get them ready to take the walk and sit quietly," McPeters said in a monotone. "We work them over, scare the shit out of them." He stopped for a second, uncrossed his legs, and sat facing Greenwood with his club of a finger pointed at him again. "We get their goddamned attention!" he said thickly, resentfully.

"I know all about that. You've preached that to me since the first time you cornered me when I came to work at Raiford in '63."

"Well, why in the hell haven't you learned it?"

"You go too far, John." Greenwood shook his head. "You don't leave a man anything—"

"*Prison* don't leave a man nothing," McPeters broke in, his eyes on fire. "Nothing, goddammit. Can't you learn that? Prison ain't supposed to leave a man nothing!"

Greenwood matched the anger in McPeters's eyes for a few short moments and then, in a measured motion, so that the act would not indicate defeat, he turned away, stared at the far wall, and thought. He sat McPeters on the left of his mind, Governor Kingsly on the right, and put the world, the press, and public opinion in the middle. He was very careful, so far as it could be done, to exclude himself and the idea of right and wrong. Two minutes ticked by as he and McPeters sat in total silence in the box of a room.

Then Greenwood turned to McPeters. "No," he said, the word spoken as if it had come from a cave. "No Preparation. If it got out we'd all go to prison ourselves—you, me, maybe even Morgan Kingsly himself. I know you can't understand my reasons, or the idea that anything from the outside could ever touch you here on the inside, but it's the truth, nonetheless. John—" he stopped himself, looking at McPeters for understanding. "I can't let you. Damn! Please see that. It can't be. . . .

"But, John," he went on, the words coming hard, "I need you. I need you to run the thing just like we planned. I've got to have you," he said finally, his voice desperate. "For once," he ended, "just give a little."

The words touched McPeters. Greenwood could see it plainly. As he came around the desk, Greenwood stood to confront him.

"Warden," McPeters said respectfully. "I don't know anything but the chain gang. It and the Army is all I've ever known. Just two things," he went on, his arms hanging limply by his side. "The Army and the chain gang. And in each of those there ain't but one way, and that's the way that comes from the power, from the top."

He crossed his arms over his massive chest. "I

don't want to cause you trouble. I want to take trouble from you. I've always been on the high side of trouble, and I know how to handle it. But if what I know can't be, then it can't be. But I tell you this—I carry out the executions as best I can. They're my job, and I've always done my job. That's my promise to you," he said. "My word."

Greenwood was silent a moment longer. He ran his hand through his thinning hair in exasperation. He shifted his weight from foot to foot. "Goddammit, John," he said, looking up to McPeters, "I know what you do around here. You hold the fucking place together. I know that. But . . ."

He meant to go on but stopped. He reached up and cautiously grasped McPeters by his rocklike upper arm. "I'm between hell and high water," he said, in a voice too loud, letting go of McPeters's arm. "This is not private like the old days. There are people out there who are waiting for us to fuck up just a fraction of an inch. A fraction." He measured it with the thumb and forefinger of his right hand. "Goddammit! Bad joke or not, we're the ones on the hot seat, not those four scumbags we're going to execute. The press, the world, wants this, but they want our balls, too.

"I don't understand it, but that's the way it is," he said, his voice building with anger. "They want it, they want us to do it, they give us the legal power to do it, and yet they want us, too. You figure it out, I can't."

There was a short silence. "John," Greenwood ventured a last time, "this is now. It has nothing to do with the past. That's over."

McPeters did not answer.

"Okay," Greenwood said to break the silence, and then he turned and walked out of the office and toward the maze back to Big Max's main hallway.

McPeters stood and looked at the empty doorway where Greenwood had been standing. He looked at the empty space as if he were studying it. Then he walked back to his desk and sat down and picked up the telephone. He dialed 618 for the main control booth. The shift lieutenant answered on the first ring.

"We do the thing its new way," McPeters said into the receiver. "Pass the word to the rest of my Death Strap squad when they come in, and to no one else."

"Yessir," the shift lieutenant answered grimly and waited for McPeters to hang up.

6:42 A.M.

Greenwood instantly felt composed as he entered the sanctity of his big, well-appointed office with its great oak desk and twelve-chair conference table. He sat down in his high-backed leather swivel chair and looked out at the warm, paneled room and the conference table that was bare except for twelve large glass ashtrays. He lit a cigarette and sat back in the chair and stared at the telephone. His feeling of composure went away at the sight of the instrument. He stared vacantly at the phone for a few seconds, then picked up the receiver and roughly punched out Morgan Kingsly's private number at the Governor's Mansion a hundred and fifty miles away in Tallahassee. Bill Tuggle, the governor's personal secretary, answered on the first ring, and in seconds Kingsly picked up an extension.

"Hugh," Kingsly said with manufactured goodwill, "there's no problem, is there?" His voice was uneven and high-pitched.

"No, sir," Greenwood replied. "I just want to report that we're on schedule and all is quiet."

"Hugh," Kingsly said politely, in his campaigner's manner, "you make me very proud. I mean that sincerely. You're a professional. I've counted on you all along with this thing; I know now that I wasn't wrong.

And I know I'm not wrong in considering you for the director's post that comes up in six months," he added, serving up the last like a steak on a sizzling platter.

Greenwood reflected on the scope of the governor's words, almost passing over the obvious bait of the director's job. The words sealed him off like a tomb and made everything else unimportant.

"Thank you," he said finally. "I'm issuing a statement to the press at seven thirty, the same statement I read to Bill Tuggle yesterday afternoon. I see no real problems on this end. I'll call back at seven forty-five as we agreed. We're still go, aren't we?" he added.

"Absolutely," Kingsly replied without a moment's hesitation.

"Fine," Greenwood answered.

"Excellent," Kingsly added. "Let me give you back to Bill now."

Tuggle came on the line as if he were speaking from a prepared text. "We're leaving for the office at seven thirty as planned," he said. "We'll be here until that time if you need us, and you have our mobile number if you need to reach us en route to the office. We'll be out of pocket for about five minutes. No, make that seven minutes, from the car to the office. I make that seven thirty-five to seven forty-two. We've got city police out on the steps of the capitol building now, and the governor will make his short prepared speech on the steps, accept no questions from the reporters, and move inside immediately. We'll be standing by for your call at seven forty-five, and we'll get you if we need you before that. Right?"

"Right," Greenwood repeated like a robot.

"Good work down there, Hugh," Tuggle commented. "Damn good work." He hung up.

Greenwood set the phone back in its cradle and pushed himself back in his chair. Suddenly the thing was clear to him. For the past month it had all seemed like some out-of-whack unrelated string of events involving the law, the courts, politics, right and wrong, religion, whatever. But it was simply politics. It was a political ceremony played out for the public's benefit, something they thought was being done for them

—something pragmatic, in the nebulous sea of bills and conferences and committees, that politicians could point to and say, "This is what I am doing for you." And like everything political it was based on the barter system, and there was a ceremony involved.

Greenwood sat back in his soft leather chair and drew an easy breath, his first in weeks. He had the vision now, and that made everything all right for him, put everything in its place. The wall clock on the opposite side of the room showed 6:47 A.M.; they would probably be feeding on the Row now, Greenwood realized.

For reasons he could not express, the thought undid his fresh confidence. He rummaged through the papers on his desk as a diversion and cursed to himself because of his uneasiness.

6:45 A.M.

The food was wheeled into the Death Facility in a steam cart at exactly six forty-five by a fat black trusty who was called Good Pussy because he always carried a pocketful of pornographic playing cards. McPeters stopped him in front of his office door with a blunt order to stand still and came out to personally inspect the food trays.

"Puss," McPeters said to the bloated trusty, beginning his examination of the steam cart, "you're right on time this mornin'. You ain't tryin' to speed these four unfortunates on their way, are you?"

"God bless you, major. No, sir." The old man grinned like a circus clown, bowing and scraping before McPeters. "Lord he'p us all, I jus' doin' my job like I supposed to." He held his hands in front of him in clear subjugation.

"You got a pocket full of pussy to show 'round this mornin'?" McPeters was totally in his element when he was speaking to a convict who was, by his definition, doing his time the right way.

"He'p me, boss," the black sputtered, blurting each word in a singsong, "these folks needs the comfort of the good Lord, not the wicked flesh. Lord bless us, Boss Mac, I shore wouldn't do nothin' like that. God he'p me, no sir, boss." He cackled on, churning his head up and down with the words.

"That's mighty fine, Puss," McPeters said, continuing his precise search of each of the four trays, picking through the contents with a big spoon. "All the same"—he stopped and looked up hard into the trusty's face—"they ask for it, you give it."

"Yessir, boss," the old man said. "You know I gon' do that."

McPeters had been stooped down over the steam cart. Now he stood up and once more towered over the trusty. "Puss," he said, putting the spoon back into the tray of spoons on top of the steam cart, "you remember an old man they called U.S. Alka-Seltzer?"

The trusty smiled ear to ear and nodded.

"Called him U.S. Alka-Seltzer 'cause he fought in World War One in a nigger rifle company and was always tryin' to bum an Alka-Seltzer for his bad stomach. Had a pot on him about like you."

Good Pussy, whose real name was Leo Dunbar, cackled again, sucking in each laugh as if he were gasping for air.

"If I had my money back from buyin' that old nigger Alka-Seltzer I could retire right now and drive a goddamned Cadillac."

"That's for shore, boss. I know you was good to that old man. An' he loved you for it," Dunbar said.

McPeters did not respond to the black man's words. He stared off behind him at the blank wall. "Old U.S. was a comfort to many a man on this Row who was goin' out. He earned his keep." He turned his cold eyes on Dunbar again. "You go on now an' earn your keep. And you have respect for that white woman, and say somethin' nice to her. You talk real good to the other three, too."

"Yessir," Dunbar said, standing still. "You know I gon' do that. God he'p all of 'em, boss."

McPeters motioned him away with his head, and Dunbar pushed the steam cart off down the hallway toward the Ready Cell, where the woman, Alice Fuller, waited. One of McPeters's three-man Death Strap squad, a knotty, muscular six-footer named Hank Chrysler, followed behind.

6:48 A.M.

Alice Fuller had asked for hot cakes with strawberry syrup both mornings since she had been transferred from the Women's Prison at Lowell on Friday.

There was no such thing as the romanticized Last Meal; once the sixty-five hours of the Death Routine began on Friday afternoon, the condemned inmates could order anything, within reason, they wanted to eat. On this last morning Alice Fuller had chosen again to have hot cakes with strawberry syrup.

Charlie Parker ordered two big sirloin steaks; George Kruger, seemingly a madman, ordered nothing but had been sent a bowl of oyster stew and two bottles of Coca-Cola; José Santos ordered fried chicken. Charlie Parker also asked McPeters for a drink of good bourbon, and Hank Chrysler, the guard, had brought a small milk of magnesia bottle of Old Grand Dad for the big black man. No one else requested whiskey; none asked for tranquilizers.

Leo Dunbar stopped the steam cart in front of the Ready Cell. The door was closed. Hank Chrysler stepped up to the door and rapped on it twice with his knuckles. In seconds, a pair of small eyes appeared in the glass slit in the top center of the door. The door could be opened from both sides; now it was opened from the inside.

A tall, thick, short-haired woman of forty, dressed in brown gabardine slacks and a brown waist jacket with a white turtleneck underneath, filled the open doorway. On both arms of her uniform there were yellow and red patches that spelled out "Women's Correctional Facility, Lowell, Florida."

She was a hard, disagreeable-looking country-woman, one of two Lowell guards who had come with Mrs. Fuller on Friday. The two were taking twelve-hour shifts around the clock; the strain of the past sixty-four hours, and her apparent lack of sleep, were written on the guard's face. Behind her, in a separate barred cage, Alice Fuller sat on her single wall bunk, wide-eyed with terror, pushed back into the corner the bars made as they came together, whining like a frightened dog, her hands held up to her cheeks.

"Hush now," the female guard said over her shoulder in a voice that seemed too pleasant for its speaker's appearance and the place. "It's just your breakfast. Hush now, there's not a thing to worry about." The big woman sounded as if she were comforting a sick child.

Hank Chrysler and the female guard, whose name was Esther Todd, eyed each other with looks that bordered on hatred; no women had ever set foot inside the deep lock of the Death Facility except to visit the condemned.

"Just hand the tray in," Esther Todd said, still blocking the doorway.

Dunbar looked at Chrysler. The guard hesitated and then sourly nodded agreement, and the tray was passed to the matron. Next Dunbar handed over a small tin pot of luckwarm coffee, a tin cup of milk and one of sugar, and a short wide-mouthed spoon as an eating utensil for the condemned prisoner. After he had finished, the matron set the items on a small bolted-down metal table out from the Ready Cell's bars; then she turned back to the black trusty and he gave her a plastic pot of hot coffee, a plastic cup, and a regular dinner spoon for her own use.

The matron placed the objects on the table beside Alice Fuller's breakfast, then turned back to the guard and the black trusty. "That it?" She clipped off the words, her hands on her thick hips.

Chrysler eyed her a second more. "Yeah," he answered, pushing himself up to full menacing height. "Just see she don't get in no mischief with that stuff. The boy'll come back and get the tray after a while." He nodded in the direction of the fifty-eight-year-old Dunbar, who stared inside at the condemned woman. "C'mon," he barked roughly to Dunbar. "Move that cart. We ain't got all mornin'."

Dunbar complied instantly, but his huge black face was strained around his puffy, permanently bloodshot eyes because he had not spoken the words of comfort to Mrs. Fuller that McPeters had ordered.

As soon as Chrysler closed the Ready Cell's outer door, Alice Fuller asked the matron the time. Her voice was thin and tiny.

"Honey," Esther Todd replied in a syrupy-soothing voice, "you've asked me that ever since I came on at midnight."

Alice Fuller's eyes pleaded. The matron looked at her wristwatch.

"It's six fifty," she said. "Just don't fret about the time. There's all the time in the world." She labored over the words, her big, bland, eyebrowless face etched with uncertainty and pity. "Just eat your breakfast. It's your favorite. It does smell good, doesn't it?"

Alice Fuller moved nervously on the bunk, clutching her forearms across her stomach. She was dressed in a gray one-piece slip-on prison dress that had no buttons, and a thick brown terry-cloth bathrobe with no waist cord. She was allowed no undergarments.

Once the Death Routine was imposed there was total supervision and no chance of suicide. The beverages given to the condemned were lukewarm so that they could not burn themselves and delay the execution. The food tray was steel, the cups were steel, and the single eating implement given, a spoon, had a base so wide it could not be swallowed and a shaft so short and blunt it could not be used as a blade. The condemned could count on being walked into the Death Chamber and carried out dead.

Esther Todd examined the contents of Alice Fuller's food tray, examined the coffee pot and the cup and the wide-mouthed spoon, and then passed them to her under a slot at the base of the cell's barred door.

"Just eat that and drink your coffee and try not to worry or excite yourself. I'm right here," she said, forcing a smile. "And I'm going to be with you." She kept on smiling.

Alice Fuller smiled back nervously and jerked her shoulders. Cautiously, she got down off the bunk and came over to the food and took it back with her. She seemed afraid of every movement she made and every sound she uttered, as if each somehow drew her deeper, took her closer to the point of no return. Back on the bunk, she set the long steel tray on her lap and poked at the stack of hot cakes with the mouth of the big spoon. Esther Todd poured herself a cup of steaming hot coffee, mixed in big spoonfuls of sugar, and added a splash of milk. She stirred the mixture together and took a small sip.

"Honey," she said, looking up at the condemned woman from her bolted-down folding chair five feet away, "you've just got to eat and drink some of your coffee. Please, now," she continued in her flowing voice, "pick up a mouthful and see how good it is. It's your favorite."

Alice Fuller cut off a small chunk of one of the hot cakes with the mouth of her spoon and brought it to her lips. As she chewed the small bite of food she started to cry; she had been crying softly all night.

"Don't do that, honey," the matron said, her voice cracking. "Please don't do that. Just eat, honey. I'm right here. Just eat. I'm right here."

Alice Fuller kept on crying dully, tears falling down her cheeks as she chewed at her food.

She had been a beautiful woman, beautiful in a brash sort of way, a critic of her looks would have said, and all her life Alice Fuller had had critics.

She was born in Evansville, Indiana, on January 26, 1945, one of four children born to Jack and Lois Keating. All his life, Jack Keating worked in the sprawling, barren Indiana-Kentucky borderline city of

130,000 as a shirttail auto mechanic. He did not fight in the war because of a bum right leg, and because of the leg injury he was not able to capitalize on big wartime factory money at one of the city's defense plants.

Alice was a woman in body before she was thirteen and had lost count of the men she had had sex with when she married a skinny, pimply-faced kid of nineteen in Memphis, Tennessee, on June 6, 1963.

In December 1960, the month she dropped out of the tenth grade at Southside High School in Evansville, she was diagnosed by the school psychologist as a nymphomaniac. She had a girl friend who worked the service bars around the Naval Air Station in Memphis, and four days before Christmas 1960, she packed her clothes in a single suitcase, had oral sex with two middle-aged factory workers in a southside Evansville bar to finance the ticket to Memphis, and by Christmas Day she had moved in with her girl friend and was working a street in the Memphis red light district for a black pimp called Chocolate Boy.

She had coarse, naturally flame-red hair that she wore shoulder length, parted in front. Her body was full and creamy white, and she had her thick, blond-red brush of pubic hair cut in the shape of a heart in front, shaved off to reveal the pink folds of her vagina. Her nymphomania made her the perfect prostitute, and her poverty and lack of education gave every assurance that she would remain one. Her life read like something out of a pulp sex book, and when she married Jerry Fuller, she added the final chapter. He was a nineteen-year-old sailor, a near virgin; she, a luscious eighteen-year-old whore.

Their sex life—the only real life they had—was like a stag movie. Jerry Fuller was endowed with an enormous, thick penis and egg-sized testicles that hung down in folds of limp skin like baskets; for Alice it was a dream sex organ, and she introduced the inexperienced Fuller into the full rites of sex.

Within two years, Alice had instilled much of her nymphomania in her husband, a condition that was expanded for both of them when Fuller, a third class Navy storekeeper, was transferred to the Miramar Naval Air Station north of San Diego, California, in 1965. In Southern California, the two of them were thrust into exactly the right place to continue experimenting with each other and with sex itself. On weekends they would ride the bus forty miles to the Mexican border at Tijuana and spend whole days in the city's *zona de tolerencia*, having sex in a small hotel room while an 8mm film projector blazed Mexican pornographic movies on the ceiling, showing young girls having sex with dogs, group sex, lesbian sex, and homosexual sex.

The act of sex took over every facet of their lives, eased only during periods when Alice accidentally became pregnant in 1966, and again in 1968 and 1971; and the more violent their sex became, the more careless Alice became, both with her sex and with her appearance. Disenchantment, for Jerry Fuller, set in with the first baby. During the final months of her pregnancy in 1966, when Alice could only satisfy her husband with oral sex or painful anal sex, Jerry Fuller took the bus ride to Tijuana by himself and got a Mexican girl for the day. The girl was slow and dull and afraid of Jerry's violence; after several hours of sexual punishment she ran out of the room and went screaming to her pimp. In a short time the pock-faced Mexican pimp, who knew Jerry from his previous trips, appeared at his hotel door with a tall Mexican boy who was dressed in a flowery silk shirt and black trousers.

"Tiko will satisfy your every need, Señor Fuller," the pimp said, grinning broadly. "I have observed you for some time, and Tiko is exactly right for you."

Jerry Fuller's instant reaction was that of rage. A queer? Him a goddamned queer? But the pimp calmed his rage and had the young boy slowly undress in front of him. The instant Jerry Fuller saw the boy naked he remembered all the nervous excitement he had experienced while having sex with Alice and watching homosexuals have sex on the movie screen ceiling above them. From that day on, Alice began to occupy less of his time. Jerry Fuller had become a practicing homosexual.

In 1967, Fuller was transferred to the Glynco Naval Air Station in the pinewoods north of Brunswick, Georgia. In the bars of nearby Savannah, he found good hunting to fulfill his homosexual needs. Two years later, he was transferred to the Pensacola Naval Air Station in west Florida. The action in the Pensacola bars was no good for gay sailors, and in desperation Jerry Fuller made the fatal mistake of beginning an affair with one of the younger sailors in the warehouse office where he was, by then, a first class storekeeper.

By 1972, Alice Fuller had all but lost her attraction for her husband. He used her for brutal sex games and made fun of her as she grew fatter with the birth of each of their three children: a girl, six, a boy, four, and an infant girl of one. In San Diego, and again in Savannah, Alice had worked as a cocktail waitress and as a topless go-go girl in several bars, but by 1972 her hips had grown chunky and her breasts sagged like water balloons about to burst. She knew she was losing her husband, and in an effort to keep him she threw herself into their sex acts with such violence that she hurt herself.

Her mind was riddled with doubt and confusion about how to win her husband back, but on a hot September day in 1972 all her doubts were erased when she came home to their trailer in a service trailer park on the grounds of the Pensacola Naval Air Station and found Jerry in bed with a young boy she knew only by the nickname of Pinky.

The two naked men looked up from the bed, shamefaced and angry, expecting Alice to go into a frenzy of contempt and rage, but she said nothing. She just stood looking at them. Finally she started to laugh.

"You dumb bastard," she said to her husband. "After all the tail I've given you for . . . how long is it, nine years? You stupid shit, I get fat and you turn queer. This is the all-time ball-busting laugh!"

Then she took off her clothes, slowly and deliberately, staring down each of the men as she went through the motions.

"Queers!" She laughed contemptuously. "Before I'm through, I'll show you that three's just the crowd you've always needed."

More out of fear that she would reveal their attachment to the naval authorities than out of desire, Jerry and his youthful lover accepted Alice, and the trio was together almost constantly until Pinky was transferred to the U.S. Naval Air Facility at Catania, Sicily, in November 1972.

From the day his lover was transferred, Jerry Fuller fell into a deep depression. He would attack Alice and the two older children, two frightened, wordless waifs, without provocation, and on one occasion he tried to drown the youngest one, a tiny, bone-thin little girl named Joyce. He became a drunk and haunted the service bars that ringed Seville Square, Pensacola's historically restored downtown area. In these bars he made clumsy, drunken attempts at picking up sailors. On November 11, 1972, he was arrested by Shore Patrol vice agents for soliciting homosexual acts; three weeks later he was given a dishonorable discharge from the Navy.

Several days after the dishonorable discharge Fuller sold his family's used house trailer for $1,450 and, with the $4,000 he had in the Navy credit union, moved Alice and the children across the Panhandle of the state to Jacksonville. The discharge had jarred him momentarily back to reality; he made peace with Alice and pledged to get a job and devote himself to her and the children.

Alice received the news like a grateful cow. She made the apartment they rented on 8th Street, in the shabby northeast section of downtown, as comfortable as possible, cared for the children with an attention she had never before given them, and even found time to help an elderly woman who lived in the apartment above them. Jerry stopped drinking and scrupulously applied himself to his job as clerk in the mammoth Sears department store some blocks away on Bay Street. Even their sex life, which had always been so violent, eased and began to take on some semblance of lovemaking.

But during the first week in January 1973, in a bar across the street from Sears, Jerry met a young sailor he had known in Pensacola. The sailor, who had just been transferred to the Jacksonville Naval Air Station, was gay, and he knew of Jerry's discharge and the reason behind it. The two formed an immediate attachment and began meeting in the bar each evening, and in a $3-a-night hotel room on Park Street that the sailor rented on the weekends.

On the afternoon of February 1, 1973, quite by accident, Alice saw Jerry and his new lover sitting together in the bar on Bay Street. She stood outside the plate-glass window of the small bar in the biting cold of the February day and watched the two men laughing and talking inside, watched them touch and look at each other fondly, and her mind snapped. She turned and raced home to her apartment building and went immediately to the apartment occupied by the old woman she had helped care for. The feeble old woman was asleep on the living room couch. Alice moved quietly into the bathroom and opened the medicine cabinet. She took out a small plastic bottle and carried it back to her apartment.

That evening before dinner she bathed each of her three children and dressed the girls in their best party dresses; the little boy she dressed in freshly pressed corduroy trousers and his favorite Mickey Mouse sweat shirt. Jerry was late for dinner that night, but Alice waited for him before she served a large pot roast, fresh carrots, mashed potatoes, and a vanilla cream dessert.

When the old woman came down to Alice's apartment several hours later, after she had missed the plastic bottle in her medicine chest, she found Alice sitting in a battered armchair in front of a small black-and-white portable TV set, smoking a cigarette and drinking a beer and watching a game show on TV. At the kitchen table, the year-old-girl was slumped over in her high chair, the two older children were lying face down on the bare linoleum floor, and Jerry was wedged back against the refrigerator, feet splayed out in front of him, his mouth slacked open in death fright.

Alice had taken 50 mg of the old woman's digoxin, a heart stimulant, and mixed the clear, tasteless, odorless crystals into the mashed potatoes; then she had mixed 50 mg of the drug into the vanilla dessert. The normal adult dose was one fourth of a milligram; all four had died of massive heart failure before any one of them could take two steps from the dinner table.

Alice's trial during the week of Mary 24, 1973, was a madness the media rushed to with unprecedented frenzy. The Duval County state attorney, in prosecuting the case against her court-appointed lawyer, noted that the death penalty had only been reinstated since December 8, 1972.

"Never," the district attorney proclaimed in his revivalist tones, "has there been a more fortuitous stroke of legal luck. Eight short weeks before she perpetrated this dastardly act, this wretched piece of nonhumanity might have gone to prison for life, but not now. *God himself,*" he roared to the witness gallery, "has ordained otherwise. Now! We can have her life for the lives she so wrongfully took herself."

On May 31, 1973, Alice Fuller became the seventh woman in Florida to be sentenced to the electric chair; two days later she was transported to the Women's Correctional Facility at Lowell, Florida, and held, since the prison had no Death Facility, in a windowless disciplinary cell in the solitary confinement unit.

She had been in the small isolation cell for the forty-four months she had been under death sentence, allowed out only once a day, Monday through Friday, for an hour's exercise by two armed male guards from the Lowell Men's Correctional Unit some miles away.

She had feigned madness, at times eating her own excrement in front of her matrons. She carried on imaginary conversations with her dead children for days; she cut her forearms with a fork. But she was not mad, and the acts fooled no one. By early 1975, she became complacent to the point of being lethargic. She refused to leave her cell to exercise. She ate very little. She did not talk, and she had the small wire-mesh-enclosed TV set taken out of her cell, the TV set being the only concession made to all Death Row inmates.

Now, where she had once been buxom and then a little fat, with her fiery red hair and inviting mouth, she was a tall, bony mass of dead white skin. Her hair was limp and blotted with gray. She was thirty-two but she looked fifty.

As the matron looked on, Alice Fuller continued to pick at her breakfast. She had stopped crying, but her cheeks were wet and her nose dripped. She did not make a move to wipe her cheeks or her nose; she simply picked dumbly at her food.

"Honey," the matron told her, when she could stand her condition no longer, "please do something with your face. Go over and get some toilet paper and clean up. Do that, honey. You'll feel better."

Alice Fuller looked up from her plate and stared at the matron, Esther Todd, as if she was aware only that the other had made sounds.

"Yes ma'am," she said. "What?" Her eyes were terror-struck and her mouth was slack with anxiety. "Is it time? What? Oh, my God! . . . God help me!" she shrieked, her breakfast tray falling to the concrete floor with a crash. "Oh, *God!*" she screamed, throwing her spoon against the bars, grabbing her hair. "God! . . . Help me! . . . Help me! . . . What time is it? What time?" She went on screaming and pulling her hair.

Esther Todd was on her feet instantly, hovering near but not against the bars of the Ready Cell. "Calm!" she shouted. "Calm! Please be calm, Mrs. Fuller. Please calm yourself! Please! It's . . . it's six fifty-two, and I'm right here with you. Please!" the matron pleaded. "I'm right here . . . I'm right here. And you've got all the time in the world," she went on, as Alice Fuller stood before her, pulling at her hair and screaming.

Beyond the double doors that led to Death Row, twenty-five cells stretched the length of the rear of the Death Facility's first floor; there was not a sound from the inmates in the cells. The only sounds were the sharp, clanking noises made as the steam cart was opened in front of George Kruger's cell and his food was taken out by the trusty, Leo Dunbar.

They had the three condemned men in the first three cells of the Row: Kruger in the first cell, José Santos in the second, and Charlie Parker in the third.

As required by law, there was a Death Watch guard posted in a chair opposite each of the three improvised Ready Cells; the guards had been there round the clock in eight-hour shifts since Friday afternoon, when Hugh Greenwood had come to the Death Facility to present the death warrants to each of the condemned.

Alice Fuller had listened quietly while her warrant was being read; Parker had listened defiantly; Santos had said the reading was not necessary and Greenwood had stopped.

"I see it," Santos told him. "I know what it is."

Only George Kruger had reacted violently to the warrant. He threw water from his toilet at Greenwood and tried to urinate on the warden and the chaplain and the Death Watch guard as they stood outside his cell door.

"He's crazy as a shithouse rat, Mr. Greenwood," the Death Watch guard said. "He don't know nothin' about what's goin' on."

Greenwood had stepped back out of range of Kruger, read the warrant quickly in a muffled monotone, and gone on to Santos's and Charlie Parker's cells.

The document was a single piece of hard, legal-

122

sized parchment with the Great Seal of the State of Florida embossed in gold at the bottom left, a standard-looking piece of legal correspondence that at once revealed itself to be singular and oppressive by the large block words DEATH WARRANT typed across the top and the presence of a two-inch black ribbon that was stapled to the center, just above the words under the title that read:

EXECUTIVE DEPARTMENT
STATE OF FLORIDA

The words of George Kruger's death warrant were:

To Honorable Hubert L. Greenwood, *Warden of our State Prison, and* Honorable Lyle B. Jorgens, *Sheriff of our County of* Hillsborough,
GREETING: WHEREAS, *as the* Summer *term of our Circuit Court for the* Thirteenth *Judicial Circuit in and for our said County of* Hillsborough, *begun on the* 7th *day of July A.D. One Thousand Nine Hundred and* Seventy-Three, *one* George Hans Kruger *was convicted of the crime of* Rape, *and thereupon by our said court the said* George Hans Kruger *was sentenced for said crime to suffer the pains of death by being electrocuted by the passing through his body of a current of electricity of sufficient intensity to cause his immediate death and until he be dead, all of which by an exemplification of the record of said conviction and sentence, which I have caused to be hereunto annexed, doth fully appear;*
THEREFORE, *I,* Morgan J. Kingsly, *Governor of said State of* Florida, *command you, the said Sheriff of said County of* Hillsborough, *that not less than five days prior to the* 21st *day of* February, *in the year of our Lord One Thousand Nine Hundred and* Seventy-Seven, *you deliver the said* George Hans Kruger *to* Honorable Hubert L. Greenwood, *Warden of the State Maximum Security Prison in our County of* Bradford, *by him to be kept securely until the sentence of death shall be executed; and that at an hour on a week day, to be decided by the said Warden of the State Maximum Security Prison,*

in the week beginning with Monday, the 21st day of February, in the Year of Our Lord One Thousand Nine Hundred and Seventy-Seven, within the permanent death chamber of the said State Maximum Security Prison in our said County of Bradford, agreeably to the Six Thousand One Hundred and Twenty-Fifth Section of the Revised General Statutes of our said State, as amended by Chapter Nine Thousand One Hundred and Sixty-Nine, of the Laws of our State, Acts of 1923, you cause the execution of the said sentence of our said Court, in all respects to be done and performed upon him, the said George Hans Kruger, for which this shall be your sufficient warrant.

You, the said Warden of our State Maximum Security Prison, or some deputy by you to be designated, shall be present at such execution. Such execution shall be carried out by the First Assistant Engineer at the State Maximum Security Prison, deputy executioner, and such deputies, electricians and assistants as he may require to be present to assist, and shall be in the presence of a jury of twelve respectable citizens who shall be requested to be present, and witness the same; and you shall require the presence of a competent practicing physician or of the physician of the prison; and all persons other than such jury and physician, the counsel for the criminal, such Ministers of the Gospel as the criminal shall desire, officers of the prison, deputies and guards, shall be excluded during such execution.

WHEREOF FAIL NOT, *at your peril, and make return of this Warrant, with your doings thereon, as soon as may be after execution.*

IN WITNESS THEREOF, *I have hereunto placed my hand and caused to be affixed the Great Seal of the State of Florida, at Tallahassee, the Capital, this 14th day of February, in the year of our Lord One Thousand Nine Hundred and Seventy-Seven.*

(signed) *Morgan J. Kingsly,*
GOVERNOR OF FLORIDA.

On the reverse side of the death warrant, Greenwood would have the names of the witnesses present at Kruger's execution typed to the left, with their home addresses to the right. The time of Kruger's death would be recorded and certified by the attending physician, and Greenwood would sign at the bottom right as the warden present at the execution. Two photocopies of the warrant would be made: one would remain in the prison records office, the other would be mailed to the clerk of the Hillsborough County Circuit Court in Tampa, to be stored there with a copy of Kruger's trial records.

The original death warrant itself would, as required by law, be returned to the governor's office and then sent to the secretary of state's office to be kept with its permanent records.

"Kruger's not crazy," Charlie Parker had told Greenwood. "He's just scared. I'm not scared. You can read that piece of paper to me all day if you want. I'll be right here." He had looked the warden straight in the eye.

Parker was right. George Kruger was not crazy, he was scared. He had been on Death Row since August 6, 1973. When he arrived he was almost twenty-four—blond, five eleven, and just under a hundred and sixty pounds. Lean and muscular. The picture of the ideal beach boy, a role he played out for almost four years before he came to prison.

Now, at twenty-seven, with over three years on Death Row, he was nearly bald, he weighed little more than a hundred pounds, and he looked feeble and hollow-eyed.

He was born on October 14, 1949, in Freiburg, Germany, the only child of Karl and Marie Kruger, and he grew up in the idyllic Black Forest country of southwest Germany, fifteen miles from the banks of the Rhine River and the French border, opposite the French mountain town of Colmar. The Kruger family had lived in the Black Forest for over four hundred years, and most of their number had been respected members of the surrounding communities and skilled workers in the famed Jols Brewery in Freiburg.

Karl Kruger was twenty-four when his son, George, was born in 1949; he was a master brewmaster and a much respected member of the Freiburg working community when he emigrated to the United States at age forty-three with his wife and son in 1968, under the sponsorship of a brewery in Tampa, Florida.

The family settled into a comfortable ranch-style house in the well-kept, middle-class Tampa suburb of Temple Terrace, about five miles from the brewery, and George, nineteen at the time, enrolled at the University of South Florida, whose campus was almost within walking distance of their home.

The Kruger home was a place of tradition and respect, a perfect example of German-style Prussian order and cleanliness. But the family was no longer in Germany. They were in America, and in 1968 the hippie movement of "turning on" and "dropping out" was in full swing; order and cleanliness were the enemy.

Within a year of his enrollment at USF, George Kruger had dropped out of his freshman studies in the College of Engineering and was living in a hippie commune on the Gulf of Mexico in nearby Clearwater Beach, Florida, completely cut off from all ties with his family.

George was good-looking, young, curious, and hungry. He had all the natural qualifications and inclinations, and he embraced the hippie–beach boy lifestyle passionately; overnight, along the Clearwater Beach strip, he became known as the Golden Kraut. He wore his pure blond hair down past his shoulders and affected a costume of loud Hawaiian-print shorts, a fringed leather vest, a braided Navajo Indian headband, and East Indian toe sandals. He made the rounds as bartender, lifeguard, beach umbrella attendant, pool attendant, and small-time dope dealer from 1970 until the winter season of 1972; from that point on, as the hippie movement began to wind down, he went solo and trafficked on his name and his looks, devoting himself strictly to making a living with sex.

He preferred women, but if the price was right he

would also do his tricks for men. During the winter season of 1973, he made over $10,000 hustling men and women along Clearwater's strip. He was famous. The *St. Petersburg Times* Floridian magazine even did a feature story on him, a slightly watered-down piece under the title, "Hustling," that played down the hardcore sexual aspect of his life, but a piece that attracted the attention of Earl Brandinghamm, a multimillionaire Ohio industrialist who spent his winters in his ten-acre beach compound in Sarasota.

Brandinghamm was a fat, red-faced drunk, five foot nine and almost two hundred and fifty pounds, whose only enjoyment in life was the sex games he designed and had acted out for him and his fourth wife, Peggy, a twenty-year-old Cleveland beautician he had married solely because of her "gifted mouth," as he called it.

Brandinghamm found George Kruger in the Gulf Hideaway Bar on Clearwater Beach three days before his fifty-eighth birthday and offered him $200 for one night's work as his own personal birthday present.

Kruger took a second look at the fat man's bulk and asked for $300; Brandinghamm laughingly agreed, with the warning that he would make him earn the extra hundred.

Like Brandinghamm's imagination, the sex game he designed for George Kruger was blunt, effective, and simple. George would pretend to break into the main house, go upstairs to Peggy's bedroom, and find her in bed, fully clothed, reading a magazine. The rest of the game was predictable: Kruger would tear her clothes off and rape her, with Brandinghamm in the room all the while as audience.

It was one of Brandinghamm's favorite games, but as he watched George and Peggy on the bed that first time, George's sexual prowess, his looks, and his total abandon added a new dimension to the sport. Brandinghamm voluntarily upped the price to $500 and had George repeat the scene. The next morning as George was about to leave the compound, Brandinghamm offered him $500 a week for the rest of the season to stay on and "play," as he called it. George accepted without hesitation and moved into one of the thatched-roof guest bungalows.

The five weeks George remained in Brandinghamm's beach compound was one long sexual sideshow, and always, even with the diverse set of girls Brandinghamm brought in, played out around the theme of rape. George got caught up in it, swept along by the sheer animalism of the act, and sex became meaningless for him without the thrill of the fight.

When Brandinghamm and his following went north on April 15, 1973, George expected to be part of the group, but Brandinghamm threw him off with an extra $500 and a limp promise that he would look him up next season. George became despondent. It wasn't the brush-off he minded. He cared nothing for Brandinghamm or his moronic wife or even for the security of the $500 a week or the comfort of the beach bungalow. It was being cut off from the act of rape that distressed him. After almost three months of the game, he had become addicted to its thrill. Confused, he wandered back into the final weeks of the Clearwater Beach winter scene and returned to hustling, but there was no pleasure or stimulation in it. He had to have the rape game in the sex act or it was no good for him.

He committed his first rape in the fashionable West Shore section of Tampa on the afternoon of April 23, and the next day he found that a new dimension had been added to the act. The *Tampa Tribune* had a page-one story that detailed his crime against the young wife of a wealthy Tampa city councilman. The *Tribune* clipping gave George almost as much pleasure as the rape itself. He cut out all the clippings in the Tampa-St. Petersburg area papers and started a scrapbook he labeled with broad felt-tip-pen letters: KNOCK KNOCK.

When he was apprehended and the scrapbook was found in his room in a cheap beachfront motel, the press began calling George the Knock Knock Rapist, but before he was arrested—as he slept in his motel room bed on the morning of June 2—he had raped five women in the Tampa Bay area. Two of the women were committed to private mental hospitals, one took her own life shortly after his trial, and the other two, both wives of prominent Tampa businessmen, with school-age children, were divorced before the fall of 1974.

No woman, no family, could stand up to the publicity surrounding the trial or the realization of the savage act itself. The joint testimony at the trial was so sickening that most of it could only be alluded to in the newspapers. In one UPI story, the writer said, "George Kruger is to rape what Charlie Manson was to mass murder. The sickness and ferocity of both almost defy description.

When he was sentenced to death in the electric chair on August 4, 1973, Circuit Court Judge Warren K. Hastings pronounced an added judgment on him. "Never," he said, "have I seen a man more deserving of legal death. I shrink from saying it, but I have no wish that God have mercy on your soul."

Two days later Kruger was transported to the Big Max Death Facility, and from the afternoon of his sentencing he had played mad. Now, three and a half years later, he had been scared for so long a time, had not made sense for so long a time, that he truly appeared mad as a hatter. But he was not; he had only forgotten how to be sensible.

Dunbar and the guard, Hank Chrysler, found Kruger lying under his wall bunk in a puddle of his own urine, wrapped in a gray prison blanket, staring out at them like a wounded fox.

"That crazy sonofabitch," said Homer Tull, Kruger's Death Watch guard, slurring his words with a chew of tobacco. "He's been layin' under that bunk like a dumb bastard since the major come in here early this mornin'."

Kruger watched the two guards, his eyes white with terror. He started to grunt and heave himself back against the wall; you could tell he was urinating on himself again.

"Goddamn," Chrysler said, looking down at the sight. He rubbed his mouth. "Goddamn this all the way to the county line," he went on. "The major's gonna be hot if this pissin' asshole don't eat somethin'."

"Boy!" Chrysler pelted Kruger with his voice, stepping up close to the bars of his cell. "You get your sorry ass out from under that bunk and come over here and eat somethin', before I come in there on you."

Kruger let out three long moans and then jammed his head under the blanket as if it were a sleeping bag.

"Dammit! Sonofabitch," Homer Tull said, standing up beside Chrysler.

The two guards looked at each other for a second, and then Tull spit a long brown wad of tobacco juice in a coffee can on the floor by his feet.

Chrysler turned back to face Kruger; after a few seconds, he told the Death Watch guard to open the cell door.

"Puss," Chrysler said to Dunbar without looking at him, "me and Mister Tull are gonna hold him, and you gonna feed him. He might try to bite us, an' that's okay. Just don't let the fucker bite you. We can't have no delays on account of other charges or any such bullshit." He watched as Tull put his key into the lock of Kruger's cell door.

"Yessir, boss," Dunbar replied dutifully, and pushed the steam cart back against the far wall of the cellblock corridor.

The second they opened Kruger's cell door he began yelling for help in his woman's voice. "Help!" he shrieked. "Help! . . . help! . . . help! . . . help!" he kept on crying like a frightened child.

Chrysler and Tull stood in the cell's open doorway, about to go in after Kruger, when all along the Row the cry was suddenly picked up by the other inmates, who had been stone quiet.

"Cocksuckers! Get away from the man!"

"Let him be!"

"Pig motherfuckers! Get the hell out!"

"Cracker motherfuckers!"

"Come in here an' suck my dick if you want something to play with!"

"Yeah, play with the man's dick, get the come for a prize!"

"Fuck you!"

"Fuck all pigs!"

The noise was suddenly deafening. Chrysler slammed Kruger's cell door shut and Tull locked it quickly. Kruger stayed pinned under the wall bunk. Dunbar stepped back against the far wall and froze in his tracks.

"Shut up! Shut the goddamned hell up!" Chrysler shouted, running down to the center of the hallway so he could be seen by most of the screaming inmates. "Shut up, goddamn you, or I'll tear-gas this block! I'll gas you bastards, so help me God," he raged at the line of defiant faces at the cell doors facing him.

They knew Chrysler would do what he said, so they began to quiet themselves, their eyes glowing with explosive hatred.

Two cells down from Kruger, Charlie Parker stood at his cell door with his hands wrapped around the bars. "Let the man alone," he said to Chrysler as the deep silence came back. "You'll get in there soon enough."

"Nigger, you shut your mouth," Chrysler yelled at him. "I'll gas you just for the fun of it, you big-mouthed coon sonofabitch."

Parker was silent for a moment; then he spoke again, never taking his eyes off the guard. "You can't wait, can you?" he said. "You want me so bad you can taste my hide. You want it, don't you, you redneck cocksucker? Well, come in an' get it," he told Chrysler, taking a half step back from the bars, poised on the balls of his feet like a boxer, his fists out in front of him like clubs.

"You sorry motherfucker!" Chrysler roared, taking a mad swipe at his own face with a wiping motion across his mouth, balling up his fists to meet the other man's, as the catcalls and noise picked up once more on the Row.

"Stick your fist up his ass, Parker!"

"Do the trick on the prick!"

"Make his shit run, Parker!"

"Put the hand on the man!"

"Go through the bars, Parker, an' pull the fucker's throat out!"

"Go right through, Parker! Like Superman! Go through the bars and kick the man's ass!"

"Kick it *good!*"

The new rebellion sent Chrysler into a frenzy. "Not one more sound!" he bellowed. "Not one more sound or I'll get the gas out!"

After a few more long seconds the noise stopped cold. On Death Row there was never any beginning, middle, or end, just the moment. After a few seconds, the moment was gone. Chrysler and Parker glared at each other in the new silence, and then the guard turned on his heel without another word and went back to Kruger's cell door.

"We're gonna feed this man for his own good," Chrysler bellowed out to the Row. "And I by God don't want to hear another fuckin' sound!"

Chrysler and Tull went in after George Kruger and pulled him out from under the wall bunk. Tull went for his arms and Chrysler went for his feet. Kruger came out like a piece of wood with his eyes closed, letting out a sickening *"Eeeaaaaooo,"* as if someone were twisting a knife in his flesh. The instant the moan faded away, he started to fight. He started kicking and screaming and snapping at Tull, with his mouth foaming like a mad dog's. Tull drew back to hit him with a right to the center of his face, but Chrysler stopped him as he drew back.

"No! Goddamn, don't hit him," Chrysler commanded. "The major don't want a mark on him. Goddamn, just get ahold of him. Pin his fuckin' arms back. Puss, get in here!" he bawled over his shoulder. "Get hold of his head and don't let him bite you."

The fat black man shook off the dread that had taken over his mind and obeyed Chrysler's order. The three of them finally wrestled Kruger out into the middle of the small cell, with Chrysler sitting astraddle his legs, Tull with his arms pulled to the right, and Dunbar, close in at the left, locking his bony neck in a stranglehold.

"Boy!" Chrysler bellowed into Kruger's wild face. "You stop now, boy! You stop and you sit still like I'm tellin' you. Nobody gonna hurt you. Nobody!" He waved his finger in Kruger's face for emphasis. "Do you understand that, boy? Nobody gonna hurt you. It ain't time yet. We're just gonna feed you. Feed you, dammit. Just sit still and let us feed you. You gotta eat somethin'."

He paused.

"Do you understand what I'm tellin' you, boy?"

Kruger's fanatic's eyes seemed to show some sign of recognition, and his rigid muscles relaxed somewhat.

"All right," Chrysler said, surveying Kruger's face, getting off his legs at the same time. "We just hafta get him up easy. Mister Tull, you keep hold on his arms. Puss, you keep a grip on his neck."

They stood Kruger up as if they were hanging up a small, wet blanket, and Chrysler motioned them back to the wall bunk.

"Sit him down there," Chrysler instructed. "We're just gonna sit you down, boy," he said to Kruger. "Just put him down easy," he said, with his hand on Kruger's chest.

"Now we're gonna turn you loose, boy," he told Kruger, as the condemned man sat on the bunk, pinned between the bulk of Tull and the trusty. "We're gonna turn you loose and nobody's gonna bother you, or mess with you, or nothin'. We're just gonna feed you somethin'. You understand that, boy?" His face was almost touching Kruger's. "We're gonna turn you loose and you're gonna sit still."

Kruger nodded his head slightly within Dunbar's grip, and they released him.

"Mister Tull, you go outside and lock the door," Chrysler said to the other guard. "Puss an' I'll feed him."

Once the cell door had been locked, Tull pushed the steel bowl of oyster stew under the food slot in the door and then pushed in a steel cup full of Coca-

Cola. Chrysler stayed near Kruger, and Dunbar went for the food and stood holding it behind the guard.

On the bunk, Kruger, dressed only in the standard issue—Death Row buttonless coveralls that were soaked with his urine—began to shiver. He clutched his shallow chest and his teeth began to chatter.

"Lord God, what a mess," Chrysler said. "What a damn smell on a grown man."

"Boss," Dunbar said from behind him, in a small voice, "I think I can get him to eat. I think I can do somethin' for him."

Chrysler turned around to face the trusty. "Go ahead, Puss," he said. "See what you can do."

The black man took two slow, deliberate steps toward Kruger, who sat with his eyes riveted on him, and then cautiously sat down on the bunk beside him. The two men faced each other on the narrow bunk in complete silence. Seconds went by, and then Dunbar smiled a small, slight smile at the little white man, a smile people smile at sick people.

Kruger's drawn face remained the same, but something seemed to ease up behind his eyes, and he slowly undid his locked hands on his lap.

Then Leo Dunbar dipped the wide-mouth spoon into the almost cold oyster stew and raised the spoon to Kruger's lips. He fed him like you would a baby, with long drips of the stew falling down the sides of Kruger's jaws.

God in heaven above, Hank Chrysler said to himself.

6:57 A.M.

José Santos stood up from his wall bunk and walked over to his cell door and picked up the steel cup of coffee and the steel tray that held four pieces of fried chicken, a lump of mashed potatoes, an ear of corn, half a lime, and two heavy biscuits, and took the food and drink back to the small bolted-down metal table attached to the wall opposite the bunk. Then he went back to the bunk and sat down and looked at the meal on the table. Each move he made was carefully planned out and deliberate; this was so in everything he did.

Hank Chrysler stood and looked through the bars. Second only to Charlie Parker, he despised Santos more than any other man on the Row. In cracker parlance, Charlie Parker was an uppity high-class nigger, but Santos was worse. He was stuckup: educated, silent, and aloof.

"Eat your damn food, Cuban," Chrysler ordered, a smirk set on his square face.

"I do not let anyone see me eat; you are aware of that," Santos said without emotion, not looking at Chrysler.

"Well, by God, spick, Mister Morris here's gonna see you eat," Chrysler said with pleasure, motioning toward the Death Watch guard.

"That is as it is," Santos answered. "But I will not eat in front of you."

"You gonna do a lot more than eat for me before this mornin's over." Chrysler smiled and looked down at Joe Morris, the Death Watch guard, who sat with his chair leaning back against the cellblock's far wall.

"As it will be," Santos repeated, looking straight at the food.

"Tough sonofabitch," Chrysler said. "This mornin' we'll see how tough you are."

Santos did not betray his thoughts with words or with a single movement of his body.

"Fuck this, and fuck you, too!" Chrysler said. "I'm not gonna stand here lettin' you put shit on me. I oughta come in there and kick your balls up around your elbow," he roared for the Death Watch guard's benefit. "You eat your goddamned food in private, you do as you goddamn please, 'cause, Cuban, you ain't gonna do what you please for much longer. That's for damn sure!" He turned away from Santos and nodded sharply for Leo Dunbar to push the steam cart on to the next cell.

As if McPeters were looking over his shoulder, the fat black convict pushed the cart near Santos's cell door.

"It's real good chicken," Dunbar said to Santos, as McPeters had ordered him, his voice loose and unsure.

Santos kept rock still.

"Dammit, Puss!" Chrysler bawled. "Get your ass *movin'!*"

When the guard and the trusty had gone the short distance to Charlie Parker's cell and were out of his line of sight, José Santos got up from the wall bunk and went over to the bolted-down metal table and sat on the bolted-down metal stool and carefully began to have his meal. The chicken tasted good. It was seasoned well with cumin and oregano. His mother had sent him the spice the week before, and Hugh Greenwood had permitted the kitchen to use it on his food once the final sixty-five hours of the Death Routine went into effect.

Santos had alternated all weekend between pork chops and chicken, each seasoned with the fragrant, bittersweet spices, but he wanted chicken for the final meal; for reasons he could not define, chicken spiced with cumin and laced with fresh lime juice conjured up the lovely, tropical, verdant, loamy image of Cuba. Cuba was his obsession in life, though he had not seen it for fourteen years, not since the day he and his mother came out on a freedom flight in 1962. Cuba represented happiness and contentment; in all his twenty-eight years, José Santos could not remember those feelings. They were too long ago; they were when he was a child in the heart of the island of Cuba.

He was born two hundred miles southeast of Havana in the colonial city of Santa Clara, the capital city of Las Villas province, a place, since the time of the Spanish in the early 1500s, where the name Santos had been royal and respected. Santa Clara sat almost at the direct center of the country from all four sides, and the Santos family had used the centrality to good advantage, becoming one of Cuba's wealthiest families, with wide-ranging trading and commercial interests in sugar cane in the east and tobacco in the west.

José's father, Ramón Santos, a third son in his family, shared in the family wealth but, in the Latin tradition of brotherhood, never took an active part in the direct affairs of the business. In the role of junior brother, he had entered one of the professions, choosing the police as his calling. When José was born on the night of September 16, 1948, in Santa Clara, Don Ramón Santos was first assistant to the chief of the provincial police force of the province of Las Villas.

Ramón Santos began his police career in Havana, where the Santos family maintained a luxurious compound of three seaview villas in fashionable Miramar, on the northwest corner of Avenida I, where it met Calle 30, and Avenida 5, off the broad Malecón. The year was 1940, and after seven years as a behind-the-scenes kingmaker in Cuban military and political life, Colonel Fulgencio Batista took office as an elected president. In 1952, after his good friend Hyman Meyer made the secret arrangements with then Cuban President Prío, Batista returned to Cuba after exile in Daytona Beach, Florida, where he had been since the end of his term as virtually self-appointed president in 1944, and seized dictatorial power in the country after a bloodless coup.

In the forefront of the anti-Prío forces which schemed to bring Batista back to the island was the Santos family, whose equally good friend and chief mainland U.S. connection was Miami's Hyman Meyer, the quiet, subdued Jew and absolute ruler of the American underworld.

Under Batista, the finances of the Santos family did not flourish quite as they had during the inflated years in the late twenties and early thirties under the tyrant Machado, but in all their history on the island their political power was never greater. José's two uncles both occupied powerful cabinet posts, and when Batista returned to power in 1952 his father, Ramón, was almost immediately made head of the provincial police in Las Villas province. Twice, as a boy, José Santos dined at the Presidential Palace in Havana, with Hyman Meyer sitting on Batista's right and his Uncle Domingo on the left.

The world had belonged to José Santos as a boy.
He received his early elementary schooling first at a
private school in Santa Clara and then at the exclusive
Lycée de Americas in Havana, beginning in 1958, when
he was ten.

The world of upper-class Cuban society rivaled
that of Bourbon Europe. But on the morning of January 1, 1959, that world crumbled and fell into history
when Fidel Castro and his army of peasants took the
capital city after twenty-five months of bitter guer-
rilla warfare.

Early in the Castro-Batista struggle, José's father
had delegated his police chief's position to a trusted
lieutenant and gone to Havana to work as senior
Cuban liaison officer with the American CIA in counter-
insurgency actions against Castro. The entire Santos
family rallied to the support of Batista, an effort that
became fanatical after Castro and his men overran the
family holdings in Santa Clara on their march to
Havana from the Sierra Maestra mountains in eastern
Cuba, near the ancient capital city of Santiago de Cuba.

Batista resigned and fled Cuba, but most of the
Santos family were not so fortunate. José's two uncles
were shot in a gun battle at José Marti airport on the
morning of January 1, and his father was captured a
day later and shot publicly within the week. José and
his mother, Maria, who had gone into hiding in one
of their servants' homes near the center of the city,
were captured on January 14 and sent to the infa-
mous political prison on the Isle of Pines.

On October 25, 1962, by prophetic coincidence
the day John F. Kennedy's Cuban missile crisis became
a reality when U-2 planes photographed the Russian
medium-range ballistic missile launch site near San Cris-
tobal, José Santos and his mother were released from
prison after Fidel Castro personally granted them
their freedom, following the intervention of an "influential American." The influential American, of
course, was Hyman Meyer, who, as a loyal family
friend, had been seeking their freedom since the early
days of their imprisonment.

Santos and his mother arrived in Miami dead

broke, anemic, and brutalized by three years on the Isle of Pines, but with Hyman Meyer as their sponsor all their needs were soon met, and after a month in a private hospital in Miami Springs they moved to a comfortable two-bedroom house in Hialeah and a ready-made existence that included ten $100 bills that arrived on the first day of each month inside a small cardboard package with the address of a New York City produce company on the label.

At age fourteen José Santos was too young and too ill to follow the developments of the missile crisis, and when the two thousand CIA-sponsored rebels landed at the beachhead on the Bay of Pigs on the morning of April 17, 1961, he and his mother had been in prison on the Isle of Pines, the hellhole where most of the surviving captives of the two-day Bay of Pigs fiasco were finally taken. But the spark of Cuban liberation burned as strongly within José Santos as it did in any uneasy heart and mind in Miami's ever-growing Cuban community.

The three years in prison on the Isle of Pines had molded an eleven-year-old pampered upper-class Latin child into a con-wise street kid, and in the early 1960s Miami scene, where Cuban street urchins and the sons and daughters of former millionaires grew up side by side in center-city tenements, José Santos had to program his mind a third time to cope with the security of the middle-class comforts Hyman Meyer provided for him and his mother.

He went to Hialeah High School and in 1966, at age eighteen, enrolled at the University of Miami. He was of average height, five feet nine inches, and he grew up strong and muscular and lean and good-looking. He did not participate in the hippie rebellion of the day. He maintained the old ways of Cuban upper-class dignity and style in all he did. He wore his thick black hair cut a medium length and parted, and throughout most of the school year at UM he wore a coat and tie to his classes or affected the Cuban countryman's pleated guayabera shirt worn loosely out over his trousers.

Within the close-knit Cuban community that had

developed in Miami by the late 1960s, as their number began to prosper in south Florida business life, José Santos was regarded as a fine, honorable, and upstanding young man.

Outwardly, when José Santos graduated from the University of Miami in 1970, cum laude, with a degree in political science, he appeared to be a young man on his way. His future in law school at the University of Virginia had been assured by Meyer, and he seemed destined for a place of prominence. There was even wishful speculation within some of the Cuban social clubs in the Miami area that he might some day become the state's first Cuban governor.

But inwardly the twenty-two-year-old Santos was eaten up with a psychotic hatred for Fidel Castro and a paranoid longing to return to his homeland, to Cuba, a place that was more an ideal to him than a reality.

Only two people in Miami knew his true feelings: Raphael Torres, the leader of the CIA-backed, anti-Castro Alpha-66 paramilitary band, and Hyman Meyer.

In June 1970, instead of making preparations for law school in the fall, José Santos said good-bye to his mother and, against her express wishes and against the bitter opposition of Hyman Meyer, was recruited into the CIA by Torres and sent to Quantico, Virginia, for indoctrination.

After a month of briefings at the CIA training facility on the Marine Corps Training Station at Quantico, José Santos was flown directly to a secret CIA training base two hours outside Santo Domingo, a sprawling hacienda thirty miles east of the posh La Romana—Casa de Campo resort complex near the village of Boca de Chavón on the Caribbean at the mouth of the Chavón River.

The Boca de Chavón training base, set up under the guise of an exclusive international retreat for alcoholics, was one of the CIA's most closely guarded secrets, known only to a handful of top agency officials as the Panther's Den. Situated in primitive La Altagracia Province, at the southeastern tip of the Dominican Republic, Boca de Chavón was acces-

sible only by four-wheel-drive vehicle, boat, or helicopter. It was staffed by twenty hand-picked CIA op-
eratives and had but one function—to train agents
especially recruited into the CIA under the top-secret
coded project known as Operation Alpha, the assasi-
nation of Cuban Premier Fidel Castro.

Santos arrived at Boca de Chavón by jet helicopter from Miami during the second week in July 1970
and was immediately thrust into Operation Alpha's in-
tensive training schedule, a ten-week routine that had
prepared eight international assassins from its inception in January 1966. All eight of his predecessors had
been killed in their assassination attempts, but CIA
officials were optimistic about Santos's chances of success. He was the first full-fledged patriot recruited for
the project, and also there was his connection with
Hyman Meyer, the man who owned the hacienda and
paid all the bills of the project, a figure which, by
July 1970, had come to just over $2.5 million.

Of all private American citizens, none had lost
more money in Cuba than Hyman Meyer. In exchange
for Meyer's intervention with President Prío in 1952,
bringing Batista back to the island, Batista had allowed him and "Lucky" Lantano and other top Mafia
leaders to establish a $200-million-a-year gambling
empire in Havana. When Castro finally closed Cuba to
the West and openly embraced communism in December 1961, more than a billion dollars in U.S. interests had been confiscated, including $10 million
in real property and fully $50 million a year in gam-
bling enterprises that belonged directly to Meyer.

When Batista fled Cuba in January 1959, he went
first to Hyman Meyer's Boca de Chavón hacienda, and
before the dictator had made his way to Portugal,
where he settled with an estimated $600 million, he
and Meyer hatched the concept of Operation Alpha.
In the years following 1959, many of Cuba's wealthiest anti-Castro families settled in the Dominican Republic, maintaining their Latin life-style rather than
relocating in Miami, and it was their profound hope
that they would one day go back to the island with
Batista as their leader, backed again by a loose-knit

coalition of extreme right-wing U.S. Republican Congressmen, U.S. and Cuban sugar barons, and Mafia czars like Hyman Meyer.

Santos proved to be the most apt pupil of those who spent ten grueling weeks at Boca de Chavón. Every moment in his life from the day in 1959 when he and his mother had been transported to prison on the Isle of Pines had prepared him for his work as Castro's executioner, and he reached out to the work with the zeal of a fanatic.

He completed his training on September 18, 1970, and was given a two-week vacation in Santo Domingo before being transferred to CIA headquarters in McLean, Virginia, for final briefings on the assassination plot. On October 2, while sitting at the pool of Santo Domingo's Hotel Jaragua, off Avenida Independencia, he read in the air edition of the *Miami Herald* that Hyman Meyer had fled the United States in the wake of Senate Crime Committee investigations and was, in the style of his close friend, Meyer Lansky, seeking political asylum in Israel. The news hurt Santos personally, as he knew Meyer better than his own father and was more indebted to Meyer than to his own father. But the news also cast an ominous shadow over Operation Alpha, the one great motivating force in Santos's life. He cut his vacation short and caught the next morning's Pan Am flight for Miami and an afternoon Eastern flight to National Airport in Washington, D.C.

From the moment he read of Hyman Meyer's troubles with the Senate Crime Committee, José Santos feared the worst for Operation Alpha; once he reached CIA Headquarters in McLean, his fears were confirmed. Until further notice, Santos was to abandon all open connections with the CIA and abort Operation Alpha completely. News of a CIA-backed plot to kill Castro, based on an alliance with Hyman Meyer, Santos was told bluntly by the CIA director, would be the bizarre link Senate watchdogs needed to begin a carryover probe into related agency activities from the crime committee hearings. For the foreseeable future, prob-

ably forever, Operation Alpha and the Panther's Den
training base were closed issues.

Santos was left like an unfulfilled bridegroom
on his wedding night, but there was no humor in his
situation. He was one of the world's most highly trained
and sophisticatedly motivated assassins, and suddenly
his objective had been taken from him.

According to CIA orders, he was supposed to en-
roll in the University of Virginia Law School as he had
originally planned; arrangements had already been
made for his late registration before he arrived in
Washington. This move would serve a twofold purpose: it would give Santos a legitimate and believable
cover, and it would also keep him relatively close to
CIA headquarters in case there was a change of status
in the Operation Alpha project.

But Santos did not enter law school as ordered.
Already functioning on a thin line between sanity and
paranoia, the fluke closing of Operation Alpha after
Hyman Meyer's flight from the United States to Israel pushed José Santos over into the gray limbo of
irrationality.

On October 6, 1970, he dropped out of sight and
was not heard from again until he was apprehended
by Miami City detectives just before midnight on December 24, 1972, the night he blew up Circulo Cubano, a pro-Castro Cuban social club in Hialeah, killing eight people, half of whom were women and young
children.

During the two years and two months he remained underground in the Miami area, José Santos
—or the Death Angel, as the press dubbed him—became the perfect terrorist: cold, totally detached, efficient, and deadly. In all, he was credited with the
deaths of more than forty pro-Castro figures in south
Florida. He was convicted by a Dade County Circuit
Court jury on eight counts of first degree murder following the Christmas Eve bombing of the Circulo Cubano on February 12, 1973, and was the first person
to be sentenced to the electric chair, sixty-six days after
Florida reinstated the death penalty.

Not one word of his involvement with the CIA or his attachments to Hyman Meyer was ever brought up at his trial. For all the world knew, José Santos was simply a lunatic terrorist whose only pleasure in life was killing.

But it makes no difference, Santos said to himself without emotion, without bitterness. *Hyman Meyer is eighty-two and in federal prison for income tax evasion. The thousand-dollar-a-month payments to my mother stopped the moment I came to prison. The CIA has disavowed any connection with me. Nothing on the outside matters now.*

All that matters is on the inside, he said silently. *What happens this morning. How it all ends.*

When he had eaten his last meal he sat and looked at the empty tray and the picked chicken bones and tried to feel some sense of loss, some sense of finality. But no feelings came. There was only emptiness, and the haunting realization that he did not belong where he was, that his life might have been completely different—a sense, a realization, that not many people ever had on Death Row.

But that is all past. What is important is now, he told himself again.

He stood and walked over to his tiny stainless-steel sink and washed his hands and face carefully, with the care that a doctor might use. Then he dried himself and walked over to his wall bunk and sat down and stared at the opposite wall so that he could not see the Death Watch guard sitting outside his cell in the hallway. He sat perfectly still, his hands crossed on his lap, waiting fifteen minutes, as was his custom, before beginning his exercises.

To Joe Morris, who leaned forward in his chair to observe him, it seemed that Santos was in a deep trance. That worried the guard. Everything about José Santos worried Morris and the other Death Watch guards who had sat with him at intervals for the past three days. He did not seem like the kind of man who would go out easy.

Charlie Parker was fifty-two years old, an enormous man, standing six feet five inches and weighing two hundred and thirty pounds, a black man who had been born in Cap-Haïtien, Haiti, on September 4, 1923, to parents who were one generation removed from African slaves.

On Death Row he was known as the Haitian, and he stood apart from the other blacks. He stood apart from everyone. There was a dignity about him that you did not often see in other men—black or white, free or convict—a dignity that had gone out of fashion in the mid-1800s.

His father was named Luke Parker, and he had been born in 1892 in Savannah, Georgia, to parents who had been freed during the Civil War. His mother was named Janet du Callies, and she had been born in 1899 on the Caribbean side of Haiti's Massif du Sud peninsula, across from Port-au-Prince in the small, poverty-stricken seacoast village of Côtes de Fer, the daughter of runaways who jumped their slave ship in the Bahamas off Matthew Town, Great Inagua, in 1859.

Luke Parker grew up a poor, uneducated black in the southeast slums of Savannah, Georgia, and went to sea as a cook's helper on a freighter in 1905, when he was thirteen. He shipped around the Caribbean and South America for seventeen years, picking up a sailor's education and the trade of a first-class ship's cook in the process; and in June 1922, while he was on a week's shore leave out of Port-au-Prince, Haiti, he met Janet du Callies, a shy, creamy-skinned girl of twenty-three. They were married in her village of Côtes de Fer three days after they met, and the day after they married Parker left his ship and the couple moved to the north side of the island at Cap-Haïtien, where Janet had relatives who worked at the plush Hotel Paris. Luke Parker was working as a salad chef at the hotel when the first of their six children, a boy they named Charles, was born the next year.

Charlie Parker's young life was pleasant. Unlike most common people in Haiti at the time, the family had good food to eat and a little money to spend. His parents were strong, independent people whose sole goal in life was to improve their position, and this was what they taught their son as soon as he was old enough to understand it.

All six Parker children—three boys and three girls, born from 1923 to 1934—were taught French as well as English, and were forbidden to speak patois, the gibberish mixture of French and English that was the common Haitian's language and, as Charlie Parker's parents saw it, their badge of ignorance and poverty. All six children were sent to school, and in 1934, when the family moved to Kingston, Jamaica, where Luke Parker went to work as salad chef at the Henry VIII Hotel, his eldest son, Charles, was enrolled in a private school run for blacks.

When the family moved back to the United States in the fall of 1940, Charlie had graduated from high school, and like his brothers and sisters he was polite, educated, and well mannered beyond his years or race. But from the moment the family members landed at the municipal dock in Savannah, Georgia, in 1940, their achievements up to that point were erased. From that moment on, although the Parkers did not know it and would not have believed it if they had, they were doomed.

They had come to America for what seemed like the golden opportunity Luke Parker had talked about from the minute he began his family in 1922: the spark, the something extra that would get him over the hump and into a business—a restaurant—of his own.

By a twist of fate, Luke Parker's two younger brothers and younger sister were dead by 1940, and when the last member of his family, his mother, died that year he became heir to a small wood-frame house off Georgia Route 17, five miles south of Savannah, a house and five acres that, as it happened, had been condemned by the Georgia State Highway Department for use in widening Route 17 and establishing a weight station for trucks.

The condemned price of the land was a meager $18,500, a figure about one third the price a well-connected white family could have gotten, but the money seemed like a million dollars to Luke Parker. He brought his family back to America with genuine immigrant glee, and, with the money, opened a small restaurant in Savannah on the corner of Hemming Street and Second Avenue, two blocks off the water-front.

Parker called his pin-clean little restaurant Brasserie Haïtien, and it opened with great success late in 1940, with Luke as chef, assisted by his two younger sons, and with his oldest daughter and wife as wait-resses, and Charlie as maitre d' and captain. It was the only black-owned restaurant in the white section of the city, but because of the family's Haitian background, and because of their general upper-class-black status —as opposed to that of the mass of poor, uneducated blacks that flocked to Savannah—they were allowed, by the white powers that be, to open their restaurant; and of course, as one local newspaper observed that Christmas season, "there was no finer continental food to be found in Savannah than in the quaint Brasserie Haïtien."

Charlie Parker always remembered the fall of 1940 and the winter and spring of 1941 as the finest time of his life, a time when he and his close-knit family were euphoric, a time when everything was beautiful.

But it all came to an end on the night of July 4, 1941, when the local Ku Klux Klan burned his father's restaurant and their three-bedroom home on 50th Street to the ground. That night changed everything in Charlie Parker's life. From that point on, for every member of his family, everything in life went sour. It was the kind of disaster, the kind of kick in the face, that most people do not come back from.

Overnight, there was nothing. The family was completely wiped out: no business, no home. Bills devoured what small savings there were, leaving a crushing weight of debts. The family, six children and two adults, walked out of Savannah a week after the disaster, penniless, with only the dirty clothes on their backs.

Luke Parker had been gone from the United States for so long he had forgotten about the racial hatred. In Jamaica it had been a matter of class structure, and Haiti, of course, was a republic set up by slaves. Parker, and the dream he had for his family, was beaten by the one thing over which he had no control. He had triumphed over every other obstacle in life, but prejudice was the one thing you could not beat in that time and place.

All eight members of the family walked most of the 120 miles from Savannah inland, west, to the little pulpwood town of Valdosta, Georgia. The trip took them a week. They stole corn and carrots out of farm fields and ate them uncooked, and at night they slept in abandoned shacks or under the wide foundations of roadside signs. They were sick and starved when they reached Valdosta and the home of Luke Parker's only living relative, a cousin who worked for a logging company.

The cousin, a gentle, illiterate giant of a man who had never married, took them in warmly and sympathetically. He was forty at the time, and he had learned well the lessons of racial hatred. When he had come to Savannah during the winter to see his cousin's fine restaurant and spend a week with the family in their spacious brick house on the edge of what was called the Colored Quarter, he had told Luke Parker, "In all my life I never seen anything like this, I never imagined anything like this. I hope it lasts for you. It's a dream." Six months later, when the same eight people stood outside his slatboard cabin, dirty and scared and bewildered, he saw the reality behind the dream.

Everyone in the Parker family saw the reality. Luke Parker was forty-nine years old, black, completely broke, marooned on the side of the road in

Georgia, with a family of six children and a wife who looked to him for support. For once in his life, as he looked at the bleak surroundings in the little slatboard turpentine camp village where his cousin lived, he had no illusions. He was down and out, beaten, and he knew it.

Charlie Parker knew it, too, but he could not accept the fact. He was seventeen: bright, educated, a handsome, lean, six-two youth and still growing. He knew who he was and what he was, but all his life he had been told that the world was his for the taking and now, suddenly, there was not even food to eat.

For a month, Charlie and his sixteen-year-old brother, Thad, caught the turpentine trucks with their father and their cousin and worked in the stifling heat of the dense slash-pine forests out from Valdosta. The Parker family was given a one-room shanty like their cousin's, a dilapidated, roach-infested box that sat on four-foot stilts that they moved into after Charlie and his father and brother drew their first week's wages of $18 apiece.

The house was a cruel copy of a Haitian shanty-town hut, a 20-by-15-foot space with two open windows and two screenless doors, a wood stove, a washstand outside by the well, and an outdoor toilet in the woods, fifty feet from the back door. The house and all that happened that year of 1941 was like a brutal object lesson in dreaming for every member of the Parker family.

On the Saturday afternoon he collected his fourth check, Charlie and Thad Parker took their money and hitchhiked back to Savannah and joined the Army. The two brothers, both Haitian citizens because of their mother's wish, took their basic training at Fort Benning, Georgia, and were then separated and never saw one another again. Thad was sent to France with an all-Negro machine-gun company, and Charlie was sent to Italy with an all-Negro infantry battalion. Thad was killed during the bitter fighting for Salerno, but Charlie seemed to live a charmed life. Men fell to his right and to his left, but in four years of fighting he was never once touched by enemy fire. He was awarded two bronze stars and a silver star and rose from the rank of private to that of first sergeant of his company. His unconcern for danger was so well known that it caught the eye of war correspondents; summing up his feeling for life in general, he said to one of them in his precise, slightly accented Jamaican English, "You have simply not got to give a damn."

After the war, Parker got himself mustered out in Italy and stayed behind in Rome and was active in the black market and in running guns to North Africa. At twenty-two, he possessed some of the airs of a British gentleman, was fluent in French and Italian, and when his application to remain in the Army as an officer was denied, his future in the black market, as far as he was concerned, was determined.

He lived well in Rome in a fine little yellow marble villa on Palatine Hill, off the Via del Cerchi, with a splendid view of the Arch of Titus. He lived with an Italian woman, a beautiful dark-haired signora whose family had been killed in the war, and she ran his household of four servants during his frequent absences.

On the surface, Charlie Parker gave the appearance of a cold, calculating, continental thug, a six-five giant who seemed the perfect product of World War II, a man skilled in the impersonal ways of death and its hardware. But inside he was possessed of a deep sorrow and of a longing for something he had forgotten how to define—the respect, the improvement in his station in life that his father had pursued so passionately.

His father had committed suicide on the afternoon of his fiftieth birthday; the news had come to Charlie Parker in a muddy ditch off Highway 7, outside the Italian town of Cisterna di Latima. His mother and youngest brother and sister had returned to Haiti after the war and were living in a small house in Côtes de Fer that he had bought for them; his middle sister had married a schoolteacher and was living in Macon, the middle brother had moved to Detroit and was working in a steel mill.

None of what had happened to his family made sense to Charlie Parker; it seemed like something out of a melodrama. He looked at other people, the people of Italy who had just come through a devastating war at home, but in all that he saw he could not find a family as destroyed as his own. He drifted through the years after the war like a man whose mind is cut off from his body. He got careless. Finally, in 1952, he was arrested by Interpol agents and was deported to Haiti.

His mother had died in 1950, and on his return he found his brother and sister living in poor circumstances in Côtes de Fer, the brother a skiff fisherman, the sister married to a fisherman and living in a shack with three small children. Soon after he arrived in Port-au-Prince, he was recruited by the advance guard of François "Papa Doc" Duvalier's Tonton Macoutes, the strong-arm gangster political police that began dominating Haiti after Duvalier came to power in 1957.

Parker's size and his background made him a natural enforcer, and his philosophy of recklessness and his desire for money made him a natural for the free-lance drug traffic that filtered through Haiti from Venezuela to the United States. By 1960, he had become wealthy in his own right as a middleman in the cocaine trade, but he had to leave Haiti by a hastily chartered plane after Tonton Macoutes officials discovered his personal business enterprises and the fact that he had been sequestering large sums of money in a numbered account in Nassau for years.

Parker landed at Palm Beach International Airport, took up residence in the fashionable northwest section of West Palm Beach on the Intracoastal Waterway, and opened a bar across the canal on Palm Beach's Worth Avenue. The Club Haïtien developed into legend, like Toots Shor's, El Morocco, and the Stork Club, becoming a mecca where high society mixed with the underworld.

He married a white woman in 1966, Ella Rice, the daughter of a Boston industrialist; that same year he and his new wife moved across the canal to a $500,000 mansion on the beach, and Parker became an American citizen. A year after they were married, Parker got back into the cocaine trade, funneling the

drug from Caracas, by air, to a deserted crop-dusting
airstrip twenty miles inland from Palm Beach, near
the farming town of Loxahatchee. The marriage of a
black to a member of Boston's sacrosanct 400 was, of
course, a strained one, but one the Rice family accepted. It put Charlie Parker in the Palm Beach social
scene, and his "colorful" background, as it was regarded by the city's high society, gave him a cameo
status that he used greatly to his advantage as a cover
for his drug business.

But Parker was always aware that he was on the
the outside, always looking in, instead of *being* in; he
continued to move through life like a man with a sev-
ered head. In 1971, his wife discovered his involvement in the drug trade, and from that point on theirs
became a marriage in name only. Although they had
remained childless by mutual consent, the marriage, as
much as any relationship could be for Parker, had
been happy and sexually complete. But the knowledge
of her husband's criminal life changed Ella Rice's
feelings. As a member of an upper-class family, she
both loathed and feared the law, and she lived in constant dread that Parker would be arrested, a fact she
feared more for her social ruin than for his personal
well-being.

When Ella Rice walled herself off from Charlie
Parker, it was the final straw. On the night of January
8, 1973, in a fit of rage at being denied her bed,
Parker hacked his wife to death with a small fireplace
ax and then threw himself on her mother, who was
visiting at the time, and cut her to death too.

Neighbors called the police, and Parker shot and
killed the Palm Beach city policeman who answered
the call with a .45-caliber automatic that he kept in
his study. After the three murders Parker composed
himself, took a shower, dressed in a $500 Cardin
suit, and drove to the police station in his $40,000
old-gold Rolls-Royce long wheelbase sedan and surrendered to the police.

When he turned himself in he made only one
statement and thereafter never said a word in his own

defense, turning over his entire estate to his four brothers and sisters.

"I did not want to kill myself," he said. "I did not want to deny society that pleasure, a pleasure that it has sought since the day I was born. I am a nigger in a white man's world, and I have come for a nigger's reward. The card game is over. I fold."

It was something he had wanted to say all his life, and once he had done so there was nothing else to say.

He had been on Death Row since February 28, 1973, and for those four years he had been like a mute. He exercised, he read, he watched the small TV set in his cell, but he would not talk to the guards, the other inmates, or the prison counselors and officials who flocked to the Row once the reality of the executions began to materialize.

Now, after all that time, it was the Monday morning he had long awaited. Hank Chrysler, with the trusty Leo Dunbar, had been at a standoff with Parker for the three minutes Chrysler had stood before his cell door, trying to get the giant black man to beg for his last meal. There was no man, no thing on earth, that Hank Chrysler hated more than Charlie Parker.

"You nigger sonofabitch," Chrysler taunted, as Parker sat on his wall bunk and stared resolutely at the far wall, unmoved, untouched by the words. "You ask me nicely and I might just slide this steak in under the door for you to wrap them big lips of yours around. Huh? What do you say, coon, you gonna do a little trick for your breakfast, or are you gonna do without?"

Still Parker remained immovable.

"Goddamn, Hank," Parker's Death Watch guard mumbled, "how the hell much longer have I got to sit here and listen to you? Give the man his food and let me be here in peace. I been sittin' here on my ass since midnight, and now I got to listen to this shit. Goddamn, man! Do what you come to do and clear out."

Chrysler turned and glared at the Death Watch guard, a fifty-eight-year-old old-timer named Ham Pervis who had come to work at the prison four years after McPeters. "Mister Pervis," he said thickly, but with some respect for a man twenty years his senior, "you wouldn't fault a man for tryin' to do his job, would you?"

Pervis looked up at Chrysler from where he sat and then looked off down the Row's corridor. "Hell," he snorted, wheeling around to Leo Dunbar, who hovered like a crow over the steam cart. "Get that slop out for this big-shot nigger and let's end this."

"Move your goddamn ass," Chrysler barked at the trusty, seeing a way out of the corner he had pinned himself into.

Dunbar made short work of setting Parker's food tray, with its thick sirloin steak, beans, mashed potatoes, piece of pound cake, and cup of lukewarm coffee, in the food slot at the bottom of the cell door.

Still Parker did not move or show any sign of recognition.

"Damn your sorry black ass." Chrysler said the words straight into the cell door, his face flush against the bars, his hands resting against the bars, his eyes wrinkled with the anticipation of going on and his mouth open to form more words, but he was stopped before he could utter another sound.

Suddenly, without warning, without reference, Charlie Parker sprang to his feet like a great black leopard; then, with seething ferocity, he pivoted and threw himself against the cell door's bars, emitting a fearsome *"Aaahhhaaaaiii"* as he moved, furiously rattling his cell door. Chrysler was sent reeling back into Ham Pervis's lap and Leo Dunbar leaped to one side, throwing himself face down on the concrete floor in fright.

"Goddamn crazy wild nigger motherfucker!" Chrysler sputtered as he pushed Pervis aside to right himself. "I'll have you on charges! Goddammit, I'll gas your sorry ass for this. Parker! Do you hear me, nigger? I'll gas your ass for this!" he bellowed, standing back from the bars, his fists clenched.

Parker, whose bulk took up most of the cell door, eyed Chrysler straight on, his great black face like a stormy winter night. He released his iron grip on the door's bars, pushed himself back with the ease of a gymnast, and started shaking with laughter as he stood up straight and watched the three men beyond his cell door.

He roared with laughter. It was the best laugh he could remember, the first laugh in years. Chrysler stood dumbfounded, glaring in silence. Leo Dunbar shakily got to his feet. The Death Watch guard, Ham Pervis, shook his head in disgust, waiting for the chain reaction to begin.

It came almost instantly—the Row filling up with the mock laughter of the other inmates—laughter and cries, hoots, catcalls, and cursing, a deafening grab bag of sounds that flooded the space like a tidal wave.

And then the noise subsided around Chrysler's cries for order; not because of his cries, but because, in the way of the Row, the moment had come and gone and there was nothing after the moment.

As Chrysler and Leo Dunbar left the Row, silence fell on it again. Charlie Parker bent down and collected his food and walked over to the small, bolted-down table in his cell and sat down and started to eat. But he was smiling. He couldn't get the smile off his face. He didn't want it off. It was the first time in two years that he had really smiled. He felt good. He ate his meal with genuine pleasure, smiling all the while.

7:10 A.M.

John McPeters was standing out from the Death Chamber's closed steel door looking directly at Death Row's closed steel door as Hank Chrysler and Leo Dunbar emerged from the Row with the steam cart.

Dunbar caught the major's eyes, ducked his chin in subservience, and thrust the cart to the right and out of the big man's line of sight. Chrysler saw McPeters's face and quickly closed the steel door and locked it.

McPeters did not move. He stood there like a boulder in the narrow hallway, huge arms folded across his chest, the thick flesh of his face pushed back into a mask, his cold eyes never leaving the Row's steel door.

"I got 'em quiet," Chrysler said as he was turning to face McPeters again. "It's that goddamned Cuban and the Haitian. Goddamned sons of bitches."

McPeters remained silent, unmoving—not menacing the guard but thinking, calculating.

"They're down," Chrysler continued, in the vacuum of McPeters's silence, facing him respectfully, with his hands on his hips. "They'll stay down."

McPeters held his eyes on the door for a few seconds longer; then he uncrossed his arms, the move slow and deliberate, ending with his shoulders squared off flush behind his chest bulge, his arms held at his sides like a weight lifter's. "That's fine, Hank," he said, his gaze on the door an instant more and then shifting to the guard's face. "That's fine," he said again, slowly, evenly, with no drawl. "We've just got to keep a hand on them."

"Yessir," Chrysler said, shifting his hands down in a motion that tried to imitate McPeters's stance. Then he fell in behind the big man and walked with him down to his office.

In the office, McPeters seated himself behind his desk. Chrysler sat on the bolted-down folding chair. McPeters looked across the room at the wall clock: 7:13. His mind filled up like a file: the other two members of his three-man Death Strap squad would be coming in momentarily; the prison chaplain would be coming in; Warden Hugh Greenwood would be coming out of his office to the entrance doors of the Administration Building to meet the first of the press corps that were being let in.

Everything was under control and on schedule. McPeters sat back and waited.

THE FACE OF DEATH

1

Lincoln Daniels had the *Jacksonville Times-Union* and the *Miami Herald* brought to his suite at seven and read them in his pajamas and bathrobe and socks. The fat Sunday editions were dominated by the executions. Both front pages had banner headlines: STARKE FOUR GO TOMORROW, LEGAL DEATH RE-TURNS. Grim-faced mug shots of the four condemned prisoners were plastered on both pages, and on both pages there were long three-column photos of the electric chair.

"Tomorrow the Thunderbolt will take its 200th victim," the *Times-Union*'s subhead read.

The *Herald*'s Tropic magazine ran a cover story entitled "The chair they call the Thunderbolt," a 5,000-word piece that took readers through the sixty-five hours of the Death Routine, strapped them in the chair, and executed them.

There was a frantic excitement about the event; one of the *Times-Union*'s feature writers, a veteran reporter who had witnessed a number of executions during the fifties and early sixties, speculated that their ultimate fascination was the fact that they were the closest man could come to actually studying death.

"An execution, therefore," the reporter wrote, "is not the ultimate punishment but rather the ultimate curiosity."

Lincoln Daniels dwelt on the words as he read them and sat and thought about them for some time. The short sentence seemed to sum it up, to bring it into focus for him, as never before.

This is an exercise, he said to himself, *not a punishment. A punishment occurs when one has consideration for the punished. In this thing there is no thought of the punished. They are merely objects in an exercise —an exercise in curiosity.*

Daniels was almost finished with the papers when Palo Reyas walked into the suite's small living room, barefoot, in his pajamas and a wool sport coat. Lincoln was glad to see him, glad to get his mind off the executions.

"You're up later than usual," he said, looking over the paper at Palo.

"American motels," Palo replied, grinning. "I always sleep late in American motels. They feel like hospitals."

Lincoln grinned too and put the paper he had been reading on the stacks of papers on the coffee table in front of him. "An interesting thought," he said. "Did the patient sleep well?" he went on, absentmindedly making small talk.

"Not likely," Palo answered, his eyes dancing with delight. "The patient in the other bed snores."

Before Lincoln could reply, the phone rang. It was Paul O'Dell of the *New York Times*.

"I know you're an early riser," O'Dell began, "so I wanted to be the first of the wolves at your door."

Lincoln liked O'Dell. They had met for the first time three years before during the Auburn Prison riot. O'Dell, with his biography of the Attica riot three years earlier, *Death in D-Yard,* was the reigning journalist on the scene; apart from that Lincoln liked the man's manner of ease and authority.

"You're the first," Lincoln answered. "It's good to hear from you. State your case."

"Just a struggling newspaperman looking for an angle and a name to tie it to," O'Dell said.

"I hear you," Lincoln came back. "You had breakfast yet?"

"No," O'Dell answered. "I'm waiting for somebody to pick up the check."

"Done," Lincoln said. "Come on over in half an hour and we'll order up a big farmhand breakfast and talk."

"We having a picnic, or are we working for a living?" Palo asked as Lincoln hung up. His face was alive at the idea of an American-style breakfast.

"My peace offering for disturbing your night's rest," Lincoln answered, standing up. "Can't have the elderly going unhappy."

Palo seized the remark instantly. "Ah," he said, rubbing his hands together, "this is turning out better than I expected, feeble old Mexican that I am."

"Everything for our amusement," Lincoln shot back, smiling, but then, breaking the smile off as his mind moved from the word amusement to the word curiosity, he added, "We could probably do with a solid meal this morning. The afternoon promises to be a long one."

Palo's look of anticipation faded. "Did you call the prison yet?" he asked.

"Yes," Lincoln answered. "I was on the phone to Major McPeters at six thirty. He'll meet us at the entrance to the Main Prison at three and take us over to Big Max and Death Row himself."

O'Dell had a powerful, block upper body, like an all-pro fullback ten years past his playing weight, with a waist and neck that sagged slightly and a wide face with precise lines that were covered by an extra layer of pinkish flesh brought on by his love of good food and good French wines and Irish whiskey. True to his aristocratic Charleston, South Carolina, heritage, he was an elegant man who affected long sideburns and slightly longish hair parted on the side; he was also an influential man, and the *Times*'s reigning authority on domestic affairs. On this biting cold morning he was dressed in a thick, reddish-brown wool suit and a finely pressed white shirt, with a green-and-orange-and-brown-striped silk tie.

Lincoln Daniels and Palo Reyas met him at the door of their suite in their shirt sleeves. "Jesus preserve us," Lincoln said, extending his hand to O'Dell. "You look like a million bucks. If there's one thing I remember about you from Auburn it's that you were the best-dressed man there."

"Working on the image." O'Dell smiled, looking past Daniels toward Palo Reyas.

"Here," Lincoln went on, pulling O'Dell inside with his handshake, "meet Mexico's worst-dressed man but one of its best artists."

The two men were introduced, and then the three of them sat down in the living room, where Daniels took the orders for breakfast. From the start, no one seemed anxious to bring up the executions. For a while it was all banter and memories of the Auburn riot, told for Palo's benefit in the style of hunting or drinking stories.

They went on with small talk—about the weather, politics, current events, Mexico, New York, the difficulty in getting to the little town of Starke, the Roman circus of reporters and TV crews going on outside—but never actually touched on the executions themselves. There was no shyness, no squeamishness: they simply avoided the subject. It was something for outsiders that did not hold up well in conversation. Ultimately, when you talked seriously about death, you were talking about your own.

They skirted the issue as long as possible, but Paul O'Dell tackled it once breakfast was over, buoyed by the fact that he had, in part, come to Lincoln's suite for an interview.

"Will you be going to the press briefing this morning?" he asked Daniels.

"No, I think I'll sit the group sessions out. The whole thing is too much like a carnival. Christ," he said, with disgust, "I walked to the motel office last night for some magazines, and I was stopped ten times on the way—everybody from a guy with the local paper to some hotshot from CBS who was upset that I didn't know his name; then I was cornered by a woman who informed me that she didn't know who I was but she wanted my autograph just the same. The phone rang till midnight, and then I had the calls stopped. You got through this morning because I had them open me back up from six to nine."

He stopped and looked at his watch—ten thirty—and laughed.

"I suppose the geniuses at *Esquire* who are paying the bills for all this are going nuts trying to get through to impart a little wisdom to me and my compatriot here." He smiled at Palo. "But we'll go it alone."

"Definitely alone," Reyas agreed. He was sitting across from Lincoln on the small sofa next to O'Dell. "There's a paranoia in the air so thick you could cut it with a machete," he added.

"I'll share this idea with you, Paul," Lincoln said abruptly. "There are two key words here: 'curiosity' and 'exercise.' I got 'curiosity' out of the Jacksonville paper this morning; 'exercise' I came up with myself. The people who are going to die don't count for a hill of beans. They're just part of an exercise, *objects* within the exercise. And the exercise, of course, is power."

"Excellent," O'Dell broke in, pounding his knuckles on his crossed leg. "Two excellent tags; I agree completely." He didn't wait for Lincoln to respond. "I've said it differently a hundred times, but your two words are the crux of my message. And dammit, that's exactly why I'm so against this thing, and why I can't understand your neutral position."

"I haven't said I'm neutral," Lincoln said quickly. "I haven't expressed an opinion one way or the other. I'm troubled by it—the act of legal death—but I can't say yea or nay right now. I just don't know. . . ." He paused and then went on. "Supposedly, the most competent legal minds in America have said that capital punishment squares with reality, religion, dignity, and Western ethics. They've worked on the question for years. Dammit, Paul, I am just not going to go up against that with a gut feeling and a few weeks of thought."

"But if you had to go on gut feeling alone"—O'Dell probed with a reporter's zeal—"how would you lean?"

Lincoln's face showed an obvious resentment to the question, but O'Dell would not relent.

"I'd go with nay," he finally said, looking O'Dell straight in the eye. "I don't like it. But, dammit, I don't know if it's wrong. I don't think it's wrong. Shit, I just don't know.

"I'm stuck between not liking it and not thinking it's wrong," he went on, as O'Dell kept silent. "When it's all over I expect to have that paradox resolved."

"That's just the point," O'Dell put in sourly. "When it's all over we'll all have a clearer understanding of it, but four people will be dead, fried to a crisp by electricity while they sit helplessly strapped in a chair."

"I know that," Lincoln answered. "That's why I came up with the word 'exercise.' "

"So," O'Dell said, gesturing with his hand, "there we are. We're on different sides, with neither one of us really able to alter the outcome." He paused for a second, disturbed at his words. "I'm just sorry that I've pressed myself and my Liberal Establishment views on you."

"Don't be silly," Lincoln said, shaking off O'Dell's self-conscious apology. "You're not pressing anything on anybody. We're just talking. That's all we *can* do: talk and report what we see and hear. We can't do one damn thing to save those four convicts—and, as I say, I'm not sure we should, if we could. Probably we should just keep our own counsel until this thing is over."

O'Dell's face showed clearly that he did not think this was the course of action to follow, but also that he knew they had no choice. The months of protests in Washington and New York, and finally in Tallahassee, had proved that point beyond contention, and the lame demonstrations during the past few days in Starke and outside Big Max had only confirmed that the executions could not be stopped.

"I suppose that's all we can do," O'Dell agreed with resignation. He changed the subject. "In any event," he said, trying to sound cheerful, "I'm one of the three pool journalists who've been allowed inside the prison today at one P.M. to see the four condemned and talk to them. Under the terms of the press agreement, I've got to give a briefing to everybody back here at six, but I'll be glad to fill the two of you in privately on anything I come across. Maybe we can have a drink this evening?"

"That'll be fine," Lincoln said, keeping silent about his and Palo's plans for the afternoon. "I'll give you a call this evening."

"Exactly what the doctor ordered," O'Dell said, seizing the exit line. "I'll wait for your call."

"Fine," Lincoln told him, knowing he would not call, knowing his plans would not allow him to call.

2

Lincoln Daniels and Palo Reyas left the motel at two thirty and drove to the prison. There was no rain, but the air was damp and the temperature had been dropping steadily since noon. The sky to the north of the prison was a solid black wall. As they approached from the Starke side, they came upon Big Max. Palo Reyas was fascinated by the first sight of the prison.

"It is a fortress," he exclaimed. "A fortress with the sterile look of a hospital, and a wire fence. But the fence looks totally out of place," he added. "There ought to be a high stone wall."

"The fence works," Lincoln said, from behind the wheel. "You examine it when we get up close. The whole place works with numbing efficiency."

"On the passenger's side in the front seat, Palo moved closer to the car's window and watched the long line of high concrete cellblocks and buildings inside the fence. When they came in line with the Death Facility, they were stopped at the roadblock that had been set up by the Highway Patrol. With the press passes that had been issued at the motel earlier that day by Pete Stokes, the prison's information officer, they were cleared quickly, but the highway patrolman in charge of the roadblock stopped them when Lincoln said they were going on across the river to the Main Prison, not to Big Max.

"Sir," the officer said respectfully, "I don't have any orders for that. You're the first one to ask to go on to the Main Prison. Everybody else goes in here for Death Row."

Lincoln was friendly and patient. "Just call Major John McPeters on your radio if you will, please," he said firmly. "The gentleman and I are going to meet Major McPeters by prior arrangement."

The highway patrolman returned to his car and made a call on his radio. Beyond the patrol cruiser, in Big Max's vast parking lot, there were clumps of TV mobile units and TV newsmen conducting interviews in front of the prison's main gate, and photographers moved along the outside of the three-tiered fence snapping photos of the prison and the front of the Death Facility. The guard dogs inside the fence runs had grown accustomed to the photographers, but occasionally there was barking, and occasionally a shrill obscenity came from one of the cellblock floors.

After a short conversation on the radio, the highway patrolman came back to the car and bent down to the window. "I'm sorry, sir," he said to Lincoln. "Go on over. I didn't know or I wouldn't have held you up."

"That's quite all right," Lincoln said. He gestured toward the prison. "Everything in order over there?" he said. "I see a good deal of activity."

The patrolman turned his head toward the prison before he answered. "I don't know," he said, his face flushed by the cold and lined with strain, "but it seems to me like something's brewing. Ever since they let those three reporters into Death row at one o'clock things have been uneasy. Every once in a while something like a crazy football cheer comes out of the cellblocks. . . . I know that doesn't sound right," he added, "but that's what it sounds like to me—a football cheer."

Lincoln looked toward the prison and the Death

Facility too, then turned back to the patrolman, whose cold face dominated the half-open window. "Well," he said, "if there's going to be cheering, let's hope the home team wins."

The patrolman cracked a tight-lipped smile. "Begging your pardon, mister, but I'd change that to the *visiting* team. As far as I'm concerned, the convicts are the home team, and I don't want nothing to do with them. I've been out here for two riots during the last three years and they're all crazy."

Lincoln returned the man's tight smile. "I stand corrected, trooper," he said. "The visiting team it is."

The trooper nodded and stood up, touching the bill of his hat in a short salute, and they drove off, leaving the man in the center of the highway, his hands wedged into his blue coat against the damp cold.

"That's the guy the public sees as the dumb sonofabitch behind the road sign, or parked in front of some café drinking free coffee. If we had his savvy, we could all probably go home and do this thing from our dens."

"The safety of the home is where we may wish we were before this thing is over," Palo injected somberly.

Major John McPeters was standing out on the two-lane asphalt circular driveway that curved in front of the gothic double towers and lower concrete structure that was the Main Prison's main gate. He stood there in the cold with his hands on his hips, dressed in his winter blues, his Sam Browne belt cinched squarely across his chest and around his waist, his peak-billed cap centered and low over his forehead.

"Jesus," Palo said, seeing McPeters for the first time. "He looks like the hill behind my house."

"Let's just say you're not likely to meet a copy of John McPeters," Lincoln volunteered.

As they pulled up and Lincoln looked through the car's window, the stern look on McPeters's immense face modified, not to a smile but rather to a look of pleasure, of satisfaction. Lincoln got out quickly and extended his hand. McPeters took it quickly.

"Lincoln," McPeters said with no drawl, "you look well. It's good to see you again."

"John, you'll live forever," Lincoln responded, smiling broadly. "You've got the look," he added, still shaking the other man's hand.

McPeters smiled, released Lincoln's hand, and stood expectantly as Palo got out of the car. Lincoln introduced the two men. "You two are both headhunters," he said. "You ought to get on well."

"If we don't get on well," Palo joked as he shook McPeters's hand, "at least I want him on my side."

McPeters gave a slight laugh at the remark; then, with an abrupt change of tone, he directed his words to the business at hand. "We've got to go to the Row now if we're going. I don't think there's much to worry about or I wouldn't take you over, but we'd better go now before things get any more stirred up. Then we can go back to my house and relax with a couple of belts and a home-cooked cracker meal. My boys, Ira and Coy, have been cooking all weekend. It's the first real work I've gotten out of them in four or five years," he added, smiling.

"Sounds like just the right medicine . . ."

Lincoln's words trailed off as a car's motor started and he turned to see a white Ford sedan, with prison markings on the front door, back out of a parking space in a long row of prison cars and trucks. The car pulled up beside them, driven by a guard in winter blues. Palo and Lincoln got in back, and McPeters sat in front. His bulk filled half the seat and his officer's cap touched the car's roof.

They drove east back toward Big Max, but before they got to the long stone New River bridge, they turned right onto a narrow two-lane road that went past the western side of the Main Prison's fence. They passed the west gate, a miniature of the prison's gothic main gate, with the dingy brick cold-storage building on a slight hill to the left; then the road jogged to the left and became a dirt road as it moved away from the Main Prison and started on line with Big Max, two miles to the front. No one said anything as they crossed a clattering one-lane wooden bridge across the river and then came up a little rise at the rear of Big Max.

To the left, a mile away, were the three stories of

the Death Facility's cellblocks. You could see the exercise yard and the single thirty-foot-high cyclone fence between the Death Facility and the long line of the other three-story-high cellblocks of Big Max, and then another thirty-foot-high fence that separated the immense athletic fields from the industrial shop buildings far to the right.

The driver, a hard-looking man half McPeters's age and half his size, turned the car right once more at the top of the rise and began running parallel with the fence. The dogs in the rear fence sections were not used to seeing cars, and they went wild. Guard towers were spaced along the fence now, and near the middle tower there was a small factory-style series of three gates through the fence. The gates were for emergencies only and were not manned. A jeep waited on the far side of the three gates, and when McPeters's driver came up outside the first gate he blew the car's horn. The driver of the jeep, a big man in blues, got out quickly and began unlocking the three gates. McPeters's driver was inside the prison compound in less than a minute. Once inside he stopped the sedan and waited for the inside guard to relock the three gates. The guard performed the task quickly and returned to his jeep and took out a small metal lockbox used for holding pistols. McPeters and his guard were carrying none, and McPeters waved the man off before he took two steps, then nodded for his driver to move off.

"You run a tight ship, John," Daniels said with admiration.

McPeters turned his head to the side. "Just country boys doing their best," he said.

"I have a rule to walk softly around country boys," Lincoln answered with good humor. "Especially the ones who tell me they're country boys."

"I got a similar rule about city boys," McPeters said with equal good humor.

McPeters was going far out on a limb by bringing Lincoln and Palo in the back door of the prison for a private audience with the four condemned prisoners on Death Row, and Lincoln had considered refusing the offer when McPeters made it the month before. But two things, his writer's sense of duty and his own personal curiosity, made him accept. Then, of course, there was the simple fact that John McPeters made his own rules; more than that, the rules of the prison *were* McPeters's rules.

But Lincoln knew what a risk it was, and the news of the disturbances along Big Max's cellblocks had made him apprehensive, both for his own and Palo's safety and for McPeter's position at the prison.

The sedan crossed the vastness of the athletic field, allowing the jeep to go ahead. Twice more the driver of the jeep had to get out and unlock single gates before the car came to a stop outside the Death Chamber.

The jeep and the sedan were protected from the view of the crush of assembled media people four hundred yards to the front by a ten-foot-high, twenty-foot-long concrete-block wall between the Death Chamber and the Witness Chamber. There was a steel door into the Death Chamber with a glass slit at eye level. The jeep's driver was standing by the steel door when McPeters and his driver and Lincoln and Palo got out of the sedan and started toward him. When they were together, McPeters nodded to the jeep driver and the man rapped on the steel door twice with one of his brass keys. A pair of eyes instantly appeared in the glass slit, and then a key sounded in the door's lock and the door opened.

McPeters stood back to let Lincoln go in first, and then Palo; within seconds all five men were inside, and the sixth man, the Death Facility guard, was relocking the heavy steel door, closing all of them off inside the Death Chamber, three feet from the electric chair. The room was warm and filled with harsh fluorescent light from the ceiling. Beyond the half-glass partition, the witness room was also lighted. The steel door that led from the chamber to the hallway and McPeters's office and Death Row was open.

Palo Reyas was the only man in the room who had not seen the electric chair. He stood looking at it with the fascination of a child. Lincoln watched McPeters come up beside him.

"This is our bad medicine," McPeters said, looking past Palo to the chair. "One dose of this and you're a believer."

"There's just one problem," Palo came back quickly, half smiling. "The patient doesn't get a chance to get sick again."

"No sir," McPeters responded instantly, his face showing appreciation of Palo's reply, "that's the beauty of the medicine: the patient stays cured forever."

"Final medicine," Lincoln chimed in, bringing a small round of grunting laughter that seemed to be physically eaten up by the room itself—as if laughter were something that could not exist in the small, acid space.

"Final medicine is right." McPeters echoed Lincoln's words. "You don't want to go through the tour again?" he asked Lincoln, who shook off the idea. "Well, then," he went on, turning his attention to Palo, "I'll have my guard here give Mr. Reyas the low-down on the chair and its workings, and he can make some drawings if he wants to. That okay with you, Mr. Reyas?"

"Please," Palo answered, "you will call me Palo, and whatever you say is fine with me. I never argue with the medicine man."

McPeters grunted another short laugh and then turned Palo over to the Death Facility guard. "You boys get yourselves some coffee and wait in the Witness Chamber," he told his driver and the jeep driver. "This will take less than an hour, and then I want to get right out."

He turned to Lincoln.

"Let's go down to my office," he said, pointing the way with his hand. "By the time my guard gets through with the tour, we'll have the first one ready for you."

They left Palo standing beside the guard, directly in front of the chair, sketching on the artist's pad he carried in his outside coat pocket, the burly guard watching with a sort of reverence as the chair took shape and form on the pad.

Out in the hall, as they walked toward McPeter's

office, Lincoln began to question him on the mood of
the men on the Row.

"It's tight," McPeters answered. "Damn tight.
We've only had one real flare-up and that was from
two brothers, the Sullivan brothers, who will probably
be the next to go, sometime next month—two crazy
sonsofbitches that are so yellow they glow in the goddamned dark," he added sourly.

As he finished speaking, they were on a line with
the Ready Cell.

"How about the woman, Alice Fuller?" Lincoln
asked.

"She's right in here," McPeters answered, stopping
their progress at the cell door. "She's scared shitless,"
McPeters went on, looking at Lincoln, "but she's quiet.
She won't be any trouble."

Lincoln stepped up to the lighted glass slit in the
Ready Cell's door and cautiously looked inside. A
matron reading a *Better Homes & Gardens* magazine
was seated to the left, outside the double cell. Inside
the tangle of bars he could see Alice Fuller. She was
sitting on her wall bunk, her legs dangling loosely over
the side, staring blankly at the far wall. He kept his
eyes on the scene for a few seconds and then stepped
back. He shook his head and exhaled. "Good God, she
looks like a sick old woman," he said.

"Like you said," McPeters answered, his face
stern, "this is the final medicine."

"It is that, John," Lincoln answered. "It is that,"
he repeated, as they started off down the hallway
once more, headed for McPeters's office.

Palo's tour took fifteen minutes. When he and the
guard appeared at McPeter's office door, Lincoln was
giving McPeters a run-down on Mexican duck hunting
on Lake Cuitzeo, going through all the intricacies of
the Tarascan Indian *reyada*.

"Jesus Christ!" Palo laughed, nodding in Lincoln's
direction. "He would rather talk about duck hunting on
that damn muddy lake than visit the local whore-
house."

"Everything in its proper place," Lincoln said. "What we've got to do," he went on, turning toward McPeters, "is get John down for some of both."

McPeters chuckled, looking first at Palo, then at Lincoln. "I don't know if a country boy like me could find his way down to Mexico—hell, I might get lost in the shuffle."

"All you got to do is get yourself to Tampa and catch a plane," Lincoln said. "Palo and I will be at the airport in Mexico City to collect you like a winning ticket on a horse race."

"That don't sound like the worst idea I ever heard," McPeters replied, smiling. "But right now you've got work to do." He stood up and moved around his desk to the office door. "I'll bring the woman in first," he said formally, all business now. "Then I'll bring in Kruger—that is, if we can walk him down here—then Santos, and then Parker. I'll have two guards outside the door at all times, and I'll be out there with them. We'll be in like a shot if you need us, but I don't anticipate any trouble.

"You didn't see Alice Fuller last time, but you got on well with the other three. They want to see you," he added, "so that means they'll behave themselves. And if they don't, like I say, I'll be here."

The words came out like rocks. Lincoln only nodded in reply. There was no need for more.

When McPeters and the Death Facility guard left, Lincoln got up from the bolted-down chair in front of the desk and moved around it to sit down in McPeters's chair.

"Sit here," Lincoln said to Palo, motioning to a metal folding chair that had been placed next to McPeter's chair.

Palo came into the room and took the chair without speaking. He opened his pad on the desk and began to thumb through the sketches he had made of the electric chair, the Executioner's Booth, the Witness Chamber, the death implements, and the Circuit Room at the end of the hall. Finally he looked up at Lincoln and spoke, his voice strained and tired. "In all my long time on this earth," he said, "I've never seen anything like this. I thought I'd seen death, I thought I'd seen it fully. But this is my first look. This *is* death."

Lincoln did not say anything; again, there was no need for words. He simply nodded his head slightly in reply, and then the two men sat in silence waiting for Alice Fuller to be brought to them.

Down the hallway they could hear the sounds of the Ready Cell being opened.

3

Alice Fuller had to be helped into McPeters's office. Billie Johnson, a tall, blond woman with thick arms—the second of the two matrons from the Women's Correctional Facility at Lowell—steadied her as she entered the room. Even with his advance look, Daniels was not prepared for the sight of the condemned woman.

As with the other three condemned pirsoners, the *Esquire* editors had provided him with a file on Alice Fuller, a thick, legal-sized folder that included a number of newspaper and 8 X 10 glossy photos. In the pictures she had the look of a tough street whore, a hearty, raunchy, seductive look. The creature that appeared before the two men was skin and bones, with skin the color of old milk. But it was her fingers that Lincoln and Palo noticed first. They were like the fingers of a skeleton. Blue-purple veins protruded over the knuckles.

At thirty-two, Alice Fuller was a hag with sharp skull curves at the sides of her mouth. Her appearance was made all the more dismal by her gray, buttonless, one-piece prison dress and brown bathrobe with no belt. She seemed to be in a daze; her movements were those of a sleepwalker. The matron steered her to the bolted-down chair and then eased her onto its seat.

"I hope this won't take long," the matron said

bluntly, in a coarse, rural accent. "She's been through it once already today. I don't see any need for interviews at all, and I'm going to report it when I get back to Lowell, this"—she glared at Daniels—"and Major Mc-Peters making me do it."

"It won't take long," Lincoln Daniels answered evenly, his gaze fixed on Alice Fuller, who sat with her bony hands folded on her narrow lap, head lowered, with her eyes on the floor. Then he faced the matron. "I don't want to cause either of you any inconvenience. If Mrs. Fuller doesn't wish to speak with me, you can leave right now."

Lincoln's tone was not aggressive; if anything, it was slightly apprehensive, the caution of someone who knows he is on completely uncharted ground. When he finished speaking, the matron stepped back and filled the open door of McPeter's office. She crossed her arms and did not respond, her eyes centered on Alice Fuller.

"Mrs. Fuller," Lincoln began, warily, "my name is Lincoln Daniels, and this is Palo Reyas. We want to talk to you. I am a writer and Mr. Reyas is an artist."

Lincoln waited for some sign of recognition from the woman, but Alice Fuller kept her eyes on the floor.

He continued. "Mrs. Fuller, do you have any objection if I take notes on our conversation?"

The condemned woman's eyes stayed riveted to the floor, and she did not move.

"Do you have any objection if Mr. Reyas makes sketches while we talk?" Lincoln asked, his voice revealing his uneasiness.

Before he could go on, Alice Fuller looked up at him. "Why didn't they handcuff me? For two, three years," she went on, sitting up fully, brushing a thick clump of limp gray-red hair back from her skull-like forehead, her voice husky and tired," I never been anywhere without cuffs."

Lincoln and Palo looked at her intently; then Lincoln looked up at the matron. The woman seemed as perplexed by the words as the two men.

Lincoln shuffled the pad and pen on the desk

top in front of him. Since she had not objected, he made a note of the remark. Beside him, at the desk, Palo began to sketch on his pad. "I don't know, Mrs. Fuller," he said, after a strained pause. "You mean that everywhere you go you are handcuffed?" He was vaguely aware of the fact, but he pressed the point for conversation.

Alice Fuller folded her arms across her flat chest and stared at Lincoln. "They always cuffed me. Even before, when I talked to the other three reporters." Her voice built higher with each word. Then her eyes broadened with terror.

"Wait, wait a minute," she shrieked, wedging herself back into the chair, her hands holding onto the seat, her head jutting back to the matron. "What's going on? What's happening?

"Oh . . . oh . . . wait!" she cried. "It's not time . . . oh, God! Wait . . . it's not time . . . *wait!* These men . . . they . . . *wait! Wait!*" She went on hysterically, her eyes searching the matron's face for comfort.

"Mrs. Fuller, *please!*" The matron went to her quickly, unfolding her arms, bracing her hands waist-high for trouble. "Nothing is happening! Nothing. Get that straight!" She was obviously embarrassed and disquieted by the outburst. "These men are reporters just like the others. *Please!*" she went on. "There's all the time in the world. Nothing's happening! They just want to talk. If you don't want to talk, we'll go back to your cell. Just say the word. It's up to you."

Alice Fuller hung on the matron's words as if she could reach out and touch them. When the woman finished speaking she released her violent grip on the seat of her chair but sat rigidly, facing Daniels and Reyas.

"I don't mind talking," she said in a low, stilled voice, as if the outburst of emotion had not occurred. "I told the other reporters I didn't mind talking. I want to do the right thing."

"Thank you," Lincoln responded tensely. "I don't mean to upset you," he added, unsure of the choice of words.

His mind momentarily split as he stared at the

woman—one half on her, the other half on a thought he had had about talking to a condemned prisoner after that first time a month before. It was like interviewing a fat person. No matter how you circumvented it, in order for the conversation to be meaningful—and no matter how many times they had been asked before—you arrived at the question of their size. It was not merely expedient or simply obvious, it was salient. And the salient fact about Alice Fuller was her death.

With the three condemned men it had been easier, if for no other reason than because they were men. Lincoln had seen men die in combat and had seen Japanese spies executed by firing squads in the Pacific during World War II. But he had no frame of reference for sitting in a room with a woman and calmly discussing her death by execution. Suddenly he became aware that there was no reference for either man or woman; that reality alone let him go on. But he was unsure of himself, unsure of how to do it.

He prefaced his questions with several lame apologies that Alice Fuller did not respond to. Then he gave up and began in the fashion he had used with the three men when he had spoken with them for the first time the month before. "Do you feel afraid? Do you feel fear?" he asked, making himself face the woman directly.

Alice Fuller looked at the floor. Then she looked up at Lincoln. She tightened her mouth and shook her head: No. Lincoln kept his eyes fixed on her tight face. Their eyes met. After a few seconds more of intense strain, Alice Fuller's eyes narrowed and she nodded her head: Yes, she was afraid.

"I'm sick scared," she said, pushing her hands back along the sides of her mouth, her fingers coming to rest on her ears. "It's like something that covers you, like a blanket. You can't get rid of it, and you don't get used to it. Just because it hurts all the time don't mean it gets so you don't notice it."

"What does it feel like? Can you describe the feeling?"

The matron eyed Lincoln with disgust, but he paid no attention to her.

Alice Fuller slowly eased her hands down to her lap, her eyes following their movement. "Like something being pulled inside you," she said. "Like somebody standing outside you pulling something inside you. Does that make sense?" Her eyes searched Lincoln's face.

Lincoln was grim. He nodded his head that it did make sense to him.

"And it's all the time. It never lets up." Her voice was husky and low with pain. She moved slightly in her seat. "In the beginning," she went on, "when I first came to prison, I didn't ever think this would happen. I . . ." Her mouth stayed open in fright and froze for a second, but then she touched her face with her hand again and regained control. "I was scared then. But it was because of not knowing. But last year when they started talking seriously about it, all that changed. Something firm happened—*firm*. That's the only word I know to describe it.

"The real fear started to take over, and then in November, when our names started to come up as the ones who might go . . . I . . . I . . . the *pulling* started. The minute my appeals ran out, it settled on me, the pulling, and I"—her voice broke—"I can't lose it. Never." She was sobbing with no tears. "Never for a second will it go away!"

The matron reached down and touched her shoulder as Alice Fuller wedged her hands together on her lap.

"Do you think of the crime? Of what you did?"

Alice Fuller inhaled deeply. The matron took her hand from her shoulder. She shook her head—*no*—and held to the answer.

Lincoln silently considered his own words, deciding, no matter how painful it was for him or the woman, to stick to specifics, as he had with the three men.

"The ones you committed the crime against—you don't ever think of them?"

"My children. I killed my children and my husband," she said blankly, as if the words were simply facts. "Yes, I think of them. At some time every day I think of them. Usually in the morning. Is that odd?" she asked, turning her chin up to face Daniels. "I suppose I should think of them at night?"

Daniels did not respond.

"Yes," Alice Fuller continued in the silence of the small room, "I think of all of them, but not of what happened."

Lincoln went to the heart of her response; it was the same as the answer given by the three men. "You make a distinction between the crime and the people?"

"Yes," Alice Fuller answered, suddenly holding onto herself as if she were cold. "You make the distinction or you go crazy. And oh, God!" Her voice rose. "You want to go crazy! But you can't . . . *you can't!*" She broke off, choking. "There's just the pulling, the gut pulling at all your insides and against all your mind."

Daniels looked at her silently, with compassion and fascination. It was like confirming a scientific discovery after long research. The woman had been kept completely separate from the three men who were to die, and yet what she said was almost identical to the statements the men had made: the separating of the crime from the victims; the wanting to go crazy, to blot all sense of reality out of the mind; the thing never going away.

The woman's words made something very clear in Daniels's mind. You did not become less human after you committed a capital crime. Your mind might have to close off certain normal mechanisms to allow you to commit the crime, but when it was over, when the heat of anger or passion had passed, you were still human and there were still the human emotions of remorse and fear. That discovery was fascination enough, but Daniels found, as he looked at the condemned woman, that the chief fascination was that the mind was capable of shutting off the valve of remorse. No one he had talked to on Death Row thought about the victims. Apparently that was a realm of the psyche that the mind of the condemned could not handle, and so it could be shut off. But the valve of fear, he knew firsthand and with certainty, could not be shut off.

"In everything you do, there's the pulling?" Lincoln probed, once Alice Fuller had regained her composure and was sitting placidly with her birdlike, vein-streaked arms crossed on her lap.

"Yes."

"In your sleep? Your dreams?"

"Yes, *oh, yes,*" she answered. "I dream about my own death every night. When I finally close my eyes, it's like dying. Sleep is supposed to be rest," she went on with great weariness, "but rest never comes: just fits, and your own death, over and over again." She rubbed her hands together.

Lincoln sat and looked at her and waited intently for her to go on, anticipating what she would say.

"That's why this is not so bad," she said, using the words he thought would come. "This will end all that." Terror welled up in her face and closed inside her eyes as she spoke. "But, oh, dear God," she moaned, her hands shooting up again to support the sides of her face, "going like this . . . like . . . *oh, God!*" she shrieked, the words blunting her shifting moves in the chair. "You don't know if there'll be any peace when you're dead. . . . *Jesus! God!*"

Then she began to weep, for the first time, with tears.

"*No peace!* God! What if there was no peace! An eternity of *pulling!* Oh, my God—!" She broke off, her bony fists clenched in front of her, eyes closed, hideous arms shaking.

"Stop, Mrs. Fuller. Stop, please!" the matron ordered, moving to the woman's side, steadying her shoulders with both hands. "You've got to stop this right now! Be quiet now. Quiet, please!"

Her voice was shrill and embarrassed, her small hard eyes trained on Lincoln Daniels with hatred. Daniels remained silent, keeping an iron hand on his own mind and emotions, conscious of the effort that it required.

Then, for the first time since Alice Fuller entered the room, Palo Reyas stopped his sketching and pushed his pad away from him and spoke, his voice filled with emotion. "Please," he said to the woman in his gentle voice. "Don't give away so much. Don't let them take so much from you."

The words fell on Alice Fuller like a soft rain. She opened her eyes and stopped her sobbing with a gasp and stared intently at Palo.

"There will be peace. All death is peace," he told her. "I am an old man, a Catholic, and I tell you there is peace. I know it."

The matron let go of Alice Fuller's shoulders and stood up, looking at Palo the way the very young look at a teacher, a look that matched Alice Fuller's.

"The important thing in life," Palo continued softly, considering every word, "is not to give away everything before the end; to be able to leave with something—something for the journey ahead, strength for the journey ahead."

Alice Fuller wiped the tears from her face and inhaled deeply, her eyes never leaving Palo's weathered face. Lincoln had to struggle with himself to retain his composure.

"That is all I have to say," Palo said. "But I have seen death many times in seven years of war, and I believe what I have said totally. You will find peace in death. I tell you that because it has been told to me and I expect it."

The silence in the room was physical until Alice Fuller broke it. "The worst thing," she said, her voice faded and spent, "the worst thing," she repeated, waving her hand in front of her as if to brush off invisible devils, "is that you don't hear anything like what you've just told me.

"Do you know that I haven't heard a kind word in four years . . . *four years!* I knew what you said four years ago, or I thought I knew it, but I had forgotten it. It went away from me like everything else." Her hand fell limply back to her lap. "Maybe that's the worst part, never hearing a friendly word. You can miss that; you can know that has been taken away from you like peace of mind itself. There has got to be peace. No punishment should last forever."

Alice Fuller lowered her head and continued in a

subdued voice, "Everything is so sorry and miserable, so cold and hard and impersonal. But goddammit"— she erupted suddenly, clenching her fists—"it all fits! It all seems to be right." She looked up toward Palo again. "My life was such shit, such garbage—this is the only way it could have ended." Her fists opened and fell back to her lap, and her eyes moved to the floor. Then, with a bolt, she stiffened and stood up quickly, swayed uneasily, and righted herself. The matron rushed in on her, but she repulsed the woman like a snake. "Get away! Get the goddamned hell away from me!" Alice Fuller screamed, her voice suddenly strong. "Stop *handling* me! *Everybody!* Everybody stop handling me! You're going to kill me, isn't that enough? Goddammit, I've been handled and pulled and pushed for four goddamned years! *Get away! Get away from me!*"

The matron stood back, silent, poised to spring on her. In seconds, McPeters and two guards appeared at the door.

"Here!" McPeters said briskly, entering the room with the ease of an athlete, taking charge immediately. "What's this? We can't have this, Mrs. Fuller," he said, without touching her. "We can't have disturbances. This has got to stop before it starts."

Alice Fuller stiffened before him. She almost seemed to stop breathing as she fell silent.

"You finished with her?" McPeters asked Lincoln his voice hard and official.

"Yes," Daniels answered, uneasily.

"Well, let's get her back to her cell," he said quickly, his words directed not at the matron but to the two guards behind him.

With the words, Alice Fuller became a robot again, swept back into the routine as if a shroud had been draped over her. Palo watched her, fighting off his own emotions. Just before she turned to face the guards, her eyes caught his.

"Do you want to hear something awful?" she said to Palo, her tone showing that she was breaking an unwritten prison taboo by speaking in the presence of

Deep Lock guards. "I never in my whole life had a dress that cost thirty dollars."

She turned and was taken away by the two guards like a broomstick before Palo could respond.

When just the three men were left in the room, McPeters shook his head and looked at Lincoln Daniels. "If you think she was bad," he said to Palo, "George Kruger will be worse."

He left the room, and Lincoln and Palo sat in silence and waited.

4

George Kruger had on clean gray overalls when he was brought handcuffed into the room by the two guards, but there was a strong smell of urine about him. McPeters entered the room the instant the guards had Kruger seated. Before anyone else could speak, McPeters hit Kruger with an order.

"One outburst, one screw-up, one piss on my floor, and I will personally kick your ass black and blue," he boomed at the hapless Kruger, who sat head down and cowed.

There was an uneasy silence as McPeters stood bent down in front of Kruger, boring a hole in his skull with his eyes. Then McPeters gave another order. "Say yessir if you understand what I've told you."

Kruger's chin stayed on his chest. "Yessir," he said.

"He's all yours," McPeters said formally, turning to Lincoln and leaving the room. The two guards remained posted on either side of the open doorway.

Lincoln Daniels watched Kruger. He seemed to have aged ten years in the past month. Lincoln dreaded the talk with Kruger more than all the rest, but at least he had spoken to him before. It was not like starting from nothing with Alice Fuller.

"George," Lincoln began in a mild voice, "do you feel all right?"

It was a lame beginning, but what did you say when there was only death to talk about? With José Santos and Charlie Parker it would be different; they were stronger men. With them there was more to talk about than death. But, like Alice Fuller, George Kruger was covered with fear, its smell, its look.

Kruger kept his face blank and expressionless and his head down for a few seconds before answering Daniels. "I wouldn't talk to the other reporters," he said. "I wouldn't open my mouth. Finally," he said, lifting his head and breaking into a grin, "I peed on the floor. I peed on myself like a little baby."

Kruger's voice was small and timid and he would often jam a smile onto his face, like an exclamation mark, when he finished speaking. But throughout the act, throughout all his acts, Lincoln Daniels could see the animal who had raped five women. He did not respond to Kruger's histrionics.

"This is Mr. Reyas, George," Lincoln said evenly, nodding in Palo's direction. "Do you mind if he makes drawings as we talk?"

Palo attempted to catch Kruger's eye, but the man avoided it.

"If he'd been here with the others," Kruger said, putting on another wide grin, "he could have drawn a picture of me peeing."

Palo did not respond to Kruger; he began his sketching.

In his mind for several hours the night before, as he lay awake in his motel bed in Starke, Lincoln Daniels had fashioned a plan, a scheme of questions that he intended to put to the four condemned prisoners. With Alice Fuller he had simply picked his way along, resolving to be content with what he got, but with Kruger he intended to press only one specific point: the fear of death, the thing that he knew had devoured him.

"George," he said sternly, "I want you to make sense. I'm glad you decided to talk to me, but I don't want to play games. I want you to tell me how you feel, in your heart and in your head. No acts, no games, just straight talk. You aren't crazy. You and I both know that."

Kruger had been sitting with his fingers locked together under the restrictions of the handcuffs, his face limp. At Lincoln's words he screwed his mouth up, his hands separated and shook violently, and his eyes suddenly caught fire.

The rattling of his handcuffs brought one of the guards into the room like a fallen hammer. Kruger took one look at him and thought better of his idea to make a move on Daniels.

Lincoln waved the guard off with his hand, and the big man withdrew to the hall, his hard eyes still on Kruger.

"You turd. You're just like the rest," Kruger whined. "I thought you came here to help me. That's why I came out. Somebody's got to help me." His hands went back together, and he began rubbing the palms spastically.

"There's nothing I can do, George," Lincoln said solemnly. "You know that. I can only take down what you say and what you do and report it. I came here to ask you how you feel about what is going to happen—what is going through your mind. But if you don't want to talk to me, I'll understand. I don't know if I would want to talk if I were in your place."

It was so miserable talking to Kruger and Alice Fuller. Lincoln knew they would have to be probed, questioned about their deaths, and as he did it he could think of nothing more distasteful or ironic, or even more nonsensical.

Yes, well, thank you very much, and how are you enjoying your death? Everything going as expected? Any surprises? Any little twists you'd like to share with the readers?

It seemed like a cheeky piece of dialogue from a 1950s British Theater of the Absurd play. But there was Kruger before him, and he was determined to press the point of fear if Kruger would respond. Leaning back in his chair, hoping to gain composure, Daniels formulated his words; then he leaned forward to begin. At that moment, Kruger broke.

"*Ooōōaaauuuu!*" he moaned, swaying in his chair like dry grass. "I want help! I want somebody to help me! I don't want to die. I can't stand it! I can't stand it!"

Again the guard burst into the room, and again Lincoln waved him off with his hand.

"Please let him be," Lincoln said to the guard. "Let him work it out his own way. Please.

"Go ahead, George, let it out," Lincoln said to Kruger, as the guard pulled back to the doorway. "Let it all out. Tell me what you're thinking, what you're feeling."

The big guard, looking disgusted at both Kruger and Daniels, turned his back on the scene and moved to the side of the door.

"I feel like I'm being sucked down a big hole and there's no bottom. I'm falling. *God in heaven, I'm falling and there's nobody to catch me!*"

Kruger's fists were balled in a knot, one holding the other, the balls of his feet welded to the floor and his legs dancing up and down as he began to urinate on himself, a puddle forming in the chair and then running down to the floor.

"Oh, Jesus!" He let out a shrill cry as he realized what he was doing. "Oh, God! Don't let the major beat me. God help me! God help me!"

The guard entered the room once more as the shrieks continued. When he saw the puddle of urine, he reached for Kruger, who slumped down in the chair in fright. Then he turned and went for McPeters, cursing loudly as he left the room.

"Go on, George," Lincoln instructed, knowing he had only seconds left. "Keep going. Don't stop. You're falling and nobody is there to catch you. . . . Who do you want to catch you?"

Kruger remained slumped down in the chair, now with his head in his hands. "I can't see. I can't see who it is I want to catch me. There's a shadow, a form, but I can't see who it is. I . . . I can't see!"

"Look, George! Look and see who it is."

"It's just a face. I see a face. It's a face . . . a face that's . . . that's mine! It's me! *Oh, Christ!* It's me that I want to catch me. Oh, God." Kruger righted himself on the chair, his handcuffed arms straight out in front of his body.

"I want to save myself and I can't. I can't do anything! I'm helpless! God, *I'm helpless!*" he cried, throwing his hands up over his head, straining under them as if he were dangling from a rope.

"You can't do anything in here for yourself!" he cried in a high voice, his hands still over his head. "Nothing! They're killing you all the time and you can't do anything to stop them. You're dying and you can't stop it! You see you're dying and you just have to sit and watch. Like you were some sort of spectator. A spectator at your own death! That's the worst thing! They make you keep watching your own death!"

Kruger's arms fell, and he collapsed into sobs and whimpers and began kicking the desk with his feet. Almost immediately the guard came back into the room. This time he disregarded Daniels completely, grabbing Kruger and jerking him to his feet as if he were weightless. "Shut up, you bastard!" the guard ordered, holding Kruger in a vice grip at his shoulders. "Shut the goddamned hell up and stand still!"

McPeters bolted into the room then, his face alive with hate, his eyes avoiding Lincoln Daniels.

"Don't hit me, major! Please don't hit me!" Kruger yelped, throwing his hands up before his face, a face twisted with fright.

Daniels got to his feet quickly. "It's my fault, major," he said formally. "Please! I caused this. George, I'm sorry. I'm—"

McPeters broke in before he could go on. "It's all right, George," he said, still avoiding Lincoln Daniels. "Just stand still and let the officers take you back to your cell. Nobody's going to hurt you. Just do what you're told and *move!*"

Kruger was mute as he was taken from the room. Lincoln could not see his face, which was still hidden by his cupped hands, but the mad act began again as soon as he was out of the doorway. He started howling like a wolf. They could hear the guard cursing and slapping Kruger on the back of his bony neck with his open palm when they got out into the hall. "Goddamn you, you sumbitch! Goddamned yellow asshole!" The words seemed to dangle in the hallway.

What in the name of God am I doing? Lincoln Daniels wondered. *I'm playing with something I know nothing about, something final and therefore uncorrectable if I'm wrong. What am I doing?*

As if he could read Daniels's mind, McPeters broke the silence. "It's not your fault, Lincoln," he said. "You didn't do anything. That boy's got one song: he's scared of dying, and he'll sing the tune to anybody who will listen. When he sees nobody's listening, he starts crying like a baby or goes into his howling act. You didn't do anything." McPeters looked across the desk at Lincoln Daniels and at Palo Reyas, who had remained seated during the whole incident.

"I don't know, John," Lincoln responded, his face grim. "I shouldn't have pressed him so hard. I shouldn't have opened up so many avenues of fear for him. I helped him with his fear, and that's no good. That was wrong of me, and I can't put it right. There's no time—"

John McPeters stopped him before he could go on. "Lincoln," he said evenly, "on the Row there is no right, and no wrong, and no time. There is only what is right at the moment. Once the Death Routine starts, there is only that: only death. Right and wrong don't matter any more; they've been forfeited. There is no use being squeamish about it or trying to avoid it. When you put a man in the Death Routine, you intend to kill him, pure and simple. He better know it and get ready, and we here at the Death Facility better know it and get ready. And you and Palo better know it, too, and be governed accordingly."

"It is so," Palo Reyas said, his voice somber. "I have watched these two people and they are pathetic, but Major McPeters is right: death is the only consideration here. We must not confuse this with life or with battle. All chance has been removed here. There is only one end."

"But honor and human dignity? Have they been

taken away too?" Lincoln asked, looking first at Reyas, then at McPeters.

Reyas answered first. "Yes," he said. "I think honor and dignity have been removed." He looked toward McPeters for the final word.

McPeters nodded. "When convicts go to prison they lose their civil rights by law, but they lost their human rights a long time before. They either gave them up or never had them to start with. I've been in this business over thirty years, and I've never seen an exception. Losers end up in prison," McPeters said, crossing his big arms over his chest, "but to end up on Death Row you have to work at being a loser."

He let those words hang in the room for a few moments, then uncrossed his arms and rubbed the palms of his hands together.

"So," he went on, forcing a thin smile with considerable effort, expressly for Lincoln's and Palo's peace of mind. "Two down and two to go. The worst is behind you. Let me get out of here so you can go to work again."

After McPeters left, Lincoln sat down and reflected on his words. He wondered if the worst was behind.

Before José Santos was brought in, Leo Dunbar, the Death Facility trusty, came in and cleaned up Kruger's urine.

5

José Santos was ushered into McPeters's office by the two guards, handcuffed and managed securely between them. He did not look at Lincoln Daniels or Palo Reyas or make any sign of recognition until he was seated in the bolted-down chair and the guards left the room. Santos stood again, then Lincoln walked around the desk to him, and they shook hands warmly and greeted each other in Spanish, the language they had used at their first meeting.

Lincoln introduced Palo. "You look well," he said to Santos, his voice even and controlled now that he was on surer ground with a man whom, if he did not respect, he had feeling for. "It is good to see you again. I have thought much about you," he went on in the formal Spanish manner. "I have wished you well in my thoughts."

"And you in my thoughts, good friend," Santos replied. "Your presence here is a great comfort to me." His eyes searched out Lincoln and then Palo, studying their outside look and feel. "My mother was here today," he added soberly, "and she wishes me to tell you that she is forever in your debt for the money and the letter you sent her."

Lincoln seemed genuinely embarrassed. His hand moved in front of him in protest. "It was a thing of need, and it is done," he said.

They separated then, Lincoln and Palo returning to their chairs behind McPeters's desk, José Santos to the bolted-down chair.

They spoke around the subject of death for a full five minutes, conversing animatedly in Spanish about things Latin—Mexico, food, bullfights, and, of course, Cuba, a place that, because of the difference in their ages, Lincoln and Palo knew firsthand far better than Santos himself.

Then there was silence, a heavy, lingering silence. The room had suddenly been emptied by the mutual recognition that it was Sunday morning and the issue of death could no longer be circumvented. In a muted, uncomfortable voice, pausing midstream to reestablish eye contact, Daniels asked Santos what he was feeling.

"You feel like a man," Santos responded, lowering his eyes in pain. "You are in control, total control of yourself and the elements around you. I know," he went on, his face knotted, "because I have not felt that way in so long a time that I have forgotten the feeling;

now, in my mind, in my heart and body, there is only the spark of that feeling, an unreachable spark.

"I feel like a man in a diver's helmet," he went on, clenching and unclenching his fists. "I can see out, but nothing can get in. Like trying to eat through the closed faceplate. The food comes right to my mouth, but there is a barrier; it cannot get to me. I'm there, but not there. No," he said, using his handcuffed hands to make the point, "I don't feel like a man. Not any more. Not for a long time. I feel like nothing, like smoke."

He inhaled deeply, looked past Daniels and Reyas for a moment, then set his eyes on Lincoln once more.

"But what difference does it make? It makes no difference!" He answered his own question. "Nothing makes any difference here. Nothing!" He looked off at the wall behind Daniels and Reyas. "We are all so small—so much smoke—and everything is so sad. In order for there to be a difference there must be a change, or room for change. Here," he said, "everything is sad and small all the time: smoke. . . ." His voice trailed off.

Lincoln could not disagree. He sat morosely and waited for Santos to go on.

"I don't know," Santos mumbled, head down. Then he looked up suddenly to face the two men before him. "You figure you can go as far in life as you can get, which is forever. And each day higher than the next. But here—here there's no future. No past. Just the dull, numbing present. And I can't, not after all this time, all this mental abuse, resign myself to the fact that this is the end. I know it is, but I just can't accept that it's happening to me. I keep thinking it's a dream, a bad dream, and I'll wake up and it will be gone. But no," he said, "it is real, and it never goes away, and I can't face it—" He stopped himself to explain. "I can face it, and I have; I just can't accept it."

Lincoln could not speak. He knew Santos was a murderer, a cold-blooded assassin, and that if anyone should be executed Santos certainly deserved to be, for all the lives he had taken. What caused Daniels great pain was the qualitative aspect. Of all the prisoners he had seen or knew about on Death Row, José Santos alone seemed not to fit the classic losers' mold.

Santos's words invaded Lincoln's thoughts as the condemned man began to speak again. "I can't accept it because it's all chance," he explained. "Chance that I'm here. Chance that I was caught. Chance that Circulo Cubano was filled with women and children instead of men, as I believed it to be. Everything—*chance*. You know how they picked the four that were to go?" He went on without pausing, again answering his own question. "They chose the four who had been under death sentence the longest. *Chance!* All chance. And chance is the one thing you can't fight, can't prepare for, can't defend yourself against. Chance makes you as helpless and as vulnerable as a baby."

As it had been in their last talk, Lincoln Daniels began to pick up flaws, huge discrepancies between fact and fantasy that were obvious to him but which escaped José Santos completely. *The people you killed,* he said to himself as he watched Santos, *it was chance for them that you took their lives. Chance rendered them as helpless and vulnerable as babies.*

Santos's words brought him out of his thoughts. "Everything here is so relative it is meaningless," he heard Santos say. "Today they bring me out to talk to you, the next time I'm taken out of my cell it will be to shave my head, the last time will be to take me to the chair." He said the words with no more emotion than if he had been reading the telephone book. "One trip will please, one will humiliate, the other will kill. Suppose they just kept bringing me out to talk to you? Over and over, playing out the same scene a million times. No harm in that at all. . . . Just a matter of what the trip is for."

Lincoln and Palo watched and waited. Santos continued, drumming his fingers on the bare ankle that protruded from the gray coveralls.

"But the Row, because of where it is and what it is, is the bottom of Deep Lock, the end of the line, the place that makes everything in the real world go away. Here, you forget it all, every bit of it," he said, bitterness at last entering his voice.

"I look at *Playboy* magazine, or some of the porn magazines, or porn playing cards—women, luscious, beautiful, lying back with their legs spread open, smooth and inviting. Or the porn pictures with sex in every form, every position, the sex organs meeting. . . . I've forgotten what it's all about. What it is like to be with a woman, what it is like to feel a woman's soft, curved body.

"Here," he went on, gripping his ankle tightly, "there is nothing soft, no curves, just straight lines and angles. I don't even remember how it is to fit with a woman, how you actually get together. I don't remember how it is to fit with the outside, either—with society. It seems as though they wait for that, for the time when you are completely out of touch with the rest of the world. Then they kill you. And there is no regret because you are different; you don't fit. It's like lopping off a diseased limb. When you get right down to the point of cutting it off, destroying,it seems the only logical thing to do. I can't accept it. But it is beginning to seem logical to me."

Santos released the grip on his ankle and let his foot move back to the floor; he seemed to be drained and, at the same time, deep in thought, looking past Daniels at the wall. His eyes remained fixed and distant for a few seconds; then he spoke again, his voice once more emotionless, clinical.

"For weeks I've followed my death in the newspapers," he said. "News stories, editorials, cartoons, bleeding-heart pieces, boil-them-alive pieces. Who's going to be the new executioner? What do they eat on the Row? Do they get TV? Do they cry? Who's got religion? Who wets the bed? Who damns God to the end? . . . The list is endless, and endlessly incorrect." He shrugged, seeking out Lincoln Daniels's eyes. "I'm going to tell you how it is to be on Death Row. If nothing else comes of this—and I can't see that anything will, or that it is supposed to—then it has stood for something.

"*Something*," he repeated to himself quickly, cupping his handcuffed hands together, using his right forefinger as a pointer. "Something," he said again, "is what you finally miss most on Death Row, because what is here is nothing. It is not a Never-Never Land. No, it is very real, but what is real is the nothingness, a condition that does not exist anywhere else on earth. Even in solitary confinement, in cells the same size as those on the Row, except that there are steel doors instead of bars, with reduced food or baby food or bread and water and darkness for weeks on end, there is something. And that something is the future. The future is something, and something is the future."

Santos was looking away as he said the words; then his eyes went straight across to Lincoln and he forced a narrow smile. "I've turned jailhouse philosopher," he said.

Lincoln and Palo manufactured smiles, but darkness for all of them came in again when Santos continued.

"On Death Row you learn once and for all that you can adapt to almost anything. Even if you can't accept it, you can get used to the idea of death, to the reality of endless days of sameness, to complete, bone-shattering loneliness . . . everything except nothingness. You never accept that.

"You find out that every man has his dignity and that it can't be taken away from him. Even if you reduce him to a vegetable, it does not go away. Every man, no matter how poorly he articulates it, how narrowly he feels it, has got to believe that his life, that *he,* stands for something. Small, large, but *something.*"

Santos stopped for a second, the words obviously causing him great anxiety. When he spoke again, his face was pained. "The newspapers talk about resignation. They say nobody ever resigns himself to the chair. That's all wrong. The word, as I've told you, is accept. You don't ever accept the idea of death, but resignation—that comes easy. It's built in from the first.

"The moment you commit a crime, you resign yourself, whether you admit it or not, to the idea of flight and fear. The idea of possible capture. The gut idea and reality of uncertainty. The idea of constant jeopardy. It's a process your mind goes through, a wearing-down process.

"People always ask why there's not normally a great deal of kicking and screaming and crying of fainting or swooning when you're caught. The answer is simple: If there's any space at all between the crime and the capture, the wearing-down process has done its work—so that the tears and kicking, mentally if not physically, are already in the past.

"Then comes jail, and you sit there for months before your case comes up, the resignation process taking greater hold. Then there's the trial, and you sit in the courtroom while the crime is played back to you in every minute detail." His eyes closed with misery.

"No one, no one on earth," Santos went on, his eyes still closed, "can know the humiliation and embarrassment of a trial unless he has gone through one. It is like being stripped naked and made to defecate in public. You are laid totally open, totally exposed." His eyes opened and scanned the room, looking past Daniels and Reyas. His hands went up, forming a V out from the handcuffs, and his fingers rubbed at his eyes as if they ached. Finally, he let his hands fall back to his lap.

When Santos spoke again, it seemed as though he had thought about the words, weighed each one for a long time before their conversation. "Then the newspapers say, 'He showed no emotion when the death sentence was passed.' Or they say, 'He smiled openly.'

"It's resignation. And even relief that the thing has come to a head, that it's being settled. By the time you get to Death Row, most of the tears are gone. You're like an empty tin can; you're ready for the rust to start collecting."

He looked away from Lincoln and Palo for a second, then came back to them, his face grim and hard. "Then finally there's the Row itself, the last part in the resignation process. A nine-by-six-by-eight-foot cell. A bunk, a stainless-steel sink, a stainless-steel toilet with no seat, a bolted-down chair, and a bolted-down table. A change of clothes twice a week. Three showers and three shaves a week. A haircut every month. A visit every month. Letter privileges three times a week on one side of two sheets of lined paper. One library book a week. A two-hour exercise period every day. Three meals a day, and a twelve-inch portable black-and-white television set, placed inside a wire cage on the cell's ceiling, that plays for twelve hours a day.

"These things make up your entire world, no more, no less, for each and every day you are here. But overriding everything is the first of the things: your cell." Santos's face twisted as he said the word cell. "You are in the nine-by-six-by-eight-foot space for twenty-two hours a day, every day. There is no way to describe the boredom, the lethargy that sets in. It is a living death." Santos brought his hands up to his chest in frustration. "And the rest is superfluous."

Lincoln kept quiet. He knew his questions would be meaningless. Palo sketched and tried to avoid contact with Santos's hungry eyes. When Santos began speaking again, his hands were back on his lap, his face was like a shadow.

"So what happens?" he said, turning his hands out at his question. "You are in a deep hole with no way to move; when you travel, when you do move," he went on, painfully, "you come to the final realization about your situation, your *place* on earth." He closed his hands together like a vice and sat up straight in the bolted-down chair. "You come to the final and absolute idea of waste. Complete waste," he said, picking up his own thought with no pause, opening his hands, leaving the fingers standing rigid, like spikes.

Santos stared at Lincoln and then his eyes moved sharply to the floor. He looked like an Indian mystic meditating in the misery of a village hut. He was deep in thought, completely withdrawn, but, as Lincoln and Palo watched, he came back to them and his fingers relaxed as he began to speak again, his voice hoarse from so much use.

"All week I have thought each day: On this day next week I will not be here, I will be dead. And now, all day today, I have thought: At this time tomorrow

I will not be here, I will be dead. Everything in steps," he said, almost to himself.

Then he spoke to both Lincoln and Palo. "I don't want to die," he told them. "But if I was released right now, I don't know how I would live.

"Tomorrow will come," he said, "and I won't be here. But," he went on, slowly shutting his eyes and pushing his head back so that his closed eyes faced the ceiling, "I haven't been here in so long that I can't say it will matter to be gone. But, oh, God," he ended, bringing his head back down, his eyes opening, *"I don't want to die."*

A small tear line began to form on his cheeks; he made no effort to conceal it. One of the guards stuck his head inside the open doorway. Santos's time was up. Lincoln and Palo got up and said good-bye to him. Santos stood and waited as the two guards closed in on either side of him.

6

Charlie Parker appeared to be smiling when the two guards brought him into McPeters's office, a closed-lipped smile that creased his right cheek. Unlike the others, he was handcuffed to a waist belt, and it was difficult for Lincoln Daniels and Palo Reyas to shake hands with him.

"You seem in good spirits," Lincoln began, when the three had taken their seats.

"Evil spirits," Parker replied, smiling cynically. "There are evil spirits everywhere."

He let out a chuckle that shook his oxlike shoulders. His eyes alternated between Daniels and Reyas. You could see that he was enjoying himself.

"More voodoo here than on the whole of Haiti. . . . No," he corrected himself. "Voodoo has life in it. This place is antiseptic, totally lifeless."

Lincoln Daniels listened intently. He had a deep feeling of sorrow about José Santos, but Charlie Parker fascinated him more than the other three put together. If Tom Jones was born to hang, Lincoln thought as he looked at the big black man, Charlie Parker was born to be electrocuted.

All his life Parker had been trying to lose, and now he had lost as big as you could and he was reveling in it. As Lincoln watched him he knew that Parker understood this completely. Parker also understood that there were only two options left to him, laughing and crying, and he had decided to laugh it off. It was a bad joke, the worst of jokes, because he had played it on himself.

Lincoln knew the laughter was a pretense, but it was the tonic Lincoln needed to cure his own misery. For the first time he launched into conversation as an animated participant rather than hanging back as a distant observer.

"An antiseptic is not for the likes of a Charlie Parker," he said with a smile.

Parker laughed, straining at the waist belt with his handcuffed hands. "These fuckers got me locked up tighter than Dick's hatband," he said, looking down at his manacled hands. "You remember Dick's hatband," he went on to Lincoln. "Hell, I even remember Dick's dick." He laughed again.

Parker's laughter and his movement caused his chains to rattle, a sound that brought the two guards rushing into the office.

"Sit your ass still!" one ordered, his arms pulled back at his sides, braced to deliver punches. "I hear any more movin' and you go back to the Row." The guard's eyes burned as they focused on Parker, but the huge black man only smiled under the unrestrained hatred.

"We're talking," Lincoln Daniels said forcefully. "There's no need for this interruption. I'll call you when we're through."

The guard met the words with the same fiery look he directed toward Parker, but after a few seconds he gave way under Lincoln's gaze and, with the other guard behind him, retreated to the hall.

"Oh, they want my big black ass," Parker said, smiling fiercely. "They want that black steak for breakfast, lunch, and dinner, and for in-between snacks. You give a cracker a chicken and he'll always eat the dark meat first. There's a real message there."

"We were talking about antiseptics," Lincoln reminded him.

"And people who get the treatment," Parker smiled his evil smile once more, an expression he seemed to have invented for the occasion. "The greatest punishment of all is having this bunch of assholes on my baby-black bottom all day long," he said loudly, for the benefit of the two guards in the hallway. "A more humorless, hateful group of people hasn't been made yet, and you're not likely to see a worse lot unless God, or whoever is running this three-ring circus, has a terminally bad day.

"In Haiti," he continued, his huge hands linked together in his lap, shoulders squared back on the chair, giving the impression of a boulder on a pedestal, "when I was a Tonton, we clapped people in jail like thunder on a summer afternoon. We roughed them up, killed some before they reached jail, crippled others. That was the way of the time." He gestured with his open hands, then locked them together once more. "We were feared and despised, and that was as it should be, because we were the enforcers, the bogeymen, the strong arm of the law, its visible vengeance.

"But in jail, in prison"—he gestured as well as he could with his hands, leaving them open for emphasis —"that was something different altogether. In jail a man was still a man. He still had needs, ideas, appetites, and if he had money or influence he could go on living like a man, could go on satisfying his appetites. But here"—he gestured again with his hands, looking around the blank little room—"there is nothing . . . *rien,*" he repeated in French and then paused for emphasis.

"In France, during the time Devil's Island was

being created, there was heated debate. 'Who will guard such rogues in so distant a place?' was the question most asked. And the answer was simple," Parker announced with obvious delight. " 'Greater rogues.' So the point here is: 'Who creates such blandness, such sterility?' The answer again, is simple: 'The most bland people on the planet.' "

Once again Parker let silence dramatize the point he was making. Then he began again. "Here I am"—looking down at his manacled hands—"as busted in the slammer as you can get, about to go out tomorrow morning, and they're worried about handcuffing me, keeping me locked in my little hole, just keeping me low and down and out—the only condition they know. Hell"—he laughed—"what I need is a five-hundred-dollar-a-night hooker, a couple of bottles of Rémy Martin cognac, and a big bed with satin sheets looking out on a yellow nighttime sea. Then"—he laughed again—"I'd get up in the morning and go out with a smile on my face.

"These motherfuckers don't know the first thing about punishment," he said thickly, shifting gears in mid-thought. "They don't regard death as an adequate punishment, because death is an intellectual thing on the one hand and something wrapped up in their chickenshit Hard-Shell Baptist religion on the other.

"Eva thang gon' be bettah in da sweet bye-'n'-bye," Parker mugged, hands upstretched, eyes wide. "Sho 'nuff, capt'n, 'cause dis down here ain't fer shit."

Then, as suddenly as he began the act, he stopped it, his face turning morose. "Death is enough," he said calmly. "Death is what it all comes down to, and it's enough. I've lived hard and I've lived rough and I've lived well, and when I think back on the good times, it's hard to leave, damn hard.

"It's damn hard, even when you've got no choice," he went on. "But it's all over." His great face was rigid, his hands cupped tightly. "I don't even watch TV any more. I had them take the damn thing out of my cell months ago. I'd watch the movies—Paris, Rome, New York, the West . . . it seemed like something from another planet. And the people—laughing, talking, kissing, touching . . . it didn't even make sense. It was like seeing something for the first time after you had been blind all your life. I just kept saying over and over to myself, What the hell are they doing? Where the hell is that?

"I don't even exercise any more," he went on, the words spoken as if they were being pieced together. "Every day the guards come to your cell, two of them, and they walk you down the corridor to the exercise yard by yourself, and when they are through making their rounds there are eight people in the yard and you play for two hours.

"Play . . . exercise . . ." He snorted. "Words that don't have any meaning here . . . so I just stopped. I've stopped everything except eating, sleeping, and excreting, the things the human body forces you into. Tomorrow morning I'll stop them. Death forces you to do that," he added swiftly, his voice blank and hard.

As with the others Lincoln kept quiet; these were the real last words of the condemned, their true last testament. There was no need for questions; questions had no place. What was going to be said would be said, and no amount of probing could bring more to the surface. It left you shattered or whole; there was no in-between.

Parker's tenseness and rigidity eased, and when he began to speak again he seemed composed, almost relaxed. "Everybody held here in the Death Facility has one thing in common besides the obvious fact of a capital crime," he said, "Like Shakespeare's characters, we've all got a tragic flaw. And the flaw has little to do with the crime. The flaw is intensely personal."

The words assaulted Lincoln Daniels's mind like a gunshot. Parker was putting into words thoughts Lincoln had held since he first came on the Row a month before, thoughts that had loomed close to the surface of his mind since that time but had never found the clarity of words.

Tragic flaw, Lincoln said to himself as he watched Parker. *That is the key.*

"My own tragic flaw," Parker said, "has little to do with my color or my place in time or geography, although none of the three helped. I had thought all three were the cause of my downfall, the cause of a lifetime of misery and nonfulfillment." He paused. "That is why I turned myself in to the Palm Beach city police so romantically and announced that I was a 'nigger in a white man's world' who had come for his final reward.

"Now I see that that was nonsense and that I should have stuck a forty-five in my mouth and gone out with a little style. But no," he added quickly, grimacing over the words and the thoughts they evoked for him, "I was a romantic fool. You see," he added sourly, "romanticism is my tragic flaw."

Lincoln watched Parker with care, taking in all the words and the concealed agony that went with them.

"I've sat here, locked away, for four years," Parker said, his eyes set on Lincoln's, "and during that time I've practiced the prisoner's occupation—the act of thinking—to perfection. I've reconstructed, re-created, my life, as they say. It hasn't been very pleasant—except the ribald parts." He forced a grin, and his shoulders shook with a clipped snort of laughter that came from within.

"No," he went on, his face turning cold. "I blew it. That's the saddest thing a man can say. I had it right there in front of me, and I blew it.

"Ah, I could blame it on my old man moving the family from Jamaica to Savannah to open his Brasserie Haïtien, on the miserable little bigots of south Georgia in the forties, on being wiped out and reduced to pulpwood-nigger status, but my father was the victim of a blind desire for something he supposed was better for his family and for himself, and the pulpwood-nigger foolishness, the temporary poverty, meant nothing. It wasn't even a test, as many like to believe. No, what I did about it was the important thing. There are endless billions of things that can happen in a person's life, the whole realm of pure chance, itself, so only the few actions we take are of real importance.

"And my actions," he said tightly, his eyes locked on Lincoln's, "were all wrong. I became a thug, a

Tonton, a dope dealer, and finally a murderer." He shrugged.

"I, too, wanted to better myself," he said. "But to me better always meant money, and the romantic's idea of money"—he searched Lincoln's eyes—"is to get it fast and in large amounts. I was a wizard at both, a natural—as you are a natural writer. I suppose I could have kept on forever, or so it seemed.

"My downfall, of course, was the killing of my wife and her mother and the policeman who came to arrest me. But not only was their killing a logical progression in the workings of my life, the act was also the positive culmination of all the hidden bitterness I'd stored up during nearly fifty years of being out of step with society and reality. At the time of the killings I charged it off strictly to race. The easy way out." He shrugged. " 'A nigger in a white man's world,' I babbled. 'The end of the card game.' " He snorted, his lips tight. " 'An idiot in the madhouse of the world' would have been more to the point," he said dryly.

"I'm ready to go tomorrow morning," he said, surveying his grim surroundings. "This place once and for all cancels romanticism."

As the words settled into the silence of the room, the three men sat and eyed each other, but before anyone could speak John McPeters filled the open doorway.

"If you're through, we'd better be on our way," he said.

Lincoln hesitated, but under McPeters's hard eyes he and Palo stood and went around the desk to Parker, who remained seated. Lincoln looked first at McPeters, then at Parker. He extended his hand to the big black man as his mind raced for words, the right words that did not come.

"Good luck," he said at last, as they shook hands hard. It was all he could think of as his and Parker's eyes locked as tightly as their hands.

"You, too," Parker came back, just before he released Lincoln's hand. The words chilled the flesh on Daniels's neck.

Down the hallway, as Lincoln and Palo moved

swiftly at McPeters's side toward the Death Chamber, Lincoln asked if there was trouble.

"No," McPeters answered. "But things don't look right, so we're leaving."

Behind them, Lincoln heard Charlie Parker's chain rattle as he stood up. The sound played all along the hall.

7

Lincoln and Palo and John McPeters were driven from Death Row back to the parking lot of the Main Prison by one of McPeters's guards. The major's tension eased somewhat once they reached the other prison. Out on the sidewalk in front of the prison's gate, he turned to Lincoln as the driver departed in a prison sedan.

"Something's brewing," he said flatly, avoiding Lincoln's eyes. "I don't know exactly what, and I may not know until it happens, but we're in for something."

"Can you put a time on it?" Lincoln asked.

"Late tonight or early in the morning," McPeters replied, his eyes surveying the gray sky as if it might give him the answer he was seeking. "Probably tomorrow morning right before we start." He paused for a few seconds. "Yeah, tomorrow morning," he said. "When the news boys are let back on the prison grounds. No use in raising much hell when you can't get on TV."

"If you can't see it on the six o'clock news it didn't happen," Lincoln agreed. "Well, happily," he added swiftly, "Brother Reyas and me don't march to that beat."

McPeters broke into a relieved laugh. "That's the ticket," he said, still grinning. "Let's eat."

"I'll second that motion," Palo Reyas added,

pleased at the sudden good cheer that had cut into the gloom surrounding them.

A quick exchange was made, with Palo riding with McPeters in his personal car, a two-year-old Oldsmobile 88 sedan, and Lincoln following behind in his rented Ford. The two cars turned left past the prison parking lot and went due west through the two miles of prison reservation land and out to the intersection. There was a long log store to the left, a railroad track to the front, and a tunnel of tall pines to the right, on either side of a highway, with the little turpentine railhead village of Raiford barely visible in the dying sunlight to the west.

McPeters regarded Lincoln in his rearview mirror for a second and then turned northeast onto another two-lane blacktop and drove off at a fast clip through the darkening tunnel of pines. The two cars moved for three miles along the highway, passing humorless little slatboard houses set in wet bottoms, cattle standing hoof-deep in icy muck, and occasional bare brown fields and strips of high-ground pasture. McPeters's house came into view just as the highway bellied out to the west and crossed the railroad track cut through more seemingly endless stretches of pines.

Lincoln pulled onto the long driveway, crossed a wide cattle gap, and followed McPeters in a long left-to-right semicircle up to the house. McPeters's two servants, a thickset cook with a bald head and three gold teeth named Ira Tuffel and a tall, skinny houseboy named Coy Deal, were standing on the open front porch when the cars stopped by the raised steps. Both convicts were in their fifties. They were wearing large white starched cotton aprons and grinning broadly. They were both murderers. Like most employees at the prison who had convict servants, McPeters always chose murderers; they usually became docile and they were predictable, whereas thieves were never predictable.

McPeters, Lincoln, and Palo were up on the front porch just as the sun fell behind the cold green tops of the long stand of pines off to the west; for a moment, the sky seemed to stand perfectly still, suspended in swirls of purple and pinkish orange and slate gray.

"The sunsets out here, John," Lincoln said, standing between Palo and McPeters, "and the stillness. I've thought about your place many times since I was here last month. You've got a fine thing here, a fine thing."

McPeters shook his head in acknowledgement, pleased but somewhat embarrassed. When Lincoln detected the embarrassment he turned his attention to the two black convicts.

"Ira, Coy," Lincoln said. "It's good to see you again. You both look fine."

The two convicts—Ira Tuffel, doing double life for shooting his wife and her sister, and Coy Deal, doing life and twenty years for the murder of two sawmill hands in a company store—stood before Daniels grinning like schoolboys.

Tuffel was the first of the two to find words. "We real fine, Mista Daniels," he drawled. "We heard your name on the TV set, too. Right on the Walter Cronkite news. Says you gon' write up the goin's-on here in the mornin'."

"That's a fact," Deal chimed in. "We said right back to the TV set that we shore knowed that gentleman. Lord, Mista Daniels," he went on, "you the first person we ever knew off TV."

McPeters looked at the two convicts and shook his head and then spoke directly to Daniels. "Don't encourage these boys," he said. "They're the sorriest two hands in the prison. I just keep 'em out here so they don't end up in solitary confinement for layin' down on the job."

Lincoln smiled at McPeters and then turned once more to Tuffel and Deal. "And how about the soap operas?" he asked Tuffel. "The both of you still following the soap operas?"

"Yessir," Tuffel answered, holding his hands together in front of him and dipping his head as he spoke. "We followin' the programs—the minute we gets through with our work," he added quickly, looking up to McPeters for approval.

"They gettin' colored folks on some of 'em now," Deal added, grinning slyly.

"That's enough," McPeters said. "There ain't no use *braggin'* about how damn sorry you are. Open the door and let these folks in the house."

Daniels introduced the two convicts to Palo Reyas and then fell silent. It was all pure antebellum South: the master and his retainers—in McPeters's case, the master and his family. McPeters, Lincoln Daniels had observed, was a man who had only one pretense, and that was when dealing with his black servants. Within the universe of the prison, he genuinely liked Tuffel and Deal and Oscar Mason, his gardener, but, as was the fashion in such things, he covered his true feelings with gruffness, indifference, and only a hint of familiarity.

The house was brightly lit and pin-clean, and there was a crackling, rich-smelling pine-log fire in the great stone fireplace.

McPeters instructed Deal to pour drinks and then excused himself and went off to the kitchen with Tuffel to check the progress of the dinner; when he emerged from the kitchen in a few minutes he was in his shirt sleeves, with his black military tie removed and his khaki shirt open two buttons at the collar showing a thick growth of long black and white chest hairs. He looked comfortable and relaxed as Deal handed him a straight bourbon over ice.

"Well, here's to the both of you," McPeters said, grinning self-consciously in the way of people who spend most of their time alone, holding his glass out to Lincoln and Palo, who were seated before the fire in two squat rockers.

"Not for one minute." Lincoln stood up. "Here's to you." Palo joined in the toast; then McPeters turned to Deal.

"You boys pour yourselves one, and drink it in the kitchen," he said. "I don't want you standing around here moonin' for a drink all night."

"Thank you, major," Deal said, bobbing his head like a fishing cork, smiling alternately at McPeters and then at Lincoln.

"By the looks of both of them that won't be their first drink of the day," McPeters said, once Deal had left the room.

They sat and talked, and the house began to fill up with the crisp aroma of meat frying in the kitchen, a meat whose vapors Lincoln thought he recognized but was not sure. In half an hour Ira Tuffel called them in to a dinner that delighted Lincoln when he saw it spread out on the big dining-room table on heavy stoneware platters.

"Jesus," he exclaimed, grabbing McPeters by the arm. "I've been sitting out there in the living room racking my brain to figure out what was going on in here, and now I feel like a moron. My old man would lay out one of these dinners every Saturday night from hunting season till spring."

On the table before them was a fine old-fashioned bird supper of deep-fried quail and dove, a heaping platter of grits and coleslaw, and two large black frying pans of cornbread.

McPeters beamed and turned to Palo. "This is nothing fancy, but I thought you might get a kick out of eating a real cracker bird supper. We never lost anybody yet from Ira's cooking," he added.

Palo laughed. "John," he said, "you're a man of constant surprises."

8

It was almost nine when they finished dinner and returned to the living room for drinks and coffee. It had been an excellent meal, with Palo delighting the table with his well-worn but well-told Pancho Villa stories of the Mexican revolution, stories that seemed to genuinely fascinate McPeters.

In the living room, as the fragrant pine fire crackled and sparked before them, the festive mood continued, but Lincoln Daniels could see that McPeters's mind was not totally on the evening.

He led into what he wanted to say awkwardly, saying that Palo's stories of Pancho Villa had put him in mind of incidents on Death Row that seemed to have some point to them, a point that he could never quite make out. But Lincoln knew from the first that what the major had to say would not be awkward, and that the point of what he had to say had not eluded him.

McPeters sat back in his big, overstuffed easy chair with his legs crossed. He seemed far away for a second, but then he began to speak, directing his first words to Lincoln, who sat at his right on a small sofa, and then to Palo, who sat in one of the rockers.

"It's like you and I meeting last month after all these years, and your telling me that you served with General Blackshear when he was a colonel in Korea," he said, his voice precise, completely devoid of his drawl or manufactured bad English. "The three-way connection between Warden Blackshear's giving me a job thirty years ago and your serving with his son in Korea, of course, means nothing, and the fact that you are here at the prison after all these years to witness executions also means nothing.

"But," he went on, looking directly at Lincoln, "if you look behind the three connections, off *around the corner*," he added, considering the words carefully, shifting his eyes from Lincoln to Palo as if he were checking their response, "you see something, you *sense* something, if not a connection then some pattern—and one that I have never been able to put my finger on.

"You're the man with the words," he said to Lincoln. "You put my old country-boy ideas into words, and we'll both retire and sit under a palm tree somewhere."

Lincoln laughed soundly in a vain attempt to break the air of foreboding that McPeters's words seemed to bring on.

"I don't know," McPeters said, brushing aside the ambiguous start with his hand. "Over the years so many things have happened on the Row. Now we've started up the executions again, and in these last few weeks I've been thinking about the thing as a whole, trying to string it together, trying to make some sense out of it. I guess I'm getting old, becoming a park-bench philosopher in my old age. But I'm not the only one," he added quickly. "There's Cabel Lasseter, the electrician, not a finer man here—not a finer man that I've met, not a better prison man I've ever met—and he's beginning to ask questions, beginning to look for answers, too.

"Don't get me wrong," he said angrily, using his meaty forefingers for emphasis. "I'm for killing every damn one of the bastards in the moning, one by one —cleaning house. But there are so many patterns," he went on, making himself ease off. "Tangles, like the wires in the walls of a big house; so many of them, and all going somewhere, but all going to a place you can't find or don't understand. People moving in and out ... thoughts ... connections ... coincidences ... meetings here, meetings there ... a tangle.

"Ah—" He broke off, pushing the sound away with his hand. "I won't try and make any conclusions. You're the ones to do that. I'll just say my piece. You see what you make of it."

Lincoln watched him as he spoke. His mind flashed back to his talk with José Santos hours earlier. As it was with Santos, Daniels again had the idea that he was watching a man who had come back from enemy territory, a man who had truths few others possessed. When McPeters began speaking again, it was evident that all preliminaries were out of the way.

"We talked about loose connections regarding Warden Blackshear," McPeters said, "but solid patterns have been known to crop up with some of the governors who signed death warrants. There are several instances where young lawyers would have clients who would get the chair and then years later these same lawyers would be governors of the state and have to sign their former clients' death warrants. But of course these things were more or less bound to happen because so many lawyers go into politics. I accept these

situations at face value, and I don't try to make anything else out of them but simple coincidence, but
how do you figure this?" He reached for his drink on
the wooden arm of his chair and took a swallow before
going on.

"In November of 1903, Milo Cloversettle was born
in a little frame house in west Florida, in a place called
Blountstown—a little wide spot on the road not too
far from where I was born, by the way. Milo was a
hard-working boy who grew up and went off to law
school at Cumberland College of Tennessee and got a
law degree and then came back home to Blountstown
and Calhoun County and set up law practice and ran
for the state legislature and got elected at twenty-two.

"Well," McPeters continued, shifting his weight
back into his chair, "Milo was delivered by a midwife, an old colored woman everybody called Aunt
Bess. And shortly after Aunt Bess delivered Milo, she
delivered a little baby boy down the road in another
frame house, a boy named William Anthony Masters.

"Milo and Bill Masters grew up together in
Blountstown and played together as kids, but by the
time they got to high school, their paths had divided.
Milo was a serious student, a good athlete, a local la-
dies' man. Bill Masters was just the opposite: a bad
student, not interested in athletics, and not really interested in girls, at least not decent girls.

"By the time Milo entered the House of Representatives in 1925, Bill Masters had already served two
jail sentences for petty theft and a six-month stretch
on the Calhoun County Work Gang for assault. He
was the worst character in Calhoun County. They
called him Wild Bill Masters. In January of 1925, he
shot and killed two city policemen in Blountstown, and
by March he was on Death Row.

"I guess you know what I'm going to say next:
Milo Cloversettle was Bill's lawyer. But that's just the
beginning. Masters's family knew Bill was guilty and
more or less expected the conviction, but they had faith
that Milo, who was in the House, could intercede with
the governor, Ben Platt, and get Bill's sentence commuted to life. But that didn't happen," McPeters said,

brushing his chin with his fingertips. "Governor Platt signed Bill's death warrant during the second week in December, 1925."

He paused for a second, took another drink, and then went on with the story, centering his attention on Lincoln Daniels. "It was the week before Christmas, and Bill's warrant was signed for the twenty-first, a death date Milo and Bill's parents took as a good sign: a good sign, because no one had ever gone to the chair that close to Christmas Day before—or since, for that matter. No, Milo and Bill's folks thought Governor Platt was just trying to scare the hell out of Bill and appease the families of the dead police officers before he commuted Bill to life at hard labor.

"But that wasn't the case. Ben Platt was a hard and fair man, and when Milo showed up at the governor's office with Bill's mother and father on the twentieth to beg for Bill's life he gave them a two-hour audience, but in the end he held firm and took Bill's mother's hand and told her that he couldn't feel right with himself and God and the dead police officers and their families if he stopped the execution.

"Mrs. Masters was sitting in a chair just to the right of the governor's big oak desk, and Milo and Bill's father were sitting out from the desk to the left, and Platt looked her right straight in the eye when he told her his decision. She didn't cry or beg any more after that," McPeters said. "She just stood up and thanked the governor and turned and walked respectfully out of the office with Milo and her husband behind her.

"The three of them drove on to Raiford that afternoon in an open-bed Model-T Ford pickup truck, the kind with no enclosed cab. (Years later, when Milo Cloversettle told me this story, he remembered that he almost froze to death in the December chill.) They visited Bill on Death Row that Sunday, and as they were leaving his mother took hold of his hand—with Wild Bill every bit of six feet and nearly two hundred pounds—and she held onto his hand as if he was a little boy. She held onto his hand and she told him, 'You be a man.' That was the last thing she said to him, and the last thing she said on the trip.

"The next morning, after the execution, she and Milo and the father went from Srarke, where they had spent the night, and collected Bill's body at the prison and drove back to Blountstown to bury him in the family plot.

"So," McPeters said. "Two boys delivered by the same midwife: one going to the chair, one defending the other. Not much of a coincidence. But I'm not through yet. Twenty-one years later, Milo Cloversettle was elected governor of Florida, and when he took office in January of 1948, the first death warrant to cross his desk was that of LeRoy Akins Masters, Wild Bill Masters's younger brother, born two years after Bill died in the chair and delivered by Aunt Bess, the same midwife who delivered both Milo and Bill."

Lincoln and Palo sat stiffly in their seats and waited for McPeters to go on.

"Young eighteen-year-old LeRoy had followed almost exactly in Wild Bill's shoes and had been sentenced to death for shooting a Calhoun County deputy sheriff.

"Almost twenty-two years to the day, in January 1948, LeRoy's mother and father, both in their late sixties by now, and their lawyer sat in the same positions before Governor Cloversettle as Cloversettle himself and the family had taken before Governor Platt in 1925. Again the mother begged for her son's life, but again it was useless; Cloversettle more or less repeated Governor Platt's words that he could not feel right with God if he spared the boy after what he had done. And again," McPeters said, his face hardening, "that woman shook hands with the governor and walked out of the office and rode to Raiford to collect another dead son and bury him.

"But this time," McPeters said, pausing, cupping his mouth with his hand, "this time," he repeated sourly, "the old woman went home from the funeral and walked into her bedroom and locked the door and took a shotgun out of the closet and stuck the barrel in her mouth and tripped the trigger.

"Governor Cloversettle signed seventeen death warrants," McPeters said, balling his fist and setting it on his knee, "but he told me he never thought about any of them except that first one for LeRoy Masters." McPeters stopped dead still and looked straight at Lincoln Daniels. "He used to tell me that he looked for a meaning from all that tangle for years, said he couldn't sleep for weeks after the boy's execution. But he said he never found a meaning. 'Maybe there's no meaning there,' he used to say. 'I don't know, but it seems like there should be some meaning. All that tangle,' he would say. 'All that tangle.'

"I saw the tangle too," McPeters said. "But like the governor, I never saw the meaning."

When McPeters finished speaking he reached for his drink once more and drained what little remained of it. He clinked the ice in the glass, and Coy Deal appeared instantly to take it for a refill. Lincoln and Palo had also finished their drinks, and Deal took their glasses away on a small wooden tray.

Lincoln was glad for the change of pace. They were coming at him too fast, these things that he wanted to digest, so he filled the time the houseboy was out of the room with small talk about nothing in particular, just idle chatter to relax his mind. Once Deal came back with fresh drinks and had departed, all three sat quietly. It was clear that McPeters still had things on his mind, things he had stored up for all the years he had worked at the prison and wanted to talk about, now that he had the right audience.

McPeters settled back in his big chair once more, sipped at his new drink, and, seeing that Daniels and Reyas were waiting for him to go on, began again, seemingly more relaxed, more comfortable with his subject and with his audience.

"There was another man I remember, Ben Stoker, who courted death and hell, too—courted them the way a man follows a woman. He was one of the meanest men I ever ran across, and on the morning he went out, hell was the only thing on his mind. Just like everything else in his life, Ben Stoker took it with a grain of salt. Stoker was set to go on the last Monday in October 1959. I remember it well, because I had just been appointed major two weeks before, and Stoker was my first execution as chief correctional officer in charge.

"About a month before his warrant was signed, Stoker and a convict by the name of Lonnie Arlis Hatcher got into a bad fight. Hatcher was a touch hog, a wild man," he explained. "The papers called him the Fair-Haired Boy of Death Row because he came from a wealthy family in St. Augustine; Stoker looked like an ape and had come from trash and had nothing. Hatcher had little Italian cigars and candy and warm socks and a portable radio; Stoker just had prison rations and home-roll cigarettes.

"But like I said, about a month before Stoker was set to go, he and Hatcher got into a knock-down, drag-out fight in the exercise yard outside Death Row. Stoker bit half of Hatcher's right ear off in the scuffle. Mrs. Hatcher wanted to have plastic surgery done on the ear." He chuckled. "Demanded it, she did. Said it was inhuman to let her son sit with only half an ear." McPeters stopped smiling and turned to face Lincoln Daniels. "Somebody reminded her that Lonnie was going to die pretty soon and that half an ear didn't matter. The poor old woman went insane on the spot, had to be carted back home in an ambulance.

"So," he went on, turning to include Palo Reyas in the story, "from the moment of the fight on, Stoker and Hatcher were on total outs. And every chance Stoker got, when he was being taken out to the exercise yard or for his shower, he would stop in front of Lonnie's cell and tell him that his ear was something all his family's money couldn't fix. My God, that would get Lonnie hot.

"Finally, on the morning he was supposed to go out, Stoker asked me if he could say something to Lonnie on his way to the chair. Hell, I thought he was going to say something like 'I'm sorry,' so I let him stop; I even felt good that he was going to get things straight.

"But, by God," McPeters continued, a thin smile forming on his lips, "this is what Stoker said to Hatcher —I remember the words exactly. 'Lonnie,' he said, 'they're going to kill me right now, and I know I'm going to hell. But there's one thing for sure: All your family's money and all their connections ain't going to keep you out of the chair much longer. In the meantime,' he said, smiling at Hatcher, 'I'm going on to hell to build up some seniority as the Devil's chief fireman, and when you get there, me and the old boy will turn up the flames on you.'

"Jesus," McPeters said, shaking his head. "That's about the toughest I ever saw a man go out."

"What did the other man say?" Lincoln Daniels asked, sitting forward on the couch.

McPeters looked at him and smiled a toothy smile. "He wasn't too happy, but as I remember it he didn't say anything."

"What did he do to get on Death Row?" Lincoln probed.

"Lonnie? Oh, Lonnie was a mighty bad boy. His car had a flat tire on the beach road between St. Augustine and Jacksonville Beach one summer day, and Lonnie, being a rich man's son, was not about to dirty his hands with changing a tire, so he flagged down the first car he saw and asked the driver to take him back to St. Augustine. Well, that's all well and good, but the first driver Lonnie flagged down was an elderly lady going toward Jacksonville Beach. She told him she'd give him a ride to Jax Beach but that she didn't have time to go back to St. Augustine.

"It all came out at the tiral," McPeters continued. "The woman was an old family friend and a well-respected person in the community, and Lonnie killed her because she wouldn't take him home on a hot summer's day. No, Lonnie was a bad boy; there was nothing fair-haired about him. And on the morning he was executed he went out like a yellow dog. I guess he knew Ben Stoker and the Devil *would* be waiting for him."

"So much meanness," Lincoln said, stiff from McPeters's last silence. "Meanness or madness. How could anyone carry on like that when he was about to die? No matter what he had done before, it seems that at the last minute he would make some sort of peace, some sort of repentance."

"I know it seems that way to you," McPeters said, "and after all the time it still seems that way to me on occasion. But the thing to remember is that the people who get on Death Row are like no other people on earth. I can't really put it into words," he went on, shifting his eyes to Palo Reyas, "but they're different.

"It's caring," McPeters added quickly, as if he were catching himself in mid-thought, his eyes returning to Lincoln. "That's probably the word. They've either stopped caring, or they never cared at all, not even the ones who go out screaming and crying and begging. They just don't give a damn. None of them."

"But they're human, they must care," Lincoln protested.

McPeters shook his head. "No."

"You're the expert, John. But I think they *do* care—but about the wrong things. Most of them seem to care about how to die, when what they should have addressed themselves to is how to live."

"Yes, but that's after the fact." Palo Reyas went back to words he had used earlier in the day. "All they have once they get on Death Row is death."

"Palo is right," McPeters said. "On the Row, death is everything."

"Yes," Lincoln Daniels agreed, pushing himself forward so that he was almost in McPeters's face, "but maybe the answer is this: Maybe the condemned don't care, or don't seem to care, because nothing they ever cared about worked out for them. Maybe, rich or poor—like Hatcher or Stoker—they have always been on the outside looking in. It's not really my idea," Lincoln explained. "It's something José Santos told me this afternoon, and it has been on my mind since. Because, like the Hatcher boy, Santos should not have ended up on Death Row."

McPeters thought for a moment. "That is a big judgment," he said softly, "and I'm glad I don't have to consider such things when I deal with convicts. You can't deal in big judgments when you guard people," he added with authority. "You deal only in what you see. And when I look at the men on Death Row

I see murderers or rapists, and the law says they should die. It is as simple and complex as that.

"I've seen men go out screaming and begging for mercy," McPeters went on. "I've seen men go out cursing God and man. And I've seen men go out so sick-scared they didn't know where they were. I've seen men who almost accidentally got on the Row, and I've seen others who killed deliberately once they were in prison—like two boys from south Florida who killed another boy from west Florida just so they could get on Death Row and have cigarettes.

"I even saw a man, a black from Miami, try to kill a guard on the morning of his execution as a favor to another inmate who was waiting to die and who didn't like the officer because he'd taken a magazine away from him. That's right," he said, nodding his head toward Lincoln's startled face. "The black made a key to his cell, and on the morning of his execution the other convict diverted the Death Watch guard's attention and called him out of his chair long enough for the black to get out of his cell and try to kill him with a knife he'd made from a Prince Albert tobacco can. An incredible story, really; a condemned murderer who died trying to kill someone else.

"That's why I say," McPeters went on, "that I don't deal in big judgments—just guarding. But I tell you and Palo this, though you probably won't believe it," he added, using his forefinger as a pointer. "With all the men I've seen die, there's nothing to going out. Nothing at all."

He sat back and took a sip of his drink and waited for a reply that did not come. After a few seconds he moved forward in his chair once more and addressed himself solely to Lincoln Daniels.

"That doesn't seem right, does it? Nothing at all."

Daniels didn't answer; he couldn't answer.

"And the last minutes," McPeters added, "go like quicksilver. Messy or not. You'll see what I mean in the morning."

9

Lincoln Daniels and Palo Reyas said good night to McPeters in front of his house just before eleven. Palo was standing on the steps having a final word with McPeters, and Lincoln stood on the ground by himself. It was ice cold and you could feel rain coming in the air, rain and a damp oppressiveness. McPeters's words would not go away from Lincoln's mind: *There's nothing to going out.* Over and over they rang in his ear: *Nothing to going out.* He wondered, the thought never leaving him; *the last minutes go like quicksilver,* he said to himself, while all the while the feeling dug deeper. *Like quicksilver.* . . .

THE ACT OF DEATH

The executioner turned onto the main street of Lake Butler at exactly seven fifteen, the instant the National Guard–Highway Patrol roadblock was lifted for the press on State Road 16 at the double entranceway to Big Max. The whereabouts and identity of the executioner had been like an unobtainable narcotic for the media; now, unseen on the deserted, damp-cold street twelve miles from the prison, he proceeded toward his appointed destination in total anonymity.

There was no more closely guarded secret in the State of Florida than the executioner's identity. It had taken six months to select the person from among the hundred and eighty-two applications that were received by the governor's office, and a full two weeks to plot the route and timetable to the prison the executioner was now following. Only three people knew who he was: Governor Morgan Kingsly, Warden Hugh Greenwood, and Major John McPeters. The executioner had refused the fee of $175 that was offered for each execution, so there would not even be pay records on file in Tallahassee. The secrecy was complete. The sole indication of his official status was the commission he carried, signed by Governor Kingsly, assigning the power to execute as prescribed by law.

As far as the world knew there was a vacuum where the executioner was concerned, and that was the way all parties desired it. There had been men and women applicants, the old and the young, the rich and the poor, the educated and the uneducated, professional people and day laborers, the socially prominent and the obscure, the sane and the mad. The cross section was unique, and the choice that Governor Morgan Kingsly made from among the top five names, after conferring with Warden Greenwood and Major Mc-Peters, was also unique.

The executioner, whose name was David Housley, was a forty-two-year-old Miami stockbroker, a man of wealth, father of four children and husband to a wife who was beautiful; a man who was bored with each and every thing he had touched for the past fifteen years.

Housley's letter of application fascinated Morgan Kingsly above all others. It was written on expensive, thick, plain bond typing paper, typed on an IBM Selectric typewriter, and mailed in a plain white envelope, and it contained only one perfectly typed and spaced paragraph. The letter read:

> I wish to make application for the position of executioner for the State of Florida. I was a clerk in the Navy during Korea and I never saw a shot fired in anger and never saw a dead body. I don't know how it would be to kill someone, but I know I could do it.

There were letters that said, "I'd kill the swine with my bare hands." And letters that said, "God has said that it is wrong to kill, but if it must be done then let it be done by one of his righteous servants." There were even letters that said, "I'm on Social Security and can't make ends meet. I don't like the idea of killing anyone, but if I've got to eat and pay my mortgage, then so be it."

Most of the hundred and eighty-two letters simply said that the applicant wanted to be considered for the job of executioner; David Housley's letter was the only one that said the applicant knew he could kill. That thought fascinated Governor Kingsly; in mid-January, when he summoned Housley to his executive office in Tallahassee, he was even more surprised by the man he saw before him.

David Housley was five-ten and weighed one-eighty—just above medium height and weight—and he carried himself like a well-conditioned athlete. He was a handsome man, rugged looking, with the acquired look of culture that comes to people who work at it. He had a long, full, high-cheekboned face, and thick straight sandy-brown hair that he combed straight back to the base of his neck with a slight, almost indistinguishable part to the left. His sideburns were cut off even with his earlobes, and he wore a thick, well-trimmed moustache that was tapered down and cut off even with the break of his lips so that there was no droop. His dress was classic stockbroker: a gray pin-striped Brooks Brothers suit, a starched white J. Press shirt, a silk maroon Christian Dior tie, and highly polished black English Church's shoes. Everything about him breathed money and security; only his eyes gave him away.

His brown eyes looked dead. In the forty-third year of his life, David Housley was terminally bored. He jogged two miles each morning on the well-sculptured streets around his two-story colonial Dinner Key home, and he worked out in a boxing gym on First Avenue three times a week, beating underfed Cubans senseless for $5 a round. During the winter billfish season he fished for sailfish off the Cay Sal rocks in the Bahamas, and in the spring when the giant tuna ran by Bimini, he was there, tying up his thirty-foot Trojan Sport Sedan to Brown's Docks, drinking himself into oblivion at night at the Complete Angler in Alice Town.

His life seemed like the Island in the Sun myth of the Great American Dream come true, but once Housley obtained it, he found it meant nothing to him. For years he had dreamed of sailing away, leaving his wife and children and heading out to the southern Caribbean or some end-of-the-line place like Belize City, Belize, or a sleepy Costa Rican seaport town, or a semideserted piece of rock like Cayman Brac south of Cuba. But he had concern for his wife and children and had not left. For years he had thought of taking a mistress. But that was too complicated.

At forty-two, he was a man cut off from everything but his business, which, after seventeen years, he performed almost by rote. He was eaten up by hate and disgust, a man who had more than once considered suicide; a man for whom death had become a fascination. He truly believed that the executions presented themselves to him as a perfect outlet for his frustrations. He had not reasoned it out, but it did occur to him that the act of execution might save him personally. As for the condemned prisoners, he had no vengeance for them whatsoever. He was not even interested in their crimes. From his distance, they did not even appear to be real.

As he drove on through the sleeping town of Lake Butler and turned northeast through swampy bottomland dotted with stands of tall pines and boggy fields dominated by small black ponds ringed with stoic gray cypresses, David Housley felt good in the warmth of the big, solid car he had rented at the Gainesville airport the previous evening. He felt almost an air of vacation. He had not jogged that morning, and there had been no forced conversation with his wife and children, and there would be none of the pressures and confrontations of his business. The idea sat strangely with him, but still the feeling of vacation tried to dominate his mind. And in the veil of secrecy that surrounded him there was also the feeling of importance.

By prearrangement, he had taken the 5:00 P.M. Eastern flight out of Miami for Gainesville. He bought the ticket with his American Express card in his own name, and when he flew into the Gainesville Airport an hour later, he rented a brown Mercury Marquis and drove into Gainesville and registered at the Flagler Inn across the street from the entrance to the University of Florida, all in his own name. He was a Miami stockbroker in town to make calls on clients; the cover was airtight. He spent a quiet evening at the hotel, taking dinner in his room. He called Warden Greenwood and reported in at eight, and then at nine he called his wife and children and told them he would return to Miami the following afternoon after he had called on his clients. He had seen no one at the hotel and no one had seen him; there was not a hint of suspicion from either family or business associates.

He had left the hotel at five thirty this morning and had coffee and a donut at an all-night restaurant, and then he drove northwest out of the city on State Road 121 into the rolling hill country, through the small farm towns of La Crosse, Worthington Springs, Dukes, and finally Lake Butler, a complete back-roads trip that cut him off from any contact with the press or, for that matter, the outside world.

Now before him the narrow black-top highway turned due east on a line for the prison, and the country raised up a bit out of the swamps and became hard-packed gray soil dotted by clumps of scrub oaks and the ever-present stands of slash pines. The cold, rainy half dark made the played-out countryside look all the more forlorn, but David Housley paid no attention. He felt a paradoxical quiet and excitement that he had not known in years; not, he was aware, since his high school days when he was the star fullback for Olney High School in the northwest rowhouse section of Philadelphia.

He passed through the sad little two-store town of Raiford at 7:23 A.M. and continued due east on State Road 16 toward the Florida State Prison's outer perimeter, two miles distant. He barely glanced at the town; he was aware only of his own supreme sense of well-being and excitement.

7:23 A.M.

At exactly 7:15, the instant the press had been let into the Big Max parking lot, the noise began. Now, eight minutes later, Major John McPeters was out in the prison's main corridor headed back for the Death Facility. He was in a frenzy. He was three minutes behind his pin-perfect schedule. In the midst of the oppressive din he rattled the first of the Death Facility's three-door maze, and instantly the maze began to open before him like a bank vault.

A second before he entered the maze, McPeters turned and stared down the completely deserted hall whose huge tunnel space was illuminated by harsh caged-in flourescent lights. At measured three-second intervals the noise came in on him; it seemed to be pushing the concrete and steel walls in; it seemed to have become part of the hall's stale air.

"No! . . . No! . . . No! . . . No! . . . No! . . . No! . . ." The chant came in like madness from a professional basketball game.

Goddammit! McPeters said to himself in silent rage. *Gone to hell in a hatbox. Goddammit it to hell!* He turned and began to bull his way through the maze.

The riot on Saturday had been violent and destructive, but now there was only noise, only the chant. Would it stay that way? McPeters asked himself as he passed the last door of the maze and charged into his office.

Standing along the left wall like three tree trunks were Bob Griffis, Earl Hancock, and Hank Chrysler, McPeters's Death Strap squad. McPeters's eyes flashed to Griffis. "How is it on the Row?" he asked through tight lips, his hands on his hips, a thick line of sweat on his forehead.

"Like they started," Griffis answered quickly, shifting his weight forward on the balls of his feet, his eyes meeting McPeters"s straight on. "Singin' that same goddamned word. Just standin' there at the front of their cells, singin' that word like crazies. All of 'em except on the first floor. Those bastards are just sittin' quiet and waitin' for a miracle."

"Okay," McPeters answered, wiping the sweat from his forehead. "I've got everybody out and standing in the corridors with tear gas, and I've called in all the other shifts. And the National Guard and the

Highway Patrol are standing by outside with riot guns. They can holler all they want, but if just one god-damned cup gets thrown, the gas starts. I don't give a goddamn if the TV cameras and every homo from New York is out front, we will by God keep order here and do our business this morning. There won't be a repeat of Saturday. If I have to use guns, then guns it will be.

"Now let's get to work," he said to the three, and he turned on his heel out the door.

As they came to the closed door of the Ready Cell, McPeters turned again to face his three guards. "Quick and firm," he said formally. "And no bullshit from us or them. We can't use the Preparation any more, and I don't know what difference that will make, but we don't have to take shit. We can't kick ass like the old days, but I tell you again"—his eyes were fiery—"we don't have to take shit."

"This sure as hell ain't like it used to be," Earl Hancock, who had helped execute Fallon and Burns thirteen years before, said with disgust.

"Nothing is like it was before. Not a goddamned thing. Now let's move," McPeters ordered. And he rapped on the cell's steel door with his knuckles—sharp, measured raps like the chanting that pulsated around them.

7:25 A.M.

Both matrons, Esther Todd and Billie Johnson, were with Alice Fuller when John McPeters entered the cramped outer area before the bars of the Ready Cell. McPeters's three-man Death Strap squad remained beyond the cell's outer door, in the corridor, as McPeters went inside to face the two matrons, who stood between him and the cell's inner door like bloated, protective hens.

The instant Alice Fuller saw McPeters she threw herself on her wall bunk and began screaming into her pillow.

"No, Jesus!" she cried. "No! God have mercy . . . *please!* I don't want to die . . . please, God . . . I don't want to die! Please . . . I beg you . . . *please!*"

McPeters and the two grim matrons sized each other up, but McPeters erased any thought of a confrontation when he spoke. "This is a thing that has got to be done, and done quick," he said, eyeing first one woman and then the other, paying no heed to Alice Fuller's cries. "We can do it the easy way or we can do it the hard way." A slight movement of his head brought his Death Strap squad into the sight of the two women.

Alice Fuller kept on with her pathetic cries as the two women looked at each other. But there was no argument. The time was almost upon them. Alice Fuller was out of their hands now, and they knew it and were secretly glad of it. The two matrons stared at each other for a few seconds and then parted to allow McPeters access to the Ready Cell's barred door.

McPeters had been holding a wide ring of Death Facility keys as he stood talking to the matrons. Once they gave way, he deftly inserted a large, worn brass key into the cell's door, turned it a strong three-quarter turn to the right, withdrew the key, and was standing inside the cell in front of Alice Fuller before the matrons or the terror-struck woman knew what had happened.

"Alice," McPeters said, in a voice that came from the back of his throat, "you have to go with us for just a minute, and then you can come right back here."

There was no reaction.

"Alice," he repeated, saying the name with a measured but subtle increase in tone and firmness, a change sufficient to turn Alice Fuller's head up in his direction, her eyes glazed with fear. "Get up and come with me. There's no need for me to touch you. You stand up and come on your own."

There was no response.

"Stand up *now*," he said in a voice that still retained its hint of understanding, but with a tone of command sufficient to bring Alice Fuller unsteadily to her feet. "Follow me," he added quickly, once the woman was standing. "Your matrons will be with you, and you will come back here in only minutes." He stepped back between the matrons and backed out into the hallway, Alice Fuller following at a distance in his footsteps as if he were the Pied Piper.

Outside the Ready Cell, McPeters turned around and took three short paces to the left to reach the Preparation Room. Alice Fuller was inside before she was fully aware of her movements, but once she saw the room's dilapidated barber chair, she panicked, thinking it was the electric chair.

McPeters was already inside the room, and the two matrons had just gone inside behind Alice Fuller. At the sight of the chair the condemned woman flung herself around, her bony arms raised in flight, and wheeled forward toward the door, screaming.

"Gaaaaad!" she cried, her cracking voice sounding all the more shrill over the muffled *No*'s that kept on as if played on a recording.

Griffis and Hancock were in the doorway, plugging the opening like a bricked-up wall; Alice Fuller hit them with her frailty and bounced back, slumping to the floor in a cold faint.

McPeters seized the moment instantly. "Get her up!" he ordered his two guards. "Up and into the chair. Quick!" He turned his attention on the two matrons. "Stand over there," he demanded, pointing to the room's bare left wall.

The two women jumped at the sound of his voice.

Then McPeters's eyes shifted to his third guard, Hank Chrysler. "Get the clippers," he ordered in a steady but biting voice. "Quick and efficient, now," he said to all three guards. "Let's move."

In seconds, Alice Fuller's slumping body was in the barber chair, her head back on the raised leather headrest, her arms held in place on the armrests by Griffis and Hancock, as Hank Chrysler moved to her rear and plugged the clippers into a wall socket. Then he stepped up directly behind the woman and turned the clippers on. The *buzzzz* filled the tiny room. Billie Johnson put her hand over her mouth and turned away from the sight.

Hank Chrysler went to work quickly, positioning his left hand on the back of Alice Fuller's bone-thin neck, pushing her head forward slightly as he started the clippers at the base of her neck and worked up the sides of her head, a system that left an eighth-inch stubble of fuzz between rows of limp, dangling reddish-gray hair. In forty-five seconds he had Alice Fuller's head clipped clean, childlike and egg-shaped.

"Quickly now," McPeters ordered Chrysler, as he saw Alice Fuller start to stir, a slight movement at first, a short jerk from her waist to her shoulder blades.

Chrysler complied instantly and with precision, bending down and unplugging the clippers, then moving swiftly toward the table on the right side of the wall near the barber chair. At the table he picked up a stainless-steel safety razor and a small white washcloth and sidestepped with the two objects to the small sink on the wall between the barber chair and the table. McPeters had the sink's single tap on. Chrysler held the two objects under the cold water for seconds; then, when McPeters turned the water off, Chrysler squeezed the cloth nearly dry and moved back behind Alice Fuller's clipped head. It was weaving as the woman slowly began to regain consciousness.

"Move," McPeters said to Chrysler.

The guard dabbed at the top of the woman's head —a point at the center of the skull, midway between the sides—with the wet washcloth. The cold water brought Alice Fuller back to consciousness. Her eyes opened with a jerk of her head just as Chrysler began to shave the circular four-inch spot where the Death Cap's contact pad would sit in place, attached to one of the electrical leads. Alice Fuller made a gulping, vomitlike sound as she came fully awake, her wild eyes searching the faces of the two guards who held her arms, her neck contorting as she attempted to turn her head up to see what Chrysler was doing above her.

"*Eeeaaaauuuupp!*" Alice Fuller gasped. "What? . . . *What?* . . . I . . . I . . . dead . . . dead . . . you . . . I . . . I . . . Oh, *God!*"

Her eyes tried to find the matrons, who stood paralyzed against the wall. In seconds, the condemned woman had located their stiff forms. "Missus Todd! . . . Missus Todd," she screamed. "I'm dying! . . . It's here . . . I'm *dying!* . . . Help me . . . help me!"

McPeters stopped the two matrons in their tracks with the outstretched palm of his right hand as they started to go to Alice Fuller. Then he turned his attention to the condemned woman herself, reaching behind her and grabbing her clipped head between his enormous hands like a vice. "Shave her!" he ordered Chrysler, his voice loud but totally controlled.

The hands shut off Alice Fuller's cries as if McPeters had disconnected her brain, but the woman's face was the mirror to her mind; it was twisted, her thin purple lips like wet putty.

Goddammit! McPeters said to himself as he held the woman's head. *The Preparation would end all this hysterical bullshit. How in hell is all this going to work out right without the Preparation?*

In fifteen seconds, Chrysler had the Contact Pad spot shaved bald; the instant it was done, McPeters shifted his position to the woman's legs, pinning each back against the chair's footrest like matchsticks.

"Now the ankle," McPeters ordered. "Let's move! Let's move!" he demanded, as Chrysler bent down by Alice Fuller's right leg, wet a wide spot six inches above the ankle, and began to shave off the short stubble of hairs for a proper connection with the Ground Pad.

Alice Fuller strained her neck down to see what the men were doing to her leg and began screaming again, but McPeters cut her off short.

"Shut up! Goddamn you, you bitch! Shut up or I'll club you!" he thundered. "Shut up, *now!*"

After a few more seconds they were through and

Chrysler and McPeters stood up, nodding for the two guards to release their grips on the now silent and stiff Alice Fuller.

As Chrysler hastily began putting the razor and washcloth away beside the clippers, McPeters gave orders to the two matrons. In the barber chair Alice Fuller remained motionless, as rigid as if she were still being held.

"I want her showered and back in her cell in five minutes," he commanded, his eyes darting to the shower stall in the rear of the room. "Change her into her other clothes in her cell," he went on, facing the two women directly at four feet. "Do it *now*," he said, as he made a motion to turn from them. "I want her dressed, and the Ready Cell's doors closed when I come back this way." He paused. "And I want no more problems."

As he turned and left the room, with his three guards in step behind him, McPeters did not look at Alice Fuller, who remained as silent as a mannequin in the barber chair.

7:30 A.M.

The *No*'s echoed on the top two floors of Death Row as they did in every other part of Big Max, but there was no chanting on the first floor. The inmates there were too close to the thing, too close to the three who were about to die.

McPeters and his Death Strap squad swept onto Death Row in full stride, the three guards first, McPeters, now in the rear, pausing just long enough to relock the Row's heavy steel door. All three Death Watch guards were on their feet the moment the door was opened. At the first cell, George Kruger's, McPeters came up to face Kruger's Death Watch guard,

Homer Tull. The broad-shouldered, broad-gutted old cracker's face was lined with strain.

"This's a helluva mess," Tull drawled, his words running together around his wad of snuff.

McPeters nodded agreement. "And it'll probably get worse," he said. He turned his attention to Kruger, who was lying face down on his wall bunk, his blanket over his head. "Kruger," McPeters said, moving over to the bars.

George Kruger shook violently and pulled the blanket tight around his head.

"Kruger!"

Kruger's knees bunched up under him, placing him on the bunk like an ostrich with his head in the sand and his rear end in the air.

"*George!*" McPeters bellowed, hands wrapped through the bars. "Up on your feet and over here. Now!" He rattled the condemned man's cell door. "*Now,* damn you! Or I'm comin' in!"

McPeters's voice had been the single sound on the Row; George Kruger's rolling off his bunk and falling onto the concrete floor became the second sound. If it was possible, George Kruger was as frightened of McPeters as he was of death itself.

"I'm up, major. *Eeeaaaahuuu!* God!" Kruger cried, holding onto the sides of his face, his teeth chattering with fright. "I'm up like you told me," he screamed in his woman's voice, bouncing on his sock feet like a drunken dancer. "*Eeeeeee,*" he whined again, still bouncing. "Major!" His mouth was pulled back so far in fright it seemed that it might tear.

"Come over here to the bars, George," McPeters commanded, his voice returned to normal.

Kruger could not move.

"You're not leaving your cell, George. No harm is going to come to you. Just do as you're told."

Still Kruger couldn't move. His mind screamed to obey, but his legs were fear-frozen.

"*Now!*" McPeters bellowed.

Kruger jumped two steps, and his hands hit the bars just below McPeter's grip. Instantly, McPeters had the thin man's hands through the bars, and in seconds Bob Griffis had handcuffs on the pale, birdlike wrists.

Kruger's mouth was shut but his teeth chattered and his eyes rolled in fear.

"Just stand perfectly still, George," McPeters ordered him, as he opened the condemned man's cell door. "We'll be through with you in a minute and then you can go back to bed. Just stand still," he said, as Hank Chrysler plugged a long extension cord into a wall socket behind the Death Watch guard's folding chair and attached the connection to the cord on his clippers.

From his vantage point at the barred wall of his cell, George Kruger watched Chrysler. He did not see or hear Earl Hancock, who came up in front of him and dropped to his knees, looping a leather belt through the bars just above his ankles. In an instant, Hancock had the belt in behind Kruger's legs and through the bars and into an open buckle. When Kruger felt the belt being cinched, it was too late. Homer Tull reached forward and grabbed Kruger's handcuffed arms and pulled his face flush with the bars, and Hancock pinned his legs to the bars with the belt.

"Major!" Kruger shrieked. "Don't kill me! Please . . . I cant' die . . . *Please!* . . . Somebody, help!"

McPeters was inside the cell with Kruger now, with Chrysler right behind him. He reached out and grabbed Kruger's hair and pulled his head back roughly. "You're a damn fool, boy," he said savagely, his lips almost at Kruger's ear. "You *can* die, but it will be a while yet . . . a while yet." His voice trailed off as he controlled himself and released Kruger's hair, wiping his hand on his trouser leg as if the hair were diseased.

The moment McPeters let go of Kruger's hair, Hank Chrysler clicked the clippers on and moved in on the condemned man as he had with Alice Fuller. He grabbed Kruger's neck and began clipping in up-and-down rows. The *buzzzz* of the clippers became the only sound in the hot corridor of Death Row, except for the unceasing *No*'s from the outside.

José Santos was standing flush with the far wall of his cell, between his wall bunk and his stainless-steel sink, when Peeping John McPeters and his Death Strap squad came in front of his cell's bars. The instant McPeters saw Santos's position, he knew there was going to be a fight. He stopped rock still at the door and found the Cuban's tight eyes.

"Son," he said in an almost gentle voice, "come over here. What you've got on your mind don't count for nothing. Believe me when I tell you that—it's been tried before and it comes to nothing."

McPeter's feet were poised like a boxer's, left before right, spread out a fraction more than shoulder length, both arms hanging down slightly crooked at the elbows. When he finished speaking, he locked his jaw and tightened his triceps and neck for a fight and waited for Santos's reply.

"It will count for something," Santos said deliberately, his eyes never leaving McPeters's face.

"You won't get a punch in, sonofabitch," Hank Chrysler broke in violently. "Motherfucker!"

Santos tightened into a steel spring and said nothing.

McPeters whirled on Chrysler. "No marks!" he barked. "No marks and no bullshit! This is not a goddamned street fight! This is work, Hank. Goddammit, when in hell are you gonna get that through your head?" McPeters's fists were balled into clubs; he towered over Chrysler.

"Major, the cocksucker!" the guard pleaded.

"Business! Goddammit, business!" McPeters drummed out. "And no marks," he instructed again, his voice like a piston.

McPeters opened the cell door. Hank Chrysler went in to the left, Bob Griffis went to the right, McPeters came in at the middle, and the Death Watch guard, Joe Morris, and Earl Hancock, the third Death Strap guard, stayed planted outside the open cell door. José Santos jammed his buttocks hard against the stone wall, balled his fists, and pushed forward slightly on the balls of his feet.

Chrysler came in just as Santos had wanted him to, and his movement into the guard was like a striking rattlesnake.

"Bum!" Santos cried out as he slammed his right fist into Chrysler's thick neck. "Scumbag!" he shouted as he kneed Chrysler in the crotch, sending the big guard sinking to the cell floor like a rubber bag full of water.

"Damn!" McPeters raged as he came in on Santos, sending the smaller man slamming back against the cell wall with a jackhammer right to his stomach.

"Fucker!" Bob Griffis shouted like a rifle shot as he clubbed Santos on the back of the neck, the thudding blow coming at the exact second that Santos's head bounced off the wall from the force of McPeters's punch.

The Cuban's head banged onto the bare cell floor.

"See to Chrysler," McPeters shouted over his shoulder to Joe Morris.

The other two Death Watch guards were on their feet, but they knew they had to stay with their prisoners.

Joe Morris dragged the unconscious Chrysler out of the cell and began to revive him in the hallway. McPeters and Bob Griffis jerked the semiconscious Santos to his feet and shoved him into the cell's barred wall. McPeters moved outside the cell and handcuffed the Cuban's hands through the bars as he had done before with Kruger. Then Earl Hancock came in and bent down quickly and cinched Santos's legs together at his ankles with the belt, through the bars. Santos came back to full consciousness, shaking the punches from his head with violent left-to-right head motions.

McPeters watched him as Hancock finished strapping his feet together.

"Give me your belt," McPeters demanded of Joe Morris, who was still working on the motionless Chrysler.

Morris pushed himself up off the corridor floor and quickly pulled his belt out of the loops of his uniform trousers. McPeters took the belt and turned back to the bars.

"Take it," he ordered Bob Griffis, inside the cell. "Put it around his neck and hand the end out to me."

McPeters got the end and ran it through the buckle. He cinched it tight—jamming Santos's nose through an opening, pushing his eyes up even with two of the bars—and held on to the loose end. "You see," he said, jerking the belt even tighter, his face separated from Santos's by only the two inches of steel bars, "it was nothing. Not even shit," he added, jerking the belt again.

Santos blinked his eyes and grimaced under the tugging of the belt at his neck, grinding his face into the bars. "Something," he made himself say, his hands grabbing for McPeters's hands, his mouth wedged so close to the bars that the words came out garbled.

"Nothing!" McPeters came back roughly, pulling at the belt again, watching Santos's hands fall away.

"Some—" Santos muttered, a choking pull of the belt finally cutting off his words.

"Nothing!" McPeters screamed into his face. *"No goddamned thing! Get that straight. Nothing!"*

Santos's eyes were closed under the strain of the belt and he was silent.

"Get on with your work," McPeters said to Earl Hancock, who had the clippers now that Chrysler was hurt. Hancock turned on his clippers and moved up behind Santos and started to cut his hair.

"Damn," Santos muttered thickly, moving nothing but his mouth.

This time McPeters let the word come out without a pull on the belt.

On the corridor floor, Hank Chrysler moaned and started back to consciousness, his knees jammed up

under his chest because of the biting pain in his
groin.

7:38 A.M.

As McPeters and his Death Strap squad started for
Charlie Parker's cell, José Santos was left strung up on
the bars of his cell like a buck deer hung for show. Mc-
Peters turned and faced him one final time before he
moved on to the next cell.

"You're gonna stay right there a while longer, son,
and get your mind right. I've seen a lot of men go out,
and goin' out like you got it planned is the wrong
way. I don't know what the right way is," he added,
"but I do know you're on the wrong track."

Santos said nothing. His eyes were closed. He did
not want to look at McPeters. They had never been
equal, and Santos had known that, but now it was
worse. Now, like the others, Santos, clipped and shaved,
had the halfway look of being between life and death.

"Watch him," McPeters said to Joe Morris, the
Death Watch guard. Then McPeters nodded to his
squad and they moved on to Charlie Parker's cell.

McPeters was sure Parker would put up a bad
fight. "You hold back," he said to the still dazed Hank
Chrysler, whose face mirrored the pain he was in, and
went on to Parker's Death Watch guard, Ham Pervis.
"Ham, you get in with us."

Pervis, fat but as violent as a bulldog, nodded in
agreement and tightened his shoulder muscles, his sour,
meaty-jowled face coming alive after the boredom of
eight hours of sitting in front of the cell. "Like old
times," he said, grinning wolfishly.

McPeters scowled, "Give me your belt," he said,
directing his words to Earl Hancock.

Before Hancock could get his hands on his belt,
Charlie Parker spoke, his words strong and clear.

"There won't be any need for that," he said, moving up close to the bars of his cell, "I'm clean," he said, turning his bald head down to McPeters, then pulling up the right leg of his gray overalls. "I don't want anybody touching me," he went on, dropping the trouser leg and standing up erect to match McPeters's height. "And I don't want any trouble," he ended, his eyes still and centered on McPeters.

"How did this happen?" McPeters said, turning to face Pervis.

"I don't know," the guard said, shaking his head, his heavy face tightening under McPeters's hard stare. "Yesterday, I guess. Hell, he don't wear no hair anyway. Goddammit, I guess the sonofabitch did it sometime yesterday. He sure as hell ain't done it since I come on at midnight."

McPeters turned back to Parker. He looked at the black man for a second and then grunted. "You're a smart fellow," he said.

Parker made no reply.

"Real smart," McPeters said.

Parker held his silence, standing like a thundercloud in his cell.

"I don't want any trouble either," McPeters said, his voice showing dissatisfaction at Parker's silence. "You gonna show your ass like Santos when your time comes?" he probed. Perhaps he should go in anyway and take some of the fight out of Parker as they had done with Santos.

Still Parker said nothing.

McPeters pushed his face up into the bars of Parker's cell. "We'll carry both of you down to the chair on stretchers if we have to," he said savagely. "That's my promise to you and the Cuban. It don't matter shit to me. There are two ways to go down there, and you know the name of both."

As he passed Santos's cell, McPeters faced Joe Morris, the Death Watch guard, and handed him the keys to Santos's handcuffs. "Let him down in a few minutes, and hand his going-out clothes in to him."

Then McPeters turned to Santos.

"He can put the clothes on or not. He can fight

or not," he said, talking past the condemned man, who still had his eyes closed. "Eyes open or closed," he went on, "however he wants it. But one thing is for damn sure"—and he turned and faced straight down the corridor toward the Death Chamber—"he is going out. *Four* are going out," he added, grinding his teeth as he started toward the steel door.

7:40 A.M.

The prison chaplain, Arthur Turner, and a Catholic priest from Starke were standing in the middle of the hallway between Death Row's steel door and the closed steel door to the Death Chamber when McPeters led his Death Strap squad off the Row. Standing with the two men, as escort, was Norman Hills, one of Hugh Greenwood's two deputy wardens.

Bob Griffis had the keys now. He locked the Row's door behind the squad and McPeters; then he and the other two guards went down the hall to McPeters's office, with Hank Chrysler still visibly in pain as he walked.

"What's the matter with him?" Hills asked McPeters, who had still not acknowledged his presence or the presence of the two ministers.

All three men were about half McPeters's size. He stood for a second watching Chrysler walk down the hall, silently evaluating, by the way he walked, whether the guard would have to be replaced. When he had made up his mind that Chrysler would be all right, McPeters turned to the three men before him, looking at his watch before he spoke.

"It's seven forty," he said roughly, without exchanging a single introductory word with the three. "I'm behind schedule. Because of that," he went on, indicating the drumming outside *No*'s.

"You've got fifteen minutes, not a second more,"

he said, without the slightest regard for Hills's paper authority, an authority that did not reach him at all. "By law, you've got to be off the Row at exactly seven fifty-five." His eyes moved between the two ministers, purposely excluding the thirty-one-year-old Hills, whom he considered to be totally worthless as a prison man.

"But, major, I think—" Hills began.

"No," McPeters boomed, going for Hills's eyes now. The younger man's face flushed blood red. "You leave at seven fifty-five. Am I clear?"

The two ministers nodded. Hills balked but said nothing, jamming his hands into the pockets of his cheap wool sport coat.

"Have you already seen the woman?" McPeters asked Turner.

"Yes," the prison chaplain answered in his nasal drawl.

"All right, then," McPeters said, stepping back to leave the three men. "Fifteen minutes!"

He turned and headed down the hall for his office. His mind was not on the ministers at all; it was on the executioner.

It was time to bring him to the Row.

7:42 A.M.

David Housley was sitting in a small windowless office in the Main Prison's Administration Building, a squat, bunkerlike structure that was separated from the Main Prison's grounds on a dead grass lawn out from the prison's Main Gate. His rented car was parked out from the Main Gate in a row of prison vehicles. The Administration Building's office workers had been told not to report for work until the regular business hour of 9:00 A.M. Positioned across New River, on the Union County side of the prison complex, two and a half miles from Big Max's Death Facility, he was completely cordoned off from the press and from all onlookers except Harley Sewell, Big Max's day lieutenant, who had been pressed into service by McPeters and given the task of shepherding the executioner to the Death Chamber.

Housley had cleared the National Guard–Highway Patrol roadblock at the Raiford side of the prison grounds at 7:27 and was allowed straight through with the letter he had produced, a document signed by the governor, stating that Housley was a state medical examiner. The name on the letter and on the clipboard lists the officers had was Dr. Calvin Landon.

From the roadblock Housley had proceeded directly to the Administration Building, where he was met by Lieutenant Sewell, an imposing six-three two-twenty figure of a man who had been standing on the Administration Building's entrance walkway at the center of the parking lot—standing there in the freezing rain in a black prison raincoat with a plastic cover over his blue officer's cap with his arms crossed in such a way that Housley had the distinct impression that the guard was actually warding off the icy rain with his own stubbornness.

The two men had never met before, but Sewell had been told that Housley was driving a brown Mercury, and he had a complete description of him from McPeters. Sewell was not to know Housley's name and was to address him only as Dr. Landon, but he knew that the man was the executioner. In the small briefcase McPeters had given him earlier that morning there was a black hood with two small eyeholes, the hood Housley would wear when he was taken from the Administration Building across New River to the Death Chamber.

Sewell sat in silence, sipping at a half-cold cup of coffee, waiting for McPeters's call. Housley had drunk sparingly from his coffee cup; he now sat staring at the blank wall opposite Sewell. The two men had not spoken—McPeters had told Sewell not to talk to Housley unless the executioner wanted to talk.

"I'm not too much in favor of the man," McPeters

had told Sewell, as he had earlier told Governor Kingsly and Warden Greenwood. "He is a smart man, and
smart men think. We need someone who won't think.
We need someone who will act, someone who will do
what he's told."

Sewell could not read Housley as he watched him
in the small room. He could not tell if the executioner
was thinking about the act or not, but to the officer
he seemed steady enough. His face was stern and un-
flinching.

Sewell checked the room's wall clock: 7:42. He
knew McPeters would call any second; when he noticed
that Housley was not looking at the clock, he took it
for a good sign. Five seconds past 7:42, the call came;
the black phone on the room's single desk seemed to
explode with the first ring. Housley held firm.

Sewell picked the phone up, almost before the
first ring had died. McPeters told him to bring the man
over, adding, "Is he okay?"

Sewell said yes, hung the phone up quickly, and
reached for the briefcase at his feet. He put the
briefcase on his knees and opened it; inside there was
only the black hood. Without speaking, he handed it to
Housley.

Housley took the small black hood quickly and
held it in his hands and looked at it. Nothing he had
done thus far had been unrehearsed. The plane ride
to Gainesville, renting the car, the hotel room, the
back-door drive to the prison from Gainesville through
Lake Butler, meeting Lieutenant Sewell, the hood,
his conveyance to the Death Chamber, and testing
the chamber's workings with Warden Greenwood,
Cabel Lasseter, the electrician, and Major John Mc-
Peters had all been practiced two weeks before, with
Housley under the curtain of the Dr. Landon identity.
Nothing he had done or seen this morning had been
a surprise or was unexpected; everything was as
planned. But now, the second time he held the hood,
it felt different. Housley's mind recorded the difference
and labeled it *active*—that was how the hood felt,
active—the difference between training with a rifle in
basic training and firing it in combat. And although

Housley had not been in combat, his mind recorded the difference with precision.

But the thought was with Housley for only a second, and he did not allow it to be transmitted from his face to Sewell. As if seeking shelter under it, Housley opened the drawstring bottom of the hood and, with a rapid motion, slipped the black egg-shaped garment over his head. It gave him the look of a man from another planet.

He stood up briskly and allowed Sewell to help him on with his tan trenchcoat; as Housley adjusted the coat, Sewell put on his wet prison raincoat, and then the two men, Sewell first and Housley one step behind him, left the office and walked across the highly buffed tile floor of the building to the front doors and out onto an entranceway that fronted State Road 16. In seconds they were in Sewell's prison sedan heading east on the highway past the Main Prison's fence.

At the end of the fencerow, Sewell turned right and followed the path McPeters had used to take Lincoln Daniels and Palo Reyas to the Death Facility the previous day. Out of the shallow eyehole recesses in the hood, David Housley watched Big Max take shape and form before him in the cold gray morning rain. They crossed the wooden bridge over New River and drove up the steep hill and came to ground level with the prison. Housley sat dead still on the car seat beside the massive Sewell, positioning the palms of his hands on the balls of his knees and keeping his head erect and staring straight forward. His gut was as tight as a knot.

As the sedan came in line with Big Max's back fence, Sewell departed from McPeters's route the previous day and turned left instead of going right for the emergency entrance McPeters had used for Daniels and Reyas. Sewell drove straight for Big Max's North Gate, the prison's regular vehicle gate. But unlike every other vehicle that passed through the gate, Sewell's did not stop for a search and shakedown. As soon as the two-gate maze was opened, Sewell sped inside and turned left and raced the car along the fence line until he came to an abrupt stop behind the protecting wall that stood before the Death Chamber's outside door. Out from the wall four gleamingly polished black ambulances stood parked, their surfaces covered with big round drops of cold rain.

The ambulances were an addition to the routine Housley had rehearsed; momentarily they threw him off, interrupted the well-planned antiseptic scheme of things for him. His bowels tightened, but he gave no sign of his feelings. There were no second thoughts in his mind. The excitement of the moment dominated him. But the ambulances did give a new dimension, a dimension Housley would not let his mind dwell on. As soon as the car stopped, Sewell darted from behind the wheel and out into the rain in front of the car, bound for Housley's side. Before he could reach the door, Housley was also outside and standing in the rain in front of the Death Chamber door. As they came together, both men were looking straight up at the three tiers of Death Row, past the fenced-in exercise yard. From the top two floors of the Row the sound was deafening and in unison:

"*No! . . . No! . . . No! . . . No! . . . No! . . . No!*"

"Jesus," Sewell muttered, as he took Housley's arm and turned him toward the Death Chamber door that came open before Sewell knocked.

"Damn," Sewell said as he led Housley inside the open doorway past McPeters.

"How long has this been goin' on?" he mumbled, still holding onto Housley's arm.

"About thirty minutes," McPeters said gravely. "Thirty goddamned minutes!"

Housley heard the Death Chamber's steel door close behind him with a rattling thud and felt Sewell let go of his arm. Then he was in the center of the room before the electric chair, facing the members of the Death Committee. His mind raced in a million directions. He felt an excitement that seemed sexual.

The Death Committee was made up of thirteen people: three convicts, nine prison officers, and the executioner.

The three convicts were two medical orderlies and Leo Dunbar, the black Death Facility trusty, who would act as clean-up man between the executions.

The prison officials were Warden Hugh Greenwood; Major John McPeters and his three-man Death Strap squad; Cabel Lasseter, the electrician; Garnett Hayes, the prison doctor; Lieutenant Sewell; and Pete Stokes.

Lieutenant Sewell's function was to transport the executioner, David Housley, to and from the Death Chamber, to provide cover and protection for him while he was on the prison reservation, and to keep order in the witness chamber.

The final member of the Death Committee, Pete Stokes, Big Max's internal investigator and information officer, was with the fourteen witnesses in a prison bus in Big Max's main parking lot, awaiting a walkie-talkie signal from McPeters to come to the Death Facility.

When they took their positions in the twelve-by-fifteen foot Death Chamber, the twelve men present were packed into two rows in front of the electric chair, with Major McPeters and Warden Hugh Greenwood standing to the left of the chair, by the chamber's open steel door, and Cabel Lasseter standing to the right of the chair. David Housley, in his hood, and Lieutenant Sewell faced McPeters and Greenwood in front of the chair, standing in front of the other two rows of men.

Except for the muffled but maddening, ever-

248

drumming *No*'s, there was not a sound in the Death Chamber. Hugh Greenwood, as warden, was the first to break the room's silence.

"We all know what we're here for," he said, clearing his throat halfway through the sentence and holding his arms at his sides in the manner of a speaker who is unsure of what to do with his hands. "This thing will not be pleasant," he added, avoiding the hooded face of the executioner, "but it's not our place to deal with the unpleasantness. We are, all of us, tools of the law, no more, no less. But I don't need to remind you that the whole damn world is outside." He gestured beyond the walls of the room to Big Max's main parking lot, where over a hundred journalists fumed like hounds after a hemmed-in fox. We've got to do our jobs—with precision, with no hesitation. The condemned don't really figure in this." He paused. "I know that might not seem right, or even proper, but it's the truth. They're finished. In a way, they've been finished for a long time. What really matters is *what* we do, and *how* we do it."

He stopped for a moment, stared down at the concrete floor in thought, and then turned his face to the group once more. For the first time, he looked directly at the executioner.

"We don't know how the condemned will take this, what they'll do," he continued, "but we can't let their actions affect us. We have to carry out our function as if we were robots. Don't think. Don't think at all. Just act."

When he had finished speaking, Greenwood moved quickly to the red wall phone on the back wall of the Executioner's Booth, took the receiver out of its cradle, and dialed the eleven digits on the direct line to Governor Morgan Kingsly's executive office in Tallahassee.

Bill Tuggle, Kingsly's secretary, answered on the first ring. "Yes?"

"Bill, we're in the Death Chamber," Greenwood said firmly. "We're ready. Do we bring the witnesses in?"

There was a three-second pause on the other end of the line. Greenwood was aware that his neck ached as he waited.

"Yes," Tuggle answered finally, the word said with loud formality.

"You say yes?" Greenwood asked, with equal formality.

"Yes," Tuggle repeated.

"I understand," Greenwood replied. "I'll make my final call to you at seven fifty-nine, and then, as agreed, I'll hang up and continue through all four executions unless the phone rings."

"Yes," Tuggle replied, as if that were the only word he knew.

"I'm hanging up now," Greenwood said.

There was no further response on the governor's end. Greenwood replaced the receiver when he heard the click of Tuggle hanging up. He came out of the Executioner's Booth and faced the Death Committee again. "The governor says bring the witnesses here to the Death Chamber," he said. "We will assume from this point on that we are go for all four executions. In the event we are not," he added, looking back toward where the red phone hung inside the Executioner's Booth, "the phone will instruct us to stop."

Then Greenwood turned and faced McPeters.

"Major McPeters is the expert here," he said. "As all of you know, the major will have charge of the workings of the executions from here on, with me giving the direct command for the executioner to engage the death controls. So, major," he said, shoving his hands into his trouser pockets with obvious relief, "it's all yours."

McPeters nodded slightly at Greenwood and took a step forward so that he was almost touching the executioner. "There will be no foul-ups," he said forcefully into David Housley's hooded face. Without pausing, he addressed himself to the others behind Housley. "No foul-ups whatsoever," he repeated.

Then he turned his back on the group and walked to the chamber's outside door. Bob Griffis was standing at the door's lock, holding a walkie-talkie. Griffis handed the instrument to McPeters and quickly opened the chamber's steel door. McPeters, dressed in his complete winter uniform, stepped out into the freezing rain and called Pete Stokes, who was standing on the steps of the witness bus five hundred yards away.

"Flypaper to Flies," he said curtly into the walkie-talkie mouthpiece, using the prearranged code names.

"Flies to Flypaper," Stokes replied instantly.

"On your way," McPeters instructed.

"On our way," Stokes answered.

McPeters was back inside the Death Chamber in seconds, and Griffis had the door locked behind him in only seconds more.

"To your places," McPeters ordered the group, handing the walkie-talkie to Griffis and slapping the cold raindrops from his officer's cap on the wall by the chamber's outside door. He replaced the cap squarely on his head and then brushed the rain off his blue officer's tunic and his Sam Browne belt.

The eleven men in the room moved on his command like a team executing a play.

Warden Greenwood moved first, going into the Witness Chamber through a small open doorway on the right side of the Death Chamber. Lieutenant Sewell followed Greenwood and took up a position beside him as the warden waited to receive the witnesses. The three-man Death Strap squad stayed with McPeters by the Death Chamber's closed steel door. Cabel Lasseter took up his position to the left of the electric chair, on the black protective rubber matting, near McPeters and his men. Dr. Hayes and his two convict orderlies went out into the main hallway. Leo Dunbar, the black trusty, followed them, holding a galvanized bucket that contained cleaning equipment.

As he had been instructed, David Housley walked to the Executioner's Booth, bent down, and opened the small cardboard box on the floor. Inside was the long black executioner's robe. He took it out and put it on as a judge would put on his robe. Then he reached inside the box and took out the pair of black skin-tight rubber gloves. He put them on. Then he turned and came out of the booth and took up a position in front of the eye-level slit, so that, after McPeters and his Death Strap squad, it would be his all-black figure that the witnesses saw as they entered the Death Chamber.

In forty seconds, everyone was in position and silent under the blanket of the muffled *No*'s that kept coming from outside.

Behind the shelter of his medieval costume, David Housley felt a sense of power his mind couldn't give words to, power he had dreamed of, power that seemed to have a will of its own. It seemed that he could hear the seconds ticking off in his head, but suddenly he was aware that his mouth was dust-dry. He clasped his gloved hands together, sending a short squeaking noise through the silent room.

McPeters turned his head back to check the sound. Housley stiffened under the big man's gray-cold stare and did not move a muscle as he and the others waited for the witnesses, waited like statues in a sealed-off world where the seconds of time seemed to fall to the floor as distinguishably as the cold rain that fell outside.

7:54 A.M.

Pete Stokes stepped inside the Death Chamber at exactly fifteen seconds past 7:54. McPeters was to the left of the door as he came in, and the three-man Death Strap squad was to the right, forming a human barrier between the witnesses and the electric chair. Stokes quickly led the way into the Witness Chamber, where Hugh Greenwood and Lieutenant Sewell waited. Once Stokes cleared the doorway of the Death Chamber, the fourteen witnesses behind him were hustled in at a trot by McPeters, who spoke two clipped words and gave each a hard look.

"This way," he instructed, pointing toward the open doorway to the Witness Chamber.

Lincoln Daniels was fifth in line behind Stokes, followed by Palo Reyas and Paul O'Dell. He was seated only seconds after entering the Death Facility, in the center of the front row, with Reyas next, and then Paul O'Dell on the second seat next to the wall.

Lincoln and McPeters did not exchange glances as Lincoln entered the Death Chamber door, and as soon as the fourteen witnesses were seated, McPeters was in the Witness Chamber standing next to Warden Greenwood. Lincoln met his eyes for an instant; as he had expected, it was as if they had never seen each other before.

The final reality of the event, *death,* came in on Lincoln Daniels fully—he had expected it—and he sat stiff-straight in his bolted-down metal chair and waited with despair as his mind raced back to the night before, when McPeters had told him and Palo Reyas that the thing would be "nothing." He looked at McPeters's stern face and wondered what had possessed him to attach such a word to what was unfolding before them.

The fourteen witnesses were silent as they faced McPeters and Warden Greenwood, with Pete Stokes and Lieutenant Sewell taking up positions in the rear of the small room. Having been requested to leave their overcoats in their own cars so there would not be added confusion or time spent taking them off once they reached the heated Witness Chamber, they were all half frozen from fifteen minutes in the unheated prison bus; now, in the twelve-by-fifteen-foot room, the air began to get stuffy with so many bodies crammed into such a small space, and most felt brittle and uncomfortable as they began to warm up.

As with the Death Committee, Warden Hugh Greenwood was the first to speak to the witnesses, but he was plainly ill at ease as he faced a group that was made up almost entirely of the headliners of international print and broadcast journalism.

On the front row from left to right were Bryson Cummings of the *London Daily Telegraph;* Brenda

Winston, ABC-TV co-anchorwoman; Evan Kerr of the Associated Press; Lincoln Daniels, *Esquire* magazine; Palo Reyas, *Esquire* magazine and all-media pool-sharing artist; Paul O'Dell of the *New York Times;* and Carl Moran of CBS-TV.

On the second row from left to right were Pierre Dervan of the *Paris Express;* Jed Niles of United Press International; Shirley Hammell of *The New Yorker* magazine; Klaus Hoffman of *Stern* magazine, cooperating with an all-Germany and Eastern Europe pool feed; Luis Delgado of Mexico City's *El Sol* daily newspaper, cooperating with a Spanish-speaking pool feed; Fred Billings of NBC-TV; and, finally, Joel Watson of the *Los Angeles Times.*

Only twelve witnesses were required by Florida state law, but because the witness assignments were made by a complicated process of news agency seniority, geographic place, and foreign language, a system that assured only one major network TV representative in the Witness Chamber, the group was expanded by Governor Kingsly, after pressure from all three major TV networks, to have network correspondents present at the executions. In point of fact, there had sometimes been as many as a hundred witnesses hustled in in shifts for executions when Florida had executed especially notorious criminals in the past, but Governor Kingsly was determined that that would be stopped, and after the first execution only the twelve legally required witnesses would be allowed inside the Witness Chamber on any given death Monday.

Warden Greenwood stuck his hands in his trouser pockets for safety and proceeded to greet the witnesses, making his short introductory remarks without looking any of them in the eye, a fact that went unnoticed by most of the witnesses, whose own eyes vacillated between the electric chair and the black-draped executioner, seven feet away beyond the protective half-glass wall of the room.

"Major John McPeters will be in charge of the actual workings of the executions from this point on," Lincoln heard Greenwood say. "I will give the commands for the death controls to be engaged, but Major McPeters will see to everything else."

McPeters began formally. First he introduced by title only the members of the Death Committee whom the witnesses could see: the electrician, the executioner, the three-man Death Strap squad, and finally Lieutenant Sewell, whom he called the Sergeant at Arms and who, he said authoritatively, had "total control over the conduct of the witnesses and was instructed" —McPeters said it bluntly—"to use whatever means necessary to keep strict order in the Witness Chamber at all times."

Next he listed the functions of those members of the Death Committee the witnesses could not see, including the prison doctor and his two inmate orderlies and Leo Dunbar, the clean-up man.

Then he paused and asked if there were any questions. There were none. It was as if no one wanted to hear the sound of his own voice. Then McPeters told the witnesses that if they became ill or needed medical assistance they tell Lieutenant Sewell, the Sergeant at Arms, who would make the fact known to him.

"I will get the prison doctor to you in seconds," McPeters assured them, still in his overbearingly formal manner. Without pausing he went on. "Each of the condemned," he said, his hands on his hips at the top of his Sam Browne belt, "will be brought in by the Death Strap squad and immediately strapped in the electric chair. Warden Greenwood will face each condemned person and ask if they wish to make a statement.

"After the statement, if there is a statement, the electrician will put the Death Cap in place and attach the final electrical lead and will turn the condemned prisoner over to the warden, who will, in turn, give the executioner the signal—a simple nod of the head—to engage the death controls.

"When the executioner throws the Death Switch, he automatically engages a two-minute, eight-cycle electrical mechanism that passes two thousand two hundred and fifty volts of electricity into the condemned prisoner's body on a high- and low-range scale for five and then twenty-five seconds until the eight parts of the cycle have been completed. From the moment the final Death Switch is thrown until the condemned prisoner is dead should be two minutes.

"You've been told all this before in the printed material the prison has supplied you," McPeters said, his words coming slower as he was obviously coming to the end of his remarks. "But I tell it to you again," he said, moving his hands forward from his Sam Browne belt, his massive shoulders cocked. And I tell you this one final thing," he said, his eyes going slowly from left to right over each of the two rows, "something else you already know, but I will say it again— there is no pain involved, only death."

McPeters stopped abruptly and looked at his watch. The time was 7:58. He gave the two rows a final sweep with his eyes, a look that seemed to plant each of the fourteen in the chairs as if they had been strapped in themselves. "That's it," he said, stepping back to leave the room. "From this point on there will be no talking. Not one word will be tolerated. The Witness Chamber and the Death Chamber are so rigged that you will be able to hear what is being said in the Death Chamber, but we will not be able to hear you. All the same, there will be no talking.

"Your chairs are bolted down and you will be locked in until all four executions have been completed. You will hear over the two speakers between the netting and the glass.

"You are State of Florida witnesses, not participants. You have a legal function here. What you do once you leave, what you make of what you have seen, is your own business. *What you do here is mine.* And there is no way that you can disrupt this thing once it starts."

He turned around and stuck his fingers through the inch-square holes in the thick netting that was attached to stall posts four inches in front of the glass shield between the two chambers. He pulled hard at the netting and it did not give. The point was made.

McPeters held his place before the group for a

brief moment more, just long enough for Warden Hugh Greenwood to leave the room and walk to the red telephone in the Death Chamber, and just long enough for him to nod to Pete Stokes and Lieutenant Sewell to take their places in front of the witnesses at the netting. Then he moved out of the Witness Chamber and locked the steel connecting door behind him with a thud. Stokes took a position to the left of the group, by Bryson Cummings of the *London Telegraph*, facing the electric chair; and Lieutenant Sewell took a position to the extreme right, next to Carl Moran of CBS.

Lincoln Daniels watched McPeters with admiration; unlike Hugh Greenwood, there had not been the slightest hesitation in McPeters's voice or actions. He was a man afraid of nothing, Daniels said to himself.

In the Death Chamber, McPeters moved up even with the eye-level slit in the Executioner's Booth. He stood there military-tall, with his hands resting on top of his Sam Browne belt. From the distance of the Witness Chamber, you could just make out the outline of Hugh Greenwood's head inside the booth. To the people sealed off in the Witness Chamber, sounds came through, muffled and uneven.

Lincoln Daniels and the other witnesses sat in total silence, all eyes on the gruesome triangle made by the executioner, Hugh Greenwood behind the eye-level slit, and McPeters ot the left. Behind the thin slit, Hugh Greenwood was on the phone to the governor. This time, as prescribed by law, it was Governor Morgan Kingsly himself on the other end of the line.

"Do we execute?" Greenwood said.

"Yes," Kingsly said. "You execute."

"Do we execute all four under warrant?"

"Yes. You execute all four under warrant."

"I understand the order to execute, and to execute all four under warrant," Greenwood said stiffly. "One moment for Major McPeters, sir."

By law, both the warden and the officer in charge of the execution had to be given dual orders to execute, as well as having the death warrants signed and in the possession of the warden at the time of the execution of sentence.

Kingsly went through the same words with McPeters as he had with Greenwood.

"I understand the order to execute, and to execute all four under warrant," McPeters repeated with the same stiffness Greenwood had used; then he handed the receiver back to the warden.

"I am hanging up the phone now, sir," Greenwood said. "We will proceed with the woman, Mrs. Fuller, first, then Kruger, then Santos, and finally Parker. And we will not stop until all the sentences have been carried out unless this telephone rings again."

"I understand," Kingsly said. "I don't anticipate making a call for any stays," he added, "but I have ten open lines to the office and I am waiting for whatever may develop."

"Then I'll hang up now," Greenwood said. "I will call you back when the sentences have been carried out."

"Right," Kingsly said, and the phone clicked off on his end.

Greenwood hung his red phone back in its cradle, took a long, deep breath as he stood looking at the blank wall of the Executioner's Booth for a second, and then turned and came out to face the witnesses.

"We have executive order to execute all four," he said in a too-loud voice that crackled over the speakers in the Witness Chamber.

It seemed to the witnesses that Greenwood said his words to their window; he sought out no eye, no face, no form beyond the glass and steel-net partition. Then Greenwood turned and faced McPeters. He looked up at the larger man's face for a second and seemed about to speak. But he said nothing. He simply nodded.

Instantly, as the power shifted to him, McPeters took full control of the situation. He turned and looked at the clock on the wall behind the electric chair. It was 7:59. McPeters regarded the clock for only a second and then turned to the men in the room and barked his command.

"Places!" he said, as he stepped back to allow the executioner to pass between him and the Executioner's Booth. The men in the room—seven now—moved, as before, with team-like precision.

Cabel Lasseter went to the green Lead Line Cabinet behind the electric chair and pulled out both thick black electric leads and laid them on the floor, one to the left of the chair, one to the right. Then he stepped to the right of the cabinet and bent down and retrieved the Contact Plate from the galvanized bucket full of salt water. He examined the implement as he had earlier that morning, then squeezed it nearly dry and laid it on top of the Lead Line Cabinet. Then he opened the Black Box on top of the cabinet and took out the Death Cap, his rubber gloves, and the Ground Pad. After a brief but thorough examination, he laid the three pieces beside the Contact Plate. "Ready," he said to McPeters, and then he stepped back into his place to the left of the electric chair, facing the witnesses, standing on the black rubber matting that surrounded the electric chair.

The executioner assumed his place inside the Executioner's Booth, standing in the center of the small opening made by the concrete side of the booth and the Death Chamber's concrete wall, standing there so that, according to law, the condemned prisoners could see him as they were brought in. "Ready," the executioner said to McPeters, in a voice that was throaty and obviously disguised.

The three members of McPeters's Death Strap squad faced him with their backs turned to the witnesses. McPeters's eyes searched the Death Chamber for a second, cataloging each and every thing and person in the small space. Everything was to his satisfaction; his stony face revealed the fact as surely as if he had said the word *perfect* out loud.

Then McPeters's head turned again to the clock on the wall behind the electric chair. He faced the mechanism at the exact instant the second hand swept from the fifty-ninth second to precisely eight o'clock; it was as if he had radar to detect the exact time to begin, as if he and the event were wedded.

The fourteen witnesses, Pete Stokes, Lieutenant Sewell, and the six principals in the Death Chamber with McPeters caught the time seconds later. The hour could not have been more apparent if it had been struck. It hung in air that did not appear breathable, that seemed to support only the Death Angel.

The silent tolling of the hour seemed completed when all at once the chanted *No*'s stopped at three seconds past eight. Everyone in the two chambers, McPeters included, jerked at the acid silence that came in on them, on the deathwork that had finally begun, as Peeping John McPeters turned in his tracks in a military about-face and led his Death Strap squad out of the Death Chamber bound for the Ready Cell and Alice Fuller, who would be the first to die.

From the vantage point of the Witness Chamber, the action was crystal clear, but it seemed to Lincoln Daniels that it came from a million miles away.

8:00 A.M.

The two ministers and the deputy warden, Norman Hills, were just leaving the first inside door of the Death Facility's maze as McPeters and his squad came out of the Death Chamber. McPeters caught Hill's eye as he turned to go through the maze's opening; his face went white with rage. He had ordered the three men out at 7:55.

"Damn you!" McPeters choked at Hills, stopping in his tracks just before the closed steel door to the Ready Cell, his arms held out in a huge T, halting his three guards behind him. *"Damn you!"* he said again, his right fist now balled, threatening Hills as the maze's steel door closed behind him with a soft thud.

McPeters held his position a step before the Ready Cell's door to let the hallway fall into absolute quiet once more. Quiet was all-important to him now. Then he took the one step up to the Ready Cell's door and rapped it twice with his knuckles, not hard, not even forcefully; the kind of knock you might expect from a friend who has come to visit.

McPeters paused for a second more and then inserted his brass key in the cell's gray steel door. He stepped inside quickly. Esther Todd was to his left, and Billie Johnson to his right; both women were ashen-faced and stiff, their hands down by their sides as if tied there.

Alice Fuller was standing between her wall bunk and the cell's stainless-steel toilet, standing against the back wall with her eyes riveted on McPeters.

"I . . . I . . ." She tried to speak, but she fell forward and vomited on the cell floor before she could get the words out, her thin arms wrapped around her flat stomach. Her spasm broke the spell that seemed to have the two matrons in its grasp. They lurched forward to the cell's bars as if to help the woman, but McPeters stopped them cold with his outstretched hands.

In the cell, Alice Fuller righted herself and stood groggily holding onto the side of the bed.

"Wash your face," McPeters said to her, his voice as soft and measured as a friend's.

Alice Fuller jerked her head sideways at the sound of McPeters's voice. Again, she tried to speak; again the words would not come, but this time she was not sick. She turned and walked past the toilet to the stainless-steel washbasin that was attached to the rear wall, bent down without hesitation, and washed her face as she had been instructed.

She raised up slowly, her eyes closed, found the white prison towel on the hook above the sink, and dried her face. She paused for a second, making sure she had hung the towel back straight and even on the hook. Then she turned back to face McPeters.

"It's time, Alice," McPeters said in a soft, even voice.

"I know," Alice Fuller said, finally able to make the words appear. "I . . . I . . . I'm glad," she managed to say before she fell mute as McPeters stepped up to her cell door and unlocked it.

She was wearing a short-sleeved, one-piece dark

green gabardine dress, her pale body scarecrow-frail
and lost inside. There was only one undergarment,
the same type of single undergarment that all four
of the condemned were required to wear: thick cotton
jockey shorts with a tight elastic top, tight legs, and a
half-inch-thick cotton fiber crotch that resembled a
woman's sanitary napkin or a baby's diaper bottom
—a repository for most of the urine that would be
passed when the current made contact with the brain
and bladder control was destroyed.

If there was one single greatest irony in the execution's nightmare of ironies, it was that the condemned were executed as they had begun life: baby
bald and diapered, handled and watched over by
others.

With the cell door open, Bob Griffis and Earl
Hancock moved inside the Ready Cell and stood in the
shallow aisle between the two matrons. Each guard
was holding an "iron claw" manacle, a single hand-
cufflike apparatus opened and closed by a horizontal
metal bar no wider than a man's palm.

"Alice," McPeters said again, this time with only a
microscopic increase in tone and intensity, but an increase that was felt by everyone in the room as if it
had been a shout.

Alice Fuller jerked forward at the sound of her
name, her legs wooden. McPeters stepped back into the
open cell door and allowed her to pass him. The moment she was even with the two guards they took hold
of her birdlike arms and clamped the iron claws on her
wrists, Hancock's left hand to her right, Griffis's right
hand to her left.

Alice Fuller let out a small cry as she was seized
by the two men. "Oh," she gargled, fright widening
her eyes. "Cold," she mouthed, her wide eyes darting
over to Esther Todd, who also stood terror-struck by
the wall to McPeters's right.

"Honey," the matron managed to say before she
turned away, holding back her weeping with her hand
over her mouth.

McPeters bristled at the matron's reaction; he
searched Alice Fuller's face and saw she was on the

verge of cracking again. *Bitch!* McPeters said silently
to Esther Todd. Then, without more hesitation, he
nodded to Griffis and Hancock to take Alice Fuller
out into the hallway.

Positioned in the hallway four paces from the
open door of the Death Chamber, the condemned
woman became lost in a mass of blue guard uniforms:
Bob Griffis on her left, Earl Hancock on her right,
Hank Chrysler in front, and McPeters in the rear,
prodding them on with his quick, thudding steps on
the hard concrete floor.

Alice Fuller balked when she saw the black-robed
executioner as she was whisked into the Death Chamber, but the 430-pound weight of the two guards who
held her 96 pounds was so great a lever that the balk
was registered only in her gaping mouth and wide
eyes.

It was her eyes that everyone noticed. They
seemed to eat up both the Death Chamber and the
Witness Chamber: wide, terrified eyes that took in every single thing and person in both rooms as if by
slow motion within the incredibly rapid pace of events
from the time she was brought through the Death
Chamber's doorway until the moment the two guards,
Hancock and Griffis, had her seated in the electric
chair and, with the third guard, Hank Chrysler, began
the strapping-in process.

After looking searchingly at all the witnesses,
Alice Fuller focused on the face of the person seated
directly in front of her on the first row: the stone face
of Lincoln Daniels.

Jesus, Daniels said to himself, his eyes remaining
glued on the condemned woman and the three guards
who worked over her, staring while his mind tried to
turn his head away, unaware that his fists were balled
at arm's length on the tops of his kneecaps.

Alice Fuller had been taken into the Death Chamber with Bob Griffis to her left and Earl Hancock
to her right, moved in front of the chair by the two
men, and then pulled back into the chair, with both
guards keeping their left-right positions on her wrists
with the iron claws as they faced the witnesses. Hank

Chrysler, standing near Griffis and out of kicking reach of Alice Fuller's right leg, bent forward and cinched the wide chest strap across the woman's wasted body just below her flat breasts.

Next, Chrysler adjusted the waist strap across the top of Alice Fuller's thighs, just at the line of her crotch. Then he and McPeters, who was standing between Hancock and her left leg, again out of kicking reach, moved down to her feet, both men dropping to one knee at the same moment.

In seconds, they had her bony ankles secured within the T-shaped stocks at the center of the chair's wide third leg that jutted down from the middle of the seat bottom. Then both men, moving together, Chrysler on her right arm, McPeters on her left, pulled the arm straps tight, five inches from the wrists that were still held down flat on the chair's heavy armrests by the iron claws.

Only after the arm straps were securely in place, and McPeters and Chrysler were standing up again after bending down for the strapping, did McPeters nod his command for the manacles to be released by Griffis and Hancock. As all four men stood up formally, two on each side of the strapped-in woman, McPeters checked the clock on the wall behind the chair: 8:04. He nodded the three guards back to the doorway of the Death Chamber and turned quickly to his right, where Cabel Lasseter stood, grimly awaiting his turn to begin.

Now it was here. In his heart he had dreaded it, but it was part of his work. And as Lasseter looked at that work—McPeters, the strapped-in woman, the executioner, the whole scene in the tight little room—he felt a sense of nothingness and futility. But Lasseter was a man who kept to honor and duty and dignity; the woman, the *object* before him, was out of his control. Like the rest, he was simply a part of the whole, a part of legally disposing of someone who had killed three small children and a grown man. But the crime did not make him act. He acted because he was doing his duty.

Lasseter reached behind him on top of the Lead Line Cabinet and grasped the Ground Pad in his left

hand and its olive-drab shoestring in his right and
walked around in front of the chair to Alice Fuller's
right leg. The woman's fright-mad eyes followed him as
if she were a staked-down sheep being approached by a
mountain lion.

"What's he . . . *oh!* . . . What's . . . what's
he . . . ?" the woman pleaded, her eyes shifting to
McPeters, who was standing out from her left arm.

McPeters shook his head for her to be silent, his
mouth close-lipped. Alice Fuller complied with a jerk of
her head down to where Lasseter had begun attaching the Ground Pad to her right leg, four inches above
her ankle.

The lead-lined leather pad, with its wide, homemade nylon stitches around both top and bottom, swallowed Alice Fuller's skinny, hairless leg. Lasseter began
to weave the shoestring between the five hooks on each
end of the pad, but he could see that it would not hold
on her leg. There was at least an inch of play. The
pad would slip down to where her ankle was strapped
in the stock recess. There would be no ground.

The electrician finished the lacing and tied the
string in a shoe knot, but it was no good; the pad
slipped to the woman's ankle. Lasseter looked up from
his kneeling position to McPeters.

"What?" McPeters was red-faced with apprehen-
sion.

Lasseter did not answer. He pushed himself up
off the floor and moved quickly to the Executioner's
Booth for his tools.

McPeters looked down at the Ground Pad. *Her
leg is too small!* he raged to himself, his eyes darting
from the pad to Alice Fuller's face and then to Hugh
Greenwood's. He shook Greenwood's unasked question
off and moved around Alice Fuller's front to assist
Lasseter, who came back from the booth with his metal
toolbox.

"I'll tape it," Lasseter said to McPeters, as both
men went down to the floor on their knees in front of
Alice Fuller. "It will work."

"My God! . . . *Lord!* . . . What are you doing?"
she began screaming in a sharp, terrified voice, fully

roused now from the dazed state she had been in when she was brought into the chamber. "Please! . . . Please! . . ." she cried, facing Lincoln Daniels and the rest of the witnesses directly. "Please help me! . . . I can't stand this! . . . *Aaaaahhh!* . . . Oh! . . . Oh! . . . Oh! . . ." She tugged hopelessly at the straps that held her down as if she were a butterfly glued to a board.

In the Witness Chamber, there were sighs and groans that could not be restrained as the scene was played out before the window.

McPeters, who was holding Alice Fuller's leg while Lasseter untied the shoestring and folded the pad into the leg, turned just in time to see Pete Stokes calling for silence. The breach of his orders set McPeters off. He flashed his face up to Alice Fuller, who kept on whining.

"Shut—up!" he thundered at her, separating the words.

The words seemed to knock the woman back into her chair. She closed her eyes and fell into rigid silence, her fingers digging at the ends of the armrests.

Hugh Greenwood picked up the tension of the moment. "John?" he managed to choke from the back of his throat.

"We're done," McPeters replied, as Lasseter finished looping the final band of black electrical tape around the Ground Pad that was now securely fastened to Alice Fuller's leg the prescribed four inches above her right ankle. He got to his feet slightly before Lasseter, but both men quickly retreated to Alice Fuller's left side and took up positions there on the black rubber matting, as Hugh Greenwood moved around in front of the condemned woman.

"Alice Fuller," Greenwood said, his voice held flat and steady by will, "as warden of the Maximum Security Unit of the Florida State Prison System, it is my duty to ask you if you have any statement before the sentence of death by the passage of electricity through your body is carried out.

"Do you wish to make a statement?" he asked formally, trying not to look at the condemned woman's twisted face and closed eyes.

There was a three-second silence so physical it seemed to everyone in both chambers that it could be touched.

Then Alice Fuller responded. *"Eeeaaaauuuuhh! . . . Eeeaaaauuuuhhh!"* she groaned in a crazed, animal-like manner, all the while shaking her head no.

"Very well then," Greenwood said, shaken, the words said half to the witnesses, half to the condemned woman. "Under the authority vested in me by the Governor and the laws of the State of Florida, I decree that the sentence be carried out."

Greenwood nodded to McPeters and moved in line with the open Death Chamber door at the center of the eye-level slit in the Executioner's Booth, a position that let him face both the executioner and McPeters, who moved a pace from him at Alice Fuller's right hand.

McPeters, in command again, gave Lasseter a single nod. The electrician moved quickly behind the electric chair to the fail-safe bar on the side of the Lead Line Cabinet next to the chamber's open door and Hugh Greenwood.

In the electric chair, Alice Fuller suddenly fell silent, her face pinched as if she were in grinding pain.

The straight, foot-long, rubber-handled fail-safe bar was in the right-handed, down, open-circuit OFF position. Lasseter bent down and touched it for good measure; then he stood and walked to the right of the electric chair, got down on one knee, and took the right lead line in his hands and began attaching it to the Ground Pad on Alice Fuller's right leg.

"Aaaahhhhaaaa!" she screamed. "God! . . . What! . . ." she yelled, bumping up and down in the chair as if the current had already hit her.

Her eyes were open now and she strained her neck, peering down to see what Lasseter was doing, her right hand grappling the air in a futile gesture to stop him.

"Please! . . . Oh, God, *please!*" she begged the witnesses, who watched her twisted face and Lasseter's hands, all of them repulsed and sickened by what they saw but all unable to turn away.

Under the cries, Lasseter worked quickly, unscrewing the copper wing nut on the Ground Pad and pushing the female opening of the lead line onto the male post of the pad, then securing the wing nut on the post again, making the tight connection between lead line and pad.

As he stood again, Lasseter nodded to McPeters, to say that the connection was properly made; then he walked past McPeters and Greenwood, behind the electric chair, to the middle of the Lead Line Cabinet and picked up the chin strap, the seventh strap attached to the condemned. He took the strap in both hands and walked directly behind the chair and with one quick motion had the strap out over Alice Fuller's clipped head and under her chin and was pulling back and upward, toward the two head posts in the center top of the chair, as McPeters's right hand moved out to cup the secured chin cup of the strap and hold her head in place until Lasseter had the strap buckled behind the head posts.

"*Eeeaaaauuuuaaaahh!*" Alice Fuller grunted, her eyes bulging out with terror, her bony fingers digging in thin air over the armrests. She kept on grunting, her hands never ceasing their digging, as the strap was cinched tight and McPeters's hand fell away to his side.

Only one strap remained to be attached to Alice Fuller, but now the restrictions on her movements were complete. The only parts of her body that she could move were her hands and her toes and her eyes, that were like those of a mad dog.

Quickly Lasseter bent down behind the electric chair and dipped his right hand into the galvanized steel bucket and withdrew the sponge-covered Contact Plate. He squeezed the plate almost dry over the bucket. In the chair, Alice Fuller flinched at the noise of the dripping water, her mad, searching eyes seemingly about to come out of their sockets.

Lasseter turned with the plate in his right hand and, with his back to the witnesses, inserted the male post of the plate into the female opening of the brown leather Death Cap. Now the Death Cap, with its black leather face mask, was supported in the electrician's right hand by the post of the Contact Plate. He moved with the joined implements up to the rear of the electric chair and slipped them down on Alice Fuller's pale, egg-shaped head.

"*Eeeaaahuuu!*" the condemned woman cried at the touch of the cold sponge, beginning her wiggling and finger grappling with renewed frenzy. "*Eeeaaahuuu! ... Eeeaaahuuu!*"

She was like a wild animal. The last thing she saw before darkness came in behind the mask was Peeping John McPeters's right hand coming in on her face to tighten into place the eighth and final strap, the Death Cap's chin strap that fit behind the regular chin strap at the point where the woman's neck began.

In a second McPeters had the eighth strap secured. Lasseter released the Contact Plate's male post, which protruded up from the cap, and bent down on the left side of the chair. He picked up the second electrical lead, turning, as he stood up, to the top of the Lead Line Cabinet and picking up the round T-screw that would join the lead and the Contact Plate's male post together.

In seconds more, Lasseter had the T-screw and the post fastened together. He stepped back and signaled to McPeters that both death connections were made. McPeters nodded his recognition. Then Lasseter turned to his right and went to the fail-safe bar on the side of the Lead Line Cabinet. He bent down and pushed the bar to the left-handed, up, closed-circuit ON position; there was a dull, close-in thud, as the connection to the Death Switch controls four feet away was made. Alice Fuller, thinking the current was coming in, jerked herself up in the chair and let out a sharp whine. When Lasseter stood up from the fail-safe bar he faced both McPeters and Greenwood.

"The connections are made," he said in a voice that was barely audible to the witnesses. "Does the warden and does the executioner accept the connections?" he added formally, in the manner prescribed by law.

Greenwood looked through the eye-level slit in the Executioner's Booth. Behind his black robes David

Housley hesitated a moment and then said "Yes," in a voice that was not heard by the witnesses.

"Yes, we do," Greenwood said in a strained, over-loud voice, assuming control of the execution once more.

"Very well," Lasseter replied. He turned on his heel and walked behind the electric chair to the center of the Lead Line Cabinet and picked up his thick black electrician's gloves. When he took his position out from Alice Fuller's left hand, a pace back on the protective rubber floor matting, he was wearing the stiff gloves, facing the hooded woman with his left shoulder to the witnesses. McPeters assumed his position opposite Lasseter, a pace out from Alice Fuller's right hand.

Greenwood reached inside his left coat pocket and took out a child's small school notebook and a twenty-five-cent ballpoint pen. He opened the notebook and prepared to write down the time the Death Switch was thrown.

The witnesses sat porcelain stiff on their chairs; there was not a sound in the Witness Chamber.

In the booth, the executioner, faced his two control panels.

McPeters and Lasseter held their places.

Greenwood turned and looked at the clock on the wall behind the electric chair. The second hand was seven seconds away from 8:06. Greenwood watched the hand sweep toward the exact minute.

"Engage," he said to the executioner without looking at him.

There was an awesome, split-second silence, and then the executioner's right hand went out to the right control panel. He turned the black thumb-shaped circuit-breaker switch to the left, and with a deep, faraway metallic thud the eight-cycle Death Machine in the Circuit Room to the left rear of the Witness Chamber was engaged.

Alice Fuller jumped again under her straps and let out a high-pitched whine.

Then the executioner pushed the red transfer button at the top of the circuit-breaker switch, and there was a dull hum as the power of the Death Machine was transferred to the Death Switch on the left panel.

Alice Fuller screamed and choked and tore at her straps. In her crazed mind she knew the current had been turned on.

On the left panel, the Ready Light silently came on over the red Death Switch. The executioner, David Housley, the bored Miami stockbroker, looked first at the light, then at the switch below it, and then out the eye-level slit to Alice Fuller, who sat strapped and wired in the chair, a thing no longer human: not dead, not alive. Housley looked at the racing clock. He looked at Greenwood. His hand went up to the Death Switch and touched it, grasped it firmly. Then, as the clock's second hand touched the bold-lettered black 12 at the top of its circle, he heard Greenwood bark, "Now!"

Alice Fuller let out one final cry before the 2,250 volts of raw electricity ripped into the top of her skull, as David Housley, without thinking—only performing, *acting*—cranked the Death Switch the lethal half turn to the left.

Whop! Alice Fuller's stick body surged up, a violent vertical jerk that started at the buttocks and shot the trunk of her body up into the electricity of the Contact Plate, into the scorching *buzzzz* of the electricity, a sound like bacon frying.

An instant after impact with the Contact Plate, the weight of the woman's body brought her trunk back down to the seat of the electric chair. Five seconds after the Death Switch was thrown, the Death Machine in the Circuit Room began the second of its eight cycles: a twenty-five-second low-range voltage sequence. On the left-hand panel in the Executioner's Booth, David Housley saw the thin red needle of the left high-range gauge above the Death Switch and the Ready Button shoot down from a register of 2,250 volts to 1,000 volts; on the right gauge he saw the thin black needle of the low-range gauge pick up the 1,000 volts on its register.

There was a *thump* as the new cycle began, and on the right-hand control panel in the Executioner's Booth

Housley saw the voltage meter to the left go down from 2,250 to 1,000, while on the amperage meter to the right he saw the amps building from 0 to 20.

Theoretically, Alice Fuller had been unconscious and felt no pain after the initial 2,250-voltage burst hit her, but this had never been proven. There were those who said the condemned felt pain in varying degrees until all life functions had been stopped. Now, as the amps climbed to 20, ventricular fibrillation set in: contractions of the muscle fibers of the heart that interrupted the synchronism between the heartbeat and the pulse beat, the first of the function-killing processes. As Alice Fuller began to fibrillate, her shallow chest heaved and sagged as the passage of blood in and out of the heart was disrupted by the amps working on the muscles of the ventricles. Her bony fingers contorted into fists that were not balled. Her knuckles began to pop. The Ground Pad caused her right leg to contract rigidly; the left leg jiggled spastically in its ankle strap. Her taut body began a rhythmic, horizontal vibration on the electric chair's seat as fibrillation continued.

The twenty-five-second low-range cycle of 1,000 volts concluded, and the gauges in front of David Housley again registered the high range of 2,250 volts, with the amps staying near 20. By now, Alice Fuller's body temperature had risen from 98.6 to 200 degrees Fahrenheit. Her hands were pinkish-purple. Under the tearing current she had lost control of her bladder, and urine trickled off the seat of the chair.

In the Witness Room, the fourteen journalists sat traumatized in their seats. In the Death Chamber none of the officials moved.

As the execution went past the thirty-second mark, respiratory paralysis in the lungs set in; behind the face mask, Alice Fuller's eyeballs began to bulge out, and her cheeks ballooned under the body's muscular strain for oxygen.

By the time the fifth cycle, a five-second high-range register, had been completed, the respiratory center of Alice Fuller's brain had been destroyed, leaving her body and brain totally without oxygen, as the last fifty-five seconds of the death cycle worked at stopping her heart and pulse with a crackling *buzzzz* of current.

When the current stopped, exactly at the end of two minutes, there was absolute quiet in both chambers. Lincoln Daniels became aware of his own breathing for the first time since the Death Switch had been thrown, aware that his own muscles were coiled like a spring.

In the Executioner's Booth all four dials on the two panels showed zero readings. The red Ready Light over the Death Switch was off. The machine was off.

In the electric chair, Alice Fuller's body was rigid; only her head sagged. Her fingers remained contorted back into her palms, her right leg drawn up in an inverted V against the right ankle strap.

The first sound after the current stopped was Major McPeters calling to the prison doctor in the hall outside the Death Chamber. Garnett Hayes appeared in the open doorway, dressed in whites, with a stethoscope hung around his neck. Hugh Greenwood stopped him from entering the room while Cabel Lasseter walked behind the electric chair to the far side of the Lead Line Cabinet and moved the fail-safe bar back to the right into the OFF position, rendering the chair safe from current. McPeters motioned the executioner out of his booth. Only then did Greenwood admit the doctor inside the chamber to do his work.

Garnett Hayes approached the chair warily, exchanging glances with McPeters before he bent forward and touched Alice Fuller's body. He reached down and undid the second button of her green dress, set the ends of his stethoscope in his ears, and put the instrument's cone over her heart. There was no sound. He withdrew the instrument and rebuttoned the dress. He felt the wrists for a pulse and snapped his fingers back as if he himself had been shocked. But it was not current, it was the heat from Alice Fuller's body; the woman's skin seemed to be boiling. The doctor's fingers went back quickly, first to the wrist, then under the face mask to the throat. As with the heart, there was no movement. Hayes stood up and turned to Warden Hugh Greenwood.

"The woman is dead," he said dryly.

McPeters looked at the clock behind the electric chair. It was seconds before 8:09. He turned to the Death Chamber's open doorway and brought his three-man Death Strap squad back into the room at a fast clip. As the squad came in, Cabel Lasseter went to work unscrewing the lead lines from Alice Fuller's stiff body: the head lead first, then the ground lead. McPeters, with his squad inside the chamber, went to his office at the end of the hall to get the first two-man ambulance crew who waited there. As McPeters came back into the Death Chamber, he saw Lasseter still bending over Alice Fuller's right ankle.

"What?"

Lasseter looked up at him and returned the stare. "The tape," he said thickly. "It's melted to her ankle. I've got to cut it off. Hand me a knife out of my tool-box. It's in the booth."

McPeters retrieved the knife quickly and handed it to Lasseter. As the people in both chambers watched, near gagging, he cut the tape from the dead woman's ankle.

As soon as the job was done, the Death Strap squad began removing the eight straps from Alice Fuller's body. Dr. Hayes and his two inmate orderlies lifted the body out of the chair and set it on the portable canvas stretcher the two civilian ambulance men carried between them. The stretcher was covered by a thick white sheet. At the bottom, they had placed the dead woman's shoes. When the two orderlies had the woman's body on the stretcher, they began folding the sheet over her, the shoes between her legs. It was not easy to cover her with the sheet. Her right leg held its inverted V position and her arms had to be forced down to her sides the way you would force a department store mannequin's arms down. There was a purple bile from her lungs that foamed out of her mouth. At the top of her head, where Hank Chrysler had shaved a bald spot, the skin was raised in a red blister, but there was no mark where the Ground Pad had been.

Bob Griffis opened the Death Chamber's steel door

to let the two ambulance men out with Alice Fuller's body. Earl Hancock raced out into the driving rain to open the rear door of the ambulance.

By the chamber's inside door, McPeters motioned in Leo Dunbar, the black trusty, with his cleaning bucket and towels. Immediately, the black man began wiping Alice Fuller's urine off the rubber matting beneath the electric chair and off the chair bottom; he seemed frightened senseless, but he had finished his cleaning and was just standing as Earl Hancock came bursting back through the chamber's open door. Griffis slammed the door behind him and locked it. The ambulance crew remained outside in their vehicle.

In the Death Chamber the electric chair was empty once more. The electrician resoaked the Contact Plate in its saline solution. McPeters turned from facing Hancock as he came back into the room and looked at the wall clock. It was 8:11. He signaled Dunbar and the doctor and his two orderlies out of the chamber and looked at his Death Strap squad.

"Let's go," he instructed them, without consulting Hugh Greenwood, and led them out of the room and to the right the two paces outside the chamber for the door to Death Row and George Kruger, the next to die.

In the Witness Chamber, the fourteen journalists and the two prison men found that they could move once more. It was like finding it out for the first time. They searched each other's faces, not for companionship but to see how they themselves looked, to see how they had come through.

In the Executioner's Booth, David Housley held himself rigid and looked out of the eye-level slit at the electric chair. He shook his head slightly, a move so small no one noticed. He kept on staring at the empty chair. His sense of power and well-being had left him, replaced only by emptiness and confusion. There were no second thoughts in his mind, but the thing had not been what he expected: three slight motions with his hand and then two minutes played out on the dials of a machine. It all seemed so empty. Not anything like what he had expected.

Like everyone else, he waited and tried to come to grips with what had happened and to imagine what was yet to come.

8:12 A.M.

All three Death Watch guards were on their feet when McPeters and his squad came through Death Row's steel door. McPeters came on the Row like a bull, his face flushed. Homer Tull, George Kruger's Death Watch guard, shook his head with disgust as McPeters approached him.

McPeters came to an abrupt halt before Kruger's door, and his eyes moved from Tull to the object of the guard's disgust: George Kruger, barefoot and dressed in his going-out suit, had wedged himself under his wall bunk, a big puddle of yellow vomit around his head.

"Damn you, boy!" McPeters raged, shaking Kruger's cell door with both hands, filling the silent Death Row corridor with the grating sound of steel on steel. Still holding onto the bars, he turned and set his eyes on Joe Morris, José Santos's Death Watch guard.

"I took him down from the bars a few minutes ago," Morris said in answer to McPeters's unspoken question. "He's dressed and sittin' on his bunk waitin'."

Without a word to Morris, McPeters turned back to George Kruger's cell door. As he put his key in the lock he gave instructions to Griffis and Hancock, who stood behind him like wrestlers about to go into the ring.

"Go in fast, get him out from under that bunk, and get his ass out here in the hall. No marks," he added loudly. "And no torn clothes if you can help it."

McPeters swung the cell door back and Griffis and Hancock lurched inside, Griffis going to Kruger's feet, Hancock, gagging at the vomit as he bent down, going for his arms.

"George!" McPeters boomed, as the two guards grabbed the condemned man. "There's an easy way to do this, and a hard way. You're pushin' the hard way all to hell and back. Get on your feet and take your medicine like a man. You're goin' down there one way or the other," he went on, standing back from the cell door, ready to let Griffis and Hancock bring Kruger out. "You might as well go like a man."

The two guards had Kruger on his feet now, both supporting his slight weight with hands under his arms. Kruger's face was spotted with vomit, his white shirt stained with yellow bile. He looked dazed, his glassy eyes staring past McPeters.

"Damn you, Kruger!" McPeters bellowed into the condemned man's hollow-cheeked face. "Damn you, you sorry sonofabitch! You could stick your dick in every woman you could get your hands on, but you can't stand on your own two feet to answer for it!"

Kruger's head snapped at McPeter's words. He seemed to come back from a deep sleep. The haze passed from his eyes, and he made a sudden effort to straighten his buckling knees.

McPeters responded instantly. "All right," he said directly into Kruger's face. "That's better. That's better," he repeated, as he turned his head to the side where the Death Watch guard, Homer Tull, was standing. "Get in there, Homer," he said, motioning with his hand, "and get me a towel."

Tull pushed his bulk past where Hancock and Griffis were holding Kruger back from the entrance to the cell and retrieved a white prison towel from the hook over Kruger's sink. McPeters took the towel and carefully wiped the vomit from Kruger's face—a motion, as with Alice Fuller, that seemed almost tender.

When he had wiped the condemned man's face and shirtfront clean, McPeters tossed the towel inside the cell and stepped back to give Griffis and Hancock room to bring the prisoner out. "Come out now, George," he said in a mild, even, almost friendly voice, "it's time." He had used these words for every condemned prisoner he had ever taken to the chair.

Kruger looked first at McPeters, a dull, barely

comprehending look of fear and agony; then he looked down at his right foot. In a clearly conscious effort, he made his right foot move forward toward the cell door. It was a cripple's step, and after he had made it, even though his eyes shifted to his left foot, he could not force himself to move again.

"I can't, major," he said frantically, his wild eyes shifting up to McPeters's now stony face. "I can't do it. I'm scared. *Please,* major," he went on, his words becoming choked by tears. "Please tell me it's not gonna hurt. . . . Please! . . . *Please!*" he cried, as McPeters grabbed both his wrists and pulled him out into the hallway, holding him at arm's length.

"Son!" McPeters stormed at Kruger. "You get a hold on yourself. I'm damned if I'm going to see a man go out like this. I've never carried a man to the chair, and I never will. You turn your ass around and walk down this corridor."

The Preparation, he raged in his mind. If only I'd been able to use the Preparation, none of this would have happened.

He turned his full attention back to Kruger, who was standing like a dilapidated statue in front of him. "You hear me?" he stormed. "You straighten up and act like a man. Don't let those people in there see a vegetable. Dammit"—his face revealed his resentment and disgust—"you asked for this without tears. Go in there and take it without tears."

Kruger choked. "Just tell me it won't hurt, major," he said. "I'll believe it if you say it."

McPeters looked him straight in the eyes. "It won't hurt, George," he answered. "And that's God's truth as I know it."

"Will I go to hell, major?" Kruger asked, his voice cracking.

The question stopped McPeters cold. "I don't know, son," he answered flatly. "That's between you and the Lord." He was obviously disconcerted. "Just turn around and start walking," he said, turning Kruger with his hands. "It's time, son—*now,*" he added forcefully, as Kruger turned to face the open Death Row door.

As he said the word "now," McPeters gave the signal with his head for Griffis and Hancock to move out past him with their iron claw manacles. The instant after Kruger came to face the Death Row door, the two guards once again had him in their grasp, this time with an iron claw on each wrist.

"Oh! . . . What? . . . *Major!* . . . Please! . . . Please!" Kruger cried. He pushed back violently, catching the two guards slightly off balance, but McPeters was there in the rear, grounded like a boulder. He stopped Kruger in mid-motion and grabbed him around the neck in a hammer lock.

"You sorry, no-good rapin' bastard. You get goin' to take your medicine. I'm through fuckin' around with you. You piss me off and I'll kick your goddamn worthless ass all the way inside the chamber, press or no fuckin' press. Now get him goin'!" he barked at the two guards, who complied by jerking Kruger forward as if he had been a bail of straw.

"Move!" McPeters ordered from behind them. "No more of your shit, *no damn more!"*

McPeters's severity and the momentum of Griffis and Hancock got Kruger past the Death Row door and inside the Death Chamber's door, but the instant he saw the black-robed executioner, he balked and went into a screaming fit.

"Aiii! . . . *No!* . . . *No!* . . . *No!"* he bleated, jerking his tall, skinny body up between the two guards like a puppet on a string. "Don't let him touch me! . . . *Please!* . . . *God!* . . . *Please!* . . ." he kept on screaming, the iron claws digging into his wrists as he kicked and pulled between his guards, pushing himself back into the hallway.

Housley, the executioner, jumped back at the sight of the berserk Kruger wedging himself against the far wall of his booth. Hugh Greenwood stood by helplessly. And there was a fever of babble among the witnesses that Lieutenant Sewell and Pete Stokes, who stood riveted to the sight, did not try to quiet.

Griffis and Hancock struggled with Kruger, who was fighting with crazed strength, but again it was McPeters who came up directly behind Kruger and put an end to the fight. Seemingly he came out of nowhere, like a giant pro defensive tackle, scooping up an end who just caught a pass on the line of scrimmage.

He dipped down under Kruger with his left hand under his back and his right hand under his leg above his knees. "Let go!" he bellowed at Griffis and Hancock. *"Let go, dammit!"* And in a savage football motion he had Kruger in the air. He took three steps and then, as if in a football tackle, he dumped Kruger into the seat of the chair. Griffis and Hancock needed no orders. Instantly they were on Kruger, Griffis to his right, Hancock to his left. Greenwood also moved as if by an unspoken command from McPeters, going behind the chair to grab Kruger around the neck from between the slats. Griffis quickly attached the chest strap. Hancock cinched the waist strap. All the while, McPeters was on his knees directly in front of the chair, pushing Kruger's feet back into the ankle stocks, his hands like vice grips. Griffis moved to the right arm strap and Hancock moved to the left arm strap; Kruger's arms were pinned in place within seconds. Then the two guards moved down to the ankles and in seconds the ankles were rendered motionless.

McPeters bolted to his feet then, motioning for Hugh Greenwood to release Kruger's head. Greenwood let go and moved back to the right of the chair to his place by the Executioner's Booth.

"John, what the hell?" Greenwood questioned, pained.

McPeters shook off the warden's words roughly, turning to Lasseter, who stood by silently in sick disgust.

"Cabel!" McPeters snapped. *"Move!"*

McPeters's words set the electrician in motion. He moved behind the chair and took the Ground Pad from the top of the Lead Line Cabinet. At the same moment, Hank Chrysler, who was standing just to McPeters's left, bent down and rolled Kruger's right trouser leg almost to his knee. Lasseter was there at Kruger's right leg in seconds. He dropped to one knee and began lacing the five hooks of the ground pad, securing it to the shaved flesh of Kruger's leg four inches above his thin, veinous right ankle. When it was in place, Lasseter immediately began attaching the right lead line to the pad with its copper wing nut. When the connection was made, both Lasseter and Hank Chrysler stood up and faced Hugh Greenwood, who came around to the front of the chair.

"George Kruger," Greenwood said, his face revealing deep anxiety, "do you wish to make a last statement before sentence is carried out?"

Kruger had been as stiff and brittle as a piece of new pottery while the strapping took place. When Greenwood spoke to him, the words seemed to trigger mechanisms lost in his fear-clouded mind. His insane, wild-animal eyes broadened and his mouth opened in an effort to speak, but the only sounds that came out were scattered, incoherent chokings, his words cut off by sheer terror.

Greenwood's face knotted with tension, and he appeared on the verge of cracking himself. "Do you have anything to say?" he piped in a shrill voice.

Again Kruger tried to speak, the pupils of his eyes eaten up by terror. In the Executioner's Booth, David Housley rammed himself against the far wall and looked out through the eye-level slit at Kruger's disgusting form. The condemned man looked like a big overgrown child, his egg-shaped shaved head and wan face giving him the appearance of a teenager in an insane asylum. *It's all so different,* Housley thought. He had expected burly, violent, defiant mad-dog killers and rapists, and instead he was confronted with sickening examples of gutless human garbage. His mind raced in a thousand directions. Suddenly he wanted to run, but there was no place, no way, to run. He pushed himself away from the wall and steadied himself at the control panels and made his eyes remain glued to the scene at the chair.

In the Witness Chamber, several people were on the verge of being sick. Evan Kerr of the Associated Press, seated next to Lincoln Daniels, turned to him and spoke loudly. Kerr, a hard-bitten AP war correspondent of ten years, a sarcastic drunk whose only means of sobriety was his work, did not have compassion on his liquor-marked face, only anger.

"This is a fucking travesty," he said to Daniels. "Taking the time to execute this garbage is like calling for an air strike on a rice paddy."

Daniels tried not to respond to Kerr, as the grim scene continued to be played out before him and the other witnesses in the Death Chamber. "I know, I know," he finally said, his voice strained, "but what the hell good does it do to talk about it here? I just want this mad thing to end."

Lieutenant Sewell stepped forward from Lincoln's right, about to call for silence in the room, but before he could speak, Paul O'Dell, the *New York Times* man seated directly under Sewell's nervous eye, banged out of his seat and confronted the prison lieutenant nose to nose.

"Why don't you give that mountain-man horseshit a rest?" O'Dell raged. "There are any number of people in this room who could kick your fucking face in, myself included."

Lincoln Daniels's attention instantly shifted from Kerr to O'Dell and Sewell. He jumped to his feet and shoved O'Dell back down into his seat. "Goddammit," he cried, "what in the hell is this, some sort of half-assed debating society? What the hell are we all doing? What the hell *can* we do? Nothing! *Nothing!*" His fists clenched. "Goddammit, man," he shouted into Sewell's face, "back off. Just back the hell off. We'll comply with your rules for the benefit of the other witnesses, but just back the goddamned hell off."

Sewell had mayhem in his eyes. He was shaking with anger, waiting like a cornered rattlesnake, trying to decide whether or not to strike. Before he could make up his mind, Pete Stokes cut in from the other side of the room.

"Please!" he shouted to everyone. "Mr. Daniels is right. There is nothing we can do. There is nothing we should do. No matter how these people look, or how sickening their actions may be, they have been sentenced to death. Why can't we all just do what we were told. Why can't we do what we're supposed to do?"

Stokes's words brought the minor rebellion to a halt. Lincoln Daniels sat down, and after a few uneasy moments Lieutenant Sewell took two steps backward and rammed himself against the Witness Chamber's outside wall.

"Please, Paul," Lincoln Daniels said, searching Paul O'Dell's beet-red, violently angry face. *"Please,"* he added in a tone that he tried to make both conciliatory and demanding.

"But it was Kruger's own wild screams that finally brought complete quiet into the Witness Chamber. "Please . . . *Please!"* Kruger shrieked. "I can't stand this! I can't stand this! . . . God!" he cried. "It's going to hurt! . . . It's going to hurt! . . . I can't stand it! . . . *I can't stand it!"*

Kruger was foaming at the mouth, his hands and ankles digging into the thick leather straps, his bald head banging back into the two vertical headrests. You could see he had retreated into a black fear-fantasy world from which there would be no return.

"Enough! *Enough!"* McPeters commanded, his words shooting out like savage punches at Hugh Greenwood's confused face. "Get on with it! . . . Get on with it! . . . *Now!"*

Greenwood snapped back to reality and motioned for Lasseter to drop the Death Cap over Kruger's head.

"Ooooohhh! . . . Ooooohhh! . . . Ohhhhhhh!" Kruger began to cry in crazy animal moans, his head still banging back into the headrests. "Pain! . . . *God!* . . . I can't stand pain! . . . I don't want pain! . . . I don't want death! . . . *Death!* . . . Oh, God, no, not death. . . . *Death! . . . Ooooohhh. . . . Ooooohhh. . . . No!* . . . Not death! . . . *No!"* His high-pitched voice was hoarse and distorted from his screaming and vain straining against the straps.

On Greenwood's command, Lasseter moved to the Lead Line Cabinet and took the chin strap in both hands. He turned and came up behind the chair; McPeters already had Kruger's head pushed back into the headrest, wedging it there with both hands locked on either side of Kruger's face, his thick thumbs pressing hard on either side of the condemned man's nose. Lasseter dropped the chin strap over Kruger's head and in one motion had the chin cup in place and was cinching the buckle tight behind the headrest. At last Kruger was totally helpless.

McPeters moved back to his position in front of Greenwood and to the side of the Executioner's Booth. Lasseter bent down and fished the Contact Plate out of the saline solution in the galvanized bucket at his feet. He squeezed it nearly dry and then returned to the rear of the chair and the Lead Line Cabinet. He took the Death Cap from the top of the cabinet and inserted the Contact Plate; then he turned back to face the rear of the electric chair once more. Kruger had been silent since the chin strap had been put in place, his eyes ravenously searching the faces in the Witness Chamber; the instant the Death Cap and its mask were in place over his face, putting him into darkness, his animal screams, now muffled and distorted by the chin strap, resumed in a frenzy. And he began to shake. Every part of his body seemed about to come apart:

"Hurry, damn it," McPeters boomed at Lasseter, unable to control his anger and disgust. "Hurry!"

Lasseter bent down and grabbed the left lead line, retrieved the Death Cap's large, round copper wing nut from the top of the Lead Line Cabinet, and came up behind the chair and began making the final connection between the Contact Pad and the lead line. When the connection was made he stepped back and took his place at Kruger's left hand. McPeters and Greenwood were already in their positions to Kruger's right. Greenwood glanced at the wall clock behind the chair: it was 8:18. He took his notebook out of his inside coat pocket and got ready to mark the time.

When he was ready, Greenwood nodded to Lasseter. The electrician moved quickly behind the chair to the far side of the Lead Line Cabinet and tripped the fail-safe bar into the ON position. George Kruger bounced violently at the thudding connection; like Alice Fuller, his crazed mind interpreted the thud as the Death Switch itself. When death did not come, Kruger stopped his shaking and gripped both arm rests of the chair with such intensity that his bony knuckles turned white. The only part of his body that moved was his head, and that movement was only in half inches under the restraint of the chin strap, the Death Cap, and the taut lead line.

With the fail-safe bar activated, Lasseter turned to the top of the Lead Line Cabinet once more. He took his thick black gloves from the top of the cabinet, put them on, and, granite-faced, once more returned to his position at Kruger's left, watching Greenwood get ready to give his signal to the executioner.

David Housley again faced the two control panels in his booth. He felt sick.

McPeters watched Greenwood as the warden turned once more to the wall clock. It was four seconds away from 8:19.

"Engage," Greenwood said, beginning the ritual again.

The executioner's hand snapped up to the right control panel. He turned the circuit-breaker switch to the left, and with a metallic thud the eight-cycle Death Machine was engaged.

Again, Kruger's body snapped at the foreign sound.

Next in sequence, the executioner pushed the red transfer button at the top of the circuit-breaker switch, and there was a grinding hum from the rear of the Witness Chamber in the Circuit Room as the power of the Death Machine was transferred directly to the Death Switch on the executioner's left control panel.

Kruger shook violently at the humming sound, again like Alice Fuller, knowing the electricity was upon him. He let out a fiendish muffled whine behind the chin strap. On the left panel, the Ready Light over the red Death Switch again flashed on. Housley's right hand moved to the Death Switch and engaged it firmly. Through the eye-level slit in his booth, he watched the clock's second hand and Greenwood's mouth. At exactly 8:19 Greenwood said the killing word *"Now!"* and Housley jerked the thumb-shaped Death Switch to the left, sending the 2,250 raw volts of electricity crashing into Kruger's shaved skull.

Because Kruger's body was so rigid prior to the switch, his toes and fingers snapped like broken twigs. After the 5-second high-range burst of electricity hit his body and the first 25-second, low-range cycle of 1,000 volts began, most of Kruger's long, thin fingers were broken at the knuckles. He had already passed his urine and it was running off the front of the chair in gushes. And from under the Death Mask, out onto his already vomit-stained white shirt, there came a slow trickle of bright red blood. Cabel Lasseter was the first to see it. His eyes flashed to McPeters and then to Greenwood. Once McPeters saw it, he could not restrain himself.

"Goddammit," he moaned, slamming his fist into his open palm. "He bit his tongue. Goddammit, he bit his tongue!"

Greenwood turned away from the sight and started for the Death Chamber's door to get Dr. Hayes. But he stopped short, seized by the irony of his action. In the electric chair, Kruger had reached the midpoint of the eight-part killing cycle. His pale body was now pinkish-purple and nearly 200 degrees. Fibrillation and respiratory paralysis of his lungs had set in, and at the end of the eighth and final cycle, the respiratory center of his brain had burned up.

When the Death Machine thumped off at the end of the two minutes, Kruger's body slumped down into the straps. His shirtfront was soaked with blood, which continued to trickle down beneath the Death Mask, and his right leg was drawn up tight in the ankle strap, in the rigid, inverted V of death. McPeters studied the body for a few seconds and then nodded for Cabel Lasseter to turn the fail-safe bar back to the OFF position. Simultaneously, Greenwood motioned for David Housley to come out of the Executioner's Booth. As soon as Housley made his way out of the booth, you could tell he was shaken. He rocked slightly as he stood outside the booth, supporting himself with his left hand against the wall.

"No, you don't," McPeters stormed at him. "No, by God, you don't. You stand up straight, or I'll beat your goddamn head in right where you are. Stand up, goddamn you!" he shouted.

Housley complied, his hands jamming down to his side, almost as if he were assuming the position of attention. McPeters kept his eyes on him a second more and then signaled Hugh Greenwood to bring Dr. Hayes into the room. But before the doctor could take the few short steps from where he stood outside in the corridor, horror visited the Death Chamber as if Hell itself had been revealed to all present.

In the chair, George Kruger's fingers began to twitch and his shoulders began to heave into the chest straps.

There was instant bedlam in the Witness Chamber; in the Death Chamber, McPeters grabbed Dr. Hayes and flung him in front of Kruger's convulsing body.

Hayes was dumbstruck. His hands trembled. McPeters had to forcibly hold him in front of Kruger.

"His pulse! His pulse! Take his goddamn pulse. Is he alive, or is it just his muscles? Move! Move! Goddammit, *move!*"

Hayes took Kruger's right wrist and held on tightly, trying to find a pulse. There was instant absolute hush in both chambers. Everyone stopped still for the doctor's finding.

After ten seconds, Hayes dropped Kruger's wrist and jerked up to his feet to face McPeters. "There's a pulse! Good God in heaven! There's a pulse! He's alive! He's alive! Jesus. The man's still *alive!*" Hayes said hysterically.

"John!" Hugh Greenwood moaned, stepping toward McPeters, his arms outstretched and pleading.

"No!" McPeters bellowed, sending him cowering backward. *"You!"* McPeters pointed to the executioner. "Get back in the booth!"

Housley's eyes were frozen on Kruger's body. He could not move. McPeters grabbed him savagely, spinning him around and toward the booth's opening.

In the Witness Chamber, shouting and cursing broke out again; Lieutenant Sewell and Pete Stokes were powerless to contain it.

Everything seemed to happen at once. The doctor fled the room, Lasseter tripped the fail-safe bar to the ON position, and as soon as the power was transferred back to the Executioner's Booth, McPeters who gave the order to throw the Death Switch as Hugh Greenwood stood by, unable to act.

"Engage the machine and throw the switch," McPeters ordered the executioner, shouting at him through the eye-level slit.

Housley's hand jerked toward the circuit-breaker switch, then the transfer button, and quickly then, without thinking, to the left-hand panel and the Death Switch.

Again, with a *whop,* Kruger's body surged up into the Contact Plate, and as it did, Cabel Lasseter turned on McPeters.

"John," he said, unmindful of the witnesses, "the pad, the pad"—he choked—"it's dry. The pad is dry."

McPeters didn't answer. His face turned gray, and like Lasseter and every other person in both chambers, he turned and stared intently at Kruger's head as the eight cycles of the two-minute killing process were played out. It was on the seventh cycle, a 5-second high-range register, that a thin, yellowish-gray line of smoke began rising from the top of Kruger's skull. But there was nothing anyone could do. They had to stand by and wait the final thirty seconds as the top of Kruger's head was seared by the bare copper wires that had eaten their way through the thin elephant-ear sponge coating.

Cabel Lasseter was standing over the fail-safe bar the instant the Death Machine cut off. He tripped the bar back to the right, to the OFF position, and then moved frantically behind the chair and unscrewed the Death Cap's wing nut. McPeters, at his side, was unfastening the Death Cap's neck strap. In one quick motion Lasseter pulled the smoking Contact Plate and the Death Cap off Kruger's shaven head. Charred flesh clung to the plate's circular surface. The top of

Kruger's skull was black, with a ring of pink inner flesh where the Contact Plate had been. And with the face mask gone, they all saw Kruger's face.

A half inch of purple tongue dangled out of the left corner of his mouth. His chin was coated with brown blood. But it was his eyes that threw most into a sick frenzy. Both eyeballs, the pupils almost indistinguishable in the center of a brown and red mass of distorted marblelike iris, were completely out of their sockets; they drooped just over the stiff bottom eyelid in a grotesque parody of a disassembled child's doll.

All of the front row of witnesses, Lincoln Daniels included, were standing when McPeters looked up from undoing the neck strap. He boiled at the sight of the witnesses out of their seats, but he let it go, turning his wrath on Hugh Greenwood, who stood paralyzed to his right.

"Get the doctor in here. *Right now!* Get the doctor in here!"

Hayes appeared instantly.

"Check him. *Check him, goddammit!* All of you," he bellowed to those in the Death Chamber, "wake the hell up! Move, dammit! *Move!*"

Hayes descended on Kruger's body; it took him only seconds to make his findings. "He's dead," he said to McPeters. "Dead. . . ." And he turned and pushed out of the room without another word.

Hayes's two convict orderlies did not want to touch Kruger's body, but McPeters shoved both of them into action as the second ambulance crew came through the Death Chamber's door carrying a portable stretcher between them.

"Get him on the stretcher, *now!*" McPeters shouted, his fists balled.

Bob Griffis had the chamber's outside door open before the two orderlies had Kruger's body on the stretcher and covered with a sheet. Like Alice Fuller's body, Kruger's right leg held its inverted V position, but unlike the woman's body, the two orderlies could not push Kruger's arms down by his sides.

As the ambulance attendants carried Kruger out into the driving rain, a gust of wind took the sheet away as if it had been stretched over a pile of sticks. Cold rain struck Kruger's face, hands, and feet, and where it made contact, gray steam rose from the still hot body. Earl Hancock retrieved the sheet from the cold, muddy ground and again draped it over Kruger's body. This time the damp, muddy sheet stuck. Hancock opened the rear door of the ambulance, and the two attendants slid the body inside. Then Hancock darted back toward the Death Chamber. Only then, as he came inside, past Bob Griffis, did he smell the dingy, charred odor of death in the room. He caught himself as he came up in front of McPeters, who was standing with Cabel Lasseter over the galvanized bucket behind the chair. He gritted his teeth and held back the strong urge to vomit. McPeters saw the reaction and ordered him back to the open door.

"Leave it open!" McPeters said through his own clenched teeth, a reaction not out of nausea but anger. He had acted too quickly. The Contact Plate was ruined. It was his fault. He believed he had allowed for all contingencies, but now it seemed that the thing itself was taking over. He fought with himself to regain control. He showed no outward emotion that he was losing control, but it was all going wrong; nothing was as he remembered it from before. *Nothing.* But the thoughts were deep within his mind. There was the reality of the thing, and that was what he had to deal with.

"Can it be fixed?" he asked Lasseter as they stood looking at the Contact Plate, with its copper mesh exposed, small pieces of blackened flesh trapped between the wires, and the remains of the elephant-ear sponge.

Lasseter stared at the object; then he turned and looked directly into McPeters's face. "No," he said. Then he took a long, deep breath. "But it doesn't matter, anyway," he went on. "It was only for cosmetics," he added, his face twisted at his choice of words. "It actually works as well or better without it. There will just be burning and smoke if we have to give another second shot. There may even be smoke from just one shot."

McPeters's eyes saw only the Contact Plate in Lasseter's hands, but his ears took in the electrician's every word. "It works," McPeters said, his eyes still fixed on the plate. "That's all I want to know—it works."

"Yes, it works," Lasseter replied.

"All right," McPeters said. "All right. Clean it. And let's get on with it."

Lasseter did not reply. He knelt down and went about the grisly business of cleaning the pad for the next execution.

Leo Dunbar had come in and was standing out from the chair, ready to clean it. McPeters motioned for him to begin. Then he started toward Hugh Greenwood and the executioner, who were standing by the chamber's open inner door.

"John," Greenwood said, pleadingly, as McPeters came up to him.

McPeters shook off his name. "It's only going to get worse," he said. "We're going after Santos."

"Dammit, John!" Greenwood said. "I never thought it would be this bad. I never thought it *could* be this bad."

McPeters shook his head again and walked out of the room without answering.

8:30 A.M.

Sounds came in on Death Row as the steel door was opened once more. José Santos was on his knees in front of his wall bunk, his elbows on the bunk as if in prayer. But he was not in prayer, and although he heard the sounds of the door opening and McPeters and his Death Strap squad entering the hall, he did not move from his position or give any sign to Joe Morris, his Death Watch guard, that he knew McPeters was on the Row, that it was his turn to die.

The indifferent priest from Starke had been gone for half an hour. He had administered the Last Rites to Santos, and Santos had accepted them, but Santos was a failed Catholic, and he knew what a terrible thing that was to be in the most consoling and damning of Western religions. On his knees, instead of praying or making the sign of God that he had been taught since he was a child, José Santos was giving himself a sort of absolution, or at the least having final moments of peace before he played out the last act of his life.

He was totally sane and completely in control of his body and mind, and he realized that he was so castrated by the thing that he could simply walk down the hall and be electrocuted without a whimper. But his will would not let him walk down the hall like a beast to the slaughter. He had lived by a code of fanaticism, a twisted, out-of-whack set of rules that had led him to kill both those he judged guilty and, inadvertently, those he knew to be innocent—a code that had brought him to Death Row, but a code nonetheless, *his* code—and to simply abandon it, to abandon what he had conceived life stood for, would be to abandon his life itself. And with death upon him, Santos still reacted to life. He knew that what he might do from his cell to the electric chair would not alter the fact of his dying, but he believed he was bound to die as he had lived. His fantasy of his homeland of Cuba, all his dreams and aspirations, counted for nothing now. All that counted was how he died.

McPeters reached Santos's cell with his squad two steps behind him. The Death Watch guard, Joe Morris, was on his feet when McPeters arrived at the cell door. He and McPeters exchanged glances but neither said anything. There was no need for words; both knew what to expect.

Standing even with the Cuban's cell door, McPeters peered inside for a second, watching as the smaller man knelt by his wall bunk. At first McPeters took it as a good sign, a sign of pacifism.

"José," McPeters said, the note of near friendship that he had extended to Alice Fuller and George Kruger present in his voice. "José," he said a second time, going silent when he saw that Santos gave no recognition whatsoever to his name. "It's time." Now there was no offer of implied friendship in his tone. He knew what was coming; he had known it all along. There was no need to try to do it the easy way.

Still without looking at McPeters or the guards at his cell door, Santos stood up from his kneeling position, his movements deliberate and catlike. He turned his back on the guards and took one step toward the rear wall, then turned about, his eyes on the five men for the first time. He placed his left foot slightly forward of his right foot. He crooked his left arm and held it just to his front, even with his waist. He crooked his right arm in similar fashion and held it just to the rear. He did not speak; his eyes did not move. No part of his body moved. He stood in total readiness to fight, to do what he had always intended to do when the time came.

"Son," McPeters said evenly, "there's no need for this. It will come to nothing. It's time for you to go, and you're going. You can buy yourself maybe five minutes. You can get off punches. You can hurt us. We can hurt you. But you'll go down that hall, and you'll sit in that chair, and that's the way it will be, fight or no fight."

McPeters had said all he had to say. He studied Santos a few seconds more to see if his words had any effect. But he knew they wouldn't. He took his key and stuck it into the door's lock. He turned the key to the right and the door clicked open. As the lock bar disengaged, McPeters gave instructions to those behind him —Bob Griffis to his left, Earl Hancock to his right, Hank Chrysler directly behind him, and Joe Morris, slightly to Chrysler's right—his eyes never leaving Santos.

"Stand pat," he said. "I'll get him and bring him out to you. We'll cuff him in the hall and then run him down to the chamber, Hank in front, Joe and me in back."

McPeters swung the door open and stood in the middle of the opening for a second, sizing Santos up like a professional prizefighter. He made his lunge straight forward; then, in mid-motion, he wheeled slightly to the right, Santos's right leg missing him by six inches, as he drove the Cuban's head back against the concrete wall with a long savage left jab that caught Santos square in the mouth and nose. Blood spattered out of Santos's face; his upper lip was split, his nose broken just below the bridge.

Santos, seemingly unmindful of the hammer blow, wheeled to his left and clipped McPeters under his left cheekbone with a knifelike right cross that opened a deep two-inch gash on the big man's face. Santos's punch did its desired work, but it left the smaller man facing his opponent head on at half a foot.

McPeters countered with an anvil-like forearm to Santos's neck, choking off all air, and followed with a right knee to his groin. The exchange had brought Santos only eight seconds. Now he slumped, semiconscious, to the cell floor, his mouth and broken nose gushing blood, his groin bruised. McPeters stepped back from Santos's beaten frame and motioned for Griffis and Hancock to come inside the cell.

"Cuff him in here," he said, breathing heavily. "We'll get him down the hall before he knows what hit him."

The two guards darted into the cell, Griffis to Santos's right, Hancock to his left. They hooked the iron claws to Santos's wrists and pulled the dull-eyed man to his feet. McPeters took the towel from above the washbasin and wiped the blood from the Cuban's face as best he could.

"You dumb sonofabitch," he said, although Santos was obviously unable to comprehend the words. "You had nothing, so you bought nothing. Goddammit, you *knew* that! You knew that, *damn you!* Damn you, you asshole, you knew that!"

The shouts brought Santos back to reality. He shook off his dizziness and nausea; his face was etched with pain. "Something," Santos said through bubbles of blood from his nose and lips, the word said as if distorted by water. "Something," he said again, with great difficulty, "I . . . I . . . had to do . . . something. . . . Have to act. . . . Have to do something . . . again.

A man," he moaned, the pain in his groin almost pushing him back into unconsciousness. "Man . . . something. . . . A man—" He broke off, pain overcoming his will. McPeters stared at him, his hand went up to wipe his face again; he seemed about to say something to the condemned man, but he held both his hands and his words back.

"Get him out! *Get him out!*" he ordered Griffis and Hancock, turning his eyes away from Santos's bloody form. "Let's go! *Let's go!*" The two guards jerked Santos to the door and through it, into the hall, bound for the Death Chamber.

"Jesus Christ, John," Hugh Greenwood choked as Griffis and Hancock dragged the bloody Santos past him. "John!" he gasped as McPeters entered the Death Chamber's doorway.

"Don't open your goddamn mouth to me," McPeters bellowed back. "You and the boy-fucking-wonder governor are to blame for all this. No Preparation. You remember that? No Preparation. You said it was too physical, too out of touch. You said nobody would buy it. Well, take a look at Santos. Take a look at me," he said, wiping at his own bloody face. "Then take a look at the witnesses. You tell me who the hell was right?

"Nobody! No-goddamn-body!" he stormed on, his mouth only inches away from Greenwood's distraught face. "Nobody keeps the old ways any more. But this is an old thing. It has nothing to do with the asshole nonsense of today, the wishy-washy, maybe-I-will, maybe-I-won't bullshit, cover-your-ass nonsense that the world runs on. This is death, *executed* death. There's a right way to do it and a wrong way. And goddamn your stinking, miserable ass, you and fucking Kingsly have done it all goddamn wrong."

"John!" Cabel Lasseter said in a loud voice, moving over to McPeters and cautiously but firmly grasping his shoulders. "Ease off!"

McPeters's rage had been spent. He glared down at Greenwood, but he had nothing else to say. They had to get on with it. That was what overrode everything else in his mind. He allowed Lasseter to pull him away from the warden and to the front of the electric chair, where Griffis, Hancock, and Chrysler had finished strapping the dazed Santos into place.

When Lasseter released McPeters, he went to the Lead Line Cabinet for the Ground Pad. He retrieved the object and came back with it to Santos's right leg. He bent down, as Hank Chrysler rolled Santos's trouser leg almost to his knee, and began securing the pad in place with the shoestring around the five hooks. When it was secured, he took the right lead line at his feet and secured it to the pad with the small copper wing nut. He tugged at the connection to see if it was secure.

The tug and the cold pad on his shaved leg brought Santos back to consciousness again. He came awake in the chair, loose and easy as if from a drugged sleep, but at once his body turned rigid as he pulled against the unyielding leather strap.

"Ah—" Santos mouthed beyond his swollen, blood-crusted lips. "Eh—" he said, seemingly able to make only grunts. Then he found words. "You! . . . you! . . ." he gulped, taking in a half mouthful of blood, spitting it out in front of the chair, his eyes searching for McPeters. "You son of a bitch! You think you won!" he shouted, spitting out the remainder of the blood in his mouth, clearing his speech. "You didn't win shit! Not shit, do you understand? *Not shit!*"

McPeters started to speak but locked his jaws and said nothing. Santos's words brought Hugh Greenwood back from his motionless state. He moved around in front of the condemned man, avoiding the blood on the rubber matting in front of the chair, as he faced him with resolution.

"Are those your last words?" he asked tightly. "You can make a last statement. Was that your statement?" He became suddenly firm and authoritative, an authority that caught McPeters's attention.

The words also had an effect on Santos. They stopped him as if they triggered something deep within his mind.

"No! . . . *No!*" Santos gulped, his eyes widening with fright as his head bent to the right to face Warden

Greenwood. "No, they're not my statement," he said, with urgency. "I don't have a statement. I wipe my ass on you. On all of you!" he screamed, his head jerking back to McPeters, then to the front toward the witnesses, and finally back to Greenwood and David Housley, the executioner, who stood just outside his booth. *"I wipe my ass on the whole world!"* he screamed, spitting out a fresh mouthful of bright red blood.

Greenwood stepped back to avoid the gush of blood. For the first time his face was marked by anger, his fists clenched. "That's it," he said directly to McPeters. "To hell with this. Get on with your work, major," he instructed.

In the chair, Santos twisted his head from McPeters to Greenwood and back between the men once more. "Wait! . . . Wait!" he cried, suddenly panicked. *"Wait!* . . . I don't want it to end like this. I didn't mean it. What I said, I didn't mean it. What I did, the killing, all of it . . . I didn't mean it," he screamed, his face a mass of confusion.

Greenwood shook his head. "It's too late," he said. "It's too late."

Santos fell silent at the finality of Greenwood's words. An absolute hush came over both chambers. Then Santos spoke again for the last time, tears beginning to run down his cheeks.

"I've got a last statement," he choked out. "Let this be my last statement." The words were distorted by blood and spittle that began to form in his mouth. "Why me?" he said. *"Why me?"* he screamed, spitting a mouthful of blood out onto his lap.

In the Witness Chamber, Lincoln Daniels finally understood John McPeters's words of the previous night. "Nothing," McPeters had said. Lincoln understood, but he preferred Santos's word: waste. *Absolute waste,* he said to himself.

Cabel Lasseter came up behind Santos with the Contact Plate inserted into the Death Cap. He dropped the implement onto the condemned man's head and down over his face, while McPeters held the head in place against the headrest. But there was no fight left

in Santos. He held his own head rigidly back against
the headrest as if he had been given prior instructions.

Lasseter cinched the Death Cap's neck strap in
place, and McPeters withdrew his hand. Quickly, Lasseter secured the left electrical lead to the Death Cap,
then tested its connection with a sharp tug that pulled
Santos's head back hard against the wooden headrest,
a motion that did not produce a sound from the condemned man.

All was done; again Lasseter conveyed readiness
to Greenwood, and Greenwood conveyed the command
for death to David Housley, the executioner. The
Death Switch was thrown at two seconds past 8:40,
and Santos was pronounced dead at exactly 8:43. But
for the time between the Death Switch and the time the
Death Machine disengaged, no one in either chamber
saw the movement Santos made in the electric chair
as his body was killed, or thought of time, or of the
idea of the man's death itself. For those two minutes,
the twenty people in the two chambers saw only one
thing: the figure of Cabel Lasseter, standing behind
the electric chair, his face gaunt and vacant, his black
rubber-gloved hands gripping the top of the Death Cap,
pressing it down onto Santos's head to assure the
lethal connection of the bare copper electrodes of the
contact plate. It was a sight that, like the electric chair
itself, had no frame of reference.

8:50 A.M.

José Santos's blood was still wet on McPeters's shirt
as he came up to the door of Charlie Parker's cell,
but the blood in the gash on his left cheek had dried.
Parker was sitting when McPeters came up; as soon as
he saw the major, he stood.

"This has sure been one hell of a morning for

you, hasn't it?" Parker said, in words that caught Mc-
Peters so off guard they stunned him.

To add to McPeters's confusion, a thin smile appeared on Parker's face.

When he didn't answer, the big black man spoke
again, the words coming out with the assuredness of a
prepared statement. "I feel sorry for you," Parker said,
"if that's any comfort. I honestly feel sorry for you.
You're the real loser here. But hell," he added, almost
smiling, "you know that. You know damn good and
well you didn't punish those three slobs you just killed.
Society didn't get shit out of it, and neither did you."

"We haven't got time for this, Charlie," McPeters
broke in, using his open right hand for emphasis. "You
can say your piece inside, you—"

"Just a minute," Parker interrupted. "I want to
say this to you. I don't give a damn about the people
out there. They don't count. What counts is you and
me. That's right," he said. "You and me. Not these
flunky guards with you, or the press out there, or the
chair—none of it. *Just you and me.*"

McPeters dropped his hand to his side and listened, not so much to hear what Parker was saying as
simply to let him say it.

"Right." Parker smiled as McPeters gave him the
floor. "You and me," he repeated. "And this is what I
have to say to you. It's short and sweet, and you can
make whatever use of it—some or none—that you
please. I'm going to be dead in a few minutes. I'm
going to walk down the hall and a few sane Christians
are going to wire me up like a Fourth of July candle
and set me off on a journey to heaven or hell or wher-
ever. Which way, I don't know, and I don't particularly
give a damn."

Parker was smiling again. Then he went on.
"What I want you to know is this: something I just
figured out, just since you started coming in here and
snatching people up like rabbits going into the stew.
Legal death," he said, his eyes on a steady, even
plane with McPeters's, "is the one and only Final Thing
that society has come up with since man first crawled

out of the cave. The first thing," he repeated, using
the forefinger of his right hand as a pointer, flashing
his manufactured smile once more. "Not Final Happiness, not Final Food, not Final Shelter, not Final
Work . . . not even Final Hate: just Death . . .
Death," he said again.

"Death," he said once more, and then broke into
a little coughing laugh, as if for his own amusement.
Then he stuck his pointing finger up and out at Mc-
Peters again as he finished his statement. "The easiest
and most obvious commodity—Thing—society could
provide," he ended, no longer smiling or laughing.

There was absolute silence for seconds that
seemed like minutes. Then McPeters answered him.
"Charlie," he said, shaking his head up and down as if
he agreed with what the man had said. "You've got
guts. I'll give you that. I'm not a philosopher," he
added quickly, "so I don't know about the things
you've said. Maybe they're true, maybe they're not.
Probably they *are* true," he said, in words that obviously came hard to him.

"I know that I do feel like a loser right now," he
conceded. "And I'll tell you this: I'll think about
what you've said. I'll do that," he repeated, half to
himself.

"Don't get me wrong," Parker broke in, his face
rigid now. "I'm no damn philosopher either. I'm just a
saloon owner, among other things, a tough guy who
got tough once too often, and with the wrong people.
And if it means anything, I agree with what you said
to Kruger when you told him he'd done his deed, and
now he'd have to take his medicine. I did my deed,
and I'm ready for the medicine. I just wanted to get
the priorities straight, first."

"Okay," McPeters agreed. "It's time," he said, as
part of his ritual. "Let's go."

"Just one thing," Parker said.

McPeters stiffened for the worst.

"I want to go down by myself. Nobody touching
me. *Nobody.* I want to do this myself, major," he said
in a tone that asked rather than told. "I don't want to
be handled."

When he finished his sentence, Parker stood back and waited for McPeters's answer, ready to fight to get what he wanted.

McPeters studied him for a moment. He started to go in and fight, but he held back, not from fear or indecision but from the last thing Parker had said. "I don't want to be handled." McPeters would not have wanted that either. His way for the thing was: "Take it like a man." Parker wanted it that way, and McPeters decided to take a chance and give it to him.

McPeters stepped back and opened the cell door. Parker waited for Griffis and Hancock to turn and take up a position that would be in front of him in the Row's corridor; McPeters and Ham Pervis, the Death Watch guard, stepped back from the open cell door to a position that would be to Parker's rear. Then Parker came out: slow and sure, unhurried and unafraid.

Once outside the door, he turned to Ham Pervis, who was holding his shoes and socks, and held out his hand.

"I'll carry those," he said.

Pervis looked to McPeters for a decision; McPeters nodded approval, and the shoes and socks were passed to Parker.

The five men turned, then, and walked down the corridor in absolute silence.

When Charlie Parker walked into the Death Chamber untouched by the guards, Greenwood, Lasseter, and the executioner were too startled to move. Parker walked slowly between Greenwood and the executioner, studying both, then his eyes fell on Lasseter, then on the chair, and lastly the gaping, dumbstruck witnesses. Then he stood in front of the chair with his back to the witnesses and carefully set his shoes and socks on the rubber matting next to the left ankle stock. He was in complete command, every move he made clean and deliberate.

He studied the chair for a few moments and then looked up at Lasseter, who was standing facing him two feet away, at the back right of the chair. He looked at him but said nothing. His face betrayed no emotion either; it was a block of ice. He adjusted his suit and tie, and then he turned and sat down without further hesitation and still with no display of emotion.

In less than a minute he was strapped in the chair, with the Ground Pad and its lead line attached to his body. Greenwood stepped up before him then, nervous and disturbed at the man's conduct.

"Do you have any last statement you wish to make before sentence is carried out?" he asked in a puzzled voice.

Parker remained serene, sitting in the chair like an African king tied to a ceremonial funeral pyre. It was a full five seconds before he answered the warden.

No man or woman there ever forgot what he answered. *"Put that cap on my head,"* he said, *"and let me go away from here."*

The mask descended over Parker's face. His fingers gripped the ends of the armrests solidly. The electrician made the Contact Plate connection and stepped back and nodded to Greenwood. The warden nodded to the executioner. The Death Machine went through its preparatory thumps. Greenwood said the word "Now," and the Death Switch was thrown.

The current crackled on. Charlie Parker's body made its death surge up into the Contact Plate's 2,250 volts of raw electricity, and the killing process started.

Outside, the savage and monotonous *No*'s began again in the freezing morning rain.

Lake Cuitzeo, Mexico

The lake was still. There was no wind or sound or movement in the small village of St. Agustín de Pulque as the three men got into the dugout canoes held by the polers and their small sons. It was a magnificent, dry October morning, and the chalk-blue sky grew amber with reflected light. The sun had not yet shown itself above the jagged, treeless peaks in the east toward Mexico City.

The men took their places in the canoes, then the sons of the polers, and finally the polers themselves. Across the muddy, brown lake their motion was measured and silent as the canoes slid smoothly through the still water so that the hidden sun was to the left of the passengers.

John McPeters sat in the first canoe, Lincoln Daniels and Palo Reyas behind him in the others. Six days before, McPeters had come in from the prison for a visit, and each day since his arrival the three men had been out on Lake Cuitzeo for the ducks before the sun came up.

Now it was Monday morning. For Lincoln Daniels, Monday morning had become synonymous with the executions at Big Max eight months before. Eight A.M. Monday morning had become death, the four deaths he had seen each Monday since they happened on that bone-cold February morning in north Florida. During the week he was able to put the deaths out of

303

his mind, but on Monday morning he would always awake early from a sound sleep, frazzled and jumpy, with visions of the deaths—visions he couldn't shake until he had replayed the bloody hour he had spent in the Witness Chamber.

He was finally convinced that the deaths were just, and he had said so in his *Esquire* article and in his book, *Small Deaths,* which he had delivered in August to William Rockbridge in New York. There he had written:

> War is so clear, so easy, because there are choices, because killing makes sense, accomplishes an objective: territory or honor, or both. Natural death is also clear and easy. There is weeping, there is sorrow and sadness and a sense of loss, of ending. But legal death is death reduced to its lowest, basest form—totally without honor, without dignity, without feeling, without any human emotion.
>
> There are no tears because we are taught that there has to be a good and just reason for weeping. Legal death, we are told, is not a condition for mourning—not a condition at all, but rather an *act*, a one-dimensional act. But never in all my life have I seen a thing that is so in need of weeping. People die and there is no grief, and maybe that is the greatest sadness, sadder than all else because it signifies a failure on the part of all of us.
>
> If you are seeking tangible evidence of the flaw of 50,000 years of human civilization, look no further. It is legal death, and it is altogether our greatest shame that we have it and that we need it. It is the sad and terrible proof that we are, after all, a society of fear.
>
> And who is more to blame than I. I took money, a great deal of it, for going to see the thing, and for telling about it.

Five days after the executions, David Housley, the executioner, had written a letter telling of his part in the executions and explaining his feelings in a jumbled, garbled fashion, and then he had taken his fishing cruiser out in the Gulf Stream ten miles off Bimini and blown himself and the boat to bits by lighting the thousand-gallon tank of gasoline on board.

Cabel Lasseter had asked for, and had been granted, early retirement with full pay, even though he was only a year away from regular retirement. The special request had never before been granted, but when he made it two weeks after Housley killed himself and three weeks before the next executions took place, no one in the state capitol objected.

A new electrician was hired, and a new executioner. The executions continued. Over a hundred people were now in Big Max's Death Facility, and the Women's Prison at Lowell held six in their Death Unit. The law was the law and it stayed the law, and people were found to carry it out.

On the lake, Lincoln watched the canoes go before him on line with the great reedbeds still two miles beyond in the center of the brown body of water. The sun was just breaking over the ridges of the bare mountains to the east as, far out on the horizon, the great flock of birds arched up into the sky. In a while they would come down to the lake's surface to escape the fiery heat of the sun, and, as was the custom, the hunters would be obliged to kill four.

Lincoln sat in the bow of his canoe and watched the birds. His eyes did not leave them once as he moved across the still and ancient lake.

ABOUT THE AUTHOR

JAMES MCLENDON lived the first eighteen years of his life at Raiford State Prison in an isolated part of north Florida—the setting for *Deathwork*. McLendon, the son of a senior prison official, was a guard in five Florida prisons, a U.S. Marine infantryman, and, after attending four southern universities, he taught the sixth grade and algebra in Baltimore, Md., area public schools. He was on the staff of a Baltimore stock brokerage firm when he decided to embark on a writing career in 1967. After working on several southern daily newspapers. McLendon took a job with the Key West, Fla. *Citizen* while he did research for his biography, *Papa: Hemingway in Key West.* From 1972 until 1977, and the publication of *Deathwork*, McLendon wrote a history, *Pioneer in the Florida Keys,* and authored more than three hundred magazine articles, which appeared in such publications as *Holiday, Saturday Evening Post,* and *Town & Country.* McLendon and his wife, Ann, an internationally published photographer, and their three children, Stacey, Ian, and Caitlin, divide their year between the Blue Ridge Mountain town of Blowing Rock, N. C., and the 437-year old city of Morelia, Mexico.

DON'T MISS
THESE CURRENT
Bantam Bestsellers

INTIMATE REFLECTIONS

Thoughts, ideas, and perceptions of life as it is.

RELAX!
SIT DOWN
and Catch Up On Your Reading!

☐	11877	**HOLOCAUST** by Gerald Green	$2.25
☐	11260	**THE CHANCELOR MANUSCRIPT** by Robert Ludlum	$2.25
☐	10077	**TRINITY** by Leon Uris	$2.75
☐	2300	**THE MONEYCHANGERS** by Arthur Hailey	$1.95
☐	12550	**THE MEDITERRANEAN CAPER** by Clive Cussler	$2.25
☐	2500	**THE EAGLE HAS LANDED** by Jack Higgins	$1.95
☐	2600	**RAGTIME** by E. L. Doctorow	$2.25
☐	10888	**RAISE THE TITANIC!** by Clive Cussler	$2.25
☐	11966	**THE ODESSA FILE** by Frederick Forsyth	$2.25
☐	11770	**ONCE IS NOT ENOUGH** by Jacqueline Susann	$2.25
☐	11708	**JAWS 2** by Hank Searls	$2.25
☐	12490	**TINKER, TAILOR, SOLDIER, SPY** by John Le Carre	$2.50
☐	11929	**THE DOGS OF WAR** by Frederick Forsyth	$2.25
☐	10526	**INDIA ALLEN** by Elizabeth B. Coker	$1.95
☐	12489	**THE HARRAD EXPERIMENT** by Robert Rimmer	$2.25
☐	10422	**THE DEEP** by Peter Benchley	$2.25
☐	10500	**DOLORES** by Jacqueline Susann	$1.95
☐	11601	**THE LOVE MACHINE** by Jacqueline Susann	$2.25
☐	10600	**BURR** by Gore Vidal	$2.25
☐	10857	**THE DAY OF THE JACKAL** by Frederick Forsyth	$1.95
☐	11952	**DRAGONARD** by Rupert Gilchrist	$1.95
☐	2491	**ASPEN** by Burt Hirschfeld	$1.95
☐	11330	**THE BEGGARS ARE COMING** by Mary Loos	$1.95

Bantam Book Catalog

Here's your up-to-the-minute listing of over 1,400 titles by your favorite authors.

This illustrated, large format catalog gives a description of each title. For your convenience, it is divided into categories in fiction and non-fiction—gothics, science fiction, westerns, mysteries, cookbooks, mysticism and occult, biographies, history, family living, health, psychology, art.

So don't delay—take advantage of this special opportunity to increase your reading pleasure.

Just send us your name and address and 50¢ (to help defray postage and handling costs).